PEGGIE

Also by Lynda Page

Evie
Annie
Josie

PEGGIE

Lynda Page

HEADLINE

First published in 1994
by HEADLINE BOOK PUBLISHING

10 9 8 7 6 5 4 3 2

British Library Cataloguing in Publication Data

Page, Lynda
Peggie
I. Title
823.914 [F]

ISBN 0-7472-1137-X

Typeset by
CBS, Felixstowe, Suffolk

Printed and bound in Great Britain by
Mackays of Chatham PLC, Chatham, Kent

HEADLINE BOOK PUBLISHING
A division of Hodder Headline PLC
338 Euston Road
London NW1 3BH

For Jenny Pullen

In grateful appreciation for all the years of unquestioning loyalty, trust and support above and beyond the call of duty. But, most importantly, for the laughs – and we've had many of those. Here's to the next forty years. Bless you, me duck!

Your friend always, Lynda

ACKNOWLEDGEMENTS

With thanks to Allison Astill Briggs, Mike Gamble, Mike French, and the staff of the Leicestershire Museum of Technology, Leicestershire Records Office and Leicestershire Libraries and Information, especially Nicky Morgan.

With extra special thanks to Mave Humphreys for . . . well . . . just everything.

Chapter One

'Right, you ready then?'

'Me ready?' Margaret Cartwright hissed harshly as she peered upwards. "I've been standing here like an idiot for the last half hour. Now if you don't hurry up and get your backside down this ladder this instant, you can forget the whole idea. And stop making so much noise. You'll wake the whole village.'

'All right, all right. I'm coming,' responded Lettice Cartwright as she gingerly lifted her plump cotton-stockinged leg over the sashed window ledge, turned her comely body and placed her booted foot on a rung of the ladder. Very tentatively she then brought her other leg over the sill to join it. The ladder wobbled dangerously and she clung to the ledge of the whitewashed, two-storey cottage in fright. 'A' you sure this ladder's safe?' she whispered as she peered nervously down towards the stone-flagged ground ten feet below.

'Of course it's safe,' her sister snapped back. 'I'm holding it, ain't I?' Peggie shivered as the cooling night air wafted under her calico nightdress and swirled around her shapely bare legs. 'For God's sake, Letty, just hurry up. If Mam and Dad catch us, we'll be skinned alive.'

Letty tightened her grip and once more looked down. 'Oh, our Maggie, I think I've changed me mind . . .'

'Changed your mind! I'll give you changed your mind. You'll climb down this ladder if it's the last thing you do, especially after all the trouble you went to to get me to agree to this stupid idea in the first place.' Peggie's large blue eyes flashed in sudden temper. 'And what did you call me?' she snapped.

Letty, clinging even tighter to the ladder, pursed her lips. 'Maggie. Well, that's your name, ain't it?' she retorted sharply.

Peggie shook the ladder angrily. 'I've told you never to call me Maggie. My name's Peggie. A' you listening – PEGGIE!'

Letty stifled a cry of anguish and felt the sweat of fear running down the bridge of her nose past her spectacles. 'All right, all right. You've made your point,' she cried, seeing the ground looming dangerously nearer.

'Well, say it then.'

'Peggie. Peggie!'

The smile on Peggie's face quickly vanished as a snow white head followed by a gnarled face and toothless scowl rose above the garden wall.

Peggie inhaled sharply. 'Hello, Old Moth— Mrs Hubbard. I

thought you'd be asleep at this time a' night.'

'I'd love to be asleep,' the old woman grumbled. 'Specially since I 'ave to rise at the crack of dawn. But the racket coming from outside wa' enough to awake the dead. I thought at the least we 'ad burglars. I might a' known it's be summat to do with the Cartwrights.'

Peggie tightened her mouth. 'I'm sorry, Mrs Hubbard. We didn't mean to wake you.'

'No, I'm sure you didn't,' Bella Hubbard replied, unconvinced. 'You youngsters ain't got no consideration for others.' She peered nosily around. 'Well?'

Peggie from below and Letty from above eyed her cautiously. 'Well, what?' they said in unison.

'What's going on? That's what.'

The girls looked at each other, then back at Bella Hubbard. 'Nothing,' they said innocently.

'Nothing! What d'yer take me for – daft? You're both up to summat. I've never known a day pass when one a' your family ain't up to summat. So what is it? And if you don't come clean I'll wake yer mam and dad. See what they have to say about all this.'

Peggie sighed loudly. 'You'd better tell her, Letty, unless you want trouble. I told you, didn't I? I told you we'd get copped if you did it this way.'

'Oh, shut up, our Mag . . . Peggie,' Letty quickly corrected herself, feeling mightily defenceless clinging to a woodworm-riddled ladder ten feet above the ground. Her elder sister, at five foot two in her stockinged feet, might be three inches shorter than herself, but with her quick fiery temper could still put the fear of God into her regardless of their love and respect for one another. Besides, she needed to get off the home-made contraption and quick, before she either fell off or it disintegrated. 'Well, if you must know,' she said haughtily, 'I'm eloping.'

'Yes,' Peggie cut in before she could stop herself. 'She is. But why she couldn't elope through the door like everyone else beats me. But no . . . our Letty has to come down a ladder.'

'You don't elope through a door, our Peggie. I've told you before, it has to be a ladder or it's not really eloping, now is it?'

'Eloping, eh!' Bella cackled, rising further above the piece of wall that divided the two cottages from the coal sheds and outside privvies. Intrigued, she rested her flabby arms on the top. Her piggy slate grey eyes widened maliciously. 'I hope it ain't with that soppy ha'porth you've bin seeing? Your mam'll have a fit.' She chuckled. 'That's if his mam don't first!'

Peggie froze.

Letty swung round and nearly overbalanced. She hastily righted herself. 'I hope you're not referring to my Wilfred?' she snapped, bravely releasing one hand from the rung and pushing her glasses further on to her nose.

'And who else would I be referring to?' Bella mimicked. 'Unless you've bin seeing someone else behind his back. If you ask me . . .'

2

'We didn't ask you, Mrs Hubbard,' Peggie said coldly, sensing her sister's anger. 'Now please, just mind your own business. If our Letty say's she's eloping with Wilfred then she is.' She turned her gaze upward. 'That right, Letty?'

'Yes,' she agreed. 'And marrying me will be the best day's work he's ever done.'

Peggie turned back to Bella. 'Right, Mrs Hubbard, if you don't mind, me and Letty would like to get back to the matter in hand. And if I were you I'd go back inside before you catch your death. Goodnight. Oh,' she added as an afterthought, 'you needn't bother rushing round in the morning to tell me mam and dad because I'll already have told 'em.'

Bella Hubbard's eyes bulged. Her mouth opened then snapped shut as she scrambled off the wooden crate she was standing on, marched inside her adjoining cottage and slammed the door indignantly, sending a cascade of early rambling rose petals fluttering to the ground.

Peggie and Letty looked at each other and giggled.

'Nosy old devil,' Letty said as she inched down the ladder and thankfully felt firm ground beneath her feet. She turned to her elder sister and sighed in relief. 'Oh, I shan't be doing that again in a hurry. I was frit to death and could have done without her sticking her nose in.' She smiled warmly. 'Thanks for sticking up for me.'

'Don't I always?' Peggie replied, returning the smile.

The two women faced each other and for an instant Peggie felt envy rise within her. In a few short moments twenty-five-year-old Letty, with her short crop of fine mousy hair and large round metal-rimmed spectacles that hid alert pale blue eyes and part of her rather attractive chubby face, would rush off to marry the man she had been courting for the last ten years. And although Peggie would deny her not one moment of happiness, she could not help but feel cheated.

A vision of Harry Machin reared up, strikingly handsome and proud, decked in his private's uniform, standing by the gate waving a final goodbye before marching off to join his colleagues on the battle fields of France. The feel of his passionate kiss still lingered on her lips, and try as she might his presence would not leave her. Oh, Harry, her mind screamed. Why did you have to die so senselessly? If the war had not intervened she would have been married by now with several children to fuss over and a loving husband to care for. But it was not fair to brood at a time like this. It would spoil Letty's happiness and that was the last thing Peggie wanted.

She held out her arms and pulled her sister close. 'A' you sure you're doing the right thing?' she asked softly.

Letty gazed down into her eyes and nodded. 'I've never bin so sure about anything. I love him, Peggie. Really I do. But if he doesn't get away from his mother now, he never will.'

Peggie nodded in agreement. 'Then I wish you all the best. I only wish I was going to be there to see you both wed.'

3

Letty gulped back the lump in her throat. 'Oh, so do I. So do I,' she said sincerely. 'And Mam and Dad, our Billy, Ronnie and Primrose. I know it's not right doing this behind their backs, but it's the only way.'

'I know, love, I know. His mother would never agree to him marrying, whoever it was to.' She sighed loudly. 'I just feel for our mam. She ain't gonna like being done out of seeing you married.' Peggie released her sister and breathed deeply to stem the tears that threatened. 'Come on, Letty. Get your bag and be off. You don't want to keep Wilfred waiting.' She grinned mischievously. 'He might be picked up for loitering.'

Letty stepped forward and once again hugged her sister fiercely. 'I shall miss you.'

'Miss me! Don't be daft. Once you're settled you won't keep me or the rest of the family off your doorstep. Now be off, I said.'

Letty picked up the old tapestry carpet bag that held the cream wedding suit she and Peggie had secretly made, sewing long into the night when everyone else was asleep, and the new cotton nightdress bought with her savings. 'You sure you don't mind breaking the news?'

Peggie shook her head. 'Of course I don't,' she lied, not relishing the idea for one moment. 'But don't forget to send that postcard once you get to Gretna Green. And, remember, not to here – care of Aggie's, else Dad and our Billy will come after you and poor Wilfred won't know what's hit him.'

'I won't, Peggie,' uttered her sister, shuddering at the thought. 'As soon as I arrive, I promise.'

Letty turned and opened the back gate. She waved before she closed it after her and hurried down the lane.

After struggling to replace the ladder against the coal shed, Peggie picked her way over the cluttered yard, careful to avoid the rusty bicycle Billy used to ride the four miles to his job down the mine in Merrylees near Desford, which was propped up against the mangle, and Primrose's old perambulator still filled with the disintegrating remains of old rag dolls and hand-knitted covers. She squatted down on the stone back step, running her fingers through her mane of long blonde curls, and sighed deeply. There was going to be hell to pay in the morning when she broke the news. But by then Letty and Wilfred would be well on their way to Scotland.

Regardless of the scene that would erupt, and despite her reservations about the mild-mannered Wilfred and his tyrant of a mother, she was pleased for her sister who deserved all the happiness she could get. After all, she had patiently courted the man for the last ten years and hadn't had an easy time of it.

Peggie lifted her head and shut her eyes as the fragrant scent of her father's two prize roses, planted by the side of the vegetables in the tiny plot of garden, wafted towards her. She smiled to herself and remembered how the family, on the strictest of instructions from her father, had tended the two precious plants whilst he had been serving his time as a store-man in one of the large transit barracks near London as the Great War had raged in Europe. The plants and her father had survived but many of the village menfolk had not.

The war had wreaked havoc with many lives but those left to pick up the pieces must surely have had the worst deal, she mused sadly. Her thoughts were interrupted by the creaking of the back gate as it slowly opened and her brother Billy crept through.

'Oh, my God, Billy,' she gasped. 'What a shock you gave me.'

He froze for a moment then clutched his hand to his chest. 'Peggie,' he whispered, striding towards her. 'What the blazes a' you doing out here at this time of night?' He squatted down to join her, pulling off his cap.

She eyed him sharply. 'I could ask the same of you? But then I know where you've been, and you should watch it, my lad. One of these days you're gonna get caught.'

'Don't start lecturing, Peggie. Not at this time a' night.'

'I ain't lecturing, Billy. I'm just stating the obvious. Bull Hammond ain't gonna take lightly to the fact that you've been messing with his wife. He ain't nicknamed Bull for nothing, you know. He'll have your guts for garters and hang your gizzards from the rafters! And then it'll be Mam and Dad's turn. That's if there's 'ote left of you, that is.'

'Look, Peggie,' Billy said innocently, 'you've got it all wrong.'

'Don't lie,' she snapped. 'I never could stand a liar and especially not me own brother.' Her eyes softened and she placed her hand on his knee and stared up into his face. No wonder Alice Hammond had fallen for her younger brother. At twenty-two years of age he lived life on the edge, charming his colleagues, friends and the women of the vicinity with his flashing smile, quick brain and his eye for a deal, whether crooked or straight. One day, Peggie felt sure, he would land in serious trouble if he wasn't careful. 'Just watch out, our Billy. I don't want to see you hurt. Not for a bit of fun, I don't.'

He took a deep breath and eyed her tenderly. 'Rest assured, I won't. Trust me. Now you still haven't answered me question?'

'What question?'

'What you're doing out here at a quarter to midnight?'

Peggie smiled. 'Couldn't sleep, that's all.'

'Oh.' He sighed knowingly. 'Still harping on the dead.'

'Don't be so callous, Billy Cartwright. You don't know what it's like to lose someone you love.'

'True. But you can't go on mourning for ever. I'm sure Harry wouldn't have wanted that.' Billy shifted himself further round to face her. 'You should get out a bit more before it's too late. If you're not careful you'll end up an old maid.'

'Old maid!' she erupted. 'You cheeky devil! I'm only twenty-seven, and if I wanted to go out I would. But I'm quite happy, thank you.'

'Happy! How can you be happy moping round the house night after night? The only time you ever go out is to Aggie's for a natter. It's a wonder you two haven't talked yourselves to death.'

Billy started at his sister for a moment. True, she wasn't beautiful but Peggie had a magnetism that made everyone sit up and take notice of all five foot two of her. She had natural blonde hair that was far too curly, like clock springs hanging down her back. As a teenager she had fussed for hours trying to tame it into some sort of style by sleeping in rags and using a flat iron to straighten it, but like its owner her hair had a mind of its own which eventually even the strong-willed Peggie had had to resign herself too.

Her attractive heart-shaped face was marred by a long straight nose which overshadowed full pink lips, and her quick temper, bossy ways and overactive tongue could drive a man to drink. But for all that Peggie had qualities that many men hankered after. He had long got over his brotherly protectiveness at the way they all stopped and stared when she marched down the street, her full breasts bouncing, her trim waist and shapely hips swaying beneath her clothes as she strove to keep her straw hat perched at a jaunty angle on top of that mane of curls. All the women he knew secretly envied her and if only she would bury the past he felt in no doubt she had a promising future.

He took a deep breath. 'I could fix you up with a date tomorrow if you'd only say the word,' he said cautiously. 'Sam Harkins . . .'

'Sam Harkins! Don't you mention Sam Harkins to me. The only reason Sam Harkins is interested is because he thinks I got some savings put past under me bed.'

'Now who's being callous?'

Peggie's features softened. 'Sorry.'

'There's nothing wrong with the bloke, Peggie. You could at least give him a go. It wouldn't do any harm to go to the pictures with him or summat.'

She sighed. She knew her brother was right. She'd had plenty of offers since word had spread she was available but couldn't bring herself to accept any of them.

'I'll think about it,' she replied to close the subject.

'Good.' He yawned loudly. 'I'm going to bed. And you'd better an' all else you won't get up in the morning.'

'In a minute,' replied Peggie.

Billy disappeared through the back door.

She raised her eyes and stared up into the star-laden sky and her fingers absently felt the locket round her neck that Harry had given her as his parting gift. Once again she saw him standing by the gate, his last words to her being his solemn promise of return. And she had believed him. No one could touch her Harry, not even the dreadful Hun.

After his departure, the then twenty-three-year-old Peggie had sat out the terrible war with the rest of the women of the village. She joined long queues for rations, helping to dig allotments for growing

6

vegetables, consoled the bereaved – and there were many of those. In fact Peggie, like the rest of the Cartwright family, had turned her hand to anything that would take her mind from the happenings in Europe.

Of an evening, by the light cast from the iron paraffin lamp hanging from the ceiling, she wrote long, cheerful letters and accosted the post lady each morning for news of her loved one. Harry's letters came regularly at first, then dwindled to a stop and for two miserable years there was nothing. Then his widowed mother received the telegram that gave her a massive heart attack which put her six foot under in the tiny graveyard at the bottom of the village. Harry, like millions of other young men, had been posted missing, presumed dead.

For months after Peggie survived in the hope that it was all a dreadful mistake, that one day he would jump off the train and come running towards her, gathering her up in his arms, just as he had promised when he had waved his goodbye. But, finally, with the help of her family, she conceded the truth of his demise and it was only through their love and support that she had learned to live with her grief.

'Harry. Oh, Harry,' she whispered thickly. 'Will I ever stop loving you? Will I ever lay your memory to rest?'

Since the day of the telegram she had made a promise in Harry's memory that she would never take another. No man would ever fill the place in her heart as completely as he had, and as time passed she could not envisage that promise being broken.

She lowered her gaze and absent-mindedly plucked at the petals of a bright orange marigold that nestled between a variety of colourful early-summer blooms planted in the half barrels by the side of the step, and listened for several moments to a dog barking in the distance. She wondered if the dog had been disturbed by Letty and Wilfred making their way down the rutted dirt lanes towards the railway station in the next village of Bagworth.

Her gloomy thoughts were quickly dispelled as she pictured Letty clinging to the ladder in fright, her glasses slipping down towards the end of her pert nose. Peggie hugged her knees and stemmed the mirth that threatened. That was a memory that would be talked of plenty when they were both old and grey with at least Letty's grandchildren hanging on their skirts.

Suddenly her spirits lifted and she rose, yawned loudly and stretched her shapely body. Her bed beckoned. In the morning she had to be bright and alert for her job as a cutter in the hosiery factory in Earl Shilton, a small town seven miles away. It didn't pay to be half asleep. The foreman was a tartar and the cutters sharp. Many a finger had been lost through absent-mindedness and she had no intention of losing any of hers, she valued them too much.

She crept into the small bedroom she shared with her sisters in the tiny two up, two down cottage, and as she lowered her body beneath the warm covers, Primrose turned over and stared up at her.

'Letty get away then?' she asked matter-of-factly.

Peggie peered at her in the darkness, frowning. 'How did you know about our Letty?'

Primrose raised herself up. 'Because nothing's a secret round here. And besides, you both made enough noise to wake the whole village. I'm surprised Mam and Dad slept through it.'

Peggie inhaled sharply. 'So you know she's eloped?'

'Yeah, with that soppy Wilfred. She wants her head examining if you ask me.'

'I didn't ask you, Primrose. I suppose you've been snooping as usual?'

Primrose shrugged her twelve-year-old shoulders and drew aside the curtain of dark brown hair that had fallen across her face. A face that, once rid of its smattering of teenage pimples and when it learned to smile more, promised to become very pretty. 'I don't snoop, you shouldn't talk so loud. Anyway, Mam's gonna go mad in the morning when she finds out.'

Peggie, too tired to battle, snuggled down beneath the covers and turned her back on her youngest sister. 'Go to sleep,' she commanded.

A muffled sob roused Peggie and she opened her eyes, taking several moments to accustom herself to the darkness. Primrose lay snoring softly, dreaming up her next batch of excuses for avoiding attendance at school. Peggie frowned, wondering who on earth was making the noise. It was with surprise she realised the sounds were coming from Letty sitting on the edge of the large bed sobbing quietly into her handkerchief. Peggie raised herself, careful not to wake Primrose.

'Letty, what's wrong?' she asked, but deep down already knew the answer.

Letty slowly turned her head, her red-rimmed, tear-filled eyes, blinking miserably behind her steamed-up spectacles. 'He didn't come,' she croaked.

'Oh, Letty, Letty! I'm so sorry,' she said, trying to stem her anger against the absent Wilfred. She drew back the covers and crawled down to the bottom of the bed, placing her arm around her sister's shoulders for comfort. 'Er . . . maybe he's ill, or you got the wrong time?'

'Don't make excuses for him, Peggie. He's let me down for the last time. I'm finished with him. I hope he's happy now he's broken my heart!' Letty bent her head and sobbed uncontrollably into Peggie's shoulder.

Finally, Peggie persuaded the distraught girl to hide her bag and get into bed and eventually, with Primrose's knees digging into her back and Letty's tearful face resting on her chest, Peggie decided exactly what she was going to do come morning.

Chapter Two

Generations of Cartwrights had lived in the village of Barlestone in Leicestershire. It was rumoured that they were even mentioned in the Domesday Book. But by the year 1920 the numbers had dwindled through war, disease and emigration, and all that remained were the seven residing in the tiny whitewashed cottage at the end of an identical row of four on Chapel Lane before the imposing Norman Church of St Giles.

At the age of eighteen, employed as a junior store-man in a local factory, Septimus Nathanial Cartwright had married Elinor Mickleby, a pretty young sixteen year old from the neighbouring village of Stanton-under-Bardon. Her hand in marriage had been won fair and square from all her other suitors, and proud and very much in love, Septimus had brought his new bride to his parents' cottage in Chapel Lane.

Sadly they were both long gone, killed before their time by the harshness of daily life. His two elder brothers had emigrated many years before to America, never to be heard from again. Septimus didn't know whether they were alive or dead and had long ago stopped wondering. His two younger sisters had been denied their right to life by a plague of measles that had struck one dreadful cold winter when the village had been cut off for several weeks by snow. The children hadn't stood a chance as the disease had relentlessly raged and many a family besides their own had been bereaved. Even the wealthy Peggs who owned the large Church Farm Estate hadn't escaped. Their young son, Miles, had been buried in the family vault in the churchyard near the other poor mites who had succumbed.

All that was left of the once large Cartwright family was Septimus and if he had his way, the next generation would always reside in the village of their birth.

For forty-six-year-old Septimus, it had been a terrible wrench to leave his family when his name had been read out along with several of his workmates. He had thought himself too old for fighting, and thankfully he was, but his skills as a store-man were desperately needed to keep the fighting men on the front well supplied. Resigned to do his bit for King and Country, Septimus had squared his shoulders and caught the troop train with several of the last remaining eligible village men – his only consolation that Billy, his elder son, who worked as a minor, was safe. Thankfully his name had not been drawn in the lottery of who went and who stayed in the pit. At least Septimus would know his beloved family was being taken care of while he was away.

He returned home, like many others, full of hope and glad the terrible fighting was over, expecting to pick up just where he had left off. It was with a dreadful shock that he found his job gone and none to replace it. Overnight his self-respect had been stripped from him through no fault of his own. But unlike others, Septimus had not wallowed in self-pity and was not resigned to his lot. He was only fifty years of age; not ready for the scrap heap just yet.

Straightening his broad back and squaring his muscular shoulders he had travelled the roads in search of work, sometimes walking miles on hearsay of a day's pay. He joined long queues to pitch against younger, more able men, all after the same demeaning handful of vacancies that offered a pittance of a wage. Sometimes he was lucky and would earn a few coppers for a long day of hard labour but these times were few and far between.

It was only his unwavering drive to support his beloved family that kept him going. Septimus believed his children should not have to tip up most of their earnings in order to keep a roof over their heads and food on the table, his adored wife should not have to skivvy for others. He was the head of the house, it should be his pay that was divided up on a Friday night for rent and food. One day he knew that something would happen to reverse the situation and give him back his self-respect. As long as he kept the faith he would one day turn the corner and his luck would change. And once again he would see pride in his family's eyes, not pity.

When Peggie arrived in the kitchen at five-thirty sharp the following morning she found her mother bustling around. Little Nell, as she was fondly referred to by her family because of her lack of inches, was tying her wrap-round floral pinafore over her black ankle-length cotton twill working skirt and white high-necked blouse. Her once shapely body, one that had caught the eye of many of the young lads in her youth, had expanded generously over the years until from a distance she resembled a ball. Placing a bowl of porridge on the table, she eyed her daughter keenly.

'You're up sharp this morning and you don't look as though you've slept a wink. You ailing for something?'

Peggie stifled a yawn. 'I'm fine,' she said lightly, not wanting to arouse any suspicions of last night's escapade. The longer her mother was kept uninformed the better. 'It was awful warm during the night and Primrose didn't stop snoring. I'm sure she needs her adenoids sorting.' She unhooked a mug from the welsh dresser and sat down at the well-worn pine table placed in the centre of the cluttered kitchen.

'Huh,' her mother grunted unconvinced, hurriedly scraping a comb through her thick, still honey blonde hair. She grabbed at the length at the back and expertly twirled it into a bun at the nape of her neck, securing it with several kirby grips. Raising herself on

10

tiptoes, she quickly glanced in the large oval mirror hanging from a nail embedded in the wall above the blackleaded range. Age was steadily creeping up on her, but despite her dumpy body she knew she still looked far younger than her forty-seven years and felt most of that was down to having a closely knit family, despite the fact that each one of them in turn was causing her heartache.

She sighed deeply as she turned and discreetly looked at her eldest daughter who, elbows on the table, was absent-mindedly sipping from her mug of tea. Peggie, so vibrant, so strong-willed, with an answer for everything, who flew through the day like the devil himself was on her heels, worried her deeply. The girl still hadn't recovered from her fiancé's death. By now she should be going out and enjoying herself, not staying in night after night moping. It was a pity there was such a shortage of young men, she needed to fall in love again, but the dratted war had seen to that and the slightest new prospect arriving on the scene was quickly snapped up by the other village spinsters and paraded before the Reverend Forest before the poor man had a chance to escape his fate.

But somehow her motherly instinct told her that Peggie was not destined to remain alone. She felt in her heart that there was someone somewhere waiting to appear when the time was right and then she would once again see the spark of happiness in her daughter's lovely blue eyes. But one thing was for sure, Peggie wouldn't find this man sitting at her kitchen table. No, the girl had to be encouraged to go out. Normally she would have spoken to Sep on such matters but he had enough on his mind. She decided to speak to Billy, see what he could suggest.

Billy . . . Now why did she have to think about him when she was in such a tearing hurry? Hurried thoughts were of no use whatsoever regarding her elder son. The best time to think about him was when she sat late at night in her ancient rocking chair by the fire doing her never ending darning and mending. She smiled to herself. Not that Billy was a bad lad, far from it. He was . . . resourceful. Yes, that summed up her Billy. In the right circumstances he would make a very good businessman, but unfortunately for him he had been born to parents who could not afford to have his keen brain nurtured by good schooling and had ended up down the mines.

Maybe that in itself had been good luck. If Billy hadn't gone down that path he would surely have ended up fighting in France and probably wouldn't be here now for her to worry over, plus the fact that the coal he procured by some means or other kept them warm many a bitter night when otherwise they would have gone cold, and the parcels of meat, odd sack of flour and other bits and pieces he brought home helped to eke out the meagre supplies she had to feed her ravenous family on.

She felt the familiar pain creeping up her legs and winced. Quickly turning her back on Peggie, she raised her skirt. Her swollen legs were getting worse. How she managed to keep them

11

hidden from Sep was a miracle. Her legs, she knew, were only swollen from the hours she had to stand on them without rest. The cure was to give up work and do less around the house, but she couldn't envisage being able to do that for a long time to come. But she knew, should her husband catch sight, he would drag her down the doctor's and demand treatment. And treatment cost money that they could not afford. When Sep found full-time work, then she would do something about her legs. In the meantime she would continue with the poultices she applied late at night when they were all asleep.

Peggie broke into her thoughts.

'Where's Dad?' she asked, sprinkling sugar over her porridge and adding the last of the milk from the jug by the huge brown teapot.

Nell dropped her skirt and turned round. 'He's managed to get a ride on a draycart into Leicester. Danny Sperry popped in last night and told him he'd heard a rumour Wolsey were looking for some Wet Finishers for their factory on the Abbey Meadows. Although your dad's never done that kinda thing before, he thought it might be worth a try.'

Peggie raised her eyes. 'If he gets work there he'd have to travel over twelve miles each way.'

Nell pursed her lips. 'Your father would walk a hundred miles if it meant work at the end of it.' She shook her head. 'Let's hope the rumour's true and your dad's first in the queue. I don't think I can stand much more of this. Not one proper job offered in all this time and it's really getting him down. I worry for him, Peggie. He's a fine man. A man that's worked hard all his life and he don't deserve this.'

Peggie swallowed a mouthful of porridge and stared up at her mother. 'Cyrus Crabbe offered him a job. Several times, in fact, and Dad refused.'

Uncharacteristically, Nell's usually good-humoured face darkened and her double chin wobbled. 'Your father would never work for that man. Not if we were in the gutter, he wouldn't. You know that as well as I do.'

'I know. I've always known there's no love lost between the Cartwrights and the Crabbes,' Peggie said slowly. 'But I don't know why.'

Nell leaned heavily upon the table, staring unblinkingly into her daughter's eyes. 'I'll tell you why. That man would sell his soul to the devil and expect change! Don't be fooled by his handsome looks nor his silvery tongue. I know first hand, and for different reasons. So does your Dad. Cyrus Crabbe is a devious, calculating liar. How he's got the nerve to stay in this village after all he's done defies belief. He only offered that job to goad your father. He knew fine well he would never take it.'

Peggie gawped at the savageness of her tones. She had never heard her mother spout forth such venom and it shocked her.

12

'What . . . what sorta things has he done?' she asked, bewildered. It must have been something terrible to make her mother so angry.

'Never you mind. It's all in the past. But I'll tell you this much. Given the chance, he'd have sold the clothes off his poor wife's back, God rest her, and still sent her out bare naked, nine months pregnant, spud picking in all weathers for a miserly few pennies. Then expect her to come home and cook and clean for him and that spineless son of his. And now she's gone the load has fallen on his daughter, poor mite. I wouldn't trust him as far as I could throw him.'

Peggie stared agog. She took a deep breath, leaned back in her chair and folded her arms. 'Oh, that bad, eh? Well, I ain't moving until you tell me all. Even if it means not going to work.'

Nell blew out her cheeks in exasperation. 'Well, you'll have to sit there all day then, won't yer? 'Cos I have to get the rest of 'em up or we'll all be late.'

'Mam, I ain't a kid any more. If there's any skeletons in our cupboard, I want to know about 'em.'

Nell drew herself up to her full height of five foot nothing. 'You're a stubborn bugger, Margaret Cartwright. I don't know where you get it from. It's not me nor your dad, that's fer sure.' She paused. 'It must have bin from your Great-granny Linney. She used to dig her heels in and not let go. She went to her grave swearing black were white.' She stared hard at her daughter, wishing she had never opened her mouth in the first place. 'Oh, all right then,' she relented. 'But don't dare tell your dad I've told you.'

'I won't breathe a word,' replied Peggie, eyeing her mother keenly.

Nell poured herself a mug of tea and sat down opposite. 'Just after you were born, your dad had a notion.'

'Notion?'

'An idea. Stop interrupting, Peggie. Do you want to hear this or not? I have to get to work as well as you.'

'Sorry,' she said contritely.

'Well, it was a damned good idea an' all. One that your father was in no doubt would give him the chance to stop working for others and do something for himself, maybe earn some decent money. It started when he heard that Farmer Bates over at Cable Farm had hit hard times and was selling a couple of his 'orses cheap. So he got to thinking that if he could scrape the money together and buy one of the 'orses and get hold of a brake he could use it to transport people to and from work etcetera.' She noticed her daughter's quizzical frown. 'You've got to remember, Peggie, in those days we never had a regular brake as we do now. We either walked or were grateful to scrounge a lift on the back of a draycart. That's provided it were going in the right direction. Anyway, your dad struck a deal with the farmer and somehow we scraped the money together to buy Dobbin.'

'Dobbin?'

13

'The 'orse. Lovely thing he was. As gentle as a kitten. Anyway, now we were 'orse owners but with nothing for the 'orse to pull and no money left to buy anything. So, your dad set about making his own brake.'

Peggie was staring at her mother in fascination. 'He never?'

'He did,' Nell said proudly. 'Your father worked all his spare hours after work, sometimes well into the night, doing any odd jobs he could, and the payment he received was wood, nails, anything as long as he could put it to good use on the brake. Worked himself to the bone he did and nobody was going to see it until it were finished. He used the old shed up the back field, the one that was later turned into the cinema.'

'Did he do a good job?'

Nell sighed. 'Well, that's just it. I don't know.'

'You don't know?' Peggie frowned hard. 'Why?'

''Cos before I could see it, it was stolen, that's why. Sep had got hold of some red paint which he thought would make it nice and bright and when he went down to work on it one night, it was gone.'

'Oh, Mam,' Peggie said, dismayed. 'Who did such a terrible thing after all Dad's hard work?'

Nell raised her eyebrows.

Peggie stared at her mother then leaned back in her chair. 'Cyrus Crabbe.'

Nell puffed out her chest. 'Well, we had no proof. But that devil took it all right or my name's not Elinor Cartwright. Four weeks later, he suddenly appears as bold as brass with a brake, identical to the one your father made, only it were painted black.'

'But didn't you do anything about it? Get the police or challenge him? Steal it back even.'

'We couldn't steal it back, Peggie. By now too many people knew about it. We did get the police only Cyrus swore blind it were his. He even showed Constable Jesson the tools he supposedly used.' Nell narrowed her eyes. 'I can still see him now. He lied that well, he nearly convinced me. It was our word against his and as he was in possession of it, we hadn't a leg to stand on. But Sep would have known that brake anywhere. Christ, he built the thing from scratch and nigh on killed himself in the process through weeks of hard graft and hardly any sleep.' She sighed deeply. 'Anyway, through his conniving, lying ways, Cyrus scuppered any plans we had of making our own living and your dad will never forgive him.'

Peggie exhaled deeply. 'It all makes sense now. I often wondered why Dad hated him so much.' Her eyes suddenly widened. 'You mean to tell me that the brake I ride to work on every morning is the one my own father made?'

'Yes. It's been mended over the years. But that's the one all right.'

'Well, that settles that. I won't ride on it again. Not if I have to get up at three to walk to work, I won't.'

Nell leaned across the table. 'Now that's just the reason why we

14

ain't told any of you this tale. You need to use that transport. There's no other way of getting to work. And you won't find anything in this village apart from skivvying for a few coppers and that's only when you can get it. Now you'll do as me and your dad have had to do and that's forget about it. Lose this job, Peggie, and we'll all be in the mire. One in the family outta work is enough.'

'But, Mam . . .'

'But Mam nothing! You'll get on the brake today, same as you do any other day, and if I hear otherwise, you'll have my foot up your backside. I don't want none of this raking up again. It was bad enough living with it then. It took Sep a long time to get over it.' Nell's eyes suddenly glazed over as another memory came to mind. She sighed deeply. 'I just thank God I saw the light before it was too late . . .' She suddenly stopped in full flow and shook herself, realising she was speaking out loud.

Peggie frowned deeply. 'Before what was too late, Mam?'

'Nothing. Never you mind,' she said hurriedly. 'That's something I'll not discuss with anyone. I was just letting me tongue run away with me. It was all this talking about the past, that's all.' She smiled, her normal good humour restored. 'And you should know about that, gel. You're always doing it.' She paused and took a breath. 'Actually, Peggie, while we're on our own, there's something I want you to do for me.'

She cocked her head, alerted by her mother's tone.

'Oh! What?'

Nell pulled up her apron and fumbled in her skirt pocket. She held out a clenched fist. 'I want you to go down the pawn and see what you can get for this.'

She opened her hand and Peggie gasped.

'But that's Grandmother's wedding ring. You said you'd never part with that.' She frowned worriedly. 'Are things that bad?'

Nell sighed deeply. 'Yes, they are, me love. Only please don't tell your father. You see,' her voice faltered, 'I never paid last month's rent. I tried, but betime the rent man came round there were n'ote left in the tin.'

'Oh, Mam. Why didn't you say? I've a few shillings I can give you.'

'No,' Nell said sharply. 'You hand over most of your wages as it is and so do our Billy and Letty. Look, your grandmother's ring is only gathering dust, I might as well put it to good use. Besides, I've managed all right up to now. It's just that I had to get Primrose those boots and Ronnie's arse was hanging out of his trousers which were third hand as it was. But you see . . . well, I told you father that I'd saved for 'em. If I tell him all this it will only make him feel worse and I couldn't bear that.' She looked at Peggie, her eyes pleading. 'So you'll do it for me? Only I ain't got the time to travel all the way into Shilton.'

Peggie tightened her mouth. 'Only if you're sure we ain't got anything else we could sell?'

15

Nell laughed ruefully. 'Peggie, us Cartwrights have never had any spare money, so you're not likely to find anything worth much more than scrap value in this house, not if you look for a month of Sundays. No, the ring is me only saving grace and knowing my mother like I did, she won't be turning in her grave. She'd give me her blessing. Not one for sentiment wasn't my mother. Not when food had to be put into mouths.'

'All right, Mam. It's Saturday tomorrow, so I can go in the afternoon after work.'

Nell smiled gratefully and patted her daughter's arm. 'Good gel.' She wagged a finger. 'Now remember, what we've talked about this morning is between you an' me. Promise?'

Peggie nodded her head slowly. 'Promise.'

'And you'll ride the brake same as always?'

'Yes, yes.'

'Good. Now I'll wake the rest of me brood.'

She walked to the door at the back of the room behind which rose the steep narrow stairs and bellowed loudly: 'You lot up now, else you'll all be going out without any breakfast.'

Primrose was first to put in an appearance, bleary-eyed as usual with her hair hanging in rat's tails down her back and over her face. She grabbed a mug and sat down at the table, picked up the empty milk jug and scowled.

Her mother grabbed a brush and scraped it through her hair then began to plait it, Primrose shrieking in protest.

'I don't know what you do with your hair, Primrose Cartwright. This lot would make a fine bird's nest.'

'Its 'cos she tosses and turns all night. What with that and the snoring . . .'

'I do not!'

'And that's enough from you two. Where's our Ronnie? I need him to go and fetch some milk and a loaf of bread. Oh, and we need some water fetching from the pump.'

'I'll do that, Mam,' Peggie offered.

'Ta, duck. Ronnie, Ronnie!' she shouted. 'Get your backside down here now, on the double.' She patted Primrose on the head. 'That's you finished. Now go and get dressed and betime you've finished, Ronnie will have done that errand.'

Primrose, rubbing her smarting head, slowly rose and made for the stairs.

'Aye, and don't forget to put your liberty bodice on,' Nell warned. 'I know you never wore it yesterday. Think I'm daft, don't you?'

Primrose's scowl grew deeper. 'Mam, I hate that thing. I ain't wearing it. Anyway, it's too hot.'

'You will, my girl,' Nell erupted. 'And don't you dare back answer me. You can still catch a chill even in this weather. Besides, it helps keep your back straight and stops you slouching. Now you'd better put it on 'cos I'll check.' Nell caught sight of the clock

16

out of the corner of her eye. 'Oh my God, is that the time? I have to go. Mrs Pegg's asked me to go in early today. She's having some visitors and wants the parlour giving a good going over and I said I'd help prepare the spread.' She grabbed her straw bag. 'See to this lot, Peggie, please. The money for the milk and bread is in the tin. Tell Ronnie to take the big jug. You don't mind, do you?'

'No, 'course I don't. Just get off, Mam.'

'Ta, me duck.' She made for the door, stopped and turned. 'I might be late home though and that means dinner'll be late.'

Peggie smiled fondly. 'Don't you worry about dinner, Mam. Our Primrose can make a start when she comes home from school. I'll give her instructions when she comes down again and me and Letty will finish off when we get home from work.'

Nell tutted loudly. 'The day our Primrose follows any instructions will be the day the sun drops out the sky, so I won't hold me breath. But you can tell her from me that if she dares even think of bunking off school she won't be able to sit down for a fortnight. And our Ronnie, warn him to keep away from the railway after school. Mr Tunley the Station Master's getting sick of seeing him hanging on the gate.'

Peggie scraped back her chair, rushed over and placed her arm affectionately around her mother's shoulders. 'Stop whittling, Mam,' she said as she kissed her on the cheek. 'Just get off and I'll see you tonight.'

Nell nodded gratefully before she departed.

Glad to be on her own for a few moments, Peggie returned to the table and sat back down in the chair, which like the table was worn thin and bleached white from years of scrubbing. She loved this room.

Unlike the rest of the house which was furnished sparsely with just the bare necessities, every available space here was filled with generations of Cartwright clutter, kept just in case it might come in useful. On the wooden mantle above the range odd pieces of chipped china, cheap trinkets and keepsakes jostled for space between sepia photographs of past relatives, staring formidably down.

The welsh dresser standing against the far wall had been her great-grandmother's, given to her husband in lieu of payment for work in the mid-1800s. It was marked from years of constant use. It had been a luxury having a piece of furniture as grand as this and the talk of the village for months when Thomas Cartwright had proudly heaved it down the street on a borrowed hand cart, going out of his way so that all the villagers saw it before finally it came to rest in the small kitchen. Like the mantle its surfaces and cupboard space were filled with items long since forgotten about.

Suspended from the ceiling hung a long wooden laundry cradle where in winter steaming wet washing hung, adding to the rivers of condensation that already ran down the windows, collecting in pools on the sills. Faded worn clippy rugs, hand-made by the girls

17

during the long winter evenings from odd bits of fabric from the rag box, were scattered across the flagstone floor and by the pot sink next to the door rested the dented tin bath, above it three blackened cast iron pans and an enormous frying pan.

Peggie fingered her chin. Her mother was right. This room might be filled to overflowing, but not one item was of any value except to the family that owned it. She sighed deeply, upset that she had been given the task of selling her grandmother's ring, knowing her mother had treasured it since the old lady had died some twenty years past. Still, needs must, as her mother was so fond of saying.

She put the ring safely in her pocket and raised her head, suddenly conscious that time was hurrying by. She had an important errand to do before she caught the cart into Earl Shilton and if she didn't get a move on she wouldn't have the time. Just then Letty appeared, her ashen face drawn and still streaked with tears. Silently Peggie poured her a mug of tea, apologised for the lack of milk and pushed it towards her.

'How are you?' she asked, knowing fine well it was a stupid question.

Letty raised swollen eyes and stared at her blankly.

Peggie had never seen her sister look so distressed and her heart cried out. 'I think you should go back to bed. You ain't fit for work today, my girl. Don't worry, we'll think of a good excuse.'

Letty, who had never before taken a day off sick from her work alongside Peggie in the hosiery factory, picked up her mug and retraced her steps. Peggie stared after her with narrowed eyes, her lips in a tight line. By the time she had finished with Wilfred Dage he would rue the day he had hurt her sister.

Dressed for work and making sure all her mother's instructions had been carried out, she left the house.

Peggie marched into the dark interior of Dage's General Store and stood before the long wooden counter. Being the only provisions shop in the village it was filled with all manner of goods stacked against walls and hanging from the wooden beams across the ceiling. Effie Dage, a sour mealy-mouthed woman, wiped bony hands on her large white apron, squared her thin shoulders and raised malicious small grey eyes to meet Peggie's.

'Yes?' she snapped. She'd been expecting a confrontation with one of the Cartwrights and she was ready.

'I'd like to speak to Wilfred, Mrs Dage, if you don't mind?'

'I do mind and he's busy,' came back the sharp reply. 'Now if you're not buying, I've no time to gossip.' She turned her back on Peggie and began to fill small blue paper bags with sugar from the sack that sat on the wooden floor.

Peggie's temper rose though she tried to stay calm. 'I said I'd like to speak to Wilfred, and I want to speak to him now. Unless you want a scene in front of any other customers, I suggest you fetch him.'

Effie swung round. 'Oh, you do, do you? Well, I've already said, he's busy. And I've told him if he's any sense he'll have no more to do with the likes a' the Cartwrights.' She leant heavily on the top of the counter, her beady eyes aflame with anger. 'You don't think I'm oblivious to what was going on last night, do you? Well, I soon put a stop to it. Locked him in his bedroom and hid his clothes. I'm having no son of mine scuttling off behind me back to wed. My son is staying where he belongs 'til a suitable woman comes along. One that'll have a bit a' respect for her future mother-in-law.'

Against her will, Peggie's tongue got the better of her. 'And what suitable women do you think Wilfred is ever going to find with you as a mother?' she blurted. 'Any girl in her right mind would run a mile. It just so happens that Letty loves your son, God help her.' She placed her hands flat on the counter, thrusting her face within inches of Effie's. 'The trouble with you, Mrs Dage, is that you thought our Letty would move in here and become your drudge. You didn't like the fact that she stood up to you and demanded she and Wilfred had their own house as far away from you as possible. And because of your self-centred, miserable attitude you made them waste ten whole years of happiness when they could have been married and raising a family.'

Peggie straightened up and glared defiantly at the gawping Effie, her temper at boiling point. 'Well, don't you fret no more on that score, you miserable old bugger. Our Letty wants no more to do with Wilfred.' She thumped her fist on the counter. 'I want to see him and make sure he understands to leave her alone. He's made false promises to her for the last time. And if I don't see him now, I'll see him after work tonight. Even you can't keep him locked up for ever!' She pushed her hat firmly back on her head and made for the door where she stopped and turned. 'No wonder your husband left you for Hatty Pringle. If you ask me, both him and Letty have had a lucky escape.' She turned and opened the door, the brass bell above jangling loudly. 'Good day, Mrs Dage.'

Once out of the shop Peggie's temper subsided and she grinned. Effie Dage's face, deeply furrowed from years of scowling, had been a picture. She wasn't used to people speaking their mind. They were too frightened she wouldn't supply them with the goods they needed. Well, Effie Dage was in for another shock soon if the rumour Peggie had heard was true. It appeared that the Co-operative Society was going to open a branch in Barlestone right across from the Dage store and Peggie wished she could be around when Effie heard about it.

Her smile quickly vanished as it struck her that neither Letty nor her mother would be pleased when they heard what she had done. Letty because she had interfered; her mother because of the harsh words she had used and her belief that elders should always be respected, no matter what.

She shrugged her shoulders. It was done now and she was glad. Maybe Letty could put Wilfred behind her and allow a man who would appreciate her worth into her heart. She sincerely hoped so at any rate.

She felt a presence behind her and turned to find Wilfred standing there nervously.

'Oh, you've come out the woodwork, have you, Wilfred? Escaped for a moment from "Mother", have you?'

Wilfred sighed deeply. 'Don't be like that, Peggie. You don't know what she's like.'

'Yes, I do. I know exactly what she's like and it's about time you acted the man for a change. Your father did.'

'Yes, he did,' Wilfred soulfully agreed. 'And because of him I can't leave Mother on her own. She wouldn't manage.'

'Of course she would. Plenty of other women manage on their own without blackmailing their children.' Peggie pulled herself up to her full five foot two and folded her arms under her full breasts. 'Our Letty only wanted her own house, Wilfred. She didn't object to your working for your mother, she just didn't want to live with her, that's all. And I don't think that was too much to ask in the circumstances, do you?'

He shook his head in agreement and Peggie stared up at him. Wilfred was actually a fine-looking man, taking after his father. He was tall, on the thinnish side, with a pleasant face and black hair just beginning to recede. He had a quiet nature which occasionally showed a flash of humour, but most importantly he loved Letty and would do anything for her bar side against his mother. Shame really, they would have been very happy together.

'Well, Wilfred,' she said, shaking her head, 'you've done it this time. You've broke our Letty's heart once too often and she wants no more to do with you.'

He stepped back in alarm. 'Oh, Peggie. I . . . I did try to meet her last night. I had my bag packed and everything. But Mother somehow found out, locked me in the bedroom and hid my trousers.'

Peggie pushed her face towards his. 'Wilfred! Stark naked with nothing to cover your modesty but your red face – if you'd have wanted to meet our Letty then you'd have found a way. Now I'm telling you: leave her be. Given time she'll get over you and meet someone who deserves her.' She narrowed her eyes menacingly. 'If you don't, I'll tell our Billy,' she threatened.

Wilfred's eyes widened in alarm. He backed away, gulping hard. With head bent and drooping shoulders, he turned and walked back around the side of the shop.

Peggie shook her head sadly watching his departure, feeling sorry for the man but not as sorry as she did for her sister.

Suddenly she jerked her head as Crabbe's brake came skidding round the corner of the street, a cloud of dust from the dried dirt road rising up behind it. All the passengers were clinging to the sides for fear of falling off. She hesitated, remembering the dreadful secret her mother had divulged earlier, and her face set hard as

20

anger rose. She felt like taking a hammer and smashing it into bits. But all the passengers on board, including herself and Letty, relied on it heavily. It took all her strength to calm her anger, and with her hand on her hat, she raced after it.

Seeing Peggie Cartwright tearing down the street, thick tendrils of her golden curly mane escaping from beneath her hat, Reginald Crabbe pulled the cart to a halt, sending his passengers lurching forward muttering grumbles of displeasure. He grinned leeringly as she arrived out of breath and patted the space on the bench to the side of him.

'You'll have to sit up front with me. There's no room in the back.' Reginald jumped down from the driving seat and raced round to join her, intent on helping her board. To have an excuse to place his hand on her backside had been his dream since he had started to help his father in the running of the family business which consisted of the brake and an old carrier cart used to haul loads of goods – when they could be bothered.

Peggie ignored his hand and raised her brows haughtily. If there was one person she detested as much as Cyrus Crabbe, it was his son, Reginald. Both were odious, leering oafs who thought that women had been created for their own pleasure and should never be seen other than in the kitchen or bedroom. At twenty-five, Reginald was the image of his father; tall, strikingly handsome, with a full head of jet black hair and a reputation for the women that stretched far beyond the county boundaries. But it was his eyes that told the truth about the man. Pale ice blue menacing eyes that made the onlooker shudder at their coldness. As she looked at him now, she knew that regardless of what had transpired in the past between her parents and the Crabbes, she would still have had an instinctive dislike of them.

She locked her gaze with his in order to reaffirm her distaste. 'I'll squash in the back, thank you,' she said coldly. She walked by the side of the brake, conscious that several pairs of eyes were watching her every move.

'Suit yerself.' Reginald grinned as he followed close behind her, seemingly unconcerned by her attitude. 'No Letty today?'

'She's ill.'

'Is she? Well then, I'll have to drop round later and see how she is.'

Peggie's eyes flashed and she turned on him. 'I shouldn't bother. You won't find a welcome in our house.'

Reginald bared his large white teeth. 'One day,' he hissed, 'you Cartwrights will rue the day you looked down on me and me father. I can't wait to see your smug faces when we push them in the dirt.'

Peggie smiled sweetly as she raised her shapely leg and placed it on the step, clasping the outstretched hand of her friend, Aggie Adkins. 'You'll have a long wait.'

Reginald clenched his fists, his knuckles glistening white against his skin. He wanted to smash Peggie Cartwright's face to a pulp for her condescending attitude. He wanted to hear her beg for mercy as his blows rained down, bruising her smooth creamy skin. But if truth be known that was not what he really wanted to do to her. Peggie Cartwright's luscious body excited him to such a pitch that he had lain awake many a night, wondering what it would feel like under his. To have her melt against him as his hands roamed over her skin, seeking out her secret places and feeling her shuddering at his touch. Instead, the woman he lusted after scorned him and one day he would make her sorry for her actions.

His eyes narrowed. That time would come. He had plenty of patience. In the meantime, it wouldn't hurt to pay a little visit to Letty. He had heard that things were far from right between her and Wilfred and if he acted quickly, they never would be again.

With no room left on the seats, Peggie squashed herself between her friend Aggie and another passenger, dangling her legs over the tail end of the brake. Several of the other passengers grumbled, 'Hurry up or we'll be late for work,' and Reginald, sullen-faced, sauntered around and climbed into the driving seat. He whipped the horse into a trot and the loaded vehicle started its journey to Earl Shilton.

Aggie, a tall, good-hearted, painfully thin woman in her mid-twenties, her plain face covered in freckles, eyed Peggie sharply. 'You should know better than to upset a Crabbe. What if he won't let you travel on the brake no more? You'd never get to work.'

Peggie smiled mischievously. 'Then I'd just have to get up earlier and walk, wouldn't I!'

Aggie grunted. 'Huh! Sooner you than me.' Her face grew suddenly serious. 'Oh, Peggie, have your heard the news about Thora Baxter? No, 'course you wouldn't, you being late. Cathy Green just told us. She found out this morning when she went round to call for her.'

Peggie looked up in interest. 'Found out what?'

'That's she's dead.'

'Dead?' Peggie was aghast. 'Thora Baxter? But I only saw her yesterday.'

'Well, she's dead today. 'Parently her mam found her in bed this morning. She had . . . What's that word that sounds like those things you get on your bum when you sit on cold slabs?'

'Piles?' Peggie answered quizzically.

'No, you daft bugger,' Aggie laughed. 'Not piles. It's that word they use when you lose all yer blood?'

'Oh, bleed to death?'

Aggie tutted disdainfully. 'The word I'm looking for means that. I know it begins with an H. Anyway, covered in it she was.' She leaned over and whispered in Peggie's ear. 'Word 'as it she was pregnant and tried to get rid of it.'

'Oh, my God, she never?' Peggie said, shocked.

'Seems she did. From one of those back street woman in

22

Hinckley. With a bent knitting needle, would you believe?'

Peggie shuddered. 'Oh, Aggie, don't! But poor Thora. Who'd a' thought it?'

Aggie pursed her lips. 'Well, there you go. I'm only telling you what Cathy said. And she would know, she wa' her friend.'

'Well,' Peggie spoke sadly, 'I didn't know Thora all that well, but I knew she liked the lads. And by the way she carried on we all knew she'd end up in trouble one of these days. All the same, though, she didn't deserve to die like that.' Peggie frowned deeply. 'I'd never go to one of those women. I'd sooner die with the shame of being pregnant than end up like her.'

Shocked, she turned her attention from Aggie and raised her face towards the sun, beginning to show above the tree tops. Firmly, she pushed Thora's gruesome end from her mind and took several deep breaths, savouring the sweet smell of the wild flowers growing profusely in the hedgerows. A patchwork of fields covered in wheat, barley and an assortment of vegetables that would soon be ripe for harvesting, swayed gently in the early-morning breeze. Cows munched on meadows of lush grasses. Sheep bleated, clustered together like patches of snow on the distant hills.

It was at these times Peggie begrudged having to be shut up all day amongst a mass of sweating bodies, scratting a living on antiquated machinery in dirty buildings. She heartily wished she could throw off her old working clothes and play truant for the day, but quickly chided herself. Her father would give anything to be in her position and she should stop being ungrateful.

She turned back to Aggie and nudged her in the ribs. 'Fancy coming round tonight?'

Aggie's plain face fell. 'I can't, me mother . . .'

'Oh, don't mention mothers!' Peggie erupted thoughtlessly. 'I've had enough of mothers today to last a lifetime.'

Aggie frowned deeply. 'If you'd just let me finish, I was going to say that tonight me mother promised to help me finish off the skirt I'm in the middle of making, so I was gonna suggest you come round to ours. Myrtle's got her night class, so the three of us will have the house to ourselves. And you know my mam, she likes a good natter, and to be honest I think some company would do her the world of good.'

Peggie smiled shamefaced. 'How is she?'

Aggie sighed. 'Bearing up. But I don't think she'll ever get over the shock of losing me dad. I know they weren't exactly bosom buddies, but they did love each other in their own way.' She shook her head. 'She still has nightmares, Peggie. Still reckons he's lying rotting in some ditch somewhere in France. And until she's convinced he's had a decent burial she won't stop grieving. Well, none of us can promise her that, can we? Not even the Government.'

Peggie turned away. She sympathised wholeheartedly with Mrs Adkins' problem. For all she knew Harry might be lying alongside him – rotting together. She shuddered and fought to push the picture to the back of her mind. A night at Aggie's sounded a good idea, and if Letty felt up to it she would take her along also. For a few hours it might help to take all their minds off their problems.

Much later that morning, Letty, still dressed in her nightclothes, tentatively opened the cottage door to find Reginald standing on the doorstep. She stared at him blankly through red-rimmed eyes.

'Yes?' she said warily.

'Fine way to greet me, I must say.'

She sighed loudly. 'What d'you want? Neither me mam nor dad's in. If it's them you want, you'll have to come back later.'

'It's you I've come to see, Letty.'

'Me! What for?'

'Peggie told me you weren't well. And I thought I'd be neighbourly and ask after you, that's all,' he replied, putting a hurt look on his face. 'I've heard about you and Wilfred.'

'How? How did you hear about me and Wilfred?' she asked sharply.

Reginald laughed. 'Through the grapevine, Letty. How else?' He looked around him, then back at her. 'Ain't you going to ask me in? I thought you'd like a bit of company and I could do with a cuppa.'

Letty frowned. Reginald Crabbe being pleasant was something unknown and the way he was looking at her unnerved her. Besides, the last thing she felt like was company. 'Er . . . not at the moment if you don't mind. But thanks for calling.'

She made to close the door but Reginald stopped her, feeling annoyance that plump homely Letty was turning him away. How dare she? Who did she think she was?

'Aw, come on Letty. What's up? Frightened of me or summat? A neighbourly chat and a cuppa ain't much to ask, is it?'

She sighed deeply. 'No. No, it's not. But to be honest I don't feel like it at the moment.' Her mind worked rapidly. 'I think I've got something catching so I don't advise you come any closer. Now if you don't mind, Reginald, I'd like to go back to bed.'

He stopped himself from saying he would join her. 'Suit yourself.' He made to walk away, then stopped. 'Fancy coming out one night?'

'Pardon?' she said in astonishment.

'I asked if you fancied coming out one night?' he repeated, trying not to raise his voice. If she agreed then he could stand her up. That way he could salvage the situation. He wasn't going to have Letty Cartwright saying she had turned him down. That wouldn't do his reputation any good. His mates would think it hilarious.

She shook her head. 'No, I don't think so, thank you.'

'Why?' he snarled. 'Ain't I good enough?'

Oh, God, Letty thought. Please go away. She smiled. 'I don't feel like going out with anyone at the moment, not 'til I'm over my illness at any rate. But thanks for asking.'

24

He stared at her crossly. It was obvious he wasn't going to get anywhere. 'Huh. Well, think about it then?'

'Yes, Yes, I will,' she agreed reluctantly. Anything to make him leave.

He turned and strode down the path and a thankful Letty closed the door after him, wondering why he had called on her in the first place.

A feeling of utter misery swamped her. Reginald forgotten, she returned to bed.

Chapter Three

Sep, hands thrust deep inside the pockets of his jacket, stared forlornly at the long queue of men waiting patiently for the gates of the Wolsey factory to open and the foreman to select the handful of workers he needed. He knew his chances of work were slim regardless of whether he joined the queue or not.

Anger at the pitiful scene suddenly filled him. Bedraggled men of all ages, in clothes unfit even for the rag bag, jostled to be nearer the front of the gates. Men desperate to take home a few coppers to their wives in order to feed their families.

A feeling of guilt filled him. Like these men he had done his bit in the war and like them had come home to find the promises of the Government for a better standard of living all lies, and the world as he knew it disintegrating around him. But the guilt he felt was for the fact that unlike the majority of these men, there was money coming into his house through the efforts of his wife and children. That money kept the rent paid and food on the table, although he often marvelled how Nell managed to eke the small sum out.

Even young Ronnie ran errands and Primrose, who strove to avoid anything that wasn't pleasurable to her, washed the breakfast dishes and fed the animals for Florrie Hewlet, the postmistress, during her lunch break from school. But for all that he had to be thankful for, it didn't lessen the gnawing ache of uselessness he felt in the pit of his stomach each morning he woke.

He stood and watched the surge of men as the gates were opened; watched as the pitiful figures fought to be selected; watched as all but a few slouched away empty handed. Sep's heart cried out for each and everyone of them. It wasn't fair. Dogs were treated better than this.

With broad shoulders hunched, he turned and made his way towards the redbrick bridge that crossed the River Soar, his hobnail boots clattering loudly against the cobbled road. He stopped and stared down into the dark waters. A canal barge, painted bright green and red, its holding bay full of coal, slipped smoothly over the waters, its wake sending a family of moorhens gliding helplessly towards the grassy bank; a barefooted young girl, no older than Primrose, guided the old grey mare that pulled it along the tow path. The girl spied him and gave a cheerful wave. Sep managed a smile back and resumed his journey towards the town. He felt he might as well have a look around while he was in the vicinity.

He wasn't a lover of towns, not many village folks were and Sep did not often feel the need or the inclination to visit more than was necessary. He would never get used to the choking fumes spewing thick black from factory chimneys, blotting out the sky; having to dodge through the increasing traffic on narrow building-lined roads; the hustle and bustle of people scurrying by; but most of all he would never get used to the noise, it was deafening compared to his beloved countryside. But, he thought sadly, the poverty here was just as bad, if not worse than the countryside. Wherever you went, there was no escaping from it.

He felt a longing to get home and quickened his pace. If he hurried, he would just about manage to catch the noon carrier cart. This town had nothing to offer him. There were too many of its own inhabitants vying for the few jobs it offered.

He sat himself for a few moments on a wooden bench in the market place. Instinctively he withdrew his pipe and pouch of tobacco from his pocket. Opening the pouch he realised he had only a barrelful of tobacco left. On deliberation he decided to keep it for later.

The marketplace was buzzing with activity and unwittingly he was soon staring around in fascination at the comings and goings. His attention was attracted by a converted Swiss Saurer 5-tonner lorry, its cargo being unloaded in front of Lipton's the grocery shop. He had apprehensively learned to drive the very same make of vehicle around the army base in order to move supplies around, and a surge of nostalgia arose. The thrill of being in control of that vehicle once his fear had left him was something he would never forget and he looked after 'his Milly' with a fierce pride, caring for her every need like he would have any good woman.

The Government had compulsorily purchased any road-worthy vehicle new or old for the war effort, leaving the civilian population mostly to revert back to horse power. This hadn't worried the country folk one iota, they very rarely saw a horseless vehicle as it was. It was the town population and industries that had suffered.

Sep frowned. Something was missing from the scene and he could not quite place what it was. He stared around thoughtfully and then it struck. Leicester was devoid of any horseless buses, something that he had grown used to seeing and travelling on during his time in London. The monstrous trams still ruled the roads here. He wondered why when there was obviously such a great need?

Regardless, though, he was in no doubt that the wealthy had certainly made up for the years of deprivation. Several Ford 'Tin Lizzies' and a 'Fiat Tipo Zero' were parked at the side of the road waiting for their owners to drive them home and it certainly appeared that industry was forging ahead on the transportation front again from the number of lorries he had seen being driven through the town centre, jostling for space on the busy roads between the trams and horse-driven vehicles. He pursed his lips.

The end of the war was certainly changing things. He wondered if it was for the better.

His eyes widened as the owner of one of the 'Tin Lizzies' came out of a draper's followed by an assistant laden down with parcels. It was a young woman, smartly dressed in a pale blue silk three-quarter-length suit and showing a trim ankle, something that would be frowned upon by the elder women in his village. She climbed behind the wheel. The assistant turned the starting handle, and after several tries, the car spluttered into life. She tightened her scarf around her dip-brimmed hat and drove off.

'God blimey,' a voice said loudly. 'What next?'

Sep turned to see a man in his mid-thirties sitting next to him.

'Women drivers, eh?' the man continued. 'First the vote, now driving. They'll be wanting us to 'ave the bloody babies next! I tell yer, if I ever copped my misses behind a wheel, I'd tan 'er 'ide.'

Sep looked at the man in disbelief.

'Fight in the war, did you?' he asked.

'I did that,' he replied proudly, puffing out his chest. 'And I didn't get a scratch, neither.'

'Lucky for you, then. But lots of men weren't so lucky and, I tell you, they were bloody grateful for the ambulance drivers.'

'Were they?' The man looked at him, perplexed. 'I don't see what yer getting at, squire?'

'Don't you?' said Sep, standing up. 'Did you go round with your eyes shut then?' His voice rose angrily. 'God damn it, man, most of them ambulance drivers were women, God bless 'em. Women practically ran the country whilst we were away. Worked the fields, humped coal and worked in the munition factories. That's half the reason why us men ain't got jobs. But we'd have had mass starvation and never won the war if they hadn't pitched in.' He lowered his voice to a harsh whisper. 'So I'd watch your mouth in future if I were you and think twice before you speak.'

The man looked on agog as Sep turned away.

He walked proudly along High Street towards the carrier cart stop. He was glad he had put the bigoted man straight. To a certain extent he agreed that women had their rightful place, but he was also in no doubt that had they stayed in that place during the conflict, the war wouldn't have been so easily won. No, praise where praise was due. The men of this land had a lot to thank their womenfolk for, his own women included.

As he neared his destination, he saw the carrier cart driving away into the distance. Damn! Either it had left early, or he was late and that meant he would either have to walk the twelve miles home or wait for the next one that the workers caught at six o'clock. His decision was quickly made. He would walk and save the fare.

He had got as far as Kirby Muxloe, a village about five miles from Leicester, when he happened upon a picturesque whitewashed public house covered in climbing roses, and the pungent smell of ale filled the air. His thirst needed quenching and the saved fare jingled in his pocket. The thought of a pint of good bitter was too much and in a trice he had crossed over the threshold and ordered one of the best.

'New to these parts?' asked the jovial portly landlord, his ruddy complexion covered in a mass of greying whiskers, as he drew long and hard on the beer pump and placed a foaming pint in front of Sep.

Sep handed over his money and took a long grateful drink from the glass. He wiped away the froth from his top lip. 'No. I live in Barlestone.'

'My brother lives out that way. Osbaston. That's the next village to Barlestone, ain't it?' He reached behind him and handed a set of darts to a customer. 'We don't see much of 'em,' he continued. 'It's too far to travel. Time you've got there, it's time to come back. Pity we didn't have one of them tram services out this way. Them townies have all the luck. Catch a tram or charabanc anywhere. But us country folk, we have to practically walk anywhere we wanna go. Mind you, in this trade you ain't got any spare time, so it's of no consequence really to me. But the missis now, she likes to visit. That's why I got the pony and trap. Quite an expert she is wi' a pair of reins.'

'Expert?' a regular standing at the side of Sep guffawed. 'In my opinion she's bloody lethal. Just about killed me the other day. Came charging round the bend like Lucifer himself was on her tail.'

'More an' likely 'cos you were drunk, Jess, and didn't see her coming,' the landlord laughed loudly.

Jess finished his drink, thanked the landlord and made to leave.

'Eh up, Jess. You going back to the farm?' the landlord asked.

'Yeah, why?'

'Yer could give this bloke a lift on the pig.'

Jess sized Sep up. 'I could that. I'm going as far as Desford. That's if you don't mind sitting on the back of the trailer? Stinks of manure though. But I've got a sack yer can sit on.'

Sep, thinking worriedly that it must be some size of pig to pull a trailer, but more to the point that it must be cruel, stared at him blankly.

The landlord gave a bellowing laugh. 'You'll be fine, squire. The pig won't bite.'

Intrigued, he followed Jess out of the pub and smiled in relief to see the 'pig'. It was one of the first petrol-driven vehicles ever to be built by Leyland, Jess informed him proudly. It had a long low front, a long flat back with room enough for at least thirty filled sacks, and a high seat behind the steering wheel for the driver. The whole vehicle was much the worse for wear.

Jess slapped him on the shoulder. 'See, Jack told yer she wouldn't bite.' He collected an old sack from a box at the back of the driving seat and spread it out across the filthy wooden trailer.

'Did I hear yer say you come from Barlestone?' he asked.

'I do, yes,' Sep replied.

30

Jess paused for a moment. 'Yer don't happen to know a lad called Billy, by chance?'

'Billy? Billy Cartwright?' Sep asked curiously.

'Could be. But I only know him as Billy.'

'Why?'

'Oh, I just wondered if you can tell him I could do wi' another pair of boots.'

'Boots?'

'Yeah. He gets 'em cheap. Good quality n' all. He gets one or two other things on the side but boots is the only thing I need.' He laughed loudly. 'Contrary to belief, us farmers ain't all rich.'

'Well, you can't be poor running a contraption like this,' Sep said, running his eyes over the 'pig'.

'Ah, that's necessity, squire. She can pull treble the load of two of my old horses, and she don't eat as much oats and hay.' He patted the long bonnet affectionately. 'Besides, I've had her that long she's part of the family. Come on then, climb aboard and we'll be off or me missis'll swear blind I've had more than me two pint quota.'

Sep sat gingerly down whilst Jess turned the starting handle. With a shudder and several loud groans the engine rattled into life.

Sep enjoyed the slow bumpy journey even though he feared that any moment the vehicle would explode beneath him. He was far from comfortable as he jolted up and down on the wooden base, feeling every little pebble, and big one, that passed beneath the large solid wooden wheels, and twice he nearly fell out when they hit pot holes in the road.

But he found himself eyeing Jess jealously. He would have given anything to be in his place and have this antiquated but marvellous machine at his disposal. It took all his willpower to stop himself from asking if he could sit behind the wheel.

Finally, Jess drew to a halt at a turning in the road and Sep alighted, walking around to where the farmer was perched on the driving seat.

'Thanks. My feet appreciate the ride.'

'My pleasure.' Jess grinned. 'First time on a horseless vehicle, is it?'

Sep took a deep breath. 'Actually, no. I learned to drive in the war, and I must say I enjoyed every minute of it.'

Jess eyed him in admiration. 'Yer don't say? Well, it's not often I bump into a fellow driver. You should have spoken up. I would have let you have a go.'

For several minutes the pair reminisced.

Jess lifted his cap and ran his hand over his mop of greying hair. 'I've another of these,' he announced proudly.

Sep gawped. 'What! Another pig? You've two of them?'

'Yes, I have that. Only the other ain't in such good nick as this 'un. I got 'em both cheap from the Dixon family in Market Bosworth. They'd had 'em since they were first made in about

1902. Not bad, eh? Nearly twenty years old and still going strong. 'Course, when I bought 'em, me wife thought I was mad. Never spoke to me for a fortnight. But she soon saw the sense and quickly realised that tinkering about wi' the engine stopped me going down the pub of an evening.'

Sep gawped again. 'What? You fix 'em yerself?'

'Oh, yes. There's n'ote to it, once yer know the rudiments. Mek most of the bits meself. What I can't, old Jones the blacksmith does.' He sniffed loudly and ran his grubby hand under his large red nose. 'Actually, I've been thinking of selling the other one if yer interested? I've got all I need with this one and it teks up too much room in me barn.'

Sep ran his eyes over the machine longingly. He dug his hands deep into his jacket pockets and rocked back on his heels. 'It's a nice idea. But what would I do with it? Besides, if I had the money to buy it, I wouldn't be able to afford to run it.'

Jess scratched his unshaven chin. 'They don't cost much to run, don't these. Ah, well, it was just a thought, you being a fellow driver. I'd best be off now.' He pressed his foot down hard on the accelerator and the engine clanked while the body of the vehicle rattled and shook. Just before he manoeuvred off he turned back to Sep. 'Oh, don't forget to give that Billy me message should you happen across him.'

Sep eyed him thoughtfully. 'No. No, I won't.'

Striding forth, he began the remainder of his journey home, his mind full of the past hour and the conversation he had had with Jess. Slowly the inklings of an idea began to form, a tiny spark that once thought out properly just might be the answer that he had been looking for since his other ill-fated undertaking many years previous. In any event, should it materialise, it would certainly smack Cyrus Crabbe right between the eyes and that thought alone was enough to spur him on.

But however good his idea might be, it would need financing and that was the one thing he lacked. He rubbed his hands together. He would work at it until he found the answer. This was one idea that was too good to shelve just because of lack of funds. In the meantime, he would keep matters to himself. At this stage it was no good building up the family's hopes, or more importantly alerting other folk.

It was well after eight when he finally strode through the back door, his aching feet desperate for a rest. He was greeted by Nell.

'Where you bin, Sep?' she asked in concern, rising from her rocking chair to take his meal out of the oven. 'I've bin that worried I nearly got the Constable. I've sent our Primrose out twice to look for you.' She wrinkled her nose. 'What's that smell?'

'Smell?' Sep eyed her blankly. 'Oh, it's manure,' he laughed. 'I've had a ride on a pig.'

Nell frowned deeply. 'Have you been drinking, Septimus Cartwright, and me worried out me mind?'

'No, I've told you the truth. I've been riding on a pig. Only the pig I'm referring to ain't got four legs, it's got four wheels. And it were grand, Nell. Took me back to when I used to drive around the army camp with supplies.'

She plonked his plate on the table. 'Sit down and eat your dinner,' she commanded.

Sep unlaced his boots, hung his old black jacket on the back of the door, unbuttoned his stiff white collar, laid it on the table and sat down, upset that his wife was dismissing his adventure.

Something Jess had said came to mind. 'Where's our Billy?' he asked. 'I need to talk to him.'

'Why? What's he done now?'

Sep raised his eyes to meet his wife's. He hesitated. He didn't want to worry her any more than was necessary on the evidence of one conversation. 'Nothing much. Just wanted a chat.' He eyed appreciatively the meal Nell placed in front of him and cut into his tripe, piling his fork with mashed potatoes and onions. 'By, this looks grand.' He glanced at her, his eyes twinkling. 'It's a bit dried up though.'

'You're lucky to get it,' she snapped. 'It nearly ended up in Florrie Hewlet's pig swill.' She plonked a steaming mug of tea in front of him and sat opposite, placing her fleshy arms on the table and eying him fondly. 'Any luck today or is it best not ter ask?'

Sep raised his eyes. 'Best not ter ask,' he said, shovelling up a mouthful of food. 'How was your day? Get her tuppenceworth, did our Mrs Pegg?'

'There's nothing wrong with Jenny Pegg, Sep, so don't be unkind. She treats me fare and square, better than some other folks I could have worked for. And I'll give Jenny her due, she gave me an extra couple a' bob today and filled me basket with leftovers.'

Sep slammed down his fork. 'Leftovers? Bloody other people's leftovers! I'm sick of charity.'

Nell narrowed her eyes as she rose, picked up her mending and seated herself again in her rocking chair. 'If we didn't get the odd bit of so-called charity, Sep, we'd really be in queer street. And before you start, I'm not blaming you, just stating a fact. It'll all change when you get work again. Now finish your dinner before it gets cold.'

Sep smiled meekly and resumed eating. Nell was right. He was in no position to be proud. But he was beginning to doubt that her forecast of work would ever materialise. He finished his dinner and pushed aside his plate.

'Where is everybody?'

'All gone out 'cept our Primrose and Letty.' Nell dropped her mending. 'Oh, Sep, I don't know what's ailing our Letty. I've never seen her look so miserable and she wouldn't eat any food. And you know our Letty for her food. Lick the dustbin clean, she would.' She frowned hard. 'I've got a feeling she never went to work today.'

Sep raised troubled eyes. Like his wife he didn't like the thought

33

of any of his offspring suffering unnecessarily and liked to keep a fatherly eye on them. 'I'll go up and have a word, eh?' he volunteered. 'See if she'll tell her old dad her troubles.'

'No, just leave it for now. She'll tell us in her own good time. She's not one to keep secrets, is our Letty. Anyway, Peggie's around Aggie's so we shan't see her for a while and Billy's on the late shift. Ronnie should be in any minute now. If he's not, I'll scalp his backside.'

Just then the door leading to the stairs opened and Primrose walked through. She hesitated when she saw her father. Before she could escape, Nell beckoned her in.

'Get yourself in here, young lady, and tell your father what you did today.'

Sep frowned quizzically at his youngest daughter, looking the picture of innocence in her long white cotton twill nightdress. Her light brown wavy hair fell down to her waist and hid most of her sullen face. 'Well?' he asked.

Primrose sat slowly at the table, her head hung low. 'I din't do nothing,' she muttered.

'Nothing?' her mother said sharply. 'You call falling asleep, forgetting to feed the chickens and letting the pigs run free for all the village to chase after "nothing"? *And* you forgot to wash the pots. It wouldn't surprise me if Florrie Hewlet sacks you after this and there's plenty of others willing to take your place.' She frowned fiercely. 'Fancy falling asleep under the apple tree.'

'Well, I was tired,' Primrose mumbled.

'Tired! How can a young gel like you be tired? Why, you'd not long had ten hours' sleep.'

'I hadn't. Not with all the racket that was going on,' Primrose said before she could stop herself.

'Racket! What racket? Sep asked. 'I never heard anything.'

Primrose bit her bottom lip. She knew she would have to tell the truth, her parents wouldn't let it rest until she had and she didn't fancy sitting here all night being questioned.

'Our Letty eloped through the window, only Wilfred never came. So she was crying most of the night.'

Sep and Nell looked at each other. Nell sighed deeply. So that was it. That was what had caused her daughter's deep unhappiness.

'You mark my words, Effie Dage is behind this,' Nell said harshly. 'Driving them to elope. I'll give 'em elope! Any daughter of mine getting married will do it with her family around her, not in some strange town, skulking in corners in case they get found out.' She realised Primrose, wide-eyed, was hanging on her every word. 'You get to bed, young lady. We'll deal with you later.' She waited while Primrose left the room and then clenched her small fat fists. 'It's about time Wilfred Dage stood up to his mother. His father had the sense to, so why won't he? I've a good mind to go round there now and knock his head off for the heartache he's caused our

Letty over the years. Well, it stops here and now. I'm going to ban her from seeing him.'

Sep raised his eyebrows. 'Calm down, Nell,' he ordered. 'Our Letty's twenty-five. She's old enough to pick and choose who she sees and how she weds. It's not like in our day when we had to do what our parents told us.'

Nell eyed him sharply. 'Is that why you married me, Septimus Cartwright? 'Cos your parents forced you?'

'You know it's not. Now simmer down or you'll start saying things you'll regret.'

Her shoulders sagged. 'I'm sorry, Sep. I'm just so angry, that's all. I just feel for the gel. I don't like it when any of me family is miserable.' She raised her eyes. 'D'yer think there's 'ote we can do?'

Sep shook his head. 'Not to ease her pain, I don't. The best thing we can do is carry on as normal and let the pair sort it out in their own way.'

'All right,' Nell agreed. 'But I'll have none of this eloping nonsense. They ain't doing me out of a wedding, Effie Dage or no Effie Dage.'

Sep grimaced. 'Well, if truth be known we can ill afford a wedding at the moment, not when we have more pressing needs, such as getting your legs seen to.' His eyes softened. 'They're bad, ain't they, Nell?'

She puffed out her chest indignantly. 'There's nothing wrong with my legs. Just swollen out a bit that's all. Nothing that a bit of rest won't cure.' She pretended to busy herself. So she hadn't fooled Sep for a moment; she'd have to be even more discreet in the future. Putting away her mending, she rose awkwardly. 'I'm off up the stairs. I've had enough for today.' She walked over and pecked her husband on the cheek. 'Will you stay up and see our Ronnie in safely?'

He smiled and patted his wife's arm. 'Just get to bed, Nell. I'll see to the rest and bring you up a fresh cuppa in a while.'

She nodded gratefully and left the room.

Several moments later there was a pounding on the back door and Sep rose to answer it.

Before him stood the village constable and a shamefaced Ronnie whose dishevelled appearance gave him the look of having slept the night in a muddy field. Most certainly he wasn't in the tidy state Sep knew Nell would have seen him off in that morning. He stood aside to allow them to enter, his face set grimly, wondering what his younger son had been up to.

Constable Jesson cleared his throat. 'This young lad was caught loading luggage.'

Sep stroked his chin. 'Oh, was he now?' His eyes settled on Ronnie. 'And were you loading luggage?'

Addressing the floor, Ronnie muttered: 'Well, the porters were busy and there was this old man, you see, struggling with this big bag, and so I offered . . .'

'That's not the point,' snapped Constable Jesson. 'You shouldn't have been near the railway anyway, let alone helping with luggage. That's a porter's job.'

'He's right, Ronnie.'

'I know.' The boy raised apologetic eyes. 'But I weren't doing no harm.'

'Yes, but all the same he got paid and that's not allowed.'

'Did you get paid?' his father asked sternly.

'Only a tanner. The man was ever so grateful and I never asked for it.'

Constable Jesson sniffed severely. 'Well, Mr Tunley wants to see you Monday night at six o'clock if that's convenient, along with the lad.'

Sep frowned hard. 'Wants to see us, does he?' He squared his shoulders and stared down at his son who was rocking uneasily on his feet, his ear still stinging from the clip he had received from the Constable. 'All right. We'll be there, Constable.'

'Righto. I'll be off then.'

'Thanks for bringing him home.'

Constable Jesson nodded and made his way out.

Sep strode forward and placed his back to the fire.

'Well, son. What you got to say for yourself? And look at me when I'm speaking to you.'

Ronnie raised his blue eyes and settled them on his father's chin.

Sep breathed deeply. 'I thought you'd been warned to keep away from the station? Apart from 'ote else, it's dangerous.'

'I'm sorry, Dad.' He sighed loudly. 'I couldn't help it. I love watching the trains.'

Sep stroked his chin. Since the day his son had first clapped eyes on a train he had been besotted by the great iron monsters. His waking and sleeping hours were filled with thoughts of nothing else.

'No,' Sep agreed sternly. 'But you're still on railway property when you'd been warned not to be. Well, lad, we'll just have to wait and see what Mr Tunley proposes to do. In the meantime, don't mention a word to your mother. She's enough worries on her mind without you adding to 'em.' He gave his son a wink. 'Save me one of the bulls eyes you buy with that tanner.' He smacked him playfully on the backside. 'Now get off to bed.'

He watched in silence as his son ran from the room, not relishing the forthcoming meeting with the formidable Basil Tunley. It was a pity that his presence had been requested instead of Nell's. She was better at this sort of thing. If there was anybody to face or any discipline to be handed out, Nell was usually the one to do it. He was too soft where his children were concerned. Somehow he always managed to see their side of things.

He made his way over to the range and shook the large black kettle. Filling it with water, he put it back on the hob and prepared to mash a pot of tea. He paused and stared absent-mindedly at the large brown tea pot in his hand, preoccupied with the thoughts that

36

had filled his mind since that afternoon.

Enthusiasm burned within him. He couldn't ever remember feeling so excited about anything since, as an unworldly young man, he had started working on the ill-fated brake. As this idea grew and took shape, so did his passion to put it in hand. But he wouldn't make the same mistakes again. That lesson had been hard learned.

He sighed at the thought of the one major obstacle that could stop the whole thing going ahead. How was he going to raise the money to get started?

Billy, bone weary from his long shift at the face, alighted from his bicycle and pushed it up the hill. As the end of the week drew nearer, the walk up the hill seemed steeper. He just thanked the Lord he had secured this rusty old bicycle in one of his deals. His other colleagues had to walk the long distance home regardless of the weather and he didn't envy them one little bit.

He hated his job. Crawling around on all fours in air filled with choking black coal dust. Hour upon hour pitting his muscles against the seams of unrelenting black gold. But it was not the thought of arduous toil that oppressed him as he entered the cage at the beginning of each shift ready to descend into the darkness – it was fear. Fear that once inside he would never leave alive, that one day some terrible catastrophe would happen as it had done to other colleagues, leaving them dead or, worse, dreadfully maimed. Wives without husbands, children without fathers, households with no main breadwinner, and all for the need for the black life-giving mineral that lay buried hundreds of feet beneath the surface.

No, it was no way to earn his miserly living but it was the only one at the moment open to him. He sighed deeply. It must be heaven to work in the fresh air, he thought longingly, seeing the countryside bathed in warm life-giving sunlight or resting beneath frost and snow. He knew many men would, given the opportunity, break his legs to get his job and they could have it as far as he was concerned. But he would have to stick it out until his sideline became more lucrative. And it would, given time, he was in no doubt of that.

He knew what he was doing was against the law, that the various items he was offered were more than likely come by illegally. But he never asked questions. As far as he was concerned, the less he knew the better. Besides, if he didn't take the stuff offered someone else would, and as it was his only means of getting out, why give the opportunity to another?

The pitch black night seemed to close in on him as he arrived at the crest of the hill and made to climb on his bicycle. He would be relieved to get home, strip off and rid himself of the grime that coated his every pore, as well as get some food inside his stomach. He jumped as a shadowy figure emerged from the hedgerow. He let go of his bike which fell to the ground with a clatter.

'Bloody hell, Mick, you frightened me half to death!'

37

'Sorry, mate,' Mick Matterson chuckled. 'Only I thought I'd missed yer.'

Billy picked up his bicycle. 'Well, you ain't, so what d'yer want?'

'Huh, fine way to act when I'm only trying to put a bit of business your way. But if yer ain't interested, some other bugger will be.'

He made to walk away but Billy grabbed his arm.

'Not so quick. What you got?'

'Stockings.'

'Stockings? What sorta stockings?'

'Ones that go on legs,' Mick mimicked. 'Ten dozen. Top quality cotton, in all colours.'

Billy rubbed his chin. 'I don't think I can shift that many.'

'Suit yerself . . .'

'Hold on. How much?'

'Two quid.'

'Two quid?' Billy shook his head. 'I can't raise that much.' He paused thoughtfully. 'How about I take half?'

'All or nothing.'

Billy calculated quickly, not wanting to let go of this lucrative deal. It might be a while before anything else came his way. 'Tell you what, I'll take 'em all, pay for half and the remainder when I've sold 'em. That's the best I can do. Take it or leave it.'

The two men stared at each other.

Finally Mick grinned. 'Deal.'

Billy nodded in satisfaction. 'Right, I'll meet you back of the church at twelve tomorrow night.'

They shook hands on it. Just before Mick disappeared through the hedge he stopped and turned. 'Oh, summat else for yer. The four-thirty tomorrow at Leicester races. Dancer's Folly.' He tapped the side of his nose. 'Had it on good authority it's worth backing. See yer.' With that he was gone.

Billy smiled to himself. He would make a good return on this little caper. He had plenty of takers lined up. And he just might risk a tanner on that tip. Mick was good with the tips. How he got his information was anybody's business but they usually came up trumps. He climbed on his bicycle and whistled softly as it gathered speed. If he hurried he would have time for a quick visit with Alice before her oaf of a husband came home from wherever he spent his time. It certainly wasn't at work. Bull Hammond hadn't done an honest day's work since Billy could remember.

The thought of Alice's inviting body sent hot blood rushing through his veins. He knew what he was doing was wrong but it was Alice who did all the running, he only accepted what was being offered. He whistled louder, picturing her peeping scantily clad through her curtains, hoping for his appearance. Good old Alice. She was at least ten years older than himself and must have been quite a looker in her youth. In fact she still was, but she hadn't much of a life married to such a ogre and he assumed his visits were just about the only pleasure she got out of life. As long as their times together gave her joy then they would continue. Providing, that was, Bull didn't find out.

As he rode past the Hammond cottage he tutted. The place was in darkness. That meant Bull was home. Still, not to worry. There were plenty of other nights and he was tired anyway. Parking the bicycle in its usual place against the mangle, he let himself quietly into the kitchen, wondering what his mother had left for his supper.

He froze as he sensed a presence. 'Who's there?' he demanded.

'What! Who is it?' came the reply.

Billy relaxed. 'Dad! What a' you doing up? And why a' you sitting in the dark?' he asked as he bent down and removed his bicycle clips. He selected a newspaper spill from the container on the hearth, placed it against the fire, and when it took hold lit the paraffin lamp hanging above his father's head.

Light flooded the room and Sep squinted as his eyes grew accustomed to the light.

'Sorry I startled you, son. Only I was doing a bit of thinking and forgot the time.' He yawned loudly and stretched himself.

Billy moved over to the sink and filled it with cold water from an enormous blue enamel jug, stripped off his clothes and started to wash, using the large block of coarse Sunlight soap.

Sep rose in the meantime and started to mash a pot of tea. When Billy had finished his ablutions, Sep addressed him.

'Sit down, son. I want a word.'

Hanging the wet towel on the hook by the sink, Billy looked around for his supper. 'Oh? What about?' he asked absent-mindedly.

Sep hooked his fingers through his braces. 'What's this I've heard about you selling boots?'

'Selling boots?' Billy reddened, giving his father his full attention. 'Er . . . I don't know what you're talking about.'

Sep banged his fist on the table. 'Don't play the innocent with me, lad. I asked a question and I want an answer.'

Billy lowered himself down on a chair opposite. 'Look . . .' he began slowly. 'I got offered a couple a' pair of boots cheap and resold 'em, that's all. Just to make a few coppers. There's n'ote wrong in that, is there? Anyway, who told you?'

'Never you mind who told me. Were they stolen?'

'Stolen!' Billy spluttered. 'No, 'course they weren't. Wadda you take me for?'

Sep sighed deeply. 'A sensible lad, I hope. It's a serious matter, selling stolen goods.' His eyes softened. 'Listen, lad, I don't mind you earning a bit on the side. Christ knows your wages are pitiful as it is. But I tell you now, if I ever have an inkling that you're dealing with 'ote crooked, I'll knock your block off. That's before I hand you over to the police. So be warned.'

Billy felt a hot flush rising up his neck. 'I wouldn't, Dad. Honest, I wouldn't. I ain't stupid.'

Sep let out a sigh of relief. 'That's what I wanted to hear.' He leaned across the table. 'Now, these boots. Can you get me a pair?

39

At cost price, mind. Mine have got nothing left on 'em to repair.'

'I'll try.'

'Good. And your farmer friend in Desford wants a pair an' all.'

'Oh, that's how you heard?'

Sep nodded. 'It all comes home, lad. You can't do anything in these parts without someone knowing. Now,' he began, then stopped and took a breath. It pained him deeply to ask the next question. But it had to be done. 'Have you any spare money?'

Billy stared at his father quizzically. Never before had he asked such a question, not even when Billy knew he hadn't a farthing in his pocket.

'How much money, Dad?'

Sep blew out his cheeks as he picked up the tea pot and filled two mugs. He pushed one in front of Billy. 'That's it, lad. I don't know. It could be a few shilling, it could be a few pounds.' He leant on the table, his eyes bright. 'See, son, I've got an idea, only it needs a bit of financing and I have to know I can lay my hands on a few quid before I go further. Look, I know you hand over most of your money to your mother but I had to ask the question.'

Billy eyed his father keenly. 'What is this idea?'

'Never you mind. I'll tell you all in good time. Now, have you got any spare or not?'

'Not at the moment. I'm a bit strapped meself.' Billy's heart plummeted. If only he hadn't committed himself to that deal with Mick, he could have helped. And he couldn't possibly break his word. If he did his major source of supply would be gone. Besides, Mick didn't take kindly to being let down. He thought rapidly. Even when he got the stuff it would take a couple of weeks to shift it. He had to do it discreetly so as not to alert suspicion. But he badly wanted to help his father. The old man needed something to get him on his feet again. Billy's inquisitive mind wondered just what this idea was. It must be something good for his father to want to borrow money on the strength of it. 'I've er . . . been asked to do a couple of extra shifts. I could give you that when I get it,' he lied to cover up the origins of his forthcoming expectations. 'Will that help?'

Sep tried to hide his disappointment. 'No, son. I'm not having you doing extra work just to help me. No, don't worry, I'll raise what I need some other way.'

Billy felt bad for telling a lie. He suddenly had a brain wave. 'I've had a good tip on a 'oss running tomorrow in the four-thirty at Leicester. Dancer's Folly.'

Sep scraped back his chair and rose. 'Don't you dare even think it, our Billy. You know I don't bet. Never have done and never will. It's money thrown away.'

'All right, Dad, calm down. But it's a winner, I'll stake me life on it. If you change your mind, just let me know.' He looked around the kitchen, then settled his eyes back on his father. 'Did Mam leave me any dinner?' he asked hopefully.

'No, she must have forgot. You'll have to help yourself to bread and cheese. She was fair worn out and went to bed early. And that's where I'm off to now, to join her. Tarra, son.'

''Night, Dad.'

As Billy cut a large wedge of bread and filled it with cheese, wondering if somehow he had missed out on some action that his father had heard about, Peggie was saying her goodbyes to Aggie at her gate. They both stood and watched as a courting couple stopped and kissed before resuming their journey. Street lighting had yet to reach rural areas and the couple were quickly lost in the darkness.

Aggie turned her gaze to Peggie. 'D'yer think I'll ever get a bloke?' she sighed forlornly.

Peggie tutted loudly. 'Course you will. It's just you haven't met anybody good enough yet.'

'Good enough?' Aggie repeated sharply. 'I ain't ever met anybody, full stop. I never get the chance to find out if they're good enough.' She sniffed loudly. 'What d'yer reckon to me getting one of them new busk-fronted corsets I've seen advertised in the paper? Marshall and Snelgrove are selling 'em in Leicester. They're new in from America. D'yer think that'll make any difference to me shape? I could always ram some paper down the front. Might make me look as though I have a chest.'

Peggie hid a smile. Aggie was built like a bean pole and the purchase of any corset let alone an expensive new design would be a waste of money. She had nothing to put inside it. But she didn't want to upset Aggie's feelings. Despite her lack of looks and figure, her friend had a heart of gold, a great sense of humour and was a wonderful cook. Any man who chose her would never starve.

'Aggie, you look fine. You don't need a corset. Having a big chest ain't the answer.' She glanced down at her own full breasts. 'They just get in the way, 'specially when you're running,' she said laughing then paused for a moment thoughtfully. 'But I tell you what I have been thinking of . . .'

'Yes' Aggie said keenly.

'Getting me hair cut in that new bob style. What d'yer think?' said Peggie, patting her great mane of blonde curls. Her large blue eyes shone wickedly in the darkness. 'Tell yer what, let's both get it done, eh? It'd suit you. It might be just the thing you need.'

'Oh, I don't know . . .' Aggie began.

'Oh, go on. Be a devil for once. If it don't suit, you can always grow it back again.'

Aggie's thin face lit up. 'Oh, d'yer think we dare? Me mam'd have a fit.'

'Aggie, we're both old enough to make up our own minds. I have to do an errand for me mam after work tomorrow so I could make an appointment with that hairdresser in Shilton. Or we could go into Hinckley, or even Leicester. We could make a day of it, eh? But

41

we won't tell anybody 'til we've had it done. It'll give 'em all a shock.'

Aggie giggled and slapped Peggie on the arm. 'Oh, go on then, and I want a perm as well. Might as well go the whole hog. Just hope I can afford all this.'

Both girls collapsed into laughter at their forthcoming adventure.

Aggie eyed Peggie. 'If we get our hair done, I want you to promise me you'll come to the annual village dance in October. You never know, we might both meet someone.'

The smile left Peggie's face. 'I wish people wouldn't keep harping on the fact that I'm on my own. I'm quite happy, thank you.'

'Are you? Well, I think it's about time you let Harry go and started looking elsewhere.'

'Elsewhere! I wouldn't give half the blokes round here houseroom, let alone 'ote else. Now change the subject, Aggie, before I lose my temper.'

'All right, all right.' Aggie tightened her mouth and folded her thin arms. 'Cold, innit?' she said sarcastically.

Peggie laughed. 'Yes, it is, and I'd better be off before the folks get Constable Jesson out. See you bright and early.' She yawned. 'I wish we didn't have to work on a Saturday morning.'

'Me neither. But I bet they'd have us in on a Sunday if they could get away with it.'

'Yeah, you're right. Anyway, I'd better go. 'Night, Aggie.'

''Night, Peggie.'

She hurried up the dirt road towards home. She had had a good night at Aggie's. It had been a pity she could not persuade Letty to come but, regardless, all three of their tongues, Aggie's, her mother's and her own, had worked overtime and her mouth felt dry. If she was lucky there might be a stewed mug of tea left in the pot when she got back.

She felt slight panic rise. She was much later than she'd intended. Her parents did not like her being out so late and she hoped they were both in bed so she wouldn't get a telling off. She smiled. Here she was at twenty-seven, old enough to be married with a family of her own, and her parents still watched her like a hawk as they did the rest of the family. Not that she really minded. It made her feel loved and wanted. Not like some of the parents she knew. They didn't give a damn what their children got up to as long as it was outside their own back door.

She stopped suddenly. Somewhere in the distance she could hear the sound of crying. She listened for a moment but the noise appeared to have ceased. Must have been an unsettled child, she thought. The night air grew chilly and she wished she had thought to pick up a cardigan to slip over her ankle-length skirt and cotton blouse. The noise began again and she frowned hard. There was definitely someone crying. But where?

She began her journey again and as she rounded a bend in the path, she almost fell over a huddled figure on the grass verge. She recognised the figure and squatted down beside it.

'Mary, what's the matter?' she asked softly.

Mary Crabbe slowly raised her head. One of her eyes was badly swollen and the beginnings of a bruise was starting to show.

'Oh, Mary,' Peggie said with emotion. 'What on earth's happened?' She placed her arm around the woman's shoulder and pulled her close.

Mary's sobs grew louder.

'Tell me?' Peggie coaxed. 'Was it your father? Did he do this to you?'

Mary shook her head savagely. 'No. no. It weren't him. I fell down the stairs, honest I did.'

Peggie froze. No one fell down the stairs and gave themselves a black eye.

'Mary, tell me the truth. I can help you.'

'No one can help me,' she cried softly.

Peggie was saddened. 'I could if you'd let me.'

Mary managed a smile. 'I would like your help, but there's others who wouldn't and you'd be in trouble and I wouldn't like that. Not on account of me.'

The breath caught in Peggie's throat. At twenty-three years of age, Mary Crabbe was a timid, frightened woman and Peggie had always had a terrible feeling that it wasn't because of her nature, just due to the years of brow beating she had suffered at the hands of her father and brother.

The Crabbes lived in a formidable, ivy-covered, redbrick early-Victorian house on the outskirts of the village and after her mother's death, at an age when other children were learning to play, Mary had been taught the only things necessary to keep house and care for Cyrus and Reginald. She was hardly ever seen outside her own garden gates and was classed as a freak by many of the villagers and pitied by the rest.

It saddened Peggie deeply to see such a mild-mannered kind young woman, who cried out to be shown a bit of love and attention, treated with such callousness and she felt a great urge to do something about it. Suddenly she had an idea.

'Mary, you can come home with me. Come on now. You can have a bed for the night at our house and I'll attend to your face.'

Mary choked back a sob. 'Why? Why should you want to help me?'

'Why shouldn't I?' Peggie replied, hurt. 'I happen to think you're a very nice person and I'd be honoured if you'd let me do something for you.'

Mary raised her head. 'Would you?' she asked in astonishment. Her shoulders sagged. 'Oh, but I'd love to come with you, Miss Cartwright.' She shuddered violently. 'But I can't. I have to get home.'

'Home?' Peggie said, her voice rising sharply. 'Mary love, I can assure you, that place you live, it ain't a home.'

'But it's the only one I've got.'

Peggie took a deep breath. She suddenly felt so guilty for having a proper home and loving family. 'Leave, Mary. Stand up for yourself. You're old enough. There's places you can go. People that would help you.'

Mary's troubled face lit up. 'Is there? Is there, Miss Cartwright? Would I be able to do things? Go to work?' She peered down at her ill-fitting, shabby dress given to her by a kindly neighbour several years past. 'Would I be able to buy some new clothes?'

'Yes, yes. You'd be free to do whatever you wanted. You might even meet a nice man and get married.'

Mary lowered her head, a sob catching in her throat. 'That's just it, I can't. I won't ever be able to leave home or get married. Not now . . . Not now that . . .' She stopped as huge tears of anguish poured down her cheeks.

Peggie eyed her, deeply worried. 'Not now what, Mary love?'

'Mary!' a deep voice sounded from above.

Both heads jerked up. Before them stood Cyrus Crabbe. Neither had heard him approach and they both stared up at him in shock. He stared back, his eyes cold, his mouth set tightly. He held out his hand.

'Come on, Mary. Say good night to Miss Cartwright. We have to go home.'

Peggie felt Mary shudder. She jumped up and stood before Cyrus.

'Mary's coming home with me, Mr Crabbe,' she announced. 'That's all right with you, isn't it? It'd be a treat for her.'

Cyrus's face darkened. 'Is that right, Mary? You want to go home with Miss Cartwright?' he asked, his cold gaze still locked on Peggie.

Mary started to shake. 'No, Dad. No, I don't,' she said hastily.

Peggie opened her mouth to protest, but quickly snapped it shut, realising that anything she said would not be in Mary's best interests.

The young woman awkwardly rose, the pain of her injuries showing deeply on her face. 'We'll go home now, Dad.' She turned to Peggie. 'Thank you for your help.'

'Oh? And what help would that be?' Cyrus asked icily.

'Nothing, Dad. Miss Cartwright just offered to bathe me eye, that's all.'

'I see. Well, she's quite capable of doing that herself.' His lips curled at the corners. 'I suggest you get off home yourself, Miss Cartwright. Never know who you might meet on such a dark night. Wouldn't want a pretty woman like you to come to harm, would we?' He made to turn away then stopped. 'How's your mother?' he asked.

Peggie's mouth gaped at such an unexpected question. 'My mother! Er . . . fine, thank you.'

'Good. Give her my regards and tell her I hope her legs are much better.' He gave a sly smile before grabbing Mary's arm and marching her down the street.

She stared after them helplessly, worried sick about what fate lay in store for Mary once she reached the place she called home. That black eye was no accident and she felt positive that Mary was in for another beating.

She clenched her fists. She would speak to her mother as soon as possible and see if she had any suggestion on what could be done to ease Mary's burdens. She couldn't let it be, not now she had witnessed first hand what the woman must suffer.

Thoughts of her mother brought back to mind Cyrus's enquiries about her welfare and she pondered for a moment why he had asked. She frowned hard. What had he meant about her legs? And more importantly how did he know? She shrugged her shoulders. Knowing the Crabbes and their reputation this was probably just his way of making trouble in the Cartwright household. It was Mary she must now think of. She was the one needing help.

Peggie straightened her back and made her way home.

Cyrus Crabbe stood over his daughter, his face malevolent. 'So what lies have you been telling, Mary? Just what was it you told Peggie Cartwright?'

'Nothing, Dad. I told her nothing, honest. She asked how I'd got me bruises and I told her I fell down the stairs and she offered to bathe me eye, that's all.'

'Liar!' he spat, scowling fiercely. 'If you think I believe that's all you told her, then you're a fool.'

Mary cowered in the corner of the room and squeezed her eyes tightly shut, waiting for the rain of blows to beat down on her. When they did not come, she gingerly opened one eye and stared up at her father. The oil lamp hanging from the ceiling at the back of him cast an eerie light and she shuddered. Why did he hate her so much? She had always done everything he had asked, not daring to do otherwise. Her days were filled with cooking, washing, cleaning. She never left the house except to collect the shopping and, on his strict instructions, never, never chatted to the other villagers.

It hadn't been so bad when her mother had been alive. She, God rest her soul, had done her best to shield Mary from her father's harsh ways. Her mother had been the only light in her miserable life and when she had died from what seemed to be a simple cold, after Cyrus's refusal even to consider paying good money for a visit from the doctor, Mary's one joy had died also. Her life now reflected her mother's. A continual round of work, all connected with caring for Cyrus and her brother Reginald, neither of whom showed one iota of gratitude. But worse, far worse, was the ever present loneliness of her existence.

She eyed him in trepidation, knowing he was deciding a form of punishment for her defiance. He was worried, she could tell. He was worried because she knew too much. She knew things that, if divulged, would bring his downfall.

She watched as he raised his head, intense fear filling her. He had made his decision.

'I know exactly what I'm going to do with you. You're nothing but a slut, a dirty, disgusting slut, and you're not going to bring shame upon my house.' Cyrus wiped away the beads of sweat pouring from his brow with the back of his hand. 'I'm going to put a stop to any gossip before it starts. I'm going to make you suffer more than you thought imaginable for what you've dared to do. And you've only yourself to blame. You knew what consequences you'd have to face if you stepped outta line.' His lips curled at the corner. 'I did warn yer.'

Mary shook as he leaned forward, grabbed her painfully thin shoulder and pulled her forcibly to her feet.

Chapter Four

'I can't give you anything for this. It's worthless, I'm afraid,' Mr Green the pawnbroker said, handing the ring back to Peggie.

She stared down at it. 'Nothing at all?' she asked in disbelief. 'But it's solid gold and very old.'

Mr Green narrowed his kindly faded brown eyes. 'That's where you're wrong, my dear. It's brass. To be accurate, it's a brass curtain ring. The type they use in all the big houses to hang the drapes.'

She stared at him agog, having terrible trouble registering what he had just divulged to her.

Mr Green stroked the side of his large hooked nose as pity for the pretty woman with the abundant mane of golden curls rose up. It pained him to see the disappointment that had settled across her face and the tears that sat behind her vivid blue eyes. He knew he would have to try and help her as he did most of the people who came into his shop. He could hear his wife's scolding, bless her, ringing in his ears. 'Joseph, this is a business we're running not a charity.' But he knew he could not let this woman leave without retaining some of her dignity. He placed his large hands on top of the counter and smiled warmly. 'I might be able to give you something for the locket around your neck.'

Peggie's hand shot to her throat. 'Oh, no,' she said, aghast. 'I can't part with this. My fiancé gave it to me just before he went off to war. He never came back.'

'Oh, I see,' he said sincerely, remembering all the family and friends he had lost. 'Well, if you change your mind, you know where you can find me.'

She left the shop downhearted. How on earth was she going to explain to her mother that her grandmother's precious ring was worthless? More importantly, her mother was counting on the money raised from it to pay the rent. She had a few shillings saved herself, but not the amount her mother had hoped to raise. She stood for several moments debating the odds before she turned and hastily retraced her steps.

Mr Green smiled as she re-entered. 'Changed your mind?' he said kindly, peering over his half moon glasses.

'Well,' Peggie began as she approached the counter, 'if I pawn this, how long have I got to redeem it before you sell it?'

Mr Green stroked his bearded chin. 'Six months. But you'll have to pay back what I give you plus the interest in full.'

She thought for a moment then unclipped the locket and thrust it at him. 'How much will you give me?'

Mr Green accepted it and pulled his magnifying glass down over his eye for the purpose of examination.

As he went about his business, Peggie gazed around the shop. It was crammed with all manner of goods. Items of clothing hung from hangers suspended from beams across the ceiling and overspilled on to racks and shelves against the walls; piles of bedding were stacked high at the side of two grandfather clocks ticking merrily away by the far wall, and Peggie was sure she could see a penny farthing bicycle poking out from behind perambulators, tin baths and several old milk churns. But the most amazing thing of all was the long glass counter behind which stood Mr Green examining her locket. It held the most amazing collection of jewellery that she had ever seen. Magnificent precious stone rings, bracelets, necklaces, earrings, and all sorts of watches and clocks glittered inside the display case, waiting to be reclaimed or sold to the highest bidder.

She began to feel better. Judging by the amount of goods in this shop, her family wasn't the only one suffering from lack of money. And judging by the quality of some of the items, it wasn't only the poor who were suffering either. She turned her attention back to Mr Green.

He flicked back his magnifying glass and looked at her. The locket was not what he had first thought it to be. It was a nice piece but not of any significant value.

'It's a nice locket,' he said slowly. 'I can . . . er . . . stretch to seven and six.'

'Seven and six?' she said sharply. 'It's worth a damn' sight more than seven and six. You can't say it isn't gold 'cos I know for a fact it is. Two pounds,' she demanded.

Mr Green shook his head. 'My dear, I'm trying to help you. As you can see from the display, I'm not short of this kind of stuff.' He sighed heavily. 'Fifteen shillings. And that's my final offer.'

Peggie tightened her lips. Although she did not want to part with her locket, she was beginning to enjoy this bartering. 'Thirty bob,' she said, and smiled hopefully at him. 'Come on, Mr Green. You know it's worth much more than that and I'll give you my solemn promise I'll be back to redeem it. This locket means the world to me.'

He frowned. If he continued giving well over the odds he would be out of business very shortly. He raised his eyes, resigned. 'All right. Thirty shillings. And that is my final offer. But to retrieve it, you'll have to pay me three pounds.'

Three pounds! Peggie thought hard. It was an awful lot of money. Well over a month's wage. But her mother needed that thirty shillings and as she had so rightly pointed out, they hadn't anything else they could raise a loan on, so it was this or nothing.

'I'll take it,' said Peggie quickly.

48

Mr Green wrote out her pawn ticket and handed over the money. After thanking him she hurriedly left the shop. She climbed aboard the brake just as it was about to leave.

'Get all your business done?' Aggie asked.

'Yes, thanks,' she replied, gripping the sides of her seat as Reginald whipped the horse into what seemed like a gallop.

'So, what time?'

Peggie turned her head and stared blankly at her. 'Time?'

'Yeah, our appointment at the hairdresser's. You said you were going to see to that while I got my buttons and tapes from the draper's.'

'Oh, damn, Aggie. I forgot. I'm sorry.'

Aggie's face fell in disappointment, then she smiled. 'No matter. I couldn't afford it anyway.'

Peggie smiled back. 'To be truthful, neither can I. What bit I have got saved I really need to buy a coat with. This one's beginning to drop to bits.'

She lapsed into silence, her thoughts on Harry. She hoped that if he was up there somewhere he would forgive her for what she had done with the locket he had so lovingly given her. Guiltily she remembered her promise to him that she would treasure it forever.

She arrived home to find the house empty except for her father who was sitting at the kitchen table staring into the palm of his hand. He shut his fist tightly as she entered.

She stared at him quizzically. 'Dad, what's up?'

'Nothing,' he replied hurriedly.

'Where's Mam?' she asked, pulling off her hat and placing it on one of the hooks on the back of the door. She picked up the blackened kettle and shook it. Satisfied there was enough water, she placed it on the hob.

Sep tutted loudly as he began to rise. 'Peggie, I'm sorry, me duck. Your mother left me strict instructions to get your dinner started and I forgot.'

'Don't worry, Dad. Sit where you are. I'll do it. I'd better make Letty something and take it up to her. I'll see to the others when they come in.'

'Letty's gone out.'

Peggie swung round. 'Out? Where to?'

Sep shook his head. 'Don't know.'

'Oh!' She paused thoughtfully. 'I wonder where she's gone?' She unhooked the large frying pan, placed it alongside the kettle, took four rashers of bacon from the dish in the pantry and put them in the pan, along with a slice of bread and four halved tomatoes. 'Do you want a sausage as well?' she asked.

'Yes please,' he replied absent-mindedly.

Peggie turned to face him. 'Well, where is Mam?'

'Oh. She's gone along to Mrs Gulliver's. The woman's gone into labour so Nell doesn't know what time she'll get home.'

'Oh, I wonder what it'll be?' Peggie said, interested. 'Mrs

49

Gulliver's hoping for a boy this time. She's had enough of girls after giving birth to seven of 'em.'

'Whatever it is, it'll still want feeding.'

'Dad!' Peggie said sharply.

Sep eyed her, ashamed. 'Sorry, love, that were uncalled for.'

Peggie picked up a metal spatula and turned the bacon and sausages beginning to brown in the sizzling beef fat. The aroma filled the air and she sniffed appreciatively, suddenly feeling very hungry.

'If our Letty's gone out she must be feeling better,' she said as she poured boiling water into the large tea pot. 'Madge Grimwell, the forewoman, played merry hell over her absence from work. By the way she went on you'd have thought our Letty was always taking time off.'

'Yes, it's funny that,' he said with a twinkle in his eye. 'Only our Letty going down with that stomach upset. After all, we all eat the same.'

Peggie eyed her father cautiously. He knows about Letty eloping and Wilfred standing her up, she thought. And if he knew then that meant her mother did also. She opened her mouth then snapped it shut. Uncharacteristically she decided it was up to Letty to disclose all the details, not her. She had enough on her mind worrying how she was going to retrieve her locket. 'Yes,' she said lightly. 'It is, isn't it.' She turned back and dished up the food on to two warm plates. She placed her father's in front of him. 'Eat this while it's hot.'

She sat down opposite and poured them both a mug of tea. As she ate she watched her father closely from beneath her lashes. It was unusual for him to be so quiet. Normally they chatted away ten to the dozen. Her father always showed an interest in what she had been doing. She pushed her empty plate away. He had something on his mind and it was something important, she was in no doubt about that.

'Come on, Dad,' she said firmly. 'Out with it.'

He raised his head. 'Pardon? Out with what?'

'Whatever's on your mind?'

'Oh, er . . . I was just thinking it's about time we got our own chickens again.'

'Chickens! Dad, you weren't thinking about getting any more chickens. Why, it just about broke your heart when they all died of that awful poultry disease while you were away at war and you said you'd never get any again.'

'I know what I said. But we must be the only family hereabouts that doesn't have our own and your mother's always complaining about the price of eggs. And we should seriously think about getting a pig. My old dad would be turning in his grave if he knew we didn't keep pigs any more. Now a pig fattened up could keep us in meat for weeks. It certainly did when we kept them before.' The mention of a pig brought back to mind Sep's real problem and he lapsed into silence again.

'Dad, our garden isn't big enough to keep chickens, pigs and Mam's copper and mangle and all the other junk we've collected. Not since Mr Brotherhood claimed back most of the gardens to extend his wood yard. Still I suppose he had a right, after all he does own these cottages.' She took a deep breath. 'Tell me what's really the problem?' She bit her bottom lip, a worried frown settling on her face. 'Is it something one of us has done?'

Sep's head jerked up. 'No, no, Peggie. None of you has done anything that I know of. 'Cept I have to take young Ronnie to see Mr Tunley the Station Master on Monday night and I ain't relishing that much.'

'So what is it?' Peggie leant across and placed her hand on her father's. 'You always expect us to tell you our troubles. So can't you trust me with yours? I'm not a kid any more, Dad. I'm a grown woman. Maybe I can help.'

Sep looked at his daughter fondly. 'Yes, you are a grown woman and a very attractive woman at that. I'm a lucky man.' He paused thoughtfully for a moment. Peggie was right. He had always encouraged his children to share their problems. Problems shared didn't seem half so bad or complicated when discussed freely. He made his decision and smiled across at her. 'Pour us another cuppa, gel, then I'll tell you all.' He gave a small laugh. 'I might as well. You won't rest 'til I do.'

Peggie quickly did as was asked, curiosity filling her.

Meanwhile Sep sat back in his chair and loosened the top button of his shirt collar. Why shirt collars had to be so stiff and uncomfortable was beyond any man's reasoning. He put the collar on the table, accepted the tea gratefully and settled his gaze upon his daughter.

'I've had an idea, Peggie,' he began. 'One that I know will be the making of us.'

'Oh?' she said, folding her arms and leaning forward, interested. The sparkle in her father's eye was not lost on her. It was something she had not seen for a long time.

'On my way back from Leicester yesterday, I was offered a ride on a motor vehicle.'

'A motor vehicle around these parts?' she said in surprise.

'Yes, but don't get carried away. It wasn't a posh car, just an old farm vehicle. Jess, that's the farmer that owns it, uses it to haul all sorts of heavy stuff on the trailer on the back and I got to thinking . . .' He stopped and eyed her cautiously, suddenly wondering if this idea was nothing more than a fanciful dream.

'Got to thinking what, Dad?' she prompted.

He inhaled deeply. 'Well . . . that if Jess could transport his farming material all over the place, maybe I could transport people.'

He paused to see Peggie's reaction. All he could see was a blank expression.

'You see,' he hurriedly continued, 'Jess has another of these

51

vehicles that he's willing to sell. Of course, it'll need some work doing to it, but with what I learned looking after my supplies lorry, I'm sure it's nothing I couldn't tackle myself.'

Peggie rested her elbows on the table, placed her chin in her hands and stared at him, mouth open in amazement. Who'd have thought that her father would have had an idea such as this?

'I know that this is the way forward, Peggie,' he continued. 'Since the motor engine was first invented, it was only a matter of time before it took over from 'orses. And I feel sure that if the war hadn't happened the motorbus business would be a lot further forward than it is now.'

'Do you, Dad?' she asked in awe.

Sep nodded. 'Yes, I do. It was only the War Department commandeering anything that moved for the war effort that put a halt to things. I learnt all this when I was on the army base. In fact, I learned lots of things whilst I was away.' He laughed. 'There's a lot more to your old dad than what you think.' He paused and breathed deeply, his eyes filled with excitement. 'Oh, Peggie, if only I could get hold of that vehicle. I've thought of so many things I could do to make it passengerworthy. I could box in the sides and put in some sort of seating arrangement and also erect a frame to throw a tarpaulin over to shield folks from bad weather.'

'Yes, you could,' she cried, swept along by her father's enthusiasm. 'We could get hold of some old blankets to cover people's legs up in the winter to make them more comfortable.'

'Now there's another idea,' he said, looking at her proudly. 'Oh, Peggie, if only I could be the first to bring motor transport out this way, I'd have the monopoly in this area like I would have done if that bastard . . .' He suddenly stopped, realising what he was about to say, and eyed his daughter apologetically. 'I'm so sorry, I should never have used a word like that in front of you.'

'Oh, it's all right, Dad. I know all about that business. Oh!' She clapped her hand over her mouth, realising that she had just broken her promise to her mother.

Sep frowned hard. 'You know about . . .?'

Peggie gulped. 'About you and Cyrus Crabbe.' Her eyes flashed. 'Yes, I do. I only found out yesterday, but I know all right.' She leaned over the table and placed her hand on her father's. 'Dad, please don't tell mam I've let it slip out. She only told me because I made her. Anyway, it was all such a long time ago.'

'I know that, Peggie,' he said harshly. 'And the Bible tells us that we should not bear grudges. But I can't help it. Not in this case I can't.' He brought his fist down hard on the table. 'That man stole from me, then blatantly lied about the fact. And in doing what he did he ruined my one chance of giving you all a better chance in life. I'll never forgive him. Never.'

'Oh, Dad,' Peggie whispered as tears of helplessness stung the back of her eyes. She suddenly realised how much getting this motor vehicle meant to him and silently vowed that she would do

52

whatever was necessary to help him realise his dream even though she could see at least one major obstacle in the way.

'It's such a wonderful idea,' she said softly. 'One too good just to be forgotten about. But how are the likes of us going to get the money to buy it?'

Sep smiled wryly. 'Pray for a miracle?'

Peggie sat back, her mind racing. She knew without a doubt the folk in Barlestone and the surrounding villages would fall over themselves to be driven around in a motor vehicle. But more important than anything, this idea would give her father back his self-respect when he desperately needed to have a purpose again. It would also damage Cyrus Crabbe's business badly and that in itself made the idea more than worth pursuing.

'There must be some way we can raise the money?' she said raising her eyes to meet his. 'How much are we talking about?'

'That's just it.' He sighed loudly. 'I don't know. But I don't think Jess wants an unreasonable amount, not from the way he spoke, and he seemed a genuine enough man to me.'

Peggie remembered the thirty shillings inside her purse, but quickly decided against it. It was no good having a motorbus if you had no house to park it outside. Besides, that money was to get her mother out of her predicament. Her father's needed a lot more thought.

'Could you not come to some arrangement with this farmer?' she suggested. 'After all, if this motor whatever it is, is just sitting in his barn, he might . . . well, he might just let you pay for it bit by bit.'

Sep frowned hard at her and shook his head. 'I shouldn't think so, me duck. Farmers like everything paid for on the nose. Anyway, it's against me principles to . . . well, it would be like asking for charity.'

Peggie sighed. Her father and his principles! She thought that for once he could lower them. 'What about our Billy? Have you asked him if he's any spare?'

'I approached him last night, but he's as strapped as the next. The only thing he had to offer was a tip for a race running this afternoon. Dancer's Folly or something like that.' He frowned. 'That reminds me, young lady, you were out rather late last night.'

'Oh, Dad, I was only at Aggie's. Actually you've just reminded me that I have to speak to Mam on a certain matter.'

'What matter?'

'Oh, nothing, Just women's talk.' She eyed her father keenly. 'That tip?'

'Tip?'

'Yes, the one you've just mentioned. Did our Billy get it from Mick Matterson?'

'I don't know. I don't abide with betting so I never delved deeper.'

Peggie's eyes shone brightly. 'Dad, if our Billy got that tip from Mick Matterson then it's a winner, I'll stake me life on it.'

Sep frowned. 'What makes you say that?'

'Well, it's a known fact that Mick gets inside information. People pay him handsomely for his tips. He must have been drunk or else owed our Billy a favour if he gave that tip away for free.'

Sep raised his hand. 'Peggie, you can just stop there. I've never been a betting man and I'm not about to start now. If I can't get this motor vehicle by honest means, I'll not get it at all.'

'But, Dad, don't you see?' she burst out. 'If we could raise the money for the bet and it won, you could buy the motor thingy. One bet wouldn't hurt. It doesn't mean to say you're gonna turn into a gambler. You're placing this bet for a purpose.'

Sep sat stunned. His daughter was right. Having one bet wouldn't harm. In fact, if he was truthful, wasn't that the very thing that was on his mind when she had come in earlier? He had two shillings in his pocket. His last two shillings. It wouldn't buy much on its own. But doubled or trebled . . . He struggled with his conscience. Peggie did have a point. One bet wouldn't damn him to hell. Besides, he could make his peace with the Lord in church tomorrow morning. If God was as understanding as He was reported to be, then He would surely turn a blind eye just this once. But Nell wouldn't. She would go stark staring mad if she found out he had spent hard-earned money gambling.

He sighed deeply, conscious that Peggie was waiting for his answer with bated breath. In his mind's eye he saw not one Cartwright motorbus but several, all painted brightly, spick and span, ready to depart for different destinations. His heart quickened. He so desperately wanted to make a go of this venture. But his conscience, his deep love of Nell and his family, plus the possibility that the horse could loose, overrode his desires.

He rose, abruptly and grabbed his coat off the back of the door.

'The answer's no, Peggie. I can't take the chance of losing what little we have left. Not when you've all worked so hard to get it.'

He strode through the door, leaving her staring after him.

Her shoulders sagged and she wrung her hands together in anguish. She felt her father was wrong not to take the gamble. What if the horse did win? The money would change their lives completely. If it didn't, what had they lost? Just a couple of shillings that would buy hardly anything of value.

She lifted her head, her vivid blue eyes shining brightly. Her father's principles wouldn't let him place that bet, but there was nothing to stop *her* from doing it. She hurriedly scraped back her chair, ran up the stairs and came down holding her tin money box. She opened it and tipped the contents onto the table. Several shillings, sixpenny and threepenny bits rolled across the green oil cloth, clattering against the crockery. This was the money she had been going to use to buy her new coat, money it had taken her months and months to acquire. Well, her coat would just have to wait until she had saved up again.

Just as she began to count it Letty stormed through the door, her hat askew, her eyes ablaze in temper. She stopped in front of Peggie and trust her spectacles further on to her nose. 'How dare you?' she spat, pushing Peggie hard on the shoulder.

She fell back in surprise. 'How dare I what?' she asked innocently.

'How dare you tell Wilfred that I don't want to see him any more?'

Peggie exhaled sharply. 'Oh, I haven't time for this now. We'll talk about it later,' she said, going back to her counting. 'Have you any money?'

'What?' Letty asked, bewildered.

'I said, have you any money? Come on, hand it over. I haven't time to explain. And where's our Ronnie and Primrose?'

Letty gawped at her. 'What's going on? What do you want my money for?'

Peggie stopped her counting and raised her eyes to meet her sister's. 'For a bet,' she announced.

Letty stared her. 'You've gone mad. I'm going to fetch Mam.'

'You'll stay where you are,' Peggie blurted, grabbing her arm. 'Mam or Dad's not to know about this 'til we know the outcome. Is that understood?'

Letty stared, agog.

'Did you hear me, Letty?' She dug her nails into her sister's arm.

Letty gave a squeal of pain. 'Yes, yes,' she cried. 'But I won't give you anything 'til you tell me what's going on.'

Peggie's temper rose. 'I told you, I haven't time to explain just now. The race'll start soon.'

'Race?'

'That's what I said, Letty. Now hand over your money.'

Reluctantly, she fished in her handbag and pulled out her purse. She handed over two shillings. 'That's my fare and lunch money for next week,' she grumbled.

Peggie grinned and put her arm around her sister affectionately. 'If we pull this off, our Letty, you'll never need to find your fare ever again.'

'Won't I?' she asked, confused.

'No, you won't.' Peggie made for the back door, yanked it open and shouted for Ronnie and Primrose at the top of her voice.

Ronnie poked his head out of the door of the outside privvy, his trousers round his ankles, a comic in his hand. 'What?'

'Get in here now,' Peggie commanded. 'I've an errand for you.'

'But I'm on the lavvy, then I'm off to play footie with me friends!'

Peggie eyed him menacingly across the yard. 'In here, now!' she shouted, marching back inside the kitchen.

Ronnie appeared several moments later. The comic was clamped firmly between his teeth and he was tucking his shirt into his short trousers.

'What's going on?' he asked, eyeing each of them in turn.

'You may well ask,' Letty said haughtily, then snapped her mouth shut as she caught sight of Peggie's frozen glare.

'Have you any pocket money left?' Peggie asked him.

'I might have. Why?'

'Hand it over,' she said, holding out her hand.

'Ah, Peggie. It's for me bull's eyes,' he wailed. 'Wadda you want it for anyway?'

'Stop asking questions and hand it over. And where's our Primrose. I want any money she's got left as well. Mind you, if I know our Primrose, she'll already have spent hers before she got it.'

'Letty!' Ronnie groaned, looking towards her to intervene.

She shrugged her shoulders. 'I've had to hand over mine, so you can do the same.'

Outnumbered by elder sisters, Ronnie dug deep into his trouser pocket and pulled out a shrivelled conker, a length of string, a penknife, a grubby handkerchief and two half-pennies.

'Is this all you've got?'

He scowled. 'I only get twopence as it is.'

Peggie sniffed. 'It'll do, I suppose.' She placed it on the table along with the rest. 'Now how much have we got?' She paused. 'It's a pity our Billy's not home 'til gone six, we might have got something from him. He got paid yesterday.' Her eyes twinkled wickedly as she made for the stairs.

'Where you going?' Letty asked.

'To see if our Billy's got any hidden,' she shouted back.

Letty and Ronnie looked at each other.

'She's gone barmy,' Letty muttered, sitting down at the table.

Peggie returned several moments later, triumphant, with a handful of loose change totalling ten and threepence-halfpenny.

'Now, let's count it up,' she said excitedly.

The grand total came to just over twenty-five shillings.

Peggie beamed. 'Well, what do you reckon? Is this enough for a good bet? Will we get a good return?'

Ronnie eyed the pile of coins, quickly calculating how many weeks worth of sweets and comics it represented. 'Depends on the odds,' he said knowingly.

Peggie looked at him in surprise. 'Odds? What do you know about odds?'

'I hear the men talking, that's all.'

'Oh, so you know what to do then?'

'Sort of,' he said cockily. 'But if we don't hurry, we won't catch the bookies' runner before he leaves for Hinckley.'

'Oh! Oh, right,' Peggie said, staring at him. Her little brother obviously wasn't as innocent as she had always thought.

She gathered the money together, screwed it tightly inside a twist of newspaper and handed it to him.

'You'd better go and do the business then, being's you know so much.'

Ronnie proudly puffed out his chest. 'Okay, sis. What's the name of the 'oss I've to back?'

Peggie eyed him blankly. That was a good point. What was the

56

name of the horse?' 'I can't remember,' she said slowly.

'Well, that's no bloody good then!' Ronnie blurted. 'You can't back an 'oss without knowing its name.'

Peggie lifted her hand and smacked him hard on top of his head. 'Don't you dare use words like that in this house, you little ruffian. I don't know, our Ronnie. Between your swearing and getting in trouble with Mr Tunley, you lead our mam and dad a right song and dance.'

Ronnie wailed loudly, rubbing his smarting scalp.

'Dance. Dance,' Peggie said slowly. 'Dancer's, Dancer's . . . Dancer's Folly!' She gave a squeal of delight. 'That's it. Dancer's Folly.' She grabbed him, hugging him tightly. 'Well done, our Ronnie,' she sang.

He broke free from her grasp. 'Ged off, sis,' he said, screwing up his face in disgust. I don't know, he thought ruefully. Adults were either playing hell or hugging you to death, and he didn't know which was worse.

'Well, what are you waiting for?'

'Eh!'

'I said, get to it,' Peggie scolded. 'Go and place that bet before it's too late.' Without thinking she grabbed the twist of paper out of her brother's hand, turned from view, rummaged in her pocket for the thirty shillings she had got for her locket, put it inside the twist and thrust it back at him. 'Go quick,' she shouted.

Hands on hips, she watched as Ronnie ran from the cottage, her mind full of mixed emotions. She couldn't wait to see her father's face when she placed the winnings in front of him. But what if it lost? She couldn't bear to think of that so crossed her fingers and said a silent prayer. She wondered how she was going to fill the time before her brother came back. Taking a breath, she turned her attention to Letty sitting at the table.

'Now, what was it you were going on about when you came in?' she asked. 'Something to do with Wilfred, wasn't it?'

Letty scowled fiercely, all her previous anger returning. 'You warned him to stay away from me, didn't you?' she hissed. She scraped back her chair, rose and strode forward, stopping just short of her sister. 'How dare you, our Peggie?' she spat. 'How dare you tell Wilfred to leave me alone?' She pushed Peggie hard on the shoulder. 'You'd no right.'

Peggie narrowed her eyes as she recovered her stance. 'Well, someone had to do it, and I had every right. It's always my shoulder you cry on when things aren't going well between you both – and that's more often than not.' She sighed deeply and her eyes softened. 'Letty, I wouldn't be much of a big sister if I just stood by and let Effie Dage get her own way. Wilfred had to be made to stand up to her and I thought confronting them both just might do the trick.'

'Well it didn't,' Letty cried. 'Me and Wilfred had a blazing row and I ended up telling him I was going out with someone else.'

'And are you?' Peggie asked in surprise.

'No, but I will be. You just watch. And I don't care who it is.'

'Letty . . .'

'Don't Letty me! I'm old enough to go out with whoever I please. Reginald Crabbe came round yesterday to enquire after my health. He mentioned going out and I said I'd think about it.'

Peggie's mouth dropped open. 'Reginald Crabbe?' Oh, of all people, not him. Her parents would commit murder.

'Yes, Reginald Crabbe. He's a good-looking bloke. I've heard he knows how to show a girl a good time.'

'But, Letty, that man has a terrible reputation and . . . and . . .'

'I don't care. I quite fancy getting a reputation meself. I'm fed up with being nice little Letty.' She stopped abruptly, suddenly shocked at what was spewing forth from her own mouth. She had no intention of going out with Reginald Crabbe. She couldn't stand the man and wouldn't be seen dead with him. But for once she had managed to strike Peggie speechless, and for this reason and only this she felt pleased and decided to carry on with it, even though it was only bravado.

'Now come on, Letty, you're upset,' Peggie spoke in alarm. 'You don't mean all this. Just give Wilfred a little time. After all, he was the one who stood you up. He's probably feeling terrible. Well, I know he is, 'cos he told me. He'll come crawling back shortly and you two'll be back together . . .'

'I wouldn't have him back if he came on a white charger in full armour,' Letty responded loudly. 'I'm gonna go and have a good time, and Reginald Crabbe is the one to do it with.' She tightened her lips, thoroughly enjoying the effect all this was having on her sister. 'And you just dare interfere, Maggie Cartwright,' she said icily, emphasising the Maggie. 'Try it just once and I'll give you a right thumping.' She threw back her head in defiance. 'Now if you don't mind I'm gonna rummage through the oddment box to see if I can find enough material to make myself a new dress. And, believe me, it'll be something that'll make all heads turn.'

She left a speechless Peggie staring after her as she ran out of the kitchen and up the stairs.

Ronnie, feeling mightily important, half skipped, half ran down the dirt street towards the Jolly Toper public house, the money for the bet tucked deep down inside his trouser pocket. The Jolly Toper was the place where all the men gathered on a Saturday lunchtime to place their illegal bets. Constable Jesson turned a blind eye to what was going on. If he rounded up all the guilty parties in the village then three-quarters of the houses would be without a bread winner.

Ronnie neared his destination and slowed down, spying his deadly enemy Godfrey Smith idling against the wall on the opposite side of the road. He was holding a thick length of birch and poking the sharp end into the dried ground, unearthing an ants' nest. As the ants swarmed out, Godfrey squashed them under his big bare feet. He spotted Ronnie and smirked. Ronnie's presence was just the thing he had prayed for to relieve his boredom.

'Wotcha, titch,' he shouted mockingly. He righted himself and strode across the road. 'What yer up to?' he demanded, towering menacingly over his prey.

Ronnie pulled himself up to his full height of five foot five, four inches shorter than his opponent. 'What's it got to do with you?' he said, looking past Godfrey towards the Jolly Toper. If he didn't get a move on he would be too late to place the bet. A run in with Godfrey Smith he could handle but not one with his sister Peggie. With his eyes fixed unblinkingly on Godfrey, he skirted round the side of him, hoping to make a dash for it.

Godfrey raised his stick and poked Ronnie in the chest. 'When I ask a question I wanna answer, you little runt.' He raised the stick in the air, meaning to bring it down heavily on Ronnie's shoulder.

Ronnie, foreseeing what was about to happen, quickly hooked his leg around the bigger boy's ankle and brought him down heavily on the ground. The birch stick snapped in two. Godfrey, his mouth gaping open in surprise, shook an angry fist in Ronnie's direction as the victor speed off.

'I'll get you for this, Ronnie Cartwright. You see if I don't.'

Still smiling to himself, Ronnie inched his way down the back yard of the public house, not wanting to be stopped from entering the building. He hadn't enlightened Peggie as he should have done. He should have told her that in order to place the bet, he would need to go into the tap room and children of his tender years were not allowed freely into such places. Regulars would turn a blind eye, but not the landlord for fear of losing his licence. He hid behind a pile of wooden barrels stacked in the yard and watched closely for his chance to slip inside.

His attention was caught by strange sounds coming from the huddle of buildings further down the yard. Apart from the dispensing of ales and spirits and the illegal gambling and betting that took place inside the rooms at the front of the premises, the Jackson family, in order to supplement their living, kept a dairy herd which supplied the villagers with milk and cheese, and also pigs and chickens which were slaughtered, cut up and sold on the premises. These were the sounds Ronnie could hear now, several pigs squealing as they met their grisly end.

He shuddered, but not from the thought that the poor pigs were having their throats cut. He shuddered at the noise they were making. Ronnie smacked his lips together at the thought of a nice leg of pork roasting inside the range back home, the sides of the tin packed with potatoes and onions. His mouth filled with saliva. His mother cooked a right tasty bit of pork and always managed to get the crackling just right. You could chew on a piece of good crisp crackling for hours. But pork was a rarity in their house. They were lucky these days to get a few pieces of ox tail for a pot of everlasting, rib-sticking soup. Well, if this 'oss won, with a bit of luck his next errand could well be to the Jacksons' slaughter house.

His attention was diverted by two village men who had suddenly appeared in the yard. They were talking in low whispers and Ronnie listened intently. Their talk made very interesting listening. Very interesting listening indeed.

The men finished their debate and walked towards the back door of the pub. Ronnie seized his chance and tucked himself behind them.

He emerged several minutes later feeling extremely pleased with himself. But then quickly frowned in concern, wondering if Peggie would be pleased when she found out what he had done.

Chapter Five

A worried Peggie paced frantically along the short cinder path that led from the cottage to the front gate. She stopped and wrung her hands together despairingly. It was two minutes past six. Surely Ronnie should have been back by now? How long did it take for several horses to run round a track and for the bookie's runner to get back to the Jolly Toper? The answers to her questions had been eating their way into her mind for the last half an hour and she could no longer ignore their significance. The horse had lost and Ronnie dare not come home.

She stopped her pacing and hung over the gate, looking up and down the road. Ronnie was still nowhere in sight. She bit her bottom lip anxiously. Her father was bound to return soon, he had already been out longer than she had thought he would be. But, more worrying, her mother could arrive at any minute and she would know instantly something was amiss and would not be satisfied until she heard all. Then the trouble would start.

On hearing a noise behind her she abruptly turned and raised her eyes to see Letty leaning out of their bedroom window, a broad smirk across her face.

'Well?' she shouted sarcastically. 'Are we rich then like you'd said we'd be?'

Peggie scowled deeply. 'Oh, shut up, our Letty, and get back to your sewing.' She made to turn away but changed her mind. 'Why don't you shout louder and let all the neighbours know our business?'

Letty leaned further out of the window. 'Well, I hope the damned 'oss lost. It'll teach you a lesson for interfering again!'

''Oss? What's this about an 'oss?' asked Bella Hubbard, beady eyes wide with interest as she emerged from her front door, a large blackened saucepan and netting bag full of early peas in her hands. She settled herself on an old wooden stool at the side of her front step, spread her legs wide, emptied the pods into her large apron and started to split them open. 'Well?' she asked, eyeing Peggie expectantly.

She shook her head. 'You must have bin hearing things, Mrs Hubbard. We never mentioned 'osses.'

'You did. I distinctly heard the word 'oss.'

Peggie tutted loudly. You couldn't go to the privvy in this house without the neighbours knowing. Ignoring Bella, she looked up at Letty.

'Haven't you a dress to finish for your special night out with your new man?' she said sweetly.

Bella's ears twitched, taking the bait. 'Dress? New man? What new man?'

Peggie turned and let herself out of the gate, leaving Letty to talk her way out of that one.

She walked slowly down the street. It had been a lovely warm afternoon and promised to be a fine evening, the type of evening to amble along the country roads hanging on to a loved one's arm. But Peggie's mind was too full to notice the weather or the fact she had no loved one to bother about.

With growing alarm she began to realise the full extent of her impulsive actions. Not only had she thrown away all her own savings, she had taken Letty's fares and dinner money for a whole week, rifled Billy's pockets, which he wouldn't take kindly to when he found out, commandeered the last of Ronnie's pocket money, but far worse than anything, she had used the money she had raised on her locket; money which her mother needed desperately to pay the rent. How on earth was she going to pay it all back without her parents finding out?

As, deep in thought, she rounded a bend in the road, she fell smack into Jim Bates, another neighbour from Chapel Lane.

'Watch it, Peggie, me duck. Yer nearly 'ad me over.'

She jumped back, startled. 'Oh, I'm sorry, Mr Bates. I wasn't looking where I was going.'

'No 'arm done, gel,' he said, hiccoughing loudly. 'But it's a good job I never finished me last pint, I might've been been on the floor if I had!'

Peggie smiled, then a thought struck her. 'Mr Bates, have you just come from the Jolly Topper?'

He shook his head. 'No. Got chucked outta there several years back for 'aving' a punch up and I ain't bin in since.' He leaned heavily against a garden fence for fear of falling down. His afternoon session was telling on him and all he wanted was to get home and fall asleep in the armchair, his wife's moaning and groaning ringing in his ears. 'Why?' he slurred.

'Oh, I, er . . . just . . . er . . . wondered if a certain 'oss won a race, that's all.'

'Did yer? Now why would you want to know that?'

Peggie innocently shrugged her shoulders. 'Just out of interest.'

'Oh! Well, sorry love, I can't 'elp yer.' He leaned towards her, a blast of his beery breath hitting her full in the face. 'Now if yer'd asked me about the cock fight last night, I could a' told yer all about that. But I don't go for the 'osses. Cocks, dogs and pigeons is more my line.' He managed to straighten up, grabbing hold of the fence for support. 'Ah,' he said, pointing across the road, 'now there's a fella that can. Wally!' he shouted to a man opening a garden gate opposite. 'D'yer know what won . . . Just a minute.' He turned back to Peggie. 'What race warrit?'

She stared at him blankly. 'I don't know.'

'Yer don't know! What race track then? Leicester?'

She nodded. 'I think so.'

'Which race? The two o'clock? The four-thirty? What?'

'Er . . . the four-thirty,' she said hopefully.

Jim Bates shouted back to Wally. 'What won the four-thirty at Leicester?'

Wally grimaced hard. 'A one-legged donkey called Shangrila. I lost a tanner. And stop shouting 'case the wife hears,' he added gruffly.

Peggie's heart sank. She grabbed Mr Bate's arm. 'Ask him about Dancer's Folly, please, Mr Bates?'

He eyed her for a second, bemused, then called back to Wally. 'What 'appened to Dancer's Folly?'

'Dancer's Folly,' he repeated thoughtfully, scratching his chin. 'Never heard on it.'

Mr Bates turned back to Peggie and shrugged his shoulders. 'I hope you didn't put much on it, gel?'

She raised her eyes haughtily. 'I don't bet, thank you very much.'

'Well, your Billy then?'

'Our Billy doesn't bet either,' she said sharply.

Mr Bates grinned. 'Doesn't he? Oh! I must be seein' things then.'

Peggie exhaled loudly. 'Thanks for your help, Mr Bates. You'd better get home before Mrs Bates comes looking for you.'

She left him watching her through blurred vision, wondering just what that was all about.

As she neared the village green, she stopped. Even in her preoccupied state, she had to smile. An unwanted threadbare Victorian horsehair sofa, propped up on several house bricks, had been dumped in the centre of the green complete with a crudely painted sign: 'The Village Seat.'

Absent-mindedly, she walked over and sank down, several hard springs digging into her. She sighed loudly as she placed her elbows on her knees, rested her chin in her hands and stared blankly at the ducks bobbing up and down by the reeds over the far side of the murky pond. How was she going to face her family after this? And what about her father? He so wanted that motor contraption. And she had so wanted to give him the means with which to fulfil his dream.

She sighed heavily as an overwhelming feeling of guilt settled upon her. Letty was right, damn her. Peggie did interfere and was far too impulsive for her own good. If she hadn't interfered in Letty's affairs by storming down to see Mrs Dage and giving her a piece of her mind – even if it was with the very best of intentions – Letty and Wilfred just might by now have managed to patch things up, and herself and Letty would not be at loggerheads. And if she had just taken time to think about that stupid bet then she wouldn't be faced with financial ruin now. But worse, far worse than financial ruin, was the prospect of her mother finding out.

She sighed even louder and more forlornly than before, closed her eyes tightly and wished the ground would open and swallow her. At least then she would be spared her family's wrath.

As Peggie sat contemplating the blessed release of an early demise, Letty slowly swung out of the gate and sauntered down the road, looking to any passerby as if she hadn't a care in the world. She inched her spectacles further on to her nose and slowly glanced around her. Wilfred usually did his late Saturday night deliveries around this time and with a bit of luck she might accidentally bump into him.

She missed him dreadfully. To others he might be soppy old Wilfred who would do anything to keep peace with his mother, but to her he was the kindest, most considerate man she could ever have hoped to fall in love with, and it had been that way since he had bashfully asked her to the village dance on her fifteenth birthday ten years previously. She sniffed back a tear. Was he missing her as she was him? She guessed he was. He had only ever had eyes for her.

She stopped abruptly. Why was it then that he hadn't come to seek her out and put things right between them? After all, it was his fault. He had stood her up, even if it wasn't his own doing. Her temper rose. Reginald Crabbe wouldn't let a mother get in his way. Nothing would get in Reginald Crabbe's way. She had heard rumours about him – rumours linking him with several married women in the vicinity – and wondered if they were true. If they were, why on earth had she half promised to go out with him? With all her heart she regretted doing so and wondered how she could get out of it.

Suddenly around the corner rode Wilfred on his bicycle, the basket on the front laden down with several boxes of groceries. On spotting her his eyes opened wide in shock and the bicycle wobbled dangerously as he brought it to a halt several feet short of her, a packet of Rinso soap powder falling to the ground. He dismounted, picked up the packet, placed it back and took a deep breath.

'Hello . . . er . . . Letty. How are you?'

'Fine,' she replied awkwardly. 'And you?'

'Fine,' he answered slowly.

Wilfred pressed his lips together and gazed intently at the ground. An uncomfortable silence engulfed them.

Wilfred, say something. For God's sake say anything, Letty screamed inwardly. Before she could stop herself she opened her mouth. 'How's your mother?' she asked sarcastically. 'Still managing to live with her conscience?' As the words left her she wished she hadn't said them. The hurt in his eyes as he raised them to meet hers cut her to the quick.

'Letty, I can't be held responsible for my mother's actions. Apart from meeting you stark naked, there wasn't much I could do, was there? Do you think I liked the thought of your standing in the dark waiting for me? But there was no way of letting you know . . .'

'Wasn't there?' she cut in. 'I'm sure Reginald Crabbe would have found a way. In fact, I'm sure *he* wouldn't have let his mother take away his clothes and lock him in his bedroom in the first place.' She raised her head and stared at him defiantly.

Wilfred narrowed his kindly brown eyes, confused. 'Reginald Crabbe? What's this got to do with Reginald Crabbe?'

As if on cue, Reginald sauntered around the corner with several other village men, all spruced up for a night of revelry around the village pubs. The corners of his mouth twitched as he spotted her. He glanced quickly at Wilfred then back at her.

'Well, if it isn't Letty Cartwright and her ex-fiancé.' He turned and winked at his friends. 'All set for our night out, Letty?' he said with amusement in his voice.

Wilfred gawped. He eyed them both, frowning deeply. 'Night out? What night out?'

Letty froze, mortified. Before she could make any response, Reginald stepped forward and placed his arm around her shoulders.

'Letty's coming with me to the dance over at Bag'orth. That right, Letty? Well, seeing's she's not interested in you any more, I thought it'd give her a chance to go out with a real man for a change.' He squeezed her shoulder as he stared at Wilfred whose face was rapidly reddening.

Letty gasped. This was the first she'd heard of it.

The four men to the side of Wilfred laughed. Letty cringed as Reginald turned his full attention on her.

'We don't have to wait for the dance to go out, Letty. What about the flicks on Wednesday? Charlie Chaplin's showing.'

Her throat closed. This situation was awful. All she wanted to do was to grab hold of Wilfred and flee. Flee anywhere as long as it was with him and away from Reginald and his sniggering cronies who were all too obviously enjoying Wilfred's embarrassment. At this moment she hated Reginald Crabbe, hated him with all her being. If only Peggie was here. She'd know what to say to get her out of this awful situation.

Her thoughts were broken by Reginald's sarcastic laugh. 'See, lads, Letty's speechless at the thought of a night out with yours truly.' He dropped his arm and turned to her. 'I'll pick you up at seven.'

It was more of a command than a request and Letty felt a hot flush creeping up her neck.

He joined his friends and, laughing and nudging each other, they sauntered off down the road.

Wilfred stared at her, mystified and hurt. Before Letty had time to speak he turned from her and climbed on the bicycle. ''Bye, Letty. Enjoy yourself with Reginald,' he muttered coldly.

She watched in despair as he rode away and huge tears flooded down her face.

Blindly, she stumbled forward. She knew this episode was the end of their relationship. Nothing she could ever do or say would repair the damage and she felt desolate. Before she knew it she found herself on the edge of the village green. She raised her head and through watery eyes saw her sister Peggie slumped on a sofa.

Without even questioning why an old sofa had been dumped there or why her sister was sitting on it, she raced over and threw herself on Peggie, wailing loudly.

'Oh, Peggie, Peggie! It's all finished,' she cried.

Peggie, distraught at seeing her sister so upset, completely forgot her own problems and their earlier heated exchanges and hugged Letty tightly. 'What's all over?' she asked, frowning deeply.

'Me and Wilfred. It was awful. Just awful. Oh, Peggie, what am I gonna do?'

Peggie stared at her hard. 'But you told me you were glad you and Wilfred were finished and that you were seeing Reginald Crabbe?'

Letty raised watery, red-rimmed eyes. 'I lied,' she sobbed, ashamed. 'I only said it to have a go at you. I never meant a word. I could never go out with him, not after what he did tonight.'

Through choking sobs she told Peggie all that had transpired.

Peggie listened intently, shaking her head. She sighed deeply and hugged her sister tighter.

'Oh, Letty, Letty, I don't know. Between us we're a right pair. You wanting to end it all because of Wilfred and me because I've managed as usual to cock things up and can't for the life of me think of any solution.' She laughed wryly. 'Between us we want a right slapping. And if I know our mam, that's just what we'll get when she hears all this.' She took a deep breath, ran a hand through her wild blonde curls and exhaled loudly. 'I know, I'll go and see Wilfred and try to straighten him out.'

'Oh, no, no!' Letty cried, horrified. 'You've done enough damage already without making matters worse.'

Peggie narrowed her eyes. 'Well, what do you suggest then? And for that matter I wouldn't have made matters worse, I'd have just made him see . . .' she paused.

'See what?'

'I don't know. See . . . see that this situation has all been blown out of proportion. That Reginald Crabbe was lying when he said you had an arrangement to go out.'

Letty sniffed loudly. 'I still think you'll make matters worse. You know how your tongue's always getting the better of you.'

'Well, in that case sort it out yourself, and in future I wouldn't ask for my help if I were you.'

Letty's shoulders sagged. 'Oh, Peggie, I'm sorry. I didn't mean all that, it's just . . . Oh, Peggie, I hurt so much. I can't bear the thought of losing Wilfred.' She burst into tears which rolled in a torrent down her plump cheeks. Her round spectacles misted up and she took them off and wiped them on the bottom of her skirt.

Peggie thrust her hand up her sleeve, pulled out her handkerchief and began to wipe her sister's wet face. 'I know, love,' she soothed. 'But it'll all come right in the end. You and Wilfred love each other. Everyone knows that. You'll make it up, you'll see. It'll just take time. In the meantime there is something you have to look forward to,' she added with a twinkle in her eye.

Letty looked at her blankly. 'Oh? And what's that?'

She grinned mischievously. 'Your night out with Reginald.'

'Oh, don't, Peggie, don't!' she erupted, putting her spectacles back on. 'I can't bear the thought of going out with him. How am I gonna get out of it?' She snatched the handkerchief from Peggie and blew her nose noisily before handing it back.

Peggie looked at the handkerchief and at Letty disdainfully. But how was she going to get her sister out of this situation? There was one thing for sure: should Letty go out with Reginald Crabbe, not only was there a strong possibility that her parents would commit murder, Letty could also wave goodbye to any chance of a reconciliation with Wilfred. She sighed heavily. She would have to come up with a plan, although she still did not quite know what.

'Don't worry,' she said softly. 'I'll think of something.'

'I should hope so,' Letty retorted. 'After all, it is your fault all this has happened.'

Peggie tutted. 'I'm being blamed for everything today.'

'So you should be. If you didn't insist on sticking your nose in where it wasn't wanted, I wouldn't be in this situation now.'

'All right, no need to rub it in. But I hardly think I can be fully to blame for your break up.' She sighed deeply, suddenly very tired and fed up with all the bickering. 'Look, can't we call a truce? I've so much on my mind and what with the other business, I can't cope with fighting with you as well.'

'Other business! What other business? I hope you're not in more trouble than you are already?'

'No, no, I ain't. It's just . . . well, it's Mary Crabbe. I saw her last night and she looked as though she'd been beaten.'

'Well, she's simple is Mary Crabbe. Everyone knows that,' Letty said unkindly. 'She probably stepped on a rake or fell down the stairs.'

'That's what she said,' Peggie said absently.

'What, that she'd stepped on a rake?'

'No. That she fell down the stairs. Only I don't believe her. I think she's mistreated by her father. And, it wouldn't surprise me, by Reginald an' all, and I'm worried. I'm gonna speak to Mam and see if she can suggest anything that could be done for her.' Peggie eyed her sister, annoyed. 'And for your information, she's not simple, she's just shy. No one has ever taken the trouble to make friends with her. Us included. We're at fault as much as the next.'

A guilty look crossed Letty's face. She had done her fair share of ridiculing Mary during her youth.

A figure heading towards them at breakneck speed alerted both of them.

'It's our Ronnie,' Peggie said, rising, noticing another, bigger, figure following closely behind.

Ronnie reached them, panting hard. The other person stopped when he spotted Peggie and Letty. It was Godfrey Smith.

Instinctively, Peggie grabbed hold of Ronnie and shielded him behind her. Letty stood up and joined them.

'What's a big lump like you chasing little boys for?' Peggie shouted to Godfrey. He took a step back. He wanted no confrontation with the sisters Cartwright. One on their own was bad enough, but two . . . But he had to keep his pride. He leaned down and pulled up his trouser leg.

'He did this to me,' he grumbled accusingly, showing a large graze covered in congealed blood on his mud-streaked shin which had happened earlier when Ronnie had legged him over.

Peggie grunted, unconvinced. 'I can just see my little brother doing that. Why, you make three of him! Now clear off, you big bully, and if you set on him again, I'll beat the living daylights outta you myself.'

'Yeah, and me,' echoed Letty.

Letty slightly turned her head and caught Ronnie full in the act of pulling a face and sticking his tongue out at Godfrey. She raised her hand and clipped him across the side of his head.

'Ouch!' he cried.

Peggie ignored the commotion developing behind her and took several steps towards Godfrey. 'Go on, I said clear off. And next time pick on someone your own size.'

Resigned, Godfrey sidled off.

Peggie and Letty turned to face their younger brother.

'Did you do that to Godfrey?' Peggie asked, placing her hands on her hips.

Ronnie stared at her innocently.

'I thought so, you little beggar.' She clipped him around his ear and he yelped again. 'Dad's told you to stay outta trouble. Now I'm telling you. All we need is his dad coming down and creating merry hell.'

'He set on me first,' wailed Ronnie.

'Huh?' Peggie and Letty grunted in unison, unconvinced.

All three sank down on the sofa.

Peggie turned to Ronnie. 'So the 'oss lost then?'

He looked up at her. 'Did it?'

Peggie frowned. 'You know fine well it did, that's why you've been hiding from me.'

'No, I ain't,' Ronnie said. 'I was hiding from Godfrey. I don't know what happened to the 'oss, I never got the chance to find out.'

All three stared at each other.

Sep strolled back along the tow path. The walk, albeit several miles, had done him the world of good. He had needed to get away and think and the tranquillity of the countryside had afforded him that pleasure. During his walk he had been able to formulate a plan and finally he knew he had found the answer. He would approach Jess and ask him if he could work for the vehicle. It wouldn't matter what the work was as long as at the end of it his payment was the pig.

He felt pleased. Jess would surely agree to his plan. After all, he would be the winner. He could name what work he wanted doing and for how long, and at this moment Sep didn't care whether he had to work for twenty hours a day for a whole year. He started to whistle and quickened his pace as his stomach rumbled with hunger. With a bit of luck Nell would have finished her midwifery and the evening meal would be well underway. If not, he'd give them a treat and start it himself.

As he neared the bottom of his road he heard his name being called and stopped and turned to see Tommy White running towards him, his hobnailed boots clattering loudly on the dried dirt path.

Tommy, a wiry little man whose meagre income came from tackling odd jobs around the village, stopped abreast of him, a broad grin across his weather-beaten face, showing large gaps where rotting teeth had fallen out. He slapped Sep hard on the shoulder.

'You lucky bugger,' he lisped enviously, pushing his threadbare flat cap to the back of his head. ''Ow did yer do it, eh? I've bin 'aving a flutter for years and never picked a rank outsider like that. And those odds. 100 to 1! Now if that ain't luck then what is it? Come on, Sep, tell us yer secret?'

Sep looked at him, deeply confused. 'I don't know what you're talking about, Tommy.'

'Don't know what I'm talkin' about!' Tommy delved into his jacket pocket and pulled out a wad of notes. 'This money sez yer do.' He slapped the notes into a gawping Sep's hand. ''Ave it yer own way, man. But next time yer get a sure bet like that,' he nudged Sep in the ribs, 'let some of us into the secret, eh?'

Tommy left Sep staring down into his hand. Suddenly the awful truth dawned. He quickly stuffed the wad of notes into his pocket and with face set firm strode home.

He was standing with his back to the range when Peggie, Letty and Ronnie burst through the door. The look on their father's face froze them in their tracks.

Primrose, who had been happily reading her comic, flicked one side of her long hair behind her ear and looked up at them. ''Bout time you lot were back. I'm starving.'

Peggie took a breath and addressed her father. 'Mam not back yet?' she asked tentatively, testing the ground.

Sep ignored her. 'Primrose, go upstairs.'

Primrose turned her head. 'Why?'

'Now,' her father demanded.

At his tone Primrose did not need another telling. Trouble was

69

afoot and although she was dying to know what was going on she did not want to be part of it. For once she was glad it was something she wasn't involved in.

Three pairs of worried eyes stared at Sep whilst Primrose hurriedly departed. Primrose gone he reached in his pocket, pulled out the bundle of notes and held them out towards his offspring, watching their faces intently.

'Which one of you would like to explain this?'

Peggie, without thinking, clapped her hands together. 'It won! Oh, Dad, it won!' she cried, jumping up and down in delight.

'What won?' he asked sharply, already knowing the answer.

Peggie gulped. She shuffled her feet nervously. 'The 'oss, Dad.' She raised her head and took several steps forward. 'I only did it for you, honest, Dad. You wanted that motor so badly.' Her eyes pleaded with him for forgiveness.

'You still placed that bet, with money we could ill afford, knowing how I felt about it?'

She raised her head and looked her father straight in the eyes. 'Yes,' she replied with conviction. 'And I'd do it again. I love you, Dad, and I wanted to help.'

Sep pressed his lips together. How could he argue with an admission like that? Many children didn't give twopence about their fathers and here he was with three whom he knew were not exactly little angels but who loved him dearly and were willing to go to any lengths to express their feelings.

He cleared his throat. As much as he wanted to put his arms around Peggie and thank her profusely, he couldn't. Inside his pocket was nearly three hundred pounds. Money that if he worked for the next twenty years, day and night, he would never see the likes of in one lump. He fought with his emotions. Half of him wanted to shout with joy. The money to achieve his dream was sitting in the palm of his hand. The other half of him disapproved of the means by which it was acquired and he had to try to point out that fact to his children.

'Where did you get the money from to place the bet, Peggie?'

She turned her head and quickly looked at Letty and Ronnie standing behind her, guilt written across their faces. She turned back. 'I . . . er . . . used me savings.'

'Yeah, and I gave her me lunch and travelling money,' Letty piped up.

'And I gave me pocket money,' chipped in Ronnie.

Peggie gave them both a quick smile of gratitude. She turned back to face her father. 'I . . . borrowed Billy's loose change an' all.' She stopped abruptly, not daring to tell her father how the rest of the bet money was made up.

'Borrowed!' Sep wiped his hand over his forehead. He walked to the table and sat down, resting his head in one hand, his other clutching the ill-gotten gains. 'Oh, what do I do?' he groaned.

Peggie rushed forward and placed her arm around her father's shoulder. 'Buy the motor, Dad, and get your business started.'

'Motor?' Letty and Ronnie asked in unison. 'What motor?'

Sep ignored their question. 'And how do I explain things to your mother?'

Peggie bit her bottom lip. 'I don't know.'

Sep sighed. 'No, nor do I.'

Just then the back door opened and Billy came through. Four pairs of eyes stared at him as he stood on the threshold, took off his thick woollen waistcoat and shook it out into the yard, a black cloud of coal dust flying through the air which for several seconds masked the early-evening sunlight. He turned and noticed instantly their anxious expressions.

'What's happened?' he asked worriedly.

Sep mentally shook himself and rose. 'Nothing, son. We were just about to get the supper started.'

'No, you weren't,' Billy said, walking towards them, the whites of his eyes shining through a coal-blackened face. 'Summat's up and I want to know what it is?'

'You'd better tell him, Dad,' Peggie said. 'He'll find out soon enough.'

Sep scratched his day's growth of beard. He took a breath, then proceeded to tell his elder son what had transpired.

Billy's face broke into a grin, his teeth shining even brighter than his eyes. 'Great. I knew that 'oss was a winner. I told you, didn't I? I told you Mick's tips are a sure fire bet.'

'No they ain't!'

Four pairs of eyes looked at Ronnie, who had, like all the Cartwright offspring, spoken before he had thought of the consequences.

He gulped.

'Speak up, lad,' demanded Sep.

He gulped again and looked at Peggie. 'I changed the bet. I heard Nobby Clarke and Will Smithers talking. They said they'd heard the 'orse had bin . . .' he paused in thought for a moment. 'Bin seen to and it weren't worth backing.'

'Bin seen to?' queried Letty.

'He means tampered with,' Billy answered.

'Yeah, that's it. That's what they said. Then they mentioned this other 'oss, Maggie's Boy, and I thought it was an omen 'cos of our Maggie.' He gave Peggie a broad grin. 'Well, it won, dinit?'

Sep scowled severely at Peggie. 'You mean to tell me you let Ronnie place the bet? You sent him, a lad of thirteen, down the Jolly Toper? Why, he's not old enough for a start. What if he'd been caught?'

Peggie squirmed, anticipating her father's wrath. But Sep, bewildered by all the day's events, sank down on the chair by the fire. He looked across at his children.

'I don't think you'd better tell me any more. I just pray your mother gets to hear none of this. If she does, our lives won't be

71

worth living.' He wagged his finger in their direction. 'You'll all go to church tomorrow and make your peace with the Lord. Is that understood?' He waited whilst they all nodded vigorously in agreement. 'Right, and I want no repetition of today's actions, for whatever reason. I know what you did was with the best of intentions and I can't say I ain't more than pleased with the outcome. But in my eyes it were wrong, and the worst of it is, you all know that.'

Like lightning he unexpectedly leapt up and shot towards the door to the stairs and yanked it open. Primrose tumbled out. 'Get all of that, Primrose, or do you want us to go over anything you couldn't hear through the keyhole?' She stared up at him guiltily, picked herself up off the floor and quickly joined her sisters and brothers.

Sep stood with his back to the range and eyed each in turn. He gave an unexpected smile. 'Come on, let's get the supper cracking. I don't know about you lot, but I'm starving.'

He smiled as he watched his daughters bustling around the kitchen: Billy stripping off for a wash down by the sink: Ronnie setting the table. In a flash the frying pan had been heated and filled and an appetising aroma was wafting around the cluttered room, and the large brown tea-pot filled with thick brewed tea, just the way he liked it.

He breathed deeply as he groped in his pocket for his pipe. Packing the barrel with the last of his baccy, he lit it and slowly puffed a plume of smoke into the air. He needed to think, think hard to come up with a good excuse for the sudden enormous windfall that burned in his pocket. And it had better be a good excuse because Nell was not an easily fooled woman.

Chapter Six

'One more push, gel, and that should do it,' Nell said firmly, poised at the bottom of Beattie Gulliver's big brass bed, scrubbed hands ready to retrieve the long awaited arrival. 'Breathe deep and give it your all.'

'I can't, I can't!' Beattie gasped exhaustedly, running her hand over her greasy hair wet with sweat, face ashen from hours of excruciating pain. 'I'm done for, Nell. I ain't got no more pushes in me. This little blighter's sapped all me strength.'

'No, it ain't,' Nell snapped sharply. 'Now come on, I ain't got all day. I've been here that long I've forgot what my own house looks like. 'Sides, I ain't had a decent cuppa since four o'clock this morning. I think that husband of yours just waves the mug past the tea pot for all the colour it's got.'

Beattie choked back a laugh. 'Oh, Nell, don't. Don't make me laugh. All right, I'll have another go. But if it don't come this time . . .'

Nell smiled, relieved. 'That's the spirit, Beattie. I'm sure one more push is all it needs.' She looked between Beattie's splayed legs. 'I can see its head. It's got black hair.'

'I don't care if it's bloody bald as long as it comes,' Beattie grumbled as she prepared for the next wave of pain.

Nell silently prayed. She was worried, worried sick. This baby should have been born hours ago. If this final onslaught didn't do the trick, then she felt sure that Beattie wouldn't survive much more.

Despite strong protests Nell had sent Beattie's two eldest daughters for the doctor over two hours ago but he hadn't appeared and Nell, used to helping out with regular village births, was no use when it came to complications. Everything seemed straightforward enough, it was just that the little mite didn't seem to want to be born. And who could blame it? It was as though the unseen baby knew what hardships faced it outside the safe warm confines of its mother's belly.

Beattie's face contorted in pain. 'Ahhhh!' she screamed.

'That's it, that's it! Push, Beattie. Push!'

'I am bloody pushin',' she cried.

Nell raised her eyes, said another prayer then stared between Beattie's legs, shouting words of encouragement and comfort.

Thankfully her prayers were answered. The innocent new life slid out on to the greying, patched sheets and gave a lusty yell.

Nell quickly cut the umbilical cord, wrapped the baby tightly inside an old towel and handed it over to its exhausted mother.

'She's lovely, Beattie,' she said encouragingly as she finished washing her down and straightened the covers on the bed. 'What a' you gonna call her?'

Beattie stared down at the bundle in her arms. 'Horace.'

'Horace!' she exclaimed in disbelief.

Beattie raised her eyes. 'Well, it's the only name I thought of. I was so adamant I was having a boy this time.'

'Well, you didn't,' Nell said, sitting on the edge of the bed. 'You had a lovely baby girl to add to the other seven.'

'Hmm,' Beattie agreed. 'She is pretty, ain't she? Even if she did nearly kill me getting 'ere.' She raised her tired eyes to Nell and smiled warmly. 'I've thought of a name.'

'Have you?'

'Yeah. Maggie, after your gel. I've always liked her. She's got spirit and I hope my Maggie,' she smiled down fondly at her new daughter, 'grows up to be like her, then I won't be disappointed.'

Nell raised her eyes again. Heaven help her, she thought. And heaven help you if our Peggie hears you calling her Maggie! She stood up and stifled a yawn of weariness. 'I'll just see you settled and then I best be off, see what me own brood's been up to.'

Several minutes later she plodded heavily down the steep wooden stairs and found the two girls she had sent to fetch the doctor huddled by the remains of the fire. Beattie's husband, Norman, was fast asleep in the threadbare armchair, snoring loudly, and the other younger children were tearing into the remains of a stale loaf of bread on the table.

Nell shook her head in disbelief. Their mother lay upstairs having just given birth and it appeared that no one downstairs cared a damn.

'What happened about the doctor?' she addressed the two older girls.

They stared at her blankly. 'Oh, he weren't in,' the older of the two replied flatly. 'Mam's okay though, ain't she?'

Nell nodded. 'But no thanks to you.' Sudden anger rose up in her and she placed her hands on her generous hips. 'Right, you two,' she shouted to the older girls. 'Get these little 'uns summat to eat. I don't know what, but toast is better than dry bread. And then get 'em washed and put to bed. Jump to it.'

The girls obeyed, wide-eyed.

Nell walked over and stood before Norman. She grabbed him by the shoulders and shook him hard. He jumped in alarm and stared up at her.

'Yes, you can look like that, you good for nothing! Your wife, God bless her, has just had a terrible time giving birth to your child and you act as if she's having a holiday. Get up, man. Tend your kids, then go and see what your wife needs. If you don't I'll get my Sep down to sort you out.'

Norman's eyes hardened. He nonchalantly scratched his greying hairy chest through his dirty vest. 'Don't you dare tell me what to do in my own 'ouse! Who d'yer think you are?'

'Who do I think I am?' Nell snapped. 'I'm just the woman who's spent the last twenty hours with your wife, while you had a skinful down the pub then came back here to sleep it off. Your kids don't know what time a' day it is, let alone when they were last fed. Now I'm warning you, Norman Gulliver. You'd better do as I say or I'll spread it around the village just what you're about.'

Norman, resigned, slowly rose. 'Damn busybody,' he muttered under his breath.

An exhausted Nell finally departed for home, twenty hours after she had left it, feeling she had done more than enough for Beattie, her newborn baby and her family. At this moment she appreciated her own family more than ever. Sep had always been there when their own children had been born. It wouldn't have entered his head to have done otherwise, and this bond had carried on through their childhood. They might argue, at times ferociously, but when the odds were against them they all stuck together like glue.

She let herself quietly into the kitchen and was surprised to see Peggie curled up in the rocking chair, reading a book.

'Hello, Mam. Sit down, I'll mash you a cuppa. Everyone else has gone to bed. 'Cept our Billy. He's still out. Dad only went up a short while ago. He's probably still awake listening out for you.' She rose and began to fill the kettle whilst Nell sank gratefully down in the armchair.

She eased off her boots, careful to replace the thick wad of brown paper that lined the worn insides, and rubbed her aching legs. She would have liked nothing more than to apply a hot poultice but with Peggie still around she couldn't risk it.

'What's she have, Mam?'

'Another girl. Ugly little thing, but she'll grow out of it.'

Peggie grinned. 'Most babies are ugly, Mam.'

'Yeah, but not to their mothers, they ain't.'

'What's she calling it?' Peggie asked, putting the teapot on the table along with two mugs. She got a cloth and took her mother's dinner out of the oven. It was dried up, but hot. Rummaging through the clutter on top of the dresser, she found a tin tray, put the plate on it and handed it over. 'Put your feet on the hearth, Mam, and eat this while it's hot.'

'Ta, love. I could eat an 'orse.'

Peggie grimaced at the mention of horses. 'Well?'

Nell looked up. 'Well, what?' she said through a mouthful of food.

'The baby's name?'

'Oh!' Nell fought to stop herself from laughing. 'Er . . . Maggie. She's called the baby Maggie.'

'I see,' answered Peggie disdainfully. 'Was that the best she could do?'

'Maggie's a nice name. Just 'cos you don't like it. 'Sides, after seven, I suppose she'd ran out of ideas.' Nell finished her food and sat back gratefully. 'I enjoyed that. Thanks, love.' She took a sip of her tea. 'So, what's been happening today?'

Peggie looked at her innocently. 'Happening?'

'Yes, happening. There's never a day when something ain't happened and I don't expect today was any different. So come on, out with it.'

Peggie froze, then gave a sudden smile. 'I did manage to get the pawn, caught him just as he was shutting. He said he'd give me thirty shillings. Only I've to collect it . . . er . . .' She thought rapidly. She needed time to come up with an idea for raising another thirty shillings and couldn't ask her father to give it her out of the winnings because then she would have to tell him about her mother's predicament. 'Friday.'

'Friday?'

'Yeah, during me lunch break.' She began to babble. ''Cos he hadn't got enough cash on him. I've already told you, I caught him just as he was shutting. And he's going away. Yes, that's what he said. He was going away for a few days to his wife's parents or something, so he couldn't settle up with me 'til then.' She held her breath. This situation was getting worse. She would have to speak to Billy and hope he could help her, if not she was done for. Nell broke her thoughts.

'Oh, Peggie. Thank God for that. Now I can settle me debts. Another few days is neither here nor there as long as I know I can get the money. Oh, I'm so relieved. I knew that ring were worth summat, although I'm sorry I had to part with it. I'll save every penny 'til I can redeem it. You did keep the ticket, didn't you?'

Peggie stared at her mother, her mind racing. 'Er . . . yeah, 'course I did. I put it away for safe keeping.'

'Good. Now fill me mug up again, please. That was the first decent cuppa I've had all day.'

Peggie did as she was asked, handed her mother the replenished mug and sat down opposite her.

'Mam, I need to talk to you about Mary Crabbe.'

Nell's head jerked up sharply. 'Mary Crabbe? Why?'

Peggie related the previous night's incident.

'Is there anything we can do, Mam? That poor gel must have a horrible life with them two. I can't seem to get her off my mind.'

Nell sighed deeply. 'There's some things that's best left alone, gel, and I think this is one of them.'

'But we can't, Mam. We wouldn't let a dog live like that, let alone a human being.'

'Peggie,' Nell snapped, 'what do you propose we do? March into the Crabbe household and demand the release of his daughter because you suspect mistreatment? Half the families in the village could be accused of that. You should have been in Beattie Gulliver's house today. Those kids are half starved and they've just brought

76

another into the world. Besides, without proof Crabbe'll have us arrested for slander. Leave things be, Peggie. Mary will leave of her own accord when she's ready, without our interference.'

Peggie's shoulders sagged. If only it were that simple. It was all right for her mother to leave well alone, but she hadn't been there the previous night and witnessed first hand Mary's obvious misery. A plan began to formulate. She would go and visit Mary, she wasn't afraid of Cyrus or Reginald. At least then her own mind would be satisfied that the girl was all right.

She took a breath. 'Cyrus asked after you, Mam.'

'Pardon?' Nell said in alarm.

'I said Cyrus Crabbe asked how you were and sent his regards. He also asked how your legs were.' As she spoke Peggie watched her mother closely.

Nell's face darkened. 'Oh, did he! Well, I don't know why, 'cos there's n'ote wrong with my legs.' Her lips tightened and she rose awkwardly. 'I'm off to bed,' she said abruptly. She reached the door to the stairs, stopped and turned. 'Heed my words, Peggie, and heed them good. Steer clear of the Crabbes or, believe me, you'll live to regret the consequences.'

She sat for a while staring into the dying embers of the fire. More and more she decided that the story her mother had divulged regarding the Crabbes and the Cartwrights was not the full one. There was something else, something between Cyrus and her mother, and she felt sure it was something that her father knew nothing about or why had her mother so abruptly ended the conversation and gone to bed? And why the harsh warning? Because it was a warning. Nell's tone of voice had left Peggie in no doubt of that.

Regardless, though, thoughts of Mary still lay heavily on her conscience. She didn't want to disobey her mother, but she knew that in order to satisfy herself she would have to pay a visit to the Crabbe household.

'Oh, my God, Billy. It's Bull, he's back early! Get up, quick. Quick!' Frantic, Alice Hammond shook Billy hard and threw his clothes at him. 'You'll have to go out by the window.'

'Eh!' Billy's eyes opened wide in horror as Alice's words struck home. 'Oh, Lord,' he groaned in panic as he jumped up and hastily pulled on his clothes. A few minutes before he had fallen into a peaceful slumber after an hour of strenuous activities between and on top of the sheets, safe in the knowledge that Bull would still be out for at least another two hours. Now here he was, in fear of his life.

Alice pulled a thick winceyette nightdress over her naked body and tried to smooth her disarrayed hair. 'I'll go down and try to stall 'im. I'll mek him a sandwich or summat. Just you make sure you're gone by the time we get back up here.'

Billy eyed her sharply. 'Ta, Alice,' he hissed crossly. 'Don't show any concern that I should break me neck or 'ote, will you?'

Alice turned on him, her hand on the doorknob, 'Billy Cartwright, if Bull catches yer, you won't have no neck to worry over. Now get gone!'

Half dressed, Billy gently slid up the sash window, grimacing as it grated loudly in its frame. When the window was pushed up as far as it would go, he knelt, backside out, on the sill, desperately seeking a hand and foothold. He could hear raised voices and knew that Alice and Bull were fighting and that time was running out.

He felt along the wall and found the drainpipe. With a manoeuvre an acrobat would have been proud of he managed to spread-eagle himself between the window frame and the drain pipe. But then disaster struck. The bedroom door opened and he heard Bull storm through followed by Alice. After several seconds she stuck her head out of the open window and gawped in alarm at the sight of Billy spread-eagled against the wall. Without a word she withdrew her head and pulled down the window.

Billy breathed shallowly, afraid that Bull would hear. His fingers began to turn numb and sudden realisation came to him that he was at least ten feet from the ground with nothing between him and the stone flags below. For the first time in his life he was really afraid. How on earth was he going to get out of this one?

Panic rose. If he levered himself fully on to the drainpipe, what if it gave way? These cottages were ancient. He could feel the pipe moving with only half his weight upon it; he dreaded to think what would happen should he climb fully on to it. Beads of sweat ran down the sides of his face. The light in the bedroom was extinguished. He was alone with no visible means of escape. He raised his eyes.

'Sorry, Lord. It don't look like I'll make it to church tomorrow.'

Ronnie ambled slowly down the moonlit road, sticking as near to the hedges and fences as possible to remain undetected. It was fun sneaking out at night, even if it was only to sit in an old shed in the bottom of Lawrence's garden eating stale cake and bread procured through various means by the rest of the gang. The fun actually lay in getting out of their houses and afterwards getting back in without being caught. As Ronnie himself still had to 'get back in', it remained to be seen whether his night had been fun until he was safely back in bed.

As he turned into Chapel Lane and his own row of cottages came into view he frowned and squinted hard in the darkness. Then he gawped. Someone was breaking into Bull Hammond's cottage. He froze in his steps, wondering what course of action to take.

Fetch Constable Jesson was his first thought. No. He hated Constable Jesson. The last time they had met over the incident with Mr Tunley the Constable clipped him hard round the ear and dragged him home to face his father. Ronnie felt he owed him nothing. Maybe he should try and wake Bull. Let him deal with the intruder. No, that thought also didn't bear thinking about. Bull was a mean man to deal with at the best of times, let alone when he had had a skinful, and it was a known fact that he had a skinful every night. Better to get his father. He'd be able to deal with the burglar. He smiled. Some burglar, though. He appeared to be stuck.

Bending low, he inched forward until he came abreast of the cottage, intending to sneak by, but something made him stop. The figure clinging to the wall seemed familiar somehow. He raised himself up and grinned broadly. No wonder the figure looked familiar. It would do, it was his own brother.

Billy was getting desperate. He could not feel his fingers and wondered how much longer he could hold on. Suddenly he heard his name being whispered and with difficulty turned his head and peered down. Relief so great he nearly slipped flooded through him. Below, trying to prop the woodworm-riddled ladder against the wall, was young Ronnie, a grin on his face so broad it split it in two.

Thankfully Billy felt firm ground beneath him. He spun round and hugged his brother tightly. 'I owe you one, Ronnie,' he whispered, and slapped him hard on the shoulder. 'In fact I'll pay you back by not telling Mam or Dad you sneaked out tonight.'

Ronnie opened his mouth to protest.

Billy grinned. 'I'm only joking. You'll never know how glad I was to see you. Now come on, let's get out of here.'

Chapter Seven

Nell sat with head erect, attired in her Sunday best, fingers clasped firmly around her hymn book as Reverend Wilberforce Forest droned out his boring sermon. It was on something to do with the righteous. The Reverend was always going on about the righteous, he had a thing about good people. Nell was only half listening. She fractionally turned her head and peered down the row at the rest of her family fidgeting beside her. Sep, Peggie, Primrose then Letty, Ronnie and lastly Billy. The latter being the most startling. She couldn't remember the last time Billy had attended Sunday morning service and wondered why he had today?

Still, it had been nice all leaving the house together, and all going in the same direction. Her brow crinkled. Something was going on in her family. She didn't know what, but she'd swear blind that all six of them were keeping something from her. She had no doubt, given time, she would find it out. In the meantime she just wanted to enjoy being with them all at the same time.

She caught sight of Primrose rising and making her way out of the pew ready to take the under-fives Bible class. She felt proud. It was an honour for her daughter even though she knew Primrose didn't want to do it. Nell puffed out her generous chest and returned her full attention to Reverend Forest. Might as well listen to what he had to say even though half of it didn't make sense to her.

At the end of the pew Billy wasn't listening to the Reverend at all. His thoughts were on the previous night and his near fatal escape. He had come to a momentous decision. He was finished with married women. Alice could beg and plead for all her worth, but he would never get into a position like that again. No, any future entanglement would be with someone single. He was just glad that Ronnie had come past when he did. Billy dreaded to think what would have happened otherwise.

He exhaled sharply and shifted his position on the hard bench. To Billy churches were a place to arrange to meet after dark, secure in the knowledge that no one but the deceased could hear the deals he struck with Mick Matherson or see when he exchanged money for goods, such as he had done the previous night before he had gone to Alice's. He grinned. Those stockings would bring in a tidy sum. Enough to strike an even better deal the next time round. The day was gradually drawing nearer when he could give up his job at the mine and work for himself. He couldn't wait. That day couldn't come soon enough for him.

He stifled a yawn and nudged Ronnie hard in the ribs. Like him his little brother was having a job keeping himself awake.

Ronnie jumped and rubbed his side where Billy had roughly elbowed him. He smiled in gratitude and averted his eyes towards the large stained-glass windows, one of which had sun rays streaming through. He stared in hypnotised fascination as dust particles floated lazily through them. He longed to be out in the sunshine, swinging on top of the station gate, watching the trains pulling their loads – and if the Reverend did not get a move on he would miss the 11.03 to Swadlingcote.

It was then that he remembered his forthcoming visit to Mr Tunley and shuddered. Mr Tunley was renowned for being a stickler for following the rule book and for a moment Ronnie wondered worriedly what the rule was about catching thirteen-year-old schoolboys train spotting on railway property.

He sighed deeply. He would be leaving school in three short weeks, his forthcoming birthday coinciding with the summer break, and it looked very much as if he would be joining Billy down the mine in Desford. It was not what he wanted and as yet there was no telling whether they would take him on. But it was better than nothing. Or was it?

They all rose to sing a hymn and in doing so Ronnie collided with Letty who dropped her hymn book.

She scowled fiercely at him before she bent to pick it up, quickly turning to the correct page. The next hymn was 'Fight the Good Fight', and it reflected her mood exactly. The only problem being she didn't know who to fight first. Effie Dage for being such a selfish woman in wanting to keep her son strapped to her side; Wilfred for seemingly letting her succeed; Peggie for her interference and making matters worse; or lastly Reginald Crabbe. Or maybe he should come first, because if he hadn't turned up last night along with his cronies, maybe she and Wilfred might have managed to patch things up.

She swallowed a sob that had caught in her throat and slowly cast her eyes around the rest of the congregation. She spotted Wilfred standing rigidly at the side of his mother, she sporting a ridiculous black plumed bonnet tied under her scraggy chin with thick black ribbon, fashionable only during the latter part of the 1890s. She also wore a triumphant look. Letty sensed Wilfred knew she was looking at him, but his eyes remained firmly fixed ahead.

She abruptly turned away with what was left of her hope of a reconciliation disintegrating. Her eyes filled with tears and she began to mouth the words of the hymn. She couldn't sing, her throat had closed up.

Singing loudly, Peggie noticed her sister's distress and turned her head to give Effie Dage a scathing look. The damned woman wanted stringing up for the part she was playing in Letty's heartache. Still the woman would suffer when the Co-operative Society moved into the village, but that wouldn't be enough to pay her back for the hurt she was knowingly causing two people, one of whom was very dear to her.

She sang even louder, wanting to try and rid herself of some of her frustration, hoping whoever was up there might hear and give her some inspiration for rectifying the situation that had arisen. Regardless, though, she was going to take matters into her own hands on one count. After Sunday dinner, she was going to pay a visit to the Crabbes. Her mind was made up on that score and nothing was going to change it.

The congregation was seated and Sep smiled at Nell, trying to keep guilt from crossing his face. He felt uncomfortable sitting in church knowing that hidden at home was a bundle of notes acquired in direct contradiction of the teachings of the Ten Commandments. He decided then to come clean with Nell, tell her exactly where the money had come from and how. Because, regardless, his omnibus company was going to be formed. He had lain awake most of the night fighting with his conscience and in the early hours felt without a doubt that this was meant to be.

He sought Nell's hand and squeezed it lovingly. She would understand. She would have to.

Meanwhile in the church rooms Primrose had managed by threats to get all twelve of the under-fives in her Sunday School class to sit still on the wooden floor. She sat on the chair at the front and opened her dog-eared Bible. With a stern air, she raised her eyes.

'Right, who's going to recite the Lord's Prayer?'

Johnny Coldwell's hand shot up. 'Me, Primrose, me. I've bin practising all week wi' me brother Arfer.'

Primrose's face darkened. 'Miss! You address me as Miss.'

Johnny's lip puckered. 'Why? Yer name's Primrose, ain't it?'

'Not here it's not, it's Miss.' She lowered her voice menacingly. 'And if you wanna be the one chosen you'd better do as I say.' She raised her eyes triumphantly. 'Now, who wants to recite the Lord's Prayer?'

Johnny's hand shot up again. "Me, Miss. Me, Miss.'

Primrose smiled. 'Go ahead.'

Johnny proudly clambered up, tucking his grubby shirt into his equally grubby short grey trousers, raised his grubby face and began: 'Our Arfer, whose king of the fighters in 'eaven. 'Arold's sister's on the game. Our chance has come, victory is won . . .'

Primrose's mouth gaped. She abruptly rose and without thinking lunged forward and smacked Johnny around the ear. 'Get out, you horrible little boy, and tell your Arthur he'll rot in hell for taking the Lord's name in vain!'

Johnny wailed loudly, having no idea why he was being so harshly dealt with, and fled the room.

Primrose resumed order, frantically hiding the mirth that erupted within her. If truth be told she would have given anything to have heard the rest of Johnny's innocent rendition, but dare not for fear the other youngsters told on her. With as grim a face as she could muster she opened her Bible again.

'I'll say it this time and woe betide any of you who don't listen.'

Eleven eager faces gave her their full attention.

Peggie stood hesitantly on the door step of the Crabbes' formidable house composing herself before she confronted the occupants. With head held high she raised the brass knocker and banged it twice.

After a long wait the door opened and Reginald stood before her. He smirked.

'Well, well. A Cartwright paying a call. Wadda you want?'

'I've come to see Mary.'

Was it Peggie's imagination or did a look of fright fleetingly cross Reginald's face? 'Fat chance of that. She ain't here.'

'Not here? What do you mean, she's not here?'

Reginald leaned forward. 'She's left. Scarpered she did in the middle of the night. And me dad swears you've got summat to do with it.'

'Me?' Peggie said, mortified, stepping backwards.

'Yes, you.' He spoke harshly, stabbing her in the shoulder with his finger. 'It were you she was talking to the other night, wasn't it? She ain't talked to no one else, so it must have been you that put ideas into her head and me dad ain't pleased, I can tell yer. And when he catches up wi' yer, you'll be sorry.'

'Oh, will I?' Peggie said haughtily, regaining her composure.

'Yes, yer will. And if you had any remorse for what you've done you'd offer to come and keep 'ouse. 'Cos now our Mary's gone we ain't got nobody to look after us.'

Peggie's temper mounted. 'Oh, now it's coming out. You're not worried about Mary, just yourself now you haven't got someone running after you. What's the matter, Reginald? Can't you or your dad fend for yourselves? Don't you know how to put a kettle on the stove or how a broom works?'

He raised his hand ready to strike.

'That's it, go on, hit a woman! That's what you used to do to Mary, ain't it? Don't forget I've seen her bruises, and if you lay a finger on me I'll make sure everyone knows about it.'

Reginald's face turned even nastier. 'Ged outta here, Peggie Cartwright, while you can.'

'Oh, don't worry, I intend to. And I'm glad Mary's gone. I hope now she has a life. Well, let's face it, living in the gutter has to be better than living with you two.' She turned and took several steps down the path, stopped and turned back. 'By the way, keep away from our Letty. She doesn't want to go out with you and never has. And if you don't, neither my dad nor Billy will take your actions lightly.'

'That right?' Reginald smirked. 'Let me tell you this – if I want to see Letty, I will. The Cartwrights don't frighten me. Just you tell her, I'll meet her as arranged.'

With that he turned, strode into the house and slammed shut the door.

Peggie froze. Now she had made the situation for Letty worse. How was she going to sort this one out?

As a worried Peggie hurried towards home, Nell lowered her darning and eyed her husband who was seemingly engrossed in the Sunday newspaper. She sniffed haughtily.

'Come on, Sep, let's have it.'

He lowered the newspaper and looked at her blankly. 'Eh?'

Nell scowled. 'Don't play the innocent with me, Septimus Cartwright. I have enough of the kids doing that. You don't live with someone for nearly thirty years and not know when they've something on their mind. Now out with it, before I drag it out of you.'

Sep slowly and carefully folded the newspaper. Sitting forward, he eyed her warily and cleared his throat. It was now or never, and if he was to have a decent night's sleep ever again it had better be now.

'Er . . .' he began. 'I've . . . er . . . come into some money, Nell.'

She gawped. 'Money! What money? I don't understand.'

Sep wiped his hand across his forehead. 'I gambled on a 'oss, Nell, and it won.' He eyed her warily, waiting for the explosion, but Nell for once had been struck speechless. 'Look, love,' he hurriedly continued, 'I know gambling's wrong but I needed to get some money together to get my motorised bus business off the ground, and taking this chance seemed the answer.'

Nell continued staring at him blankly, her mind racing. She had known something was going on but she's expected nothing on this scale. 'What motorised bus business?' she finally managed.

'The one I told you about the other night.'

'No you never! You never mentioned nothing of the sort else I'd have remembered. Besides, what do we need a motorised bus for out here? If we want to go anywhere we've always used the 'orse and cart or our legs. I can't see the need for 'ote else.'

'Oh, but there is, Nell. Motorised transport is the way of the future. It's big business down in London.'

'London, London! You've never been the same since you came back from that place. I sometimes wonder if some of the things you saw there didn't turn your brain. We live in Leicestershire, Sep. It's a far cry from the rich South.'

'They ain't all rich, Nell,' he cut in. 'And they work as hard as you and me for what they get.'

She bent her head, ashamed. 'Ah, well, maybe they do.' She looked up, eyes flashing. 'But you still ain't explaining very well what's going on.'

Sep leaned forward, not really knowing where to start. 'Look, Nell, you know that when Crabbe stole my brake it broke my heart. Not just because I'd built it from scratch but because it was going to be our living. Crabbe's made a decent living out of it, more than decent in fact. He bought his own house and he can afford meat. We can't. Now if Crabbe was as clever as he thinks he is, then by now he would be thinking on the lines that I am. He's obviously not and that's his fault. I'm going to step in where he's failed and if I pinch his customers in the process then that's his look out. I've now got the money to do it, Nell. Not like before, when I had to work my guts out for every piece of wood and nail I used, but hard cash that will buy what I need. And that's the difference. I can build this business properly and do things like they should be done.' His face softened. 'I can't pretend it's going to be easy. I'll need the family's support if I'm going to succeed and we'll all have to pitch in. But as God's my witness, this is gonna be the making of us, Nell. It is, I promise you.'

She sighed deeply. It had been a long time since she had heard her husband talk with such passion about anything and her heart gladdened, despite her misgivings. 'I've no doubt it will be if you're behind it,' she said sincerely. She shifted position in the chair and stared hard at him. 'But I want the truth on one thing.'

'Oh? What's that?'

'This bet.'

'What about it?' he gulped.

'I don't believe for a minute you gambled on a 'orse. Never in all our married life have you ever condoned such things, let alone done 'em.' She shook her head. 'No, I've a strange feeling it's more than likely got something to do with our children, because they've all been acting really strangely, especially when they all attended church this morning. Now, am I right?'

Sep shifted uncomfortably. 'Well . . . yes, sort of.'

'Sep.' She frowned deeply. 'I think you'd better start from the beginning.'

He clasped his hands firmly together and related the whole truth, starting where it all began with his trip into Leicester several days before.

She stared at him, many emotions passing through her. When he finished she shook her head gravely.

'I knew it,' she said sharply. 'It's only just beginning to dawn on me just what kinda kids we've raised. Gambling, stealing. Don't look at me like that. Our Peggie going through Billy's pockets amounts to stealing, and to top it all, our Ronnie actually placing the bet. Why, he's only thirteen. He shouldn't even be thinking on things like that, let alone knowing how to go about 'em.' She stared hard at him, then suddenly started to laugh. She laughed so hard fat tears of mirth poured down her rotund face.

Sep jumped up and knelt before her. 'Nell, Nell, a' you all right?' he asked, concerned.

She wiped her eyes on her apron. 'Oh, yes, Sep, I'm fine, just fine. What else could I be with such a family? I love you all, and so much it hurts.' Unexpectedly she leaned forward and hugged him tightly. 'You're right, me old duck. We're meant to start this business and the Lord in His infinite wisdom has given us the means in the best way He knew how. Who am I to question the reasons why?' She drew back from him and looked at him proudly. 'Do it, Sep. Make this business of yours into the best there is and I'm behind you all the way.'

Sep's raised eyes filled with delight. 'D'yer mean it, Nell? Really?'

She looked back at him, love radiating from her eyes. 'I ain't never meant nothing so much. Now when do we get started?'

Chapter Eight

'Can I 'elp yer?' Winny Burridge asked as she stood on the doorstep of the redbrick farm house. She had a smudge of flour on the end of her nose which she wiped off with the aid of her snow white apron.

'I'm looking for Jess,' Sep answered awkwardly, his eyes quickly scanning the farmyard.

During his lifetime, he had been in many farmyards but never such a hotchpotch as this one. An assortment of animal noises filled the air, and poultry as well as cats and dogs roamed freely. Rusting farm implements lay scattered on the hard mud ground and leaned haphazardly against old wooden outbuildings. It reminded Sep somewhat of his own back yard but on a far grander scale, and a strange feeling of belonging settled momentarily upon him.

Finding the farm had been easy. He had only to mention Jess's name as he had entered the village of Desford and he had been pointed in the right direction.

He returned his attention to the woman standing before him and whipped off his cap respectfully. She was just as a farmer's wife should be. Fat, rosy-cheeked, with a merry twinkle in her large brown eyes.

'Oh, he's long gone,' she said. 'You have to be up with the lark to catch our Jess. He's gone to market today, won't be back 'til late.' Her gaze suddenly darted past Sep towards a large barn across the yard. 'Benny!' she scolded. 'What a' you doing?'

'Nothin',' came back a sullen reply.

'I can see that!' She spoke sharply, glaring angrily at the tall, lanky youth hovering by the barn door. 'Them cows should have been back up the pasture an hour ago. Now get to it.' She turned her attention back to Sep and smiled broadly, her double chins wobbling. 'I dunno. I have to be up his backside every minute of the day. Lazy dollup. I can't understand why Jess keeps him on, especially considering the amount of men that'd jump at his job.' She eyed Sep searchingly. 'Is it a job you're after?'

'Oh, no, no,' he answered quickly.

Winny looked relieved. If truth be known she would have liked nothing more than to help all the travellers that happened onto her doorstep, and especially this one standing before her now. His appearance, although threadbare, was clean and he looked cared for. Her eyes twinkled. He was quite a handsome man and for all her fifty years and happy marriage she still appreciated a handsome man when she saw one. 'Well, can I help being's Jess ain't available or do you want to call back?'

Sep inwardly groaned. If he came back that meant another round trip of ten miles and he did so want to sort out this business of the vehicle. Cap in hand, he scratched his head.

'Well, I don't know if you can,' he began.

'Try me.'

He relented. 'Well, I've come about the pig Jess mentioned to me.'

'Pig! Oh, Bertha. Yes, she's round the back. Follow me.' She began to walk across the farmyard, Sep following. 'I don't know how much Jess is asking. Did he mention a price?'

'No, he replied. 'We never got that far.'

The woman stopped before a low wooden shed. 'Well, here she is. She comes from good stock. Do you intend breeding her or just fattening her up for Christmas? Though to me that would be a shame 'cos she's many a good breeding year left in her still.'

Sep stared down at the large pink animal grubbing about in the wet mud below. He bit his bottom lip as mirth threatened. 'I'm sorry er . . . Mrs . . . er . . .

'Call me Winny. Everyone else does.'

'Winny. Look, I don't think this is quite the pig I'm interested in.'

'Oh! Which pig then? I didn't know we were getting rid of any of the others just yet.'

'The pig that your husband said is in the barn. It's a motor vehicle.'

Winny burst into laughter. 'Oh, that pig. Oh, I see. Well, I think I see.' She looked quizzically at him. 'You want to buy that old thing. What for?'

'For moving things,' he replied cagily.

Winny tutted loudly. 'You'll have a job with that contraption. Look, I don't know what tale my old man has been spinning but it's been in our barn for the last, well, I don't know how many years and all it's good for is housing the chickens. Come on, I'll show you.'

She led a dismayed Sep back across the yard to a small barn and pulled open the large wooden doors. With a flurry, an assortment of chickens flew up in the air, sending a cascade of straw and feathers along with them. Sep looked at the sight of the rusting nose of the 'pig' peeking out through bales of straw stacked roof high and his heart sank. Jess obviously hadn't paid any heed to this vehicle since he had first parked it here.

Winny sensed his mood. 'Come into the house and have some tea. I was just about to mash when you came by.'

Without waiting for his answer she hurried off towards the house. Sep continued to stare at what he could see of the vehicle. She was right. It was nowhere near good enough even to begin revamping for his requirements. Sighing heavily, he turned and followed her, wondering where he went from here.

Seated at an enormous pine table in the centre of the well-

90

stocked kitchen he gratefully accepted the mug of strong brewed tea and took a sip. He eyed appreciatively the plate of freshly baked scones she had placed before him and selected one. Winny sat her ample frame down opposite.

Sep thanked her for her hospitality.

'My pleasure,' she responded sincerely. 'Least I could do after my dear husband brings you all this way on a wild goose chase.' She eyed him quizzically. 'As a matter of interest, just what kind of things were you planning to transport?'

Sep hesitated. 'Er . . . well, people to begin with.'

'People, eh?' she repeated keenly. 'What, like an omnibus service, the sort they operate in the big cities?'

Sep nodded. 'Yes. I'd really have liked a proper bus but I could never afford one of those.'

Winny shook her head. 'No, definitely not. Cost a king's ransom, I'd say. At least four or five hundred pounds.'

'As much as that!' Sep sighed heavily, seeing his dream fading rapidly.

Winny leant back in her chair and folded her fleshy arms under her bosom. 'If it's any consolation, our old Leyland truck would be no good for transporting people. Done up it'd be all right for ferrying folks up and down to the fields, but not for charging fares.'

Sep's face fell. 'No. You're right. It wouldn't be.'

Winny frowned in thought. 'For something like that you'd need a . . . let me see . . . something like a Ford Model T lorry.'

Sep raised his head and stared at her. 'Would I?' he asked, bemused. It suddenly struck him that this farmer's wife was very knowledgeable on the subject and he wondered why?

'Yes,' she continued. 'A good second hand Model T could easily be converted.' She began to laugh at Sep's expression. 'I don't know what yarn my dear husband has been spinning you, but in this family it's me that knows all about motor vehicles. You see, before I married I used to work as a lady's maid for the Dixon family in Market Bosworth and they were motor mad. The whole lot of them were, Lady Dixon included, and of course being landed gentry they could afford to dabble in such costly pastimes.'

Her eyes grew misty. 'Oh, you should have seen some of the motor cars that passed through their hands, especially the Renault limousine. It was a beauty and I was driven in it many times when accompanying Her Ladyship on shopping expeditions or visits.' She leaned forward and lowered her voice. 'Before I met Jess I used to go out with the chauffeur and he knew all there was to about engines and such like. Had to, you see, in case they broke down anywhere. It wouldn't do to have Her Ladyship stranded in the middle of nowhere.' She leaned back and guffawed loudly. 'And when we went out that's all he would talk about. Blooming engine bits and pieces. Oh, I know all about chassis and clutches.' She picked up the teapot, replenishing Sep's mug. 'I've never lost my interest. Have another scone,' she offered.

Sep smiled. 'Ta very much. These are good. Nearly as good as my own wife's. And I can assure you, that's a compliment,' he added hastily.

Winny chuckled. 'Don't worry, I took it as one.' She picked up a scone, cut it open and spread it thickly with freshly made butter. 'Well, as I was saying. Between the Dixon family and their chauffeur there wasn't much they didn't know about motors.' She smiled broadly. 'That's how we came by the pigs. When Jess and I married they were given to us as a wedding present. The Dixons thought they'd come in useful on the farm and they were right. They've been a Godsend one way or another.'

'Oh, I thought Jess said he bought them?' Sep queried.

'He would. He likes strangers to think he's a cut above the other farmers around here. But, truthfully, we would never have been able to afford them.'

'And you think I could afford one of those . . . what did you call it?'

'A Ford Model T. Well, of course, I don't know how much money you have to spend, but a second hand one, I do, considering you were thinking of buying that rusty old thing from us.' She leaned back and eyed him thoughtfully. 'You should consider buying one that was used by the army during the war.'

'Should I? How do I do that?'

'Look in the newspaper. I read the other day that a garage in Leicester had several for sale.'

'Did you? Did you notice how much for?'

Winny shook her head. 'No. Can't say as I did. But I reckon they'd be a sight cheaper than a new one. Anyway, one thing's for sure, at least you'd know you were getting a good deal. The army would have kept them in pristine condition. Then all you'd have to do would be convert it for passenger carrying like the Dixons did with theirs.'

Sep rested his arms on the table. 'How did they do that?' he asked keenly.

'What, convert it? Oh, that was simple. Well, simple to them but the likes of us would never have thought on it. Hang on.' She rose, walked over to the large dresser at the back of the room and returned with a piece of paper and a pencil. She sat down again and proceeded to make a sketch, Sep looking on in fascination. When she had finished she pushed the paper towards him. 'See,' she said, pleased with her handiwork. 'The Model T has a long flat back and this seating arrangement when needed was lifted on manually and bolted into place. When the lorry was used for shifting other loads it was unbolted, and so it went on.'

After studying the crudely drawn sketch, Sep sat back. He scratched his temple. 'I see.'

'Yeah, clever, isn't it?'

'You can say that again. It's so much better than the plans I had for the pig. And you've given me another idea.'

'Have I?'

'Yes. When I've done the passenger runs I could use the lorry for other things such as coal or flour.'

'You've got it!' Winny spoke in delight. 'I can see this venture of yours is going to be a tremendous success.'

'Oh, I've a lot of hurdles to cross yet.' He smiled broadly at her. 'But one thing's for sure, I'm glad I missed Jess this morning. If he had been here I would have bought that old pig and been on my way home with it now.'

'I doubt that, my dear,' Winny said, frowning. 'I doubt that it would have got as far as the farm gate before it fell to pieces.'

They both looked at each other then burst into laughter.

'Oh, Winny. Thank you, thank you so much.'

'My pleasure. Now you get yourself off into Leicester as soon as possible and make enquiries. Try Sturgess's. I'm sure they'll be able to help. Eh, and make sure you keep me informed on your progress. Because when your omnibus service is in operation, I want to know the times you go into Leicester.'

Sep walked towards her and grabbed her hand. 'Winny, you can ride on my omnibus any time and for free.'

''Ere, don't you go talking like that. It'll be a business you'll be running. You don't give nothing away for free in the future to nobody.'

'You're right. Half price then.'

'That's better, and I accept. But only if you'll take that wife of yours a dozen of my fresh eggs. Oh, and when you next see Jess, don't let on about our chat. I wouldn't like him to think I was belittling him. In fact, I won't mention you've called today. That'd be best. The fewer people who know about your venture the better 'til you've had chance to get it going.'

Sep grinned. 'Exactly my thoughts, Winny. Thank you.'

His feet hardly touched the ground on his journey home. First thing tomorrow he would travel into Leicester and visit the garage. As much as he would have liked to have gone that very minute, he couldn't, he had to take Ronnie along to see Mr Tunley. Despite that one blight, his heart pounded with excitement. He had so many plans to make, so much work to do, and for the first time in an age he felt properly alive.

Chapter Nine

'Mam, do I have to go?' Ronnie asked forlornly as he stood by the kitchen door dressed in his Sunday best trousers, the ones with only one patch on the backside, his short fair hair wetted and slicked down.

'Yes, you do,' his mother scolded. 'If you do things you know you shouldn't then you should be prepared for the consequences. Ah, here's your dad. Now try to liven yourself up and take that look of doom off your face.'

She eyed Sep as he entered the kitchen from upstairs. Like his son he was presented as smartly as she could manage. Straightening his tie, she nodded. 'Well, whatever Mr Tunley's got to say, at least he can't tell anyone you were badly turned out.' She pulled her husband aside. 'What do you think he'll do, Sep?'

He shook his head grimly, 'I don't know, Nell. I must admit I'm worried. It wouldn't have been so bad if Constable Jesson hadn't been involved but as he is . . . well, because of the number of times Ronnie has been warned in the past, he's probably advised Mr Tunley to press charges.'

Nell clasped her hand to her mouth. 'No, surely not? Why, the lad wasn't doing any damage. Besides, what could they charge him with?'

Sep shrugged his shoulders. 'Trespassing? Oh, I dunno, Nell. But standing round here won't get it sorted out. What are you doing?'

'I coming with you, that's what I'm doing,' she said, pulling on her shawl. 'No son of mine is landing up in the correction house without a fight.'

Sep's face hardened. 'Nell, you ain't going anywhere. In a mood like that you'll just make matters worse. Now make yourself a cuppa tea and leave it to me.'

'Sep . . .'

'Nell!'

She exhaled loudly and watched in silence as they departed. Slumping down in her chair by the fireside she picked up her mending and stared at it blankly, wondering worriedly what the formidable Station Master had in store for her son.

Seated behind his desk, Mr Tunley, his face severe, raised his head and eyed Sep and Ronnie standing nervously before him. He picked up a pile of papers, shuffled them together and cleared his throat.

'Well, I've listened to all you have to say and the way I see it there's only one course of action I can take.' He paused and eyed them each in turn. 'Persistent offenders like young Cartwright have to be dealt with properly and he can't say I didn't give him fair warning.'

'Look, Mr Tunley, you have my word,' Sep pleaded. 'My son won't come near the station again . . .'

'Ah,' Mr Tunley cut in. 'I might have your word, Mr Cartwright, but I've no guarantees Master Cartwright will take any notice.' He eyed Ronnie sharply from behind his thick-rimmed spectacles. 'How old are you, lad?'

'Thirteen, fourteen in July,' he muttered.

'Old enough to know better,' replied Tunley, picking up a piece of paper from the pile. He pushed it across the desk. 'Report to that address next Friday morning at ten-thirty sharp.'

Sep grabbed the paper and scanned it. He raised his eyes, confused. 'It's an appointment to see the doctor!'

'That's right. Dr Runcorn. He's the official Midland and Great Northern Railway Doctor. I've arranged for young Cartwright to attend a medical.'

'Medical?'

Mr Tunley leant back in his chair, took off his spectacles, wiped them with his handkerchief and replaced them, Sep and Ronnie staring at him blankly.

'All potential candidates for jobs on the railway have first to take a medical. We can't take anyone on who isn't fit.'

Both gawped and stared at each other, then back at Mr Tunley. 'Job?' they said in unison.

'That's right. I've thought long and hard about this matter and the way I see it is the only way to cure young Cartwright is for him to earn money doing something he's so obviously interested in, and it so happens that due to promotion I have a vacancy. What d'you say, lad?'

Ronnie was struck speechless and Sep nudged him. 'Answer Mr Tunley, Ronnie.'

'Er . . . Thanks, Mr Tunley,' was all he could manage.

Mr Tunley coughed. 'Working on the railway is no picnic, lad. It's hard work so you'd better be prepared. And, believe me, you've a lot to learn about the workings of an outfit like this. Now, when you've had your medical, which I've no doubt you'll pass, you'll need to go to London to see the Superintendent.'

'London.' Ronnie mouthed in awe. 'How do I get there?'

'Why, on a train. How else do you think?'

Ronnie's mouth dropped even further. 'Train! By train. Did you hear that, Dad? I'm going on a train.'

'I heard, son, and I think you should thank Mr Tunley again for what he's doing.'

'His thanks to me will be shown by hard work and no slacking.' Mr Tunley rose. 'Now, if you don't mind, I have to check the

96

sorting office before the mail train arrives from Rugby.' He offered his hand to Sep which was readily accepted and shaken. Mr Tunley turned to address Ronnie. 'Come to see me after your medical and we'll take it from there.'

'I will, I will,' he cried in delight.

Mr Tunley showed them to the door and watched as they departed down the platform, hoping that this decision was going to prove one of his better ones.

'Can you believe it, Dad?' Ronnie spoke excitedly as they made their way home. 'I'm going to be working for the railway and I'm going to London on a train.'

Sep exhaled deeply. 'Son, things are happening just lately that several weeks ago I would never have thought possible.' He stopped, turned, and placed his hands on his younger son's shoulders. 'Ronnie, you're being given a great opportunity and you must make the most of it.'

'I intend to, Dad. I want to end up a Station Master like Mr Tunley.'

'Good, and you make sure you do.' He lowered his hands and resumed walking. 'Come on, let's get home and tell your mother. I can't wait to see her face.'

'Oh, Sep, Sep!' Nell cried, clasping her hand to her mouth. 'Am I hearing right?'

'You are. Our Ronnie's got a job and one with a bright future.'

'Oh, Sep, Ronnie!' she uttered, her eyes shining proudly. 'And here's me been expecting all sorts. But I tell you, I never expected this.' She turned to the rest of her family seated at the table, listening intently. 'Billy, go down to the Three Tuns and get a jug of beer and a quarter bottle of port. And mind you get it straight from the barrel, I don't want palming off with any old rubbish.'

'Beer and port?' Peggie uttered, shocked. 'Mam, you never touch the stuff.'

'Well, I do now. I need a drop of something to calm me nerves. What with all that's going off at the moment, I need something to make me sleep. Besides, Mrs Pegg swears by it.'

Sep laughed. 'I see. If Mrs Pegg endorses it, then it's all right, is it?'

'For one night it is, yes. Anyway,' she paused and eyed her family in turn, 'I think you'd all agree we've something to celebrate.'

'Me un' all, Mam?' piped up Primrose.

'No. You can have tea.'

'Ah, Mam,' she wailed.

'Just a sip won't hurt, Nell,' Sep said persuasively.

She eyed her daughter. 'Oh, all right. But just a sip.'

Primrose clapped her hands in glee. 'Yippee!' she sang. 'I bet none of my friends has had a drop of port.'

97

'No, and you won't again if you don't keep it to yourself,' she chided. 'Go on then, Billy. Get off before I change me mind.'

Sep bought the Ford Model T to a precarious halt at the side of the country road, climbed down from the cab and walked around it several times, taking in every detail. His heart swelled as an enormous feeling of pride filled him. This motor vehicle belonged to him, he owned it all, every bit of metal, wood, rust and rattle, and he wanted to savour these few moments with it before he introduced it to the rest of his eagerly awaiting family, and of course the villagers. There was no chance of getting such a phenomenon home without anyone seeing it. He realised now how his grandfather must have felt when he brought home the welsh dresser, parading it through the village for all to see.

He smiled broadly. How the news would spread! Well, let it. Let them all wonder what Septimus Cartwright and his family were up to, and wouldn't they be surprised when they found out – one family in particular.

With head held high, his pocket filled with the winnings from the bet, he had gone into Leicester and struck a deal. He could easily have bought a better-looking vehicle, but the one he had chosen, although in need of sprucing up, had as good an engine as a more expensive model and by his sensible decision he had a few pounds left to allow for the conversion and other incidentals to get the Cartwright Omnibus Service off to a good start.

Driving home had not been without incident. Roads leaving the city and onwards were very narrow, vision was restricted by high hawthorn hedges, and there were plenty of pot holes to negotiate, but after having travelled ten of his twelve miles, he was getting used to his new acquisition. He felt at home in the driving seat and 'Mabel', as he had affectionately christened her, was performing admirably. Won't the family be proud? he thought, giving her one last inspection.

Finally, he climbed aboard and began the rest of his journey. Not long after he crossed over the boundary of Barlestone, people were gawping, curtains were twitching, and a crowd of barefooted children were trotting behind him, for the majority their first ever sight of a motorised vehicle.

He brought it to rest at the side of his cottage, the family already gathered by the gate. News of his arrival had travelled quicker than he had. Nell, one hand clasped to her mouth, the other to her chest, stood speechless. He jumped down and ran to join her, placing his arm around her shoulders.

'Well, what do you think?' he asked, gazing at each of them in turn.

Primrose, after first giving the gathering crowd of onlookers a superior stare, scrambled into the driving seat.

Billy walked around in scrutiny and rejoined his father. 'Not bad, Dad. Not bad at all.'

'Oh, and you're an authority?' he replied with a twinkle in his eye.

Billy laughed. 'She looks good, Dad.' He nodded towards the crowd. 'She's causing quite a stir.'

Sep smiled. Having never been a vain man, the awestruck stares he was receiving made him uncomfortable. 'Let's all get inside. We've plenty to talk about.'

With the whole family seated around the table, replenished by mugs of tea and home made potted meat sandwiches, Sep gazed round at his family, all looking back at him expectantly. He suddenly realised that this was the very first meeting of the Cartwright Omnibus Service and took a deep breath, pencil poised against the piece of blank paper on the table in front of him.

'Firstly, I want none of our business discussed outside these walls. Is that understood? That way, no one will know what we're doing before we ourselves do.'

Six heads nodded.

'Good. And should anyone ask why we have a lorry, you don't know. It's bad enough them all knowing how we got the money for it, let alone anything else.'

'Why?' Letty asked. 'Wouldn't it be better for everyone to know we're starting an omnibus service?'

'Not at this stage,' her father replied hurriedly. He eyed Nell knowingly. 'Case anyone else should jump in before I've had the time to carry out the necessary work.'

'Oh, I see,' Letty uttered.

'Now, this is going to be a family business and I'll expect you all to chip in.'

'Yes, and that means you, Primrose, and you, our Billy,' Nell cut in. 'You'll expect to reap the benefits, won't you? And there won't be any unless we all pull our weight.'

'What will I have to do then?' Primrose asked forlornly. Her face suddenly lit up. 'Will I be able to drive?'

'No, you won't,' Peggie scolded. She turned to her father. 'But I will, won't I?'

'Don't be stupid. You won't be able to drive a lorry,' Billy scoffed. 'Especially not one loaded with passengers.'

Peggie turned on her brother. 'And what makes you such an authority? Dad has often told us women drove in the war, so what's wrong with me driving now?' She turned to her father for confirmation. 'Dad?'

'I'm not having any daughter of mine driving a lorry. So you can put that idea right out of your head,' Nell said haughtily, leaning back in her chair and folding her arms under her bosom.

'Ah, Mam . . .'

'What about me?' Ronnie grumbled. 'I'll be working on the railway. I won't have time.'

99

'The railways don't work twenty-four hours a day,' Letty said sharply.

Sep scraped back his chair, stood up and banged his fist on the table. 'Order!' he shouted. 'This is supposed to be a business meeting, not a slanging match.' Six pair of eyes fixed upon him, mouths clamped firmly shut. 'That's better.' He settled himself down again. 'Any more of that and none of you'll be involved. I'll employ whoever I need when necessary.' He waited as mutters of apology were made. 'Right, you've all been warned. Now, first things first. I'm going round to see Mr Brotherhood to ask him if I can put the lorry in his yard for the time being. If not, well, I'll have to come up with something else. There's one thing for sure, I'm not leaving it out in the open while I'm working on it.'

'I could ask Jenny Pegg, see if she has any room in one of her outbuildings.'

Sep eyed his wife thoughtfully. 'Do you think she would, her being gentry un' all?'

'I've told you before, Sep, Jenny's all right. She might have money, but she's down to earth.' Nell grinned as a memory occurred to her. 'She'd have to be to agree to be pushed through the village in a wheelbarrow to help raise money for the church roof fund, wouldn't she? And she enjoyed every minute of it.' She sniffed haughtily. 'If Mr Brotherhood ain't got any spare space, I'll approach her. There's no harm in asking, after all.'

Sep nodded. 'I suppose.' He turned to his elder son. 'Billy, I need you to get me some wood, nails and other bits on the cheap.'

He raised his eyes innocently. 'What makes you think I can get things like that?'

Sep leaned across the table, his face inches from his son's. 'Well, it seems to me you can get everything else on the cheap so why not what I need?' He leaned back, his eyes narrowing. 'I'll tell you what I want and you see what you can do.'

'Okay, Dad.'

'Thanks, son. Now, Ronnie. I know you'll be starting this new job soon but there's still plenty for you to do helping me with the heavy work, and it'll keep you out of mischief.'

'What about us?' Peggie asked. 'What will me and Letty be doing?'

Sep looked at them both fondly. 'Girls, you two will have to continue going to the factory for the time being. We need your money. I'm sorry.' He turned to Billy. 'And you as well, son. We still have to eat.'

Peggie and Letty tried to hide their disappointment, which Sep could not help noticing.

'Look, it can't be helped,' he said sincerely.

'Course it can't,' chipped in Nell. 'I'll still be working for Mrs Pegg.'

Sep smiled gratefully at her. 'Hopefully not for long.' He turned his attention back to the rest of them. 'I've no doubt in time this venture will keep all of us more than occupied. But let's not run before we can walk.' His eyes twinkled. 'Or drive.'

'Oh, funny, Dad,' Primrose sniggered. 'Dad's cracked a funny.'

'That's enough from you,' Nell snapped.

Sep rested his elbows on the table. 'Well, that's it then. That's the end of our first business meeting. Now remember what I've said. Not a word to anyone.'

They all nodded, each filled with exciting thoughts on what this new venture might hold for them.

When they had all dispersed, Sep turned to Nell. 'What did you think of our first meeting then? Did I do all right?'

She walked over and put her arms around him. 'You did fine. I'm right proud of you. The way you put our young 'uns in their place, why, anyone would think you'd been doing it for years.'

Sep frowned hard. 'If it hadn't have been for Crabbe's thieving I might have been, Nell. By now we could've been living in a big house, with a thriving business and no money worries. Our gels wouldn't be scratting in a factory nor our Billy down the pit.'

Nell pulled back from him and raised her eyes angrily. 'Stop that, Septimus Cartwright. Stop that right now. This is a new beginning for us. For all you know you might not have made a living with that brake. Any number of things might have gone wrong.'

Sep nodded in agreement. 'Yes, you're right as usual, me old love. I've got to think of now, and to be honest this is a far more exciting venture than the brake ever was.'

'Good. Leave the past where it belongs, Sep. In the past.'

He gazed absently across the room. If others will let it, he thought, and rested his eyes on Nell. 'I'll go round and see Brotherhood.'

She reached up and kissed him on his cheek. 'I'll have your supper ready when you return. I'll do something special.'

Kenneth Brotherhood readily agreed to Sep's request. 'I've a shed you can use over there.' He pointed over the far side of the large yard. A lean to, big enough to hold two Ford Model T lorries, lay half hidden by planks of wood, old railway sleepers and uncut tree trunks. 'You'll have to clear the way through yourself. Unfortunately I've had to lay off my spare man for the present.'

'That's no problem. Me and my boys will do it in no time. I appreciate this, Mr Brotherhood, and I'll pay you rent. Keep things all above board.'

'Too right you will,' he replied, laughing.

Kenneth Brotherhood paused. He took great pleasure in giving a helping hand when he thought it was the right thing to do, but he'd known Septimus Cartwright a long time and knew the man wouldn't take kindly to an offer of a shed for free even if only for the interim.

He liked Septimus, they had always been on sociable terms since they had knocked around together as boys, but his own life had

101

been relatively easy compared to his tenant's. The Brotherhoods'
futures had all been secured when his great-great-grandfather had
had the foresight to purchase the parcel of land the cottages and
woodshed now stood on for a tiny sum of money for which he had
worked night and day. The Brotherhoods had prospered since
then, never becoming rich, but comfortable enough not to have to
worry. The Cartwrights hadn't been so fortunate, but nevertheless
had worked just as hard, if not harder than ever his family had had
to do, and all because of his ancestor's farsightedness. Strange, he
thought, how lives are shaped by just one small action. It could just
be that the Cartwrights' futures were being secured now by Sep's
gamble on buying the lorry.

He eyed his tenant warily, knowing he would have to tread
carefully if his offer of help was to be accepted in the vein it was
meant. 'Ha'penny a week. How does that sound?'

Sep stared at him. 'Ha'penny?' he repeated, bewildered.

Kenneth Brotherhood laughed loudly. 'Are you saying that's too
dear?'

Sep blew out his cheeks. 'No, no, not at all. It's far less than I
expected.'

'Well, being realistic, I couldn't charge more than that. The
shed's falling down. So if I were you I'd accept before I change my
mind.' He slapped Sep on the shoulder. 'What are you proposing
to do with this lorry?'

He tightened his lips. As much as he respected Kenneth
Brotherhood, and was grateful for his generosity, he did not feel he
wanted to divulge his plans to anyone just yet, as much as he trusted
them.

'Oh, this and that,' he said cagily. 'Nothing definite. I've some
work to do on her first.'

Kenneth nodded. 'I see. Well, I must say I envy you. She's a fine-
looking lorry.' He rubbed his large work-worn hands across his
chin. 'I could put some business your way if you're interested.'

'Oh? What kind of business?'

'Delivering my wood. And I'll pay a reasonable rate for the job.
I've always used Crabbe when my own cart is spoken for, but he
gets more and more unreliable as time goes by. Says he'll come at
a certain time and turns up hours, sometimes days, late. Only
because he knows he's got the monopoly in this area.' His eyes
twinkled. 'Well, now he'll have to look out, 'cos if my hunch is right,
I don't think he will have for much longer, will he?'

Sep scratched his ear, ignoring Kenneth's probing. 'I'm sure we
can do business together, when I'm in a position to.'

'Good. Just give me the nod. But if you'll take my advice, you'll
get that lorry on the road as soon as possible, get it earning money
for you. In the meantime, if you need any bits and pieces, just ask.
I've all sorts lying round here.'

They shook hands and parted. As Sep went to fetch the lorry to
move it into the yard until he cleared the frontage to the shed, a

feeling of wellbeing enveloped him. He had only just acquired the vehicle and here he was already with an offer of work. He couldn't wait to tell Nell.

Later that night, Peggie sat propped up in bed reading a book whilst Letty sat on the edge brushing her hair. Primrose was sound asleep, snoring softly, the top of her head just visible above the blankets.

Peggie closed her book and prepared to settle down. 'It's exciting ain't it? she said, pulling the covers beneath her chin. 'I can't wait to drive that lorry. It looks easy enough. And I wonder what it's going to look like when Dad's built the conversion thingy-me-gig? Letty, a' you listening to me?'

'What?' She turned her head and stared at her sister blankly.

'You never heard a word I said, did you? She sat up. 'Letty, what's wrong?'

Letty lowered her head, fingering the hair brush. 'I'm worried, Peggie.' She raised her eyes. 'I'm worried about this date with Reginald Crabbe. How can I get out of it?'

Peggie frowned and sighed deeply. 'I don't honestly know.' She ran her fingers through her dishevelled curls, making them stick out even further. 'If you stand him up, he's the type that'd come round and cause a stink and that would never do. Mam and Dad would have a fit.'

'Why would they have a fit? What is it that they have against the Crabbes anyway?'

Peggie reddened. 'I dunno,' she lied hurriedly. 'Just always disliked each other, I guess.' She sat further up, drew up her legs and hugged her knees tightly beneath the covers. 'Look, the way I see it is, you'll have to go just this once, Letty, and make the best of it. If he asks to see you again, tell him you don't want to. That way it'll keep him away from the house and Mam and Dad will never find out.'

'Oh, I can't, Peggie. I can't stand the thought of spending all that time in his company.'

'You'll just have to. It's your own fault. You should never have agreed in the first place.'

'But I didn't!' Letty cried. 'I only said I'd think about it.'

'You must have. And keep your voice down, you don't want to wake nosy knickers,' she said quickly, eyeing the sleeping Primrose. Her face softened. 'It won't be that bad. Tell him halfway through the night you have a headache and need to come home.'

Letty sighed forlornly. 'All right. But what excuse will I have for not seeing him again, apart from telling him he makes me feel sick, that is?'

Peggie hid a smile. 'Tell him . . . I know, tell him you're still hurting after the business with Wilfred and you need time to recover. Even he'll see sense in that, and in the meantime he'll meet someone else and forget about you.'

'Thanks very much,' Letty muttered. 'You saying I'm easily forgettable?'

'You know I'm not. But you know as well as I do of Reginald's reputation.'

'All right. I just hope it works.'

'Good. Now get into bed or we'll never get up in the morning.'

As the Cartwright household settled down for the night, on the outskirts of the village two men faced each other across a table laden with dirty dishes and utensils, the floor in dire need of a sweep and scrub, the air pungent with the smell of body odour, stale food and tobacco smoke.

'Have you heard about the Cartwrights, Dad?'

Cyrus head jerked up. 'Heard! Heard what?'

Reginald smiled slyly. 'About them buying a lorry.'

'A lorry?' Cyrus repeated, scratching his day's growth of beard.

'Yeah, you know, one of them mechanical things.'

'I know what a bloody lorry is,' he snapped sharply. 'A' you sure about this?'

'Yeah, 'course I am,' Reginald replied tonelessly through a mouthful of bread and cheese. He drank noisily from his mug of strong tea. 'John Vaughan seen it with his own eyes. Said Cartwright's parked it up in Brotherhood's wood yard.'

'Oh, has he?' Cyrus leaned back in his chair, raised his long legs, cleared a space with his booted foot, and rested them on the table. 'Now what is he doing with a lorry, and for that matter where's he got the money from to buy it?' He spoke thoughtfully.

'Oh, that's easy. He won it. Had a bet on the 'osses.'

Cyrus lowered his legs and leaned across the table, his dark eyes narrowing to two thin slits. 'Sep Cartwright had a bet on the 'osses? I don't believe it!' he spat. 'You're lying?'

'It's true, Dad. Damned good odds an' all. Luck of the devil if you ask me.'

'You can say that again!' Cyrus handsome face scowled deeply. 'I need to find out what he's up to.' He fixed his gaze on his son. 'I need you to do some checking around. See if any of those so called mates of yours know anything.'

Reginald wiped his mouth with the back of his hand, then rubbed it over his grimy shirt. 'I can do better than that,' he said cockily.

'Oh! How come?'

'I've got a date with Letty Cartwright tomorrow night.'

A slow smile spread across Cyrus' face. 'How the hell did you manage that?'

'Charm. Chip off the old block, eh?'

'Not quite, son. You'll have to go a long way 'til you can match me.' He paused thoughtfully, then nodded. ''Course, her and that Wilfred Dage have parted. I suppose you got in there quick while she was off her guard?' His eyes glinted wickedly and he leaned back in his chair, folding his arms behind his head. He started to laugh. It grew to a bellow. 'Oh, this'll be one in the eye for the high and mighty Septimus Cartwright. One of his precious daughters going out with a Crabbe.' He stopped laughing, eyes narrowing again. 'Reginald, you've given me an idea.'

'Eh!'

'Just shut it and listen,' snarled Cyrus. 'Tomorrow night Letty Cartwright is going to be swept off her feet. Do you hear me, lad?'

'I hear you. But I don't understand.' Reginald shrugged his shoulders. 'Why? Why should I wanna sweep her off her feet. She's too homely for my liking and I don't go a bundle on women who wear spectacles.' He grinned. 'Now if it were Peggie . . .'

'Forget her. You'll never land Peggie Cartwright in a million years. It's Letty you must concentrate on. You're gonna win her over. She's gonna see a side of the Crabbes she never thought existed.' He slammed his fist hard on the table. Reginald jumped. 'I want you to make her forget Wilfred Dage. Do you understand me?'

He gulped. 'Yes, Dad.'

'Good.' A smile twitched at the corners of his mouth. 'You never know, you might end up marrying her and that would really finish that bastard Cartwright. He'd never live it down.' His eyes scanned the filthy room. 'Besides, we could do with someone cleaning up this place and cooking us some decent meals.' He smirked. 'You did say she was homely.'

Reginald grunted scornfully. 'I can think of plenty of things to do with Letty Cartwright but I ain't going so far as to marry her. I draw the line at that. I only made her go out with me in the first place for a laugh. Just to have a dig at the gutless Wilfred.'

Cyrus leapt to his feet, leaned over the table and grabbed Reginald by the throat. 'I don't care what led up to this,' he hissed. 'You, Reginald Crabbe, will do as I bloody well say.' He lowered his voice menacingly. 'Or you'll end up like your sister.'

Reginald gulped painfully in fright. 'All right, Dad,' he whispered hoarsely as the grip on his throat tightened.

After what seemed an eternity Cyrus relaxed and sat back in his chair. 'You should know better than to question me, my lad.'

Reginald gulped again. 'Yes, Dad. I'm sorry, Dad.'

'I should think so. Now, you'd better clear up this pig sty. You can't bring a Cartwright back to a stinking hole like this. And we want to make the right impression, don't we?' He kicked his son beneath the table. 'Don't we?' he repeated angrily.

'Yes, Dad, yes,' Reginald uttered.

He jumped up and hunted for the broom, his father looking on mockingly. The worst thing he could have done was to question Cyrus. He should have known from past experience to keep his mouth shut. Instead, for the sake of bragging about a rumour regarding the lorry and a conquest of Letty that was based on lies, he had landed himself right in it. He took a deep breath. It didn't pay to disagree with his father. Many people had found that out to their cost, including his own sister. But then, she had been stupid which was something Reginald wasn't. He shuddered. Under no circumstances was he going to end up like her. So to keep the peace he would go along with his father's wishes in the hope the idea palled and he subsequently forgot about it. Reginald brushed the floor so vigorously the handle of the broom snapped in two.

Cyrus watched him with growing satisfaction. It gave him a feeling of immense power to know that he frightened his son. Especially now that Mary was out of the way, he had to have someone to vent his anger on. Well, now he had a distraction again and it was to do with his old adversary.

Cyrus couldn't remember a time when he hadn't hated Septimus Cartwright. It had all begun at school when the pair had been forced to sit together on a low wooden bench behind a worn desk and Septimus had beaten him in a spelling test. The rest of the class had jeered at him, egged on by the spiteful school master. He knew they were jeering because he had a mother who drank herself silly and a father not much better; because his clothes were threadbare and he smelt. So did a lot of the other kids but it was him they jeered at.

As if losing the test wasn't bad enough, his mother had arrived at the school on prize giving day, in a drunken stupor, and made a scene. None of his class mates or the teachers had ever let him forget it.

At the time he had been too young and puny to take out his anger and hurt on the people who scorned him, so he took it out on Septimus who was smaller than him and because he was envious of the fact he had parents who cared for him; parents who were concerned over his welfare; a mother who sent him to school each day clean and tidy and with something for his lunch and a father who took him fishing and gave him a patch in his garden and taught him to care for the land. Cyrus' own mother never knew what time of day it was, let alone whether he had risen and gone to school, and his father, when he condescended to be at home, worried more about his beer and betting money than whether his family was being fed.

Those early days had ignited sparks of dislike and as the years passed those sparks were fanned into flames. Now a fire burned in the pit of his stomach which wouldn't die until he had done his rival down for good. It made him feel better when he achieved success, no matter what the cost, and equally as important, he usually prospered in the process.

He dreaded to think how his life would have worked out if Septimus hadn't come up with the idea of the brake and he had not by chance found out about it. That had been his making. The brake had been so easily stolen and the authorities so easily fooled. Now he was being presented with another opportunity through, of all things, his son. If Cyrus could get him married off to one of Cartwright's daughters he would be triumphant.

He eyed his son scornfully as he swept the room. 'Put yer back into it,' he snarled.

Chapter Ten

Wednesday evening came around far too quickly for Letty's liking. The rest of the family were all too preoccupied with helping on the lorry to notice her anxious state. Pity the foreman at work hadn't. She had been reprimanded three times for turning out poor quality work. Once more and she would surely get the sack. Even Peggie, her closest ally, seemed to have forgotten what night it was. She was in the shed now alongside Ronnie, holding tools in readiness for their father and Billy, and Letty felt anger mount, masking her worry for a moment. Peggie had let her down and it hurt. Now more than ever before she needed and wanted her support and she hadn't got it.

Dressed as dowdily as she could manage, her usual fashionable bob parted unbecomingly down the middle and gripped severely back behind her ears, she checked herself once more in the mirror and nodded. She looked dreadful, just the effect she had striven for. She picked up her bag and made her way down the stairs. She found her mother bustling around the kitchen making enormous sandwiches for the ravenous workers. Primrose was sitting at the other end of the table reading a comic. She lifted her head as Letty entered and grinned broadly.

'I didn't know we had a tramp lodging upstairs,' she spluttered laughingly.

Letty let the remark pass. She was not in the mood for a confrontation, she had enough on her mind.

Nell looked up, quickly took in her daughter's attire and frowned. 'Primrose is right. I thought you'd thrown that dress in the rag box long ago.' She turned and slapped her youngest lightly over the head. 'But you still shouldn't have said that. Now get up the shed with these sandwiches before they all down tools in hunger,' she said, shoving the basket of food across the table towards her youngest daughter.

Primrose grabbed the basket, stuck her tongue out at Letty and skipped out of the cottage, banging the door shut behind her.

Nell, watching all this, shook her head. 'That child will be the death of me.' Wiping her hands on her apron she turned her attention back to Letty. 'Are you going up the shed to help the others? Is that why you're dressed in that old thing?'

Letty breathed deeply in order to be careful of what she said next. 'I was but I've changed my mind. Thought I might go for a walk and get some fresh air.'

'Why? Ain't you feeling well?'

'Bit of a headache, that's all. If it clears I might go to my friend, Brenda's, for a bit.'

Nell nodded. 'All right. It might do you good, you've had a face like a condemned man for the last few days. I hope this walk and natter with Brenda helps to put a smile back on that pretty face of yours.' She smiled fondly, walked towards her daughter and put her arms around her, pulling her closely. 'It'll all come right in the end, you see if it don't.'

Letty smiled ruefully. 'Do you reckon?' she replied despondently. She pulled back from her mother's embrace. 'I'd better go, before this headache gets worse.'

Nell watched silently as her daughter slouched out of the door, feeling mightily glad she wasn't young any more and having to put up with all the problems youth entailed.

Letty walked quickly down the dried dirt street, praying that Reginald had been struck down with Yellow Fever, the Black Death, anything as long as it meant he couldn't keep their appointment. Her heart banged painfully in her chest as she spotted him coming towards her from across the village green.

He smiled in greeting, bought his hand from behind his back and presented her with a bunch of flowers. She accepted, surprised.

'Er . . . thanks,' she gulped.

'My pleasure, Letty. I picked 'em myself.' What he didn't tell her was that he had picked them from several gardens on his way to meet her on his father's instructions. He quickly eyed her. What a sight she looked, he'd seen travelling women dressed better than she was, and what on earth had she done with her hair? He just hoped to God none of his mates saw him. 'You look nice,' he lied.

Her face flushed with embarrassment, she could feel her cheeks burning. 'Do I?' she asked in surprise, fingering her spectacles nervously.

'You always do, Letty.' He placed himself at her side. 'Right, where would you like to go?' he asked, frantically searching his mind for a location unfrequented by anyone he knew.

'Where would I like to go?' she repeated. 'Er . . . Well, er . . . I have this headache you see and . . .'

He hid a smile of relief. Letty herself had handed him the solution. 'Oh, well then,' he said, grabbing her arm, 'we'll take a walk down by the river. That should clear your head. Then we'll stop by the Wayside Inn for a drink. Only lemonade,' he added hurriedly. 'Come on.'

Reluctantly, she found herself being led towards the narrow red brick hump-backed bridge crossing the river where steps led down to the tow path. His attitude and manner had surprised her. She hadn't expected him to be like this. This Reginald Crabbe was a reformed character to the one who had confronted her and Wilfred the other night. She quickly switched her thoughts. She must not think of Wilfred. If she did, she would cry and she couldn't do that in front of Reginald.

She glanced discreetly at him as he held her elbow while descending the steps. He looked smarter than she had ever seen him before. His jacket and trousers had obviously been pressed and his shirt she could tell had been freshly laundered. He had made this effort for her and suddenly she felt guilty for her own unusually slovenly appearance. The Cartwrights had never had much money, but they had always made the best of themselves, especially the women.

They walked for quite a way down the picturesque waterside. Letty unwittingly found herself warming to her escort, feeling more and more as the evening wore on that Reginald Crabbe was not the brash, foul-mouthed womaniser he made himself out to be.

Reginald himself was feeling thoroughly bored. It was hard keeping up the act of playing the gentleman. He would much sooner have been in a pub with his mates, ending the evening with a roll in the hay with an accommodating female. It was only his father's threats that spurred him on. When he returned home that night he would have to give a full account of the proceedings and was terrified at the thought that he just might not be able to captivate the dowdy Letty.

They stopped at a grassy part of the bank and rested for a while. 'Is your headache any better?' he asked her.

She looked at him blankly. 'Headache? Oh, my headache! Yes, thank you, it is. I feel much better.' She turned her head and gazed out across the river. Her thoughts were of Wilfred. The last time she had sat by the river she had been with him and they had been discussing their elopement. She had been happy then, happy in the knowledge that he loved her and was willing to defy his mother in order that they should marry.

'Penny for 'em?'

'Pardon?' She turned her head and looked at him blankly.

'I said, penny for them,' he repeated.

'Oh, nothing. I was just thinking about things, that's all.'

'About Wilfred?'

She sighed. 'Yes, actually, I was.'

Reginald fought hard to find suitable words. 'Er . . . well, it's understandable you should think of him, I suppose. But if it were me that had been made a fool of I'd want to knock his block off.' He realised this was his chance and seized it. He grabbed her by the arms and pulled her round. 'But it's him that's the fool, Letty. He must have been mad to let you go as easily as he did. If some bloke did to me what I did to him the other night, I'd have punched him in the gob . . . mouth.'

'Wilfred's not like that,' she snapped. 'He's not a violent man.'

'No, more's the pity. But I'm not talking about violence, Letty. I'm talking about standing up for yourself and the one you love. If

111

he'd more gumption about him you wouldn't be sitting here with me now. Would you?'

She slowly shook her head. 'No, I suppose I wouldn't.'

'You need a man, Letty. A proper man. One that'll show you his feelings. That man's me, Letty. I've liked you for a long time and I'm glad it's all over between you and Wilfred. It means I have a chance.' He stared at her searchingly. 'I have got a chance haven't I, Letty?'

He was quick to notice her look of apprehension. He dropped his arms, a hurt look crossing his face. 'I know people don't think much of me and my dad. But I can assure you it's only because we've tried to make an honest living and keep ourselves to ourselves. It's jealousy, Letty. Jealousy 'cos we've tried to do something with our lives.' He raised his eyes to meet hers. 'We've had to live for years with lies and rumours and they've all been untrue. I bet you've heard and believed them all?'

She stared at him, ashamed. 'Yes, I must admit I have.'

His face fell forlornly. 'Well, 'course you would, not knowing any better.' He looked at her pleadingly. 'Give me a chance, Letty? Give me a chance to prove myself to you?' You'd better or I'm done for, he thought worriedly 'You will, won't you? You will agree to see me again?'

She stared at him for a moment then compassion filled her. She wanted to see him again and he was right. If Wilfred had truly loved her he would have put up a fight. But he hadn't and now he was the loser. But if she agreed to see Reginald again what would her family's reactions be, especially Peggie's? Oh, what the hell? she thought, suddenly not caring about her family. Besides, they were all too interested in the lorry to care what she was doing. 'Yes,' she said hurriedly before she changed her mind. 'I'd like to see you. But it'll have to be in secret.' Her mind fought frantically for a plausible excuse. 'You see, my family wouldn't be pleased if they thought I was seeing someone so soon after Wilfred.'

Immense relief crossed his face. 'That's all right, Letty. I understand. What about Saturday night then? We could take a walk or maybe go in the brake to Desford or Ratby to the cinema?'

She nodded. 'Yes, that would be nice.'

They rose and made their way back towards the village. Saying goodbye at the bridge, a light-hearted Letty made her way home. She had enjoyed herself and on Saturday decided to take greater pains with her appearance. Reginald was a good-looking man and she wanted to look nice for him.

Momentarily she felt guilty for betraying Wilfred, then mentally shook herself. If he had really wanted her she wouldn't be planning what to wear for her date with Reginald. What was wrong with having a bit of fun? It was better than moping around, and if she went out with Reginald Wilfred would surely get to hear. With a bit of luck it just might be the jolt he needed to make him do something about their situation once and for all.

* * *

Cyrus raised his head expectantly when his son entered the room.

'Well, how did you get on?'

'All right. I'm seeing her Saturday night.'

'Saturday night! Why that far away?'

'You can't rush things like this, Dad, she might get suspicious.'

'Huh. Yeah, well. You could be right, I suppose.' He sat forward in his seat. 'Did you find out anything about this lorry?'

'No. I didn't get the chance.' He eyed his father nervously. 'A' yer worried?'

'Worried! Why should I be worried? Septimus Cartwright having a poxy lorry don't worry the likes of me. Wadda you think he's gonna do with it anyway?'

Reg shrugged his shoulders. 'It did cross my mind he might be going to use it to haul loads, like we do on the dray cart.'

Cyrus scowled deeply. The thought had crossed his mind and if it had also crossed his brainless son's then maybe he should be worried. 'Huh,' he spat. 'And what loads is he going to haul? I've got the monopoly in this area. Folks have been using me for years and they ain't gonna change just 'cos Cartwright's bought a lorry, now are they? He ain't got my years of experience.'

Reg gulped. He had always thought his father a bright man, but he was obviously wrong. Did his father not realise how disliked he was, how people would jump at the chance to use a source of transport other than his? But Reginald wasn't going to be the one to tell him. Let him find out in his own way.

'Yeah, yer right, Dad. Nobody in their right mind would use him. That's if he is planning that anyway. I'm maybe wrong. Oh, I forgot to tell yer, I did manage to convince Letty that we Crabbes are just victims of malice and jealousy by the villagers. So if her family find out we're seeing each other, she'll think on what I said and question their motives.'

Cyrus stared at his son in surprise. 'Well done. I can see you learn quick.'

'Yeah, well, I've got a good teacher, ain't I?' He kicked off his shoes, slung his jacket across a chair and loosened his tie. 'I just hope to God I can keep up this pretence. She's hard going, is Letty Cartwright, and she's still carrying a torch for that spineless creature, Wilfred.'

'I thought I told you to make sure she forgot about him?'

'Oh, come on, Dad. Wadda you want in one night? A miracle?'

Cyrus' face darkened. 'Yes,' he snarled. 'If that's what it takes.' He tented his fingers. 'Bring her round here so she can see for herself what a nice home you come from. Let her see that by sticking with you she could better herself.'

'Eh! And how do you propose I do that?'

'Use your brains. That's if you've got any. Just you make sure you get her here, and the sooner the better.' And the sooner I can

113

pump her and find out what her father intends doing, he thought worriedly.

Peggie was waiting up for Letty, and as she entered, sprang out of her chair and bounded towards her.

'Where have you been? she demanded.

'You know where I've been,' replied Letty coolly. 'And before you start, I'm seeing him again.'

'You're not!' Peggie exclaimed.

'Oh yes I am. He's a nice man, Peggie. He never put a foot wrong tonight. He told me all about the lies and rumours that have been spread around the village, and all because the Crabbes wanted to better themselves. It ain't fair, Peggie. People should just learn to mind their own business.'

She gawped in disbelief. 'He's lying, Letty.'

'Oh, don't be stupid. Why would he lie? He's got nothing to gain by lying to me. It's not like I've money or anything, is it?'

Peggie stared at her blankly. 'No, it's not,' she agreed. 'But you can bet your life he's seeing you for a reason.' She frowned hard. 'You didn't tell him anything about the lorry, did you?'

'No, 'course I never. Besides, he didn't ask.'

'Didn't he? Oh!' Peggie bit her lip worriedly. 'Just be careful, Letty. That's all I ask?'

Letty's face darkened. 'I'm not stupid, Peggie. I am old enough to make up my own mind about things.' Her face softened. 'I've only agreed to go to the pictures on Saturday night, nothing more, and you needn't worry, we're going out of the village so no one will see us.' She sighed deeply. 'I need this, Peggie. I need to feel wanted right now. Just leave it at that, please. Now if you don't mind, I'm tired. I'm off to bed.'

Without another word, she turned and made her way up the stairs.

Peggie sank down in the chair she had just vacated and stared deep into the dying embers of the fire. What if she was wrong about the Crabbes? What if they were all wrong about the Crabbes? She shook her head. No. No way had anyone misjudged them. Her father and mother would never make up such a tale. Besides, it wasn't just her parents who didn't think highly of them, it was most of the villagers.

There was no doubt about it, somehow Reginald Crabbe had managed to hoodwink her sister. Letty was vulnerable at the moment and couldn't see what was staring her in the face.

She rose and grabbed the poker, thrusting it into the grate to rake the ashes vigorously. She just hoped to God Letty saw sense before it was too late.

Outside in the warm night air, Billy alighted from his bicycle, deciding to push it the last few yards home. He whistled softly. Life wasn't too bad at the moment, apart from his job that was. He had managed to off-load all but a few of the stockings and was going to show a nice profit, half of which he could put towards financing another deal when it presented itself. In the meantime he found he was enjoying himself working alongside his father and watching the transformation of the vehicle taking place. The seating contraption, something they had worked long and hard on, was just about finished. They just had to hope that it fitted and did the job intended of it.

What a change had come over his father these last couple of weeks. The man was positively glowing with enthusiasm for his new venture. He had even hinted at the possibility of Billy's giving up his job down the mines eventually and he planned to agree. Giving up his job would not hinder his business dealings with Mick. If anything he could expand. He now had a motorised vehicle at his disposal; he could sell further afield.

As he approached Alice Hammond's cottage he slowed down and looked cautiously across, relieved that the place was in darkness. He hadn't seen hide nor hair of her since that fateful night and if he was honest with himself he wanted to keep it that way. The memory of clinging to that wall, a deep void between him and the stone slabs below, was still very vivid and never again did he want to find himself in a predicament like that.

Not that he hadn't missed her. Who wouldn't miss the accommodating Alice? She was a single man's dream. Besides, he had grown quite fond of her during their illicit meetings and did hope she was faring all right. Those thoughts though did not stop him from going out of his way to avoid any contact.

Suddenly she was there, standing before him, dressed in her nightdress, her shawl wrapped tightly across her full breasts.

'Oh, my God, Alice, you gave me a scare,' he spluttered, startled.

'I should bloody well 'ope so,' she said sulkily. 'And where 'ave you been 'iding yerself? I ain't seen nothin' of yer for over a week. I've missed yer.'

'Now, Alice,' he said regaining his composure. 'What did you expect after Bull nearly catching us like that? I don't know about you, but that episode half scared me to death.' He looked at her fondly. 'I've missed you an' all, Alice, but I thought it'd be better if we cooled things for a while.'

'Cool it! Wadda yer mean, cool it? One small 'iccup and you're off, is that what yer mean? Wadda about all those things yer said to me?'

'What things?' he asked, perplexed.

Alice's jaw dropped. 'You told me you loved me.'

Billy froze. Yes, he had. But didn't all men say things like that when they were enjoying themselves between the sheets? 'And so I do, Alice. But you're a married woman . . .'

'You've got somebody else, ain't yer?' she asked, a catch in her voice.

'No, I haven't. I haven't, honest, Alice. But I can't go on like this, scared out my wits every time I hear a noise. Why, it's enough to put a man off his stride.'

'I'll leave him then, Billy. We can run away together.'

He gawped. That was the last thing he wanted. He was fond of Alice but not that fond. Why, she was nearly ten years older than himself and beginning to show the signs. Besides, the idea of being a stepfather to her six boisterous children didn't bear thinking about. It was a wonder one of them hadn't woken up and caught them at it.

'Oh, yes, Alice, and we'd spend the rest of our lives in fear of Bull finding us. And what about your children? Surely you couldn't leave them?' He looked worriedly around, wondering if Bull was on his way home from the pub having enjoyed after hours drinking or in bed about to realise Alice wasn't beside him. 'I couldn't live like that. It wouldn't be fair on either of us, now would it? Besides, I can't afford to get married, there's talk of lay-offs down the mine.' That part was true. Things were still bad after the trouble last year when the mines across the country went on strike for more pay. And they still hadn't fully recovered from the effects. 'Alice,' his voice lowered tenderly, 'ours is a love that's not meant to be.'

'Oh, Billy, don't say that. Please don't say that!'

Tears of anguish welled up in her eyes and started to trickle down her face, he could see them shining in the moonlight and suddenly felt compassion for this woman whose body he had so often enjoyed.

'Don't cry, Alice. I hate to see a woman cry.' He pulled out a rag from his pocket, not realising it was covered in coal dust, and wiped her face. 'I'll try and pop in on Friday night.' As the words left his mouth he regretted saying them but what else could he do? He couldn't leave her so distressed.

'Will yer, Billy? Will yer?' she said, her coal-smudged face lighting up in pleasure.

'Yeah, I'll try. Now please go back to bed, Alice, before Bull catches us.'

'I will, Billy. I'll see yer Friday than, about the usual time.'

He nodded. She reached up and kissed him on the cheek, turned and scampered happily down the path and into her cottage.

Once home, he strode through the back door and slammed it shut behind him. Peggie, raking the fire, her mind still full of Letty and Reginald, jumped in fright. She turned, wielding the poker.

'Oh, Billy, it's you,' she snapped. 'What on earth's the matter?'

'Nothing's the matter,' he said angrily, stripping to his waist and heading for the sink. 'Did Mam leave me any supper?' he asked, tipping cold water into the tin basin from the large jug on the window sill.

'In the oven. The remains of the shepherd's pie. And if nothing's the matter why did you slam the door so hard? It's a wonder you haven't woke Mam and Dad.'

Billy swung round, the top half of his body covered in a thin

116

lather. 'Shut up, Peggie. I'm not in the mood for one of your lectures tonight.' He returned to his ablutions.

Peggie smiled knowingly. 'Oh, I see. Had a run in with Alice, have you? Want to talk about it?' she offered, mostly out of nosiness.

Billy strode into the kitchen, drying himself on a rough piece of towelling. 'Peggie, I'm warning you, keep your nose out. I've had enough of women for one night.'

Peggie, knowing when she was treading a fine line, decided it was best to do as she was told. Besides, she needed to get Billy in the right frame of mind to ask her favour. She retrieved his supper from the oven and placed it on the table.

'Eat this while it's hot.'

He eyed it gratefully, sat down and began to tuck in. She sat opposite and watched him for several moments.

'Billy,' she ventured.

'What?' he responded, tearing a piece of bread from the loaf in front of him.

'I . . . er . . . need to borrow some money.'

He raised his head. 'I haven't got any. You cleaned me out when you rifled my pockets for that bet.'

Her face darkened. 'No, I didn't. I only took your loose change. You must have some from your deals.'

His head jerked up. 'Deals! What deals?'

Peggie narrowed her eyes and leaned across the table. 'Don't play the innocent with me, Billy Cartwright. You might pull the wool over Mam and Dad's eyes but I know what you get up to with Mick Matterson.'

Billy wiped his hand across his mouth, pushed away his empty plate and leaned back. 'Oh, you think you do, do you?'

'I don't think anything, Billy. I know. Now all I'm asking for is a loan and if I wasn't desperate I wouldn't ask.'

Billy eyed his sister sharply. 'Why d'yer need a loan, Peggie?' he asked, concerned.

She scratched the back of her neck. She told Billy the tale of her mother's predicament, the ring, the locket, and how she had foolishly put the thirty shillings in with the rest of the stake.

He shook his head, laughing. 'Oh, Peggie. One day you're going to get yourself into serious bother. Why didn't you just tell Mam the truth about the ring being worthless. It would have saved you all this trouble in the long run.'

'I couldn't, Billy. It would break her heart.'

He sighed. 'Yeah, it would, and I suppose if you hadn't risked it on that 'oss, Dad wouldn't now be planning his business.' He ran his hand over his chin. 'So you want to borrow the thirty bob from me to give to Mam so she can pay the rent that Dad thinks is already paid? And meanwhile the locket that Henry gave you is sitting in the pawn and you have to find the money to retrieve it before Mam notices it's gone and asks what you've done with it?'

117

Peggie nodded.

Billy stared at her. He just about had thirty shilling, it was all the profit he had earned flogging the stockings and with it he had been going to finance his next deal. He had no choice, not when a member of his family needed his help and he had the means at his disposal. His next deal would have to wait, his next step towards leaving his dreadful job would have to take a temporary step back. At this moment his sister's need was greater than his.

'I'll get it,' he said, rising.

'You will! Oh, Billy, thank you. You've saved me skin.'

'Yeah, well, make sure you don't forget that fact the next time you lay into me over summat trivial.'

'Trivial! Billy Cartwright, you never do anything trivial.' She leapt from her chair, raced over and threw her arms around him. 'I won't forget this, I promise.'

Billy eyed her. 'Mmm. We'll see.'

Chapter Eleven

Early-evening on the following Saturday found all the Cartwright family gathered in the shed at the back of Brotherhood's wood yard staring in admiration at the transformed vehicle. The metal trailer had been panelled around and a framework erected over the top to take a tarpaulin cover when the weather deteriorated. Inside, a removable wooden base, across which six wooden benches had been fitted; room enough for fifteen people to sit. When cargo was being transported, the seating base could be unbolted and lifted off. The whole lot had been painted black with bold white lettering: Cartwright and Family, Transportation Services.

Sep placed his arm around his wife's shoulders. 'Well, what do you think?' he asked proudly.

'Oh, Sep,' was all she could manage.

'Yes, I agree,' he said, laughing. 'If I say it myself she looks good, don't she? Let's hope we get plenty of business coming our way.'

'Oh, I hope so too,' said Nell sincerely. 'Especially after all the work you've done.' She turned to him, her eyes shining. 'I'm so proud of you, Sep. I really am.'

He smiled down at her, lovingly. 'I couldn't have done it without your backing, Nell. Don't forget that.' He turned his attention to the rest of his family. 'In fact, I couldn't have done it without all your help. Thank you.'

Loud demurrals were expressed.

'When are you going to take her out, Dad?' Ronnie asked.

'Good question.' He grinned. 'How about right now?'

A cheer rent the air and without further ado the Cartwright offspring clambered eagerly aboard, pushing and shoving each other to get the best seats.

Nell stepped back. 'I'll wait here,' she said.

'You'll do no such thing. This is as much your bus as it is mine.'

'I know, Sep,' she said softly. 'But, well,' she lowered her head, 'I'm scared.'

'Scared! What of?'

She nudged him hard in the ribs. 'Shush, not so loud. The young 'uns will hear.'

He lowered his voice. 'What are you scared of, Nell?'

'Well, that,' she replied, inclining her head. 'The bus. I've never been on one before and it makes such a noise.'

Sep guffawed loudly. 'Of course it makes a noise, but I promise it won't bite you. Come on,' he coaxed. 'You can sit up front with me, 'cos I ain't leaving this shed without you.'

Nell shuffled her feet apprehensively.

'Come on, Mam,' Peggie shouted, irritated. 'We're waiting.'

'Oh, all right,' she snapped. 'But if I'm sick, don't say I didn't warn you.' She made towards the back. 'Billy and Ronnie can sit up front, I'll go in the back with the girls.'

They pulled her aboard and she settled herself between them.

'Now hold on to me tight,' she ordered, grabbing Peggie's and Letty's arm and gripping them hard.

Before his wife could change her mind, Sep rushed around to the front of the vehicle and bent down, ready to turn the starting handle. He raised his head and addressed Billy. 'Well, here goes. Lets hope all our tinkering with the engine has worked.'

Holding his breath and using all his strength, he yanked the handle hard. Nothing happened. On the third try the engine roared into life and the noise was deafening. Clambering aboard, he released the brake, pressed his foot on the accelerator and eased the bus, filled with his family, out through the shed doors.

Folk working in the wood yard stopped and stared in wonder, the same happened as they drove through the village, and before long a procession of men, women and children was trotting behind, waving and cheering in excitement. For the villagers of Barlestone this was a first and they delighted in the knowledge. The whole Cartwright family, Nell included, sat proudly, waving now and again like royalty, as Sep continued his tour of the village at a speed of fifteen miles an hour.

Nell turned to Peggie. 'Tell your father to slow down, he's going too fast.'

Finally, with the bus bedded down for the night after performing faultlessly, the family trooped into the kitchen and sat down. Nell put on the kettle.

'Well, what now?' she asked her husband.

Sep took his pipe from his pocket, tapped the barrel against the inside of the fireplace, filled it with baccy and lit it. 'Well, I think we should have another meeting to discuss our next step.'

'I can't, Dad,' Letty said. 'I'm going out.'

'Not tonight you're not, miss,' Nell responded. 'A family meeting means all the family and that includes you. Where were you going anyway?'

Letty looked at her. 'Just out with . . . er . . . Brenda.'

'Well, you can go out with Brenda any time. Tonight you stay in and that goes for the rest of you.'

Letty pouted. She'd been really looking forward to her night out with Reginald, had pressed her best dress and polished her boots, and if she didn't show he probably would not ask her again. 'But . . .'

'But nothing, Letty. Now help me with this tea then we can get on with it.'

Letty tried to contain her frustration. Reginald would be waiting at the bridge for her as arranged and she had been so looking forward to their evening together. What was he going to think of her now? Oh, damn this bloody bus lark, she fumed inwardly. What difference would it make whether she was at this meeting or not? For a fleeting moment she realised how Wilfred must have felt when he had had to leave her standing that fateful night through no fault of his own.

Her thoughts were interrupted by her father requesting her presence at the table.

'Right,' Sep began, raising his mug. 'Here's to the Cartwright Omnibus Service. Long may they all ride in her.'

As the meeting got underway Sep soon realised that there was more to the transportation business than he had envisaged and if his family, who knew next to nothing of matters of this nature, raised the kind of queries that they were, what was left that they hadn't thought of?

After heated exchanges and long deliberations many of the obstacles were thrashed out. The supply of petrol: it was decided to keep their own in drums with the help of Jim Carpenter who kept the bicycle shop in the village and also repaired motor cycles. The routes which the bus would travel: Sep, with help, worked out that he could do the early workers' run to Earl Shilton and Hinckley, get back to change the vehicle over for freight and carry out any deliveries he had picked up, then change the vehicle over again ready to transport the workers back at night. It was going to be hard work and long hours, but the rewards at the end would be well worth it.

'Seems to me we need another lorry and more hands,' Billy said.

'You could be right, son,' his father agreed. 'But in the meantime we make do with one and use it to its full capacity.'

Peggie, Letty and Primrose were landed with the job of writing leaflets and their distribution.

Primrose didn't like the thought one bit and sat racking her brains as to how she could get out of it. Apart from breaking her hand which would be very painful she couldn't think of anything, so she was lumbered with the task of sitting with her bossy sisters writing out numerous leaflets and sticking them up around the village.

Ronnie, who had passed his medical with flying colours and was waiting impatiently for instructions to visit the Superintendent in London, would help as much as possible cleaning down the lorry and helping with the maintenance along with his brother. Further duties would be sorted out when his working hours were settled. Nell would as usual keep their bellies full and a warm fire burning.

It was decided, after further discussion, to give every passenger their first ride free. That was bound to create interest and in the long run it would be money well spent. As Nell pointed out, she'd yet to meet anyone who didn't grab at something for nothing.

When their offspring had all retired to bed – all apart from Letty and Primrose fired with enthusiasm for the part they were to play in the venture – Sep placed his arm around his wife's shoulder and gazed into her eyes.

'Nell, when we've made our fortune, what would you like?'

She frowned. 'Like?'

'Yes, there must be something that you've always hankered after?'

She shook her head. 'Hanker? I don't hanker after nothing, Sep. I'm just grateful for what I've got.'

He smiled warmly. 'I know that. But there still must be something that you've always wanted.'

Nell gave a little laugh. 'Matter of fact, there is.'

'Oh?' He looked at her, interested.

'A piano.'

'A piano? But you can't play.'

'I know. But it's never stopped me from wanting one.' She stared wistfully into space. 'It has always been my dream that one of the children would learn to play and we could have a sing-song round it of an evening. Especially at Christmas. All those lovely carols.' She mentally shook herself. 'It's just dreams, Sep. A piano's not a necessity in my book.' She pulled away from his embrace. 'Now come on, let's get to bed. We've another busy day tomorrow.'

Sep watched her thoughtfully as she bustled about settling down the cottage for the night. A piano. Of all the things he'd expected her to say – a new stove – new clothes – a bigger house even – he'd never expected a piano. Well, if that's what his Nell wanted then that's what she would have. It might take him years to achieve but he would get her one. It would be his main goal.

When Letty did not arrive for their appointment earlier in the evening, Reginald brutally kicked a passing dog, laughing when it yelped pitifully in pain, and retired to the Jolly Toper, his mind fully occupied; not with Letty's non-appearance but with the story he was going to make up to tell his father. Luck was not on his side. As he sullenly propped up the bar, Cyrus walked through the door.

'What happened?' he hissed angrily as he joined his son. 'I waited in and you didn't show and all that special food we bought was a waste of good money.'

Reg gulped on his beer and turned apprehensively to face him. 'She didn't show.'

'You stupid good for nothing!' spat Cyrus. He raised his hand in readiness to strike then realised where he was. He thrust his face within inches of his son's. 'Why didn't she show? I know why. You must have scared her off. What did you do?'

'Nothing, Dad. I played it straight, I told you. She must be ill or summat.'

'Ill! If a woman wants yer bad enough she comes crawling on all fours, whether she's ill or not.' His eyes narrowed menacingly. 'I can't trust you to do anything. You're just a waste of time. But don't think you're getting out of our plan. Far from it. Just make sure you make other arrangements to see her, and quick.'

Reginald nodded vigorously. Anything to keep his father happy.

Cyrus leaned heavily on the bar top, sipping at his pint. Rumours about the Cartwright lorry were spreading rapidly round the village and he didn't like what he was hearing one little bit. An idea suddenly struck him and he smiled. There was only one thing for it if he wanted to find out first hand what was going on and that was to renew old acquaintance. That thought gave him great pleasure but he wondered if it would the recipient.

The following Monday morning Nell bustled happily around the grand home of Hubert and Jennifer Pegg, a house that had been in Hubert's family for generations. Nell liked her job with the amenable Jenny and her solicitor husband. They might have money but they always treated her fair and square and always thanked her for the work she had done, even though they paid her.

Hubert had his own office in Hinckley. It was just a small practice but he made enough money to keep them in what Nell would term luxury.

As she gave the antique walnut dining table a final flick of her duster, Jenny popped her head around the door.

'Ah, Nell,' she said with a smile. 'If you've finished in here come through to the morning room and have a coffee with me.'

Nell replaced the lid on the beeswax polish and accepted, probably just a little too enthusiastically. She liked it when Jenny asked her for a coffee. It meant she could sit in the plush surroundings she helped to care for and imagine what it would be like to own and live in such a house. The house, built in the middle of the seventeen hundreds for a then wealthy landowner, was sited the other side of the church and could be seen from her own tiny cottage bedroom window. It was surrounded by a high redbrick wall and had a short driveway lined with laurel and other evergreen bushes. The grounds had diminished over the years as had the family money, but there were still several remaining outbuildings and stables and Nell imagined the upkeep, especially the coal bill in winter, to be enormous by her standards.

She entered the morning room whose french windows overlooked a small well-kept garden and sat down in the Regency wing-backed chair opposite Jenny Pegg, accepting the minute cup of coffee that was handed to her. She looked at it, imagining her own family's reactions should she dare dispense beverages in such delicate pieces of china. Knowing the clumsy Primrose, it wouldn't last two minutes.

Jenny sat back in her chair, took a genteel sip of her drink and replaced the cup back in its saucer. 'I hear your husband has acquired a lorry,' she said as casually as she would when discussing the weather.

'That's right, Mrs Pegg,' Nell answered proudly. 'We . . . er . . .

had a windfall and it was Mr Cartwright's idea. How did you hear about it?'

Jenny smiled. 'Oh, my dear, through the village grapevine, of course. And rumours are rife about what you intend doing with it.' She leaned forward, gracefully adjusting her pure silk shirt. 'What do you intend doing with it?'

It was Nell's turn to smile. 'Mr Cartwright's idea is to operate an omnibus service and he's also hoping to get some freight to deliver.'

'Is he?' replied Jenny, impressed. She sat back in her chair and crossed her legs. 'Well, I can put business his way straight off.'

'You can?'

'Yes. As you know I sit on the committee for several women's societies and if we have any transporting to do we hire Crabbe's brake. Well, I for one will be delighted to dispense with his services.' She smoothed her hand over her thick greying hair. 'Between you and me, Nell, I've never liked the man. Too full of his own importance. We've only used him in the past out of necessity. From now on it's Cartwrights for us. You are reliable, I hope?'

'Oh, very. And reasonable,' Nell replied firmly, hoping they were.

'Good. Ask Mr Cartwright to call on me when it's convenient. Now in the meantime I've a leg of pork that will go off if I don't use it up quickly. So I hope you'll do me a favour and take some of it home for that ravenous family of yours?'

A while later, her basket laden down with pork and other odds and ends thrust upon her by her generous employer, Nell left the house and made her way down the short driveway. She jumped as she turned out of the large iron gates. Leaning against the outer wall was Cyrus.

'Nell,' he addressed her. 'How a' yer?'

'What's it to you?' she asked frostily, aiming to walk straight past him.

He caught her arm. 'I asked how you were and I expect an answer.'

'Oh, you do! Well, I'm fine,' she snapped, pulling her arm free. 'Now if you don't mind, I'm busy.'

He sneered at her. 'You weren't too busy to dally with me while that husband of yours was away during the war.'

Nell froze and turned on him, her face thunderous. 'Dally! I've never dallied with you, Cyrus Crabbe, and you know it.'

'Didn't you? Well, what d'you call it then?'

Nell paled at thoughts of the past. Cyrus had happened upon her one bitter cold day, snow lying thickly, as she trudged the narrow isolated road back from Barton-in-the-Beans, a village two miles from Barlestone. She hadn't wanted to go in the first place but had heard of a possibility of extra work. The journey turned out to be a waste of time.

The Great War had raged for three dreadful years and for all that time she had striven to support her children alone. Coped with the growing shortages of basic foodstuffs and necessities; the fear of the German Zepplins dropping their bombs. She witnessed the poverty the war was causing, the disease and hardships, but worse, far worse than all of this, she missed the love of her life, her husband, and wondered if she would ever see him again.

After three years of continual struggle, even she was questioning the point of it all. It appeared only to be achieving the terrible loss of many lives on both sides. Men who should be with their families were lying rotting on the battle fields and she felt so helpless. The thought of spending another Christmas without Sep was more than she could bear, but for the sake of showing a brave face to her children, she soldiered on regardless.

As she plodded homeward through the snow, the bitterly cold weather seeping through her old clothes, her foot slipped down a hidden pot hole and she badly twisted her ankle. She lay for over an hour and it was with great relief that she heard the muffled noise of hooves in the distance. Relief until she saw it was Cyrus driving his empty cart.

Rounding the bend, he couldn't believe his eyes or his luck when he saw Nell sprawled on the ground. He thought maliciously that it would be nice to relieve his boredom with a little fun at her expense.

He pulled the brake to a stop just short of her and slid out of the driving seat to stare down at her.

'Need a hand?' he asked casually.

Her temper flared. It was obvious to anyone she needed a hand and his mocking tone didn't make her feel any better.

Shivering uncontrollably, she decided it was best to humble herself. Cyrus was the type, if riled, just to leave her where she was and she knew if she was left much longer in this predicament there was a possibility she would never see her family again.

So she accepted his offer and with difficulty he helped her aboard. Silently, they continued the slow journey homeward. All the way she was conscious of the terrible deed he had done with Sep's brake. The vehicle she was travelling on should have been theirs by rights. Regardless of this, and much against her nature, she could not help noticing what a good-looking man he was, how his body was still firm and fit for a man of middle age, and she speculated that many women must think so also and never doubted he would have much trouble in that department, especially since he was now a widower.

She was glad when they finally reached the outskirts of the village, she wanted to get home, away from this man and all he stood for. She gasped when he turned the brake into his own yard and drew it to a halt.

'Why are we stopping here?' she asked in horror.

He climbed down, walked round and held out his hand. 'You want that ankle seeing to and I thought you looked in need of a hot drink.'

A hot drink sounded inviting but instinct warned her to decline his offer. 'It's all right, thank you, I can manage,' she said offhandedly.

He cocked his head and stared at her, a smile on his lips. 'What's the matter, Nell? Frightened I might make advances to you? I could have done that on the journey home. Come on, you've had a shock and I'm only being neighbourly, that's all. My daughter Mary will bandage your ankle.'

Shame filled her and before she knew it she was allowing him to assist her down and inside his house. Settled in a comfy chair by the fire she gazed around in admiration at how clean it looked. Mary obviously did a good job in looking after her father and brother.

She entered the room carrying a pot bowl filled with warm salt water and several clean rags. She looked tired and pale and well over her nineteen years.

'Hello, Mary,' Nell said kindly. 'It's good of you to help me like this.'

A smile so brief it was hardly visible crossed the young girl's face and without a word she knelt before Nell.

Frowning, Nell raised her long skirt, showing her badly swollen legs, and with difficulty managed to get off her boot. To her, having three boisterous girls, it was unnatural to see one so quiet and withdrawn. She noticed Mary staring at her legs.

'Oh, never mind them, dear,' she said quickly. 'I've had trouble with them for a while now. It's my ankle, I think I've twisted it.'

'You need those looking at.'

Nell's head jerked up in shock as Cyrus entered the room carrying two mugs of tea. Instinctively she dropped her skirt, angry that he had seen her legs. She felt a hot flush of acute embarrassment race up her neck.

Undeterred he sat down. 'Come on, Mary, get a move on. Mrs Cartwright's in pain.'

As gently as possible, Mary bathed and bandaged Nell's ankle and once finished left the room as quickly and quietly as she had arrived.

'That better?' Cyrus asked politely.

'Yes, much, thank you.'

'And your tea?'

'Fine.' She took a deep breath, his charm was beginning to unnerve her. 'Look, if it's all the same to you I must get home.' She managed to smile. 'My children will start arriving back from school soon, then the others from work, and if the supper's not ready . . .'

'Yes, all right. I'll take you now.'

They journeyed back to her cottage again in silence and once there he helped her to her back door.

She raised her eyes to meet his. 'Please thank Mary for me. I never got a chance.'

'I will.'

'Yes, right . . . Goodbye then.'

Cyrus smiled. 'Goodbye, Nell.'

If she hadn't hobbled as quickly as she could into her cottage she would have seen the satisfied smile playing on his lips as he boarded the brake and manoeuvred it down the road. As it was she missed it and spent the rest of the day wondering why he had been so kind after what had transpired in the past.

She said nothing to her children when asked about her ankle, only that she had fallen in the yard.

As she was hobbling around the kitchen the next morning after the family had all left a knock sounded on the door. She opened it to find Cyrus standing before her.

'You left this,' he said, holding out a paper parcel.

'What is it?' she asked perplexed.

Cyrus smiled. 'Sausages, I think.'

'But I never bought any sausages so they can't be mine.'

'Oh, well, have them anyway. I'm sure you could put them to good use.' He made to walk away then stopped. 'How's your ankle?'

Oh . . . er . . . fine. Much better,' she said awkwardly.

'Good.' He stared at her boldly. 'I don't suppose you have the kettle on?'

Her mouth dropped open. Her first instinct was to refuse but how could she when he had been so kind to her the previous day? Against her better judgement she stood aside and he entered.

After that initial call he took to visiting on a regular basis, always when she was alone, and she found herself unwittingly looking forward to his visits. His masculine attentiveness, something she had been starved of during the last three years, soon began to have the desired effect.

She began to take extra special care with her appearance and even lost a little weight. Her children would be rushed out in a morning just in case he happened to knock on her door.

None of this was lost on Cyrus and bit by bit he wormed his way into Nell's affections, biding his time until the right occasion presented itself. He was having fun trifling with her and was spurred on by thoughts of who her husband was.

The occasion presented itself one hot summer morning when Cyrus, in between runs, was cosily seated in Nell's cluttered kitchen sipping home-made lemonade. The postwoman called and Nell accepted the letter that was cheerfully delivered, careful not to open the door too wide for fear Cyrus was seen. That would never do. The news would be around the village before she'd had time to think of a plausible excuse for his presence.

The letter was from Sep. Once again he was informing her that his leave had been cancelled. Cyrus quickly spotted her dismayed expression.

'Bad news?' he ventured.

She raised her eyes. 'Oh, yes, actually it is. Sep's leave has been cancelled again.'

'Seems to be becoming a habit,' he said casually.

Nell frowned. 'What do you mean?'

He shrugged his shoulders. 'Oh, nothing. I was just making an observation, that's all.' He gave her a winning smile. 'This lemonade is good, Nell.'

'Thank you,' she said graciously. 'But I still want to know what you meant by that remark?'

He ran his hand through his thick thatch of jet black hair. 'Oh, me and my big mouth.' He sighed loudly. 'It just seems to me, Nell, that Sep is using any excuse he can to avoid coming home. This is the third time, ain't it?'

'Yes, but what of it? There's a war on. My Sep keeps the supplies moving. Without the likes of him the war on our side would grind to a halt.'

Cyrus leaned over the table and rested his hand gently on top of hers, his eyes kindly. 'Nell, even fighting men get leave. Are you sure that Sep ain't making up excuses?'

Her frown grew deeper. 'Yes, 'course I'm sure.' She stared at him blankly. 'Are you trying to tell me he's got someone else, is that it?'

'I'm not trying to tell you anything, Nell. But these things happen, especially during wars.'

She shook her head with conviction. 'No, no. My Sep would never do that.'

'Wouldn't he?' He stared hard at her. 'I'm not so sure. Besides, you're doing it yourself, Nell.'

'Doing what?'

'Come on now. You've got to admit you've taken a fancy to me like I have you. Mind you, I've liked you for many years and it was a sad day for me when you married Sep.'

'Pardon?' she uttered, perplexed.

A pained look crossed his face. 'Don't tell me you never knew, Nell?' He groaned loudly and buried his face in his hands. Finally he raised his head, his eyes boring into hers. 'Nell, that husband of yours has always been jealous of me, right from when we were kids and I beat him in a stupid spelling test at school. Trivial, I know, but it was enough to start him plotting ways of beating me at everything I did from then on.' He raised his eyes. 'Apart from the business about the brake, his one major success was in marrying you.'

Nell gawped. 'Marrying me? But I don't understand.'

'No, I don't expect you do. Nell, I don't think you know that husband of yours at all. To all and sundry he's a fine man, but I know better. He made my name mud in this village and beyond, and I've spent years trying to live with the consequences.' He took a deep breath. 'It was me that first spotted you, Nell. It was at the village dance. You had on a blue dress and your hair hung down to your waist. You were as pretty as a picture and you haven't changed. Anyway, Sep knew I was about to make a move. He should do, he'd been standing behind me all night, watching. So he got in first and there was nothing I could do about it. Then there

128

was the brake. I made that brake, Nell. As God's my witness I did. Sep got wind and made out it was his and the rest is history.'

She stared blindly across the room, her mouth gaping in horror. He surely couldn't be telling the truth, surely not? You couldn't live with a man all these years without knowing his true nature. Regardless of how much you tried to hide it, your true self always won through in the end. But what if he was telling the truth, what if their life together had been a sham and Sep only married her to get one over on Cyrus?

She turned her gaze to the man seated before her, his handsome face a picture of sadness. She tried to picture Sep, so unlike Cyrus in every way, but the man nevertheless that she loved – or did she still? She was beginning to have doubts. Three years was a long time to spend without company in your bed or sharing your life. Memories gradually faded as days went by. Cyrus interrupted her thoughts.

'I'm so sorry, Nell. I never meant for any of this to come out. And I suppose you've got no reason to believe what I say. But I can't stand by any longer and see you made a fool of.'

'Fool! Is that what I am? Well, we'll see about that.' She rose abruptly and headed for the door. 'I'd like you to leave, Cyrus, please. I need to be on my own.'

He rose and joined her. 'Yes, you do. This must all be a shock. But I've got to stress, Nell, it is the truth, you've got to believe me.'

He stared down at her, his ice blue eyes boring into her very soul, and mesmerised she raised hers to his. He bent his head, intending to kiss her, when the old clock on the mantle chimed the hour and Nell jumped. The moment was gone.

With difficulty Cyrus controlled his temper and smiled sweetly. 'I'll come and see you tomorrow.'

She nodded slowly and let him out of the door.

The rest of the day she performed her tasks in a daze. Her whole world had fallen about her. Confusion about her feelings for Sep and Cyrus clouded her every minute. Finally she could stand it no longer and, much to the bewilderment of her family, threw down her mending and informed them she was going out and it was none of their business what time it was. She had to see Cyrus regardless of the fact that people might observe her.

The night was pitch black when she arrived at his house just after ten o'clock and, getting no answer at the front door, made her way around the back. As she turned the corner of the house voices reached her ears through the open window. She froze. Cyrus was drunk, very drunk, and he was shouting at his son.

'See, lad,' he was saying. 'Women can't resist me. I set my cap and they jump. I've waited a long time for this and she's took the bait, hook line and sinker.'

'And she believed everything you said, Dad?'

'Everything,' came the smug reply. 'But I'm warning you now, son, you breathe a word and I'll break your bloody neck. And you!'

129

There was a loud thud as something heavy was thrown across the room and a scream, which was obviously from Mary, rent the air. 'Get me another drink, you lazy little cow. You're just like your mother was. She was a poor excuse for a woman. No gumption. Wouldn't say boo to a goose. Not like Nell Cartwright, eh? She'd give any man a good run for his money. I wouldn't like to be in Sep's shoes when she confronts him. By God, he won't know what's hit him, poor sod!' He laughed loudly. 'How d'yer fancy Nell as your new mother, eh? Well, shouldn't be long if my plan goes accordingly, and one thing's for sure – Sep Cartwright won't be able to hold up his head in this village no more.'

Nell shrank back in humiliation. What a blind fool she had been. How close she had come to nearly wrecking her life, and all because of the lies of that man. The letter she had written to Sep earlier burned in her pocket and she quickly snatched it out and crumpled it savagely. Turning on her heel, she flew down the path and back home.

That night she sat staring for hours into the dying embers of the fire, contemplating the predicament she had got herself into. More than anything she felt humiliated. Cyrus had taken her for a complete fool and she had fallen for his charm and lies without question. And what about Sep? Terrible guilt burned inside her for the fact that she had so nearly put their marriage, something they both held so precious and worked hard at, in jeopardy. She silently thanked the Lord that she had gone to pay a visit to Cyrus earlier. If she hadn't, well, she dreaded to think of the consequences.

As first light began to filter through the tiny windows she had made her plan. Instinct told her that tackling Cyrus head on was the wrong thing to do. He wouldn't take her rejection of him kindly and his wrath, she had no doubt, would be vented against her family. No, it was far better to fight her dreadful urge to strike back.

When he arrived she calmly and quietly told him that, regardless of the past, she had married Sep for better or worse and would have to abide by those promises for the sake of her children.

Cyrus was not happy and Nell could see he was fighting anger.

'You're making the wrong decision, Nell. He doesn't love you. Your marriage is a mockery.' His voice fell to a harsh whisper. 'Besides, how can you stay with someone now you know what a liar he is?' He walked towards her and for an instant she thought he was going to embrace her. She took several steps backwards and he sighed loudly. 'Nell, I could make you happy.' He was fighting now, fighting for his pride. After all, he had bragged openly to his own children of his conquest and that prospect was fading rapidly. 'I have my own house, a business. What have you got with Sep? A rented hovel and work when he can get it.'

Yes, thought Nell angrily. You have a house that was paid for on the strength of the Cartwright's idea and at least the work Sep tackles is honest and above board.

She held up her hand. 'Please, Cyrus. Don't make this any

harder for me. I meant what I said. I'm staying with Sep and that's my final word. Now I'd be obliged if you'd leave.'

'Oh, would yer?' he said icily. 'And what if I don't want to?' he advanced upon her.

She grabbed at the nearest thing she could lay her hands on which just happened to be the bread knife. She waved it in front of him. 'I'll use it,' she said with conviction.

He backed away, grinning mockingly. 'I ain't fooled you, have I, Nell?'

She shook her head. "Fraid not. Now get out while you can.'

'All right, I'm going. But even you've got to admit I took you in for a while and if you say otherwise I'll call you a liar. Good day, Nell, and you know where I am if you change your mind and fancy a bit of fun.'

Laughing loudly, he turned and sauntered out of the door. Nell sighed deeply in relief and sank down on to a chair.

For months after she lived in fear that Sep would somehow find out about that episode, especially after his return from the war when things were strained between them due to their prolonged parting, but as time went by her worries faded and for the most part she'd managed to forget all about it – until now.

Returning her thoughts to the present, she stared up at Cyrus, her face dark. 'Don't you ever dare say I dallied with you! You're just a liar, Cyrus Crabbe. You were born a liar and you'll die a liar. Now get out of my way.'

He blocked her path. 'Not 'til you tell me what that husband of yours is up to?'

'Ah, so that's it? Well, if you're that concerned, why don't you ask him yourself?'

'I'm asking you.'

Nell grinned wickedly. 'Well, I ain't gonna tell you. You'll find out soon enough, and if I were you I'd look for other ways to earn a living because, believe me, the Cartwrights have at long last got something better than you. And it ain't before time neither!'

Throwing back her head, she marched past him and across the green.

Cyrus breathed deeply. So that was it. Sep was going to use the vehicle to run a bus service and that meant Cyrus would have competition. He clenched his fists in temper, then suddenly smiled. Village folk didn't like change. They preferred to stick to the old ways. But if that wasn't the case then there was plenty he could do to hinder his old adversary's plans, including one idea that he had been playing around with for a while. It was guaranteed to get one of the Cartwrights out of the way.

'Septimus Cartwright,' he said aloud, 'I'd watch your back if I were you. Cyrus Crabbe ain't done for yet. No, sir, not by a long chalk.'

Later that night he tackled his son as they sat eating their evening meal. 'I want you to do two runs tomorrow morning.'

'Two runs?' Reg queried, wiping his mouth on the back of his hand and making a grab for another piece of bread. 'But what about that big delivery of wood for Brotherhood's? Will yer manage on yer own.'

'Sod Brotherhood's. He'll have to wait. I want you to do two runs. One to Shilton for the workers and another to Coalville for the shoppers.'

'But you've always told the folks who wanted to go shopping to use their bloody legs. Said you couldn't fit in another run. What yer playing at, Dad?'

Like lightning, Cyrus leaned across the table and grabbed Reg's hand, crushing it hard. 'Don't you question me, lad. Just do as I say or face the consequences.' He narrowed his eyes menacingly. 'And I don't want you blabbing none of my business to your cronies down the pub. If I hear one word, I'll break your bloody neck. And another thing. Have you seen Letty yet and made arrangements to see her again?'

'No, I ain't had chance.'

'Ain't had chance?' His eyes twinkled as an idea struck. 'I think it's about time you proposed to her. You two'd make a lovely couple. You make sure you see her tomorrow. I want you two married as soon as possible. Is that understood?'

Grimacing in pain, Reg managed to pull away his hand and nursed it. 'Married!' he exclaimed, horrified.

'You heard me. Your marriage to Letty would be one in the eye for Sep and Nell Cartwright. That'd teach 'em to go into business against me.'

He laughed harshly as he returned to his meal.

Reginald stared at him, horrified. Marriage had never figured high on his list of priorities. The only good thing about marriage was a regular supply of conjugal rights but as he never went short in that department, marriage had never warranted a serious thought. Still he supposed if it kept his father off his back he would go along with it. Letty would be easily managed and wouldn't interfere at all with his life. He'd make sure of that.

He shook his head. Just what was his father up to? He would have given anything to know but it was far better not to ask, not when his father was in this mood. Besides, it would all come out soon enough.

Later that night, when Reginald had gone out, Cyrus let a visitor into his house.

'Come in and make yourself comfy. I've a proposition for you.'

Mick Matterson eyed him cautiously. Cyrus Crabbe was bad news and the thought of being involved with him did not appeal at all.

'I'll stand, thank you.'

'You'll sit.'

Mick sat.

Cyrus placed his back to the fire. 'I hear you get things cheap?'

'Cheap? No, not me,' he said, shaking his head. 'You've got me mixed up with someone else.'

Cyrus clenched his fists. 'Don't play games with me, lad. I hear you get things – well, let's say, not exactly kosher, shall we? And then you sell them on to the likes of Billy Cartwright. Now I know I'm correct. My sources of information don't come any better and if you know what's good for you, you'll come clean. Unless you fancy a long prison sentence, that is. Now I'll ask you again.' He paused slightly. 'I hear you get things cheap?'

Mick lowered his head worriedly and took a breath. 'Yes, I do.'

'That's better, lad.' Cyrus smiled in satisfaction. 'Now when's your next deal coming off? I want all the details.'

Chapter Twelve

The weather was fine for the first day of business. Sep, with Peggie and Letty sitting excitedly on the seats in the back, carefully manoeuvred the vehicle out of the woodyard and down the dirt road in the direction of the Three Tuns public house. He was surprised to see a good crowd had already gathered, even though it was only just approaching six-thirty.

He addressed his daughters. 'Well, if the leaflets have done n'ote else they've pulled us a good crowd.'

He halted abreast of them and jumped down, grinning broadly. 'Well, them that's riding, climb aboard.' He ran round the back, unhooked a wooden box from under the trailer and placed it on the ground for use as a step.

Several people clambered aboard. The sceptics stepped back and watched disapprovingly.

'A' yer sure yer can work it proper, Sep?' Ma White shouted. 'It don't look safe to me.'

'It's as safe as the Tower of London,' he bantered back. 'Why don't you get aboard and see for yourself?'

'Not me,' she replied disapprovingly. ''Orse and cart's done me all me life and it'll see me out, thank you very much.'

Several voices mumbled loudly in agreement.

'Suit yourself, it's your loss.' He raised his eyebrow at her. 'First ride's free.'

Ma White frowned thoughtfully. 'Is it? I din't know that. Oh, in that case, I might as well. 'Ere, someone gimme a leg up.'

Without realising, Ma White had given the Cartwright Omnibus Service the best start it could have. If she, one of the oldest and most cantankerous residents, was willing to have a go on this new contraption then the rest were not going to be left out and all but a few scrambled aboard, their saved fares sitting comfortably in their pockets. Sep cranked the engine and the journey began amid loud cheers from the passengers and onlookers.

As the bus moved off, Reginald pulled the brake to a halt outside the Three Tuns, dismayed at the sight of the back of the bus loaded with passengers disappearing round the corner. He turned to the two women waiting to board the brake and his heart sank. His father would not be pleased when it came to handing over the day's takings.

Later that night a tired but happy Sep walked through his back

135

door. His wife and offspring greeted him enthusiastically.

'Well?' Nell asked as she placed his meal before him.

Sep sat down and eyed it appreciatively. 'This looks good, Nell.'

'Sep,' she scolded. 'How did it all go?'

He grinned up at her. 'Grand. Just grand. Best day's work I've ever done and I enjoyed every minute.' He looked across at his daughters. 'Didn't you tell your mother, girls?'

Peggie shook her head. 'No. We've kept her in suspense. We thought you should have the honour.'

He smiled in appreciation. 'Ah, thanks.'

'And they ain't told me a damned thing, so come on, I want to hear all about it,' Nell said, sitting down and folding her arms.

Sep proceeded to tell her all the day's happenings, beginning with the first trip with the workers and then the deliveries for Mr Brotherhood and then back to collect the workers.

'You should have seen it, Nell. Talk about the grapevine. As we drove down the lanes people were flagging me down and by the time we got to Shilton the bus was crammed. They were packed into the seats and hanging on the back.'

'Yeah, and we were squashed, weren't we, Letty?' Peggie grumbled laughingly.

'Like sardines,' replied her sister.

'It's all right for you,' Primrose pouted. 'I didn't even get a go. I had to go to rotten school.'

'Ah, we'll soon put that right, gel,' her father laughed. 'You can help me on Saturdays.'

'Doing what?'

He scratched his ear thoughtfully. 'You can be my conductress, that's what you can do.'

'Conductress? What's that?' She pouted even harder. It sounded to her like hard work.

'They have them on the London buses. They collect the money and keep the passengers in order.'

Primrose smiled happily. 'Oh, I like the sound of that. I could help you in the week if you like?'

'Good try,' said her mother. 'Not on school days. I don't want the board man paying me a visit.'

'Sounds like a job for me, Dad,' Peggie said keenly.

Sep nodded. 'Yes, you could be right. But not just yet. Maybe in the future.'

'That's not fair,' Primrose wailed. 'You gave me the job of conductressing . . .'

'Shut up, Primrose,' Peggie hissed. 'Conductressing's a job for an adult, not a silly kid.'

'That's enough from you two,' Nell shouted. 'If you don't give over neither of you'll do it.' She turned her attention to her husband. 'So you think it's going to be a success then?'

'Well, if today was anything to go by, I'd say so. I've already been asked if I've any plans to go into Leicester for shopping trips.

136

Thought I might do that on Fridays after I've done the work run.'

Billy swallowed a mouthful of food. 'The lads at work are asking if you've any plans to do a run to the mines? Said if they can promise the bus will be loaded each shift, you might do it cheaper.'

'Were they?' Sep rubbed his chin thoughtfully. 'I'll have to give it some thought.'

'Yeah,' chipped in Ronnie. 'What about fitting in the train station an' all? It's a fair walk and folks are usually laden with baggage.'

Sep exhaled loudly. 'I'll give that some thought as well.' He shrugged his shoulders. 'Seems to me you were right, our Billy, about needing another vehicle. But I don't want to jump in too quickly. I feel I should give it a bit more time. Besides, vehicles cost money and we ain't made any yet.'

Nell relaxed back in her chair. 'Oh, Sep, I am glad it's all gone well. I've bin that worried today in case it didn't.'

'Well, for once I'm glad to say you worried needlessly.' He raised his mug of tea in the air. 'Here's to us.'

'Cheers,' they all sang in unison.

Nell eyed her husband hesitantly. 'Did you see 'ote of Crabbe?'

'Not Cyrus I didn't. But I certainly saw a glimpse of his son. And he didn't look very happy.'

'Oh, dear,' Nell muttered, worried.

'Now, Nell,' he said sharply. 'Don't you go bothering yourself. Cyrus Crabbe can't do anything about this. The bus is ours and all the villagers know that. And besides, it's fair competition. And going by what's been said tonight, there's enough work in this village for both of us, and more besides.'

'Yeah.' Nell smiled. 'You're right. I only hope he sees it that way.'

'He'll have to. Besides, if he carries on running his business as haphazardly as he's done in the past, then he can't expect anything else but to go under.'

'And that can't be bad for us, eh, Dad?' laughed Peggie.

'I'll say.'

As the months passed by the business gradually flourished. Nell watched her family, proud that each, in their own particular way, helped as much as they could, even Primrose who had found out to her delight that the family's owning a business had boosted her prestige amongst her school friends and used it to full advantage.

Many obstacles had had to be overcome and when faced each was discussed and thrashed out in the usual Cartwright style – around the kitchen table.

Running a bus service, as they all soon realised, was not just a case of acquiring a vehicle and hoping for passengers. Regular routes and timetables were now in place with proper calculated fare structures; a supply of petrol was stacked in huge drums in Brotherhood's wood yard; spare parts, tools and equipment –

137

mostly second or third hand – filled shelves and spaces on the floor in the shed; they had their own setting down and picking up place in Applegate Street in Leicester along with a few other county operators that had sprung up since they had begun. Sep had found out to his acute embarrassment that passenger vehicles of any description were not allowed past the town boundary. That was reserved for trams and horse cabs only.

Most of the other operators were friendly and like him had started up with practically nothing. They swapped stories and information and Sep felt himself belonging to this growing band and relished the feeling.

The whole family began to look forward to the future with optimism, secure in the knowledge that their hard work and commitment was going to pay off.

Much to Peggie's delight and excitement, Sep, tired of answering her endless questions and fed up with her continual begging and nagging that if Billy was allowed then why not she, took her out one Sunday afternoon, found a straight piece of road and allowed her to sit behind the wheel.

The heavy vehicle jolted and juddered, hissed and stalled several times, but Peggie undeterred, finally managed to drive. Adrenaline flowed through her as the wind whipped her curls and smarted against her face, but she knew then, knew without a doubt, what had spurred her father on after his initiation to such feelings during the war; she knew what spurred any man on to forge further forward, breaking speed records never thought possible as they raced around the tracks in their dangerously small cars.

The feeling was inexplicable but once possessed was in the blood forever and she craved for more. She vowed then that her goal was to join her father as a driver. Sep knew also and was secretly proud of his daughter's natural ability and commitment and decided as soon as the time was right to take her fully on board.

Normal life continued, such as it could with long hours of hard work. Ronnie's interview with the Superintendent in London was successful and he talked incessantly of his ride on a train and his visit to the depot. Now they all waited for news to arrive of his starting date.

Letty's secret assignations with Reginald continued. She liked him. Liked him a lot. What woman wouldn't? He was a good-looking man and such a charmer, and for a time she had been happy to go out with him. But she knew in her heart it could never amount to anything more than friendship because she still loved Wilfred. Even though it was painfully obvious to her that he was going out of his way to avoid her.

Several times recently she had tried to break it off with Reginald but somehow her words were either misconstrued or Reginald blatantly ignored what she was trying to tell him. He was beginning to alarm her. He was hinting at marriage and pressurising her to meet his father and she didn't want either. But somehow she found herself being swept along, unable to stop the flow.

She couldn't talk to Peggie. Her sister would go mad if she knew she was still seeing Reginald. Peggie believed that the association had ceased weeks ago and, like the rest of the family, thought that she was visiting friends when she disappeared of an evening. Besides, Peggie, as did the others, spent every spare minute in the shed with that confounded motor bus getting it ready for the next day's work. She barely noticed what was happening to her sister. So what could Letty do? Carry on, she supposed, and hope that something happened to stop it all before it was too late.

Chapter Thirteen

One morning in early October, just as the first signs of winter were setting in, Nell pulled her shawl tightly round her shoulders and prepared to leave the cottage. If she didn't hurry she would be late. Jenny Pegg had asked if she would help get several of the bedrooms aired and ready for visitors she was expecting over the weekend and that meant mattresses had to be turned, extra bedding sorted, and all manner of other jobs undertaken.

She sighed. She would be fifty years old very shortly and if she was honest with herself she felt she was getting too old and tired for this kind of work and would be secretly glad when she could give it up and relax a little. She would have to do something soon; she doubted her legs would hold up for much longer. The swelling was getting worse these days and the hot poultices were not easing them as much as they used to.

She managed a smile. As if she could ever relax with her family to look after. Still, with the bus business continuing to progress the way it was, then maybe in the not too distant future she might be able to give serious thought to cutting down on her hours.

A commotion outside startled her and she stared at the closed door, wondering for a second what was happening behind it. It burst open and Primrose charged through, followed closely by Constable Jesson.

'What the . . .' she began.

'I caught this young madam red handed, I did. Red handed.'

Nell frowned deeply at her breathless daughter. She looked an utter disgrace. She had gone out to meet her friends that morning eager to enjoy the few days of the autumn school holidays wearing a clean pinafore over her grey dress. That white pinafore was now badly stained, her dress crumpled and her woollen stockings round her ankles. The plaits in her hair had come undone and she had lost her ribbons. 'Caught you what, Primrose? What you bin up to now?'

'Scrumping,' Sidney Jesson erupted. 'In broad daylight in Major Allot's orchard.'

'I weren't, Mam. It weren't me. I was only watching the others doing it. 'Sides, Major Allot said we could.'

Nell just managed to stop herself from saying aloud that the miserly Major Allot wouldn't donate the scrapings from his potatoes to the starving, let alone give permission to help themselves to his precious fruit – fruit that he had so much of he left it to rot year after year rather than distribute it to the villagers. Instead she raised herself up to her full height and addressed the Constable. 'My daughter says she had permission.'

'And she's lying, 'cos Major Allot fetched me himself.'

'Oh! Oh, well, er . . . where's the evidence? Where are these confounded apples she's supposed to have scrummped!'

'Dropped 'em, they did, when they saw me coming.'

'And I suppose it was only Primrose you chased, was it? Well, I'm sorry, Constable, you can't expect me to chastise the child when I've no evidence to go on. But I take your word for it and I'll see she's sent to bed with no supper,' she said firmly, ignoring the dismayed expression on Primrose's face. 'Please give my apologies to Major Allot. Now if you don't mind, Constable, I have to go to work and I expect you have all the other scrumpers' parents to see. Good day.'

Seeing he was going to get no further with the matter he reluctantly left.

Nell turned to Primrose. 'Primrose . . .'

'Mam, we weren't doing no 'arm. We were only picking up the fallings. And they were filled with maggots and going rotten, so they weren't no good to anyone. It's just that Constable. Now our Ronnie's behaving himself, he follows me everywhere, just waiting to catch me doing summat I shouldn't.'

Nell frowned. 'Yeah, and he doesn't have much of a wait, does he, Primrose? 'Cos you're always doing summat you shouldn't!' She paused thoughtfully. 'But you're right. He does seem to have something against the Cartwrights.' She frowned even deeper. 'Still, that doesn't excuse what you did, madam, does it? Or the fact that you told a lie about having permission?'

'No, Mam. I'm sorry.' She raised her eyes and gave her mother a winning smile. 'I just thought you might make an apple pie for tea, that's all.'

Nell managed to keep her face stern. 'That would've been nice.' She walked slowly round the table. 'Did you . . . er . . . drop all the apples when the Constable chased you?' she asked casually.

Primrose grinned and pulled up her dress. Several apples were stuffed down inside her long drawers.

Nell could not suppress her smile any longer. 'Apple pie it is.'

Later that afternoon Nell stared at her younger son in disbelief. 'Oh, Ronnie. No, I can't bear it.' She closed her eyes tightly and sank down in a chair, the half-made pastry for the apple pie forgotten. Her eyes began to water and she sniffed loudly.

Ronnie stared at her bewildered. He could not understand why his mother was taking his news so badly. 'I thought you'd be happy, Mam.'

She raised her head and tried to put a smile on her face. 'Happy! Oh, Ronnie.' She wiped her eyes on her apron. 'It's just that I never expected you'd have to go so far away. I thought Mr Tunley said he had a job for you at the station in Bag'orth.'

'So he has, Mam. I'm only going to Rugby for part of me training. I'll only be gone six months, then I do the rest of me time in Bag'orth and roundabout.'

'Six months! Oh, Ronnie,' she wailed. 'I won't see you for six months. But what if you're ill and what about your washing and . . . and . . . who'll make sure you eat proper?'

Just then Sep walked through the door, wiping his oily hands on a rag. He looked at his wife and frowned hard. 'What's up, Nell, Ronnie?'

Ronnie divulged his news.

Sep strode over and slapped him on the back. 'Well done, lad. Proper training, eh?' He grinned broadly. 'Your mother's crying 'cos she's pleased for you. Ain't you, Nell? Nell?'

She sniffed loudly. 'Yes 'course I am. But this place, Rugby. How far away is it?'

'From here . . . about thirty miles or so.'

'Thirty miles? Oh, Sep, I'll never see him. Thirty miles . . .'

'Now, Nell, stop it,' Sep said sternly. 'The lad's got to go for his training and we can always visit in the bus. Besides, six months is nothing. He'll be back under our feet before we know it.' He strode forward and put his arm around her shoulders to comfort her. 'Now pecker up, love. The lad's got a great opportunity here and we should all be happy.'

Nell wiped her eyes. 'Yes, all right, Sep.' She smiled bravely at her son. 'I'll sort your clothes for you.'

'Ta, Mam,' he replied, relieved. 'So, you'll sign the apprenticeship papers, Dad?'

'Yes, 'course I will and proud to do it.' He puffed out his chest. 'A Cartwright apprenticed to the railway. Now that's something. When do you report?'

'First thing Monday morning and Mr Tunley says they've got me good digs. With a Mrs Piddlesworth. She takes in all the apprentices and looks after them proper. I'm starting with another lad so I won't be on me own.'

'Glad to hear it, ain't we, Nell?'

'Yes, yes. She sounds right . . . right . . . nice, does Mrs Piddlesworth. Is the clean?'

''Course she's clean, Nell. The railway wouldn't entrust her with their lads if she wasn't. Now stop worrying and let's get cracking. I've a load to deliver and you've a son to sort out. But first I'd like me dinner.' He smiled at her fondly. 'If that's all right with you?'

Several minutes later Ronnie skipped happily down the path with his signed apprenticeship papers clasped firmly in his hand.

Nell placed two chunks of bread and a piece of cheese in front of her husband. 'He will be all right, won't he, Sep?'

'Yes' he replied firmly, then his voice softened. 'If things had been different, Nell, Ronnie wouldn't be the first to leave. Both Peggie and Letty would have been married. We've had the children

143

round us for longer than most, so for that we should be thankful.'

She sighed. 'Yes, you're right.' But for all that it would not stop her from missing him every moment he was away. She folded her fleshy arms under her ample bosom. 'I'll need some brown paper to wrap his stuff up in, and a clean piece of string. Can you get some on your travels?'

Sep looked over towards the cluttered welsh dresser. 'A' you sure we ain't already got some?' He shook his head. The thought of rummaging through the assortment of articles on the overspilling dresser did not appeal to him at all. 'It's all right. I'll get some new. We want our lad sending off proper.' He looked up at his wife thoughtfully. 'Tell you what, Nell. How about if we all see our Ronnie safely to Mrs Piddlesworth's? We could all go on Sunday morning after church in the bus. That'd put your mind at rest, and Mrs Piddlesworth will see that Ronnie comes from a good family. We could visit the station where he'll be working as well, if you like?'

Nell's face beamed in delight and she flung her arms around him. 'Oh, Sep. Thank you. Thank you!'

On his way home from handing in his papers, Ronnie encountered Mick Matterson. 'Tell your Billy I'll meet him usual time, usual place on Sunday night. Got that?'

Ronnie nodded. 'What for?'

'Never you mind what for. Just tell him, and make sure you do or you'll have me to deal with.'

'Okay, okay.'

Ronnie continued on his way and after several seconds his mind filled with thoughts of his forthcoming adventure and he promptly forgot the encounter with Mick and his message for his brother.

The following Sunday morning after church, wrapped up warmly to ward off the October chill, and with a picnic basket filled with cold belly pork sandwiches, fruit cake and bottles of cold tea, the whole family, excited at the prospect of a day out, happily boarded the bus in order to see Ronnie settled with Mrs Piddlesworth.

The journey was eventful. Several false starts and many wrong turnings on unfamiliar narrow roads delayed their arrival by several hours. Regardless, they were greeted warmly by Mrs Piddlesworth, a tall, thin, no-nonsense widow whose house was unexpectedly cosy and comfortable. After a long talk and welcome cup of tea and slices of home-made Madeira cake, Nell was content that her son was in good hands.

The whole family was impressed by the station. It was far bigger and busier than the one that served Bagworth, it even had a large tea room, overseen by two jolly women serving beverages from huge aluminium urns along with an assortment of sandwiches and cakes. The Station Master seemed a nice enough man and assured Sep and Nell that their son would be well taken care of. Railway rules were strict and the lads were made to stick by them.

As they prepared to leave, a tearful Nell hugged her son tightly and had to be forced by her husband and children to board the bus ready for the long journey home.

They finally arrived back after two in the morning and all fell into bed, tired but happy. Happy that they had all seen parts of the beautiful countryside that had been denied them before and happy too that Ronnie was settled.

They were woken an hour later by Constable Jesson banging loudly on the door. A bleary-eyed Sep let him in.

'It's Billy I need to speak to,' Constable Jesson said firmly, looking all around him.

'He's in bed,' Sep replied, frowning. 'What do you want to see him for anyway?'

'That's for me to discuss with your son.'

Sep's face set grimly. 'And I'm his father. Now why d'you want to see him?'

Just then Billy appeared, running his hands through his tousled hair. 'What's up, Dad?' he asked, worried at the sight of the constable.

Constable Jesson strode over and grabbed Billy by the arm, gripping it tightly. 'I'm arresting you, Billy Cartwright, for being in possession of stolen goods.'

Billy froze. 'Eh?'

Sep leapt over and forcibly removed the Constable's hand.

'Don't you manhandle my son like that in my house.' He turned to Billy. 'Is what the Constable's saying true?'

Just then Nell appeared dressed in her nightgown, her hair hanging loosely past her shoulders. 'What's going on?' she asked, pulling her shawl tightly across her chest.

'Go back to bed, Nell,' Sep commanded. 'I'll deal with this.'

'I'll do no such thing. Now I asked what was going on? What's the Constable doing in our house at this time a night?'

'He's arresting our son, that's what he's going.'

'Arresting our Billy!' she exclaimed, horrified. 'What for? Billy, what have you been up to?'

'N'ote, Mam,' he said hurriedly. 'I ain't been up to nothing.'

Constable Jesson grunted. 'I wouldn't say that, lad. I'd say you've definitely been up to no good.'

'And what's he supposed to have done?' she demanded.

'He's bought stolen goods, that's what he's done. And going by my information, it wouldn't be the first time neither.'

'What!' Nell cried as she sank down on a chair. 'Is this true, Billy? Is this true?'

Sep turned to him. 'Well, answer your mother?'

Billy paled. He had been several weeks back and he'd managed to sell the lot almost immediately, so technically, no, he wasn't. And Peggie, when she had borrowed his capital, had put paid to his buying any more for the time being.

Just then Peggie, Primrose and Letty appeared.

Peggie spoke first. 'What's going on?'

Primrose went over and sat on her mother's knee, resting her head on her shoulder.

'Back to bed,' Sep ordered.

His request fell on deaf ears.

Too tired and worried to fight with his stubborn daughters who would only listen to the proceedings on the stairs anyway, he turned to Constable Jesson. 'When was my son supposed to have bought these goods? And for that matter, what goods are we talking about?'

'I'm sorry, Mr Cartwright. I'm not obliged to divulge information of that nature.'

Sep slammed his fist hard on the table. 'You damned well will when you're accusing my son. Now I want answers before I demand to see your superiors.'

Constable Jesson froze. The last thing he wanted was his superiors involved any more than was necessary in this matter. He gulped. 'A load of stockings were stolen from the main Co-op depot in Leicester early last night and the information we have received is that they were then sold on to Billy here.'

'Who? Who sold them to Billy?'

'Er . . . I'm not in possession of that information. And if I was, I couldn't divulge it.'

'Oh, you couldn't!' Sep folded his arms. 'What you're trying to tell me is that you know some stockings were stolen, but not by whom. But you definitely know that my son then bought them. Huh, sounds mighty fishy to me!' He inhaled deeply and turned on Billy. 'Is what the Constable's saying true? Did you buy stolen stockings last night?'

Billy shook his head. 'No, Dad, I didn't,' he said truthfully. 'Besides, what would I want with stockings!'

'I'm sorry, but that's not what we believe and I'd like you to accompany me down to the station . . .'

Peggie suddenly stepped forward. 'Just a minute, Constable.'

'Peggie, you keep outta this.' Sep turned to face her. 'And didn't I tell the rest of you to go back to bed?'

'No, just a minute, Dad,' she interrupted, refusing to be quietened. 'Constable Jesson, did you just say that those stockings were stolen early last night. You mean Sunday night?'

'Yes, about eight o'clock. Why?'

Peggie smiled in satisfaction. 'Well, I'm sorry, Constable, but our Billy couldn't possibly be involved.'

Constable Jesson swallowed hard. 'He couldn't?'

'No, he couldn't. Because we were all in Rugby seeing our Ronnie safely off to his new job on the railway. So Billy couldn't possibly have bought them then. Unless, of course, you're going to accuse us of all being involved?'

'Yes, that's right,' Sep said, relieved, looking at Peggie in surprise. In all the confusion he had forgotten all about their trip. 'And we didn't get back 'til an hour or so ago and our Billy was with us all the time.' He moved towards the door. 'If you need to check our story out, I can give you the name of the landlady our Ronnie is staying with. She will vouch for us – all of us.' He opened the door. 'Now if you don't mind, we would all like to get back to bed. And in future, Constable, I'd make sure your information was correct before you come knocking on my door again in the middle of the night with such baloney.'

Constable Jesson's face reddened profusely. 'I'm sorry to have bothered you,' he stuttered, embarrassed, as he sidled swiftly out of the door.

Sep turned to face his family. 'Up to bed all of you, 'cept Billy. I want a word with you.'

When they had all departed Sep turned to him. 'Sit down. Me and you need to have a talk.

Billy, ashen-faced, still in shock from what had transpired, did as he was told, eyeing his father.

Sep sat down opposite and leaned heavily on the table. 'Billy, have you been up to things you shouldn't have? Those boots you got me. Were they stolen?'

Billy lowered his head. 'I never asked.'

Sep groaned. 'No, you never asked because you already knew the truth.' He took a deep breath. 'Have you any idea what trouble you could have been in. And for what?'

Billy raised his head. 'Money, Dad. That's what. A way to get myself out of that hell hole I work in.'

Sep shut his eyes tightly and shook his head. 'Yes, but at least that hell hole is honest work.'

Billy sighed. 'Look, Dad, I weren't doing anything really wrong. I never stole the goods, if they were stolen that is. I just brought 'em. And if I hadn't, then someone else would have.'

Sep raised his eyes, angrily. 'But that doesn't make what you did right, Billy.'

'I know that, Dad. But is it wrong to want to improve your lot? And it's the only way I could see of doing so.'

Sep eyed his son in concern. 'Do you really hate your job so much that you're willing to put your neck on the line to get out?'

Billy nodded. 'I've detested every minute I've spent down that pit and I don't regret what I've done.'

'You wouldn't be saying that if you were facing a jail sentence, lad. And what about us – your family? How d'you think we'd have coped, 'specially your mother?' He watched his son's face closely. 'No, you didn't think of the consequences, did you?'

He rose, picked up his pipe from the mantle and took several moments to pack it with tobacco and light it. He puffed long and hard as he thought.

During the last two months the business had done far better than he had dared hope. Glad to turn to someone far more reliable and civil than Cyrus Crabbe and his son, people had bombarded him

147

with work. Apart from his regular passenger runs, he now delivered overloads for Brotherhoods and for Scott's the coal merchants; the latter was a pain – delivering sacks of coal was heavy work and it took an age to hose the vehicle down to rid it of coal dust afterwards – but the money he got was worth it. He had received several enquiries regarding transport for special occasions and more would come in once word spread further.

The trip they had taken to deliver Ronnie safely had also got his mind working on other possibilities, such as day trips to the country and even the seaside. But those possibilities he had put to one side until later when he felt more able to cope.

Expansion at this time was something that frightened him. To expand would mean the acquisition of another vehicle. It meant obtaining money from a bank and he didn't like the thought of that. He liked to pay his way in hard cash. He looked across at Billy. But did he have a choice?

He made a decision, one he hoped he would not live to regret.

'Right, that settles it.'

'Settles what, Dad?' Billy asked, horrified. 'You're not going to turn me in, are yer?'

'I will if anything of this nature happens again. So be warned.' He paused to let his words hit home before he spoke again. 'I've made a decision. We should really have a family discussion but as it is, well, as the head of the family I'm going to do this off my own bat. There's money left from the winnings and a bit that I've been able to add to since we started up, being as things have gone better than I thought and because you, Peggie, Letty and your mother have continued to work.' He paused. 'We'll see about getting another vehicle. You can come into the business.'

Billy, expecting the worst, stared in surprise. 'D'yer mean that, Dad? A' yer sure?'

'If it'll stop you going to prison, I'm sure. It's not enough money to buy as good a vehicle as the one we've got, but I'm sure the garage will do me a good deal and we can do it up between us.'

'Ah, Dad. I won't let you down, I promise.'

'You'd better not. Now get to bed before I change my mind.'

Billy smiled gratefully, turned and made for the door.

Sep stopped him. 'Just a minute, Billy.'

'Oh?'

'Who did you buy the stuff off?'

'Eh? Dad, I can't tell you that,' he said, striding back into the room. 'It'd be betraying a confidence.'

'Your loyalties are misplaced, son. Someone didn't think like that when they gave your name to the police.'

Billy swallowed hard. He hadn't thought of that. It must have been Mick. Mick Matterson was the only one he had dealt with and the only one as far as he was aware who knew of their arrangements. His face grew grim.

'I'll sort this out, Dad.'

'Billy . . .'

'Dad, leave me to sort it out. I'll find out who shopped me and they won't be doing it to anybody else, believe me.' He turned on his heels and left the room.

Sep stared after him with mixed emotions. He didn't like the thought of any of his family being mixed up in any kind of criminal activities, whether innocently or not, and prayed that this business had frightened Billy enough to put paid to such activities once and for all.

He tapped his pipe out against the side of the fireplace, placed it on the mantle and peered at the clock. He had better get to bed. He had a long day of hard work facing him and Nell would be waiting, needing calming down and reassuring that all was well before he could resume his sleep for what was left of the night.

'Wadda you mean he ain't locked up! You caught him red handed, didn't yer?'

'Well, no. Not exactly.'

Cyrus Crabbe spun round, his face furious. 'I think you'd better explain, Jesson. I give you a Cartwright on a plate. I give you dates, times and places, and you tell me you didn't catch him? I wanna know why and it'd better be good.'

Sidney Jesson fought hard to stop himself from shaking. Cyrus Crabbe frightened him, had always frightened him. Why, oh why, had he allowed himself to get into such a position in the first place?

But he didn't need to ask. His fate had been sealed that day many years ago when he had so innocently helped Cyrus Crabbe move the brake from the shed across the field and into the back of his own yard. His brake, Cyrus had told him. The brake he had worked on night and day for the past few months. And although it wasn't quite finished, the owner of the shed wanted it back – plans to turn it into a moving picture house and he couldn't do that whilst the brake was taking up valuable space.

The young officer of the law, new to the village, had believed him, feeling sorry for the fact no one else would lend a hand. Between them they had pushed the heavy brake across the fields. Gullible with youth, it never occurred to Jesson at the time to question why it had had to be done in the middle of the night.

But not long after he had known. It had had to be done that way because Cyrus had been stealing the brake – and the Constable had unwittingly helped him. Sidney felt in no doubt that he had been chosen because of the nature of his job. Cyrus had used this situation to get a hold over him for future use.

Many times since, Sidney Jesson had been blackmailed into helping Cyrus with a devious act, usually against someone who had dared to cross him, and the longer Sidney had allowed it to go on, the more Cyrus had over him. But he knew he could never come clean. One hint of scandal and his career and standing in the community would be in tatters. He would be booted out of the

149

force and, because of the seriousness of his actions, would also be facing a long prison sentence. That he could not stand. Not only would his life be ruined but also his wife's and children's, and he could not allow that.

So there was nothing he could do but carry on and hope that he was never caught.

He raised his eyes. 'I never got a chance to go to the churchyard. I got waylaid by proper police work down at the station, so I had to assume that all went to plan. But it seems that Billy Cartwright never met Matterson. He was over at Rugby.'

'Over at Rugby? What was he doing there?'

'Seeing young Ronnie settled into his new job on the railway. The whole family were present.'

Cyrus reddened angrily. 'Pity you never found all this out before you accused Billy. If you hadn't I could still have used that ploy. As it is . . .'

'Yes, yes. Well I'm sorry. But I wasn't to know, was I? You told me everything was arranged. All I had to do was turn up at the church and nab him. Well, as I couldn't get to the church in time, I went round his house. I wasn't to know Billy never kept his appointment in the first place or that the whole Cartwright clan would be able to vouch for him.'

Cyrus leapt up, his eyes sparkling. 'It's their word against yours. You can break their alibi.'

'No, I can't. They had tea or summat with a woman in Rugby. Plus they visited the station master, and as Rugby is a fair distance away, even Billy Cartwright couldn't be in two places at once.'

Cyrus's face darkened in rage. 'Get out. Just get outta my sight, Jesson.' He bounded forward and grabbed him by the shoulders. 'Next time I ask you to do summat, you'd better do a good job. Or I'm warning yer.'

Jesson gulped in fright. 'But I did that big favour for you several months back and you said that would be the end.'

'I lied,' Cyrus said icily. 'And don't you dare ever mention that again,' he snarled. 'A' you listening? I told you what would happen if any of that got out. Your career in the police force will be finished and you'll never get another job of any description, believe me.'

Sidney gulped. He knew first hand that Cyrus's threats were not idle and it didn't matter to him who was at the receiving end, family or foe. If they got in the way or were a threat, they were dealt with in Cyrus's own particular way and he had no doubt that if he himself stepped out of line he would be dealt with just as harshly.

The Cartwrights had always annoyed Cyrus though Sidney couldn't fathom for the life of him why he was so determined to destroy them. He himself had known the Cartwrights for over twenty-five years and they had always been God-fearing people who, like others, went quietly about their business. Apart from Billy's trading activities, not one of the Cartwrights would dream of doing anything against the law.

Cyrus broke in on his thoughts.

'Get out,' he shouted. 'Before I do summat you might regret.'

Sidney didn't need another warning. He left while he could.

In a burst of temper, Cyrus picked up the tea pot and threw it across the room where it smashed into smithereens. Broken pieces of pot scattered along with the remains of cold tea and leaves.

'Damn and blast,' he fumed loudly. Now he'd have to wait for another opportunity to blacken the name of the Cartwrights' and in the meantime his business was suffering, suffering badly. If he didn't come up with something soon his livelihood would be lost completely. Between himself and his son they'd hardly earned enough to buy food this week, let alone anything else.

Septimus Cartwright had only been in business a few months and during that time had picked up work that should have been Cyrus's. If he wasn't careful nothing would come his way in future. Why, why, he thought angrily, hadn't he himself thought of getting a lorry before Septimus had?

He shook his head. Something had to be done and done quick.

Just then Reginald sauntered in. He quickly detected his father's mood and eyed the mess across the far side of the room.

Cyrus turned on him before he could escape. 'Seen Letty tonight?'

'No,' he answered casually. 'I'm not meeting her 'til . . . er . . . next Saturday. We're going to the village dance.' That was not exactly true. She had reluctantly informed him that she was going with her friend Brenda and maybe her sister Peggie, and he had told her he would see her there.

'Next Saturday?'

'Look, Dad, before you start, I can't rush her, she'll get suspicious.'

'Suspicious! She'll only get suspicious if you let her. And yer still ain't bought her round here like I told you to. Why not?'

'Because the opportunity ain't arose, that's why not.' He surveyed the mess across the room whilst his mind sought desperately to change the subject. If his father probed deeper he would quickly realise that Letty was not the pushover first envisaged and Reginald was encountering problems with her. 'How am I supposed to mash a cuppa in that?'

'Sod the tea pot. I've more important things on me mind. Have yer found out 'ote else about the Cartwrights?'

'Such as?'

'What they're up to, you dozy bugger?'

'Dad, you know what they're up to. They're running a transport business, like the one we used to . . .'

Cyrus swung his hand and brought it back heavily against the side of Reginald's head, knocking him sideways. 'Don't you be sarcastic with me.'

Reginald took several seconds to regain his composure. 'I didn't mean to be sarcastic, but what else can I find out?' he said, rubbing his head. The pain was excruciating but he wouldn't let his father

151

have the satisfaction of knowing that.

Cyrus grunted. That was true. What else was there? Septimus had bought a motor vehicle, cleverly converted it and was now running a transport business that was promising to become very successful. Successful, in Cyrus's eyes, at his own expense.

Reginald watched his father pacing up and down, his temper worsening. He knew if he wasn't careful he would get another beating before the night was out. Before there had always been two of them to weather the storms but since Mary had gone, there was only him. He searched his mind for something to lighten his father's mood and spoke before he could stop himself.

'I asked Letty to marry me. That's why I ain't seeing her 'til Saturday. She's gonna give me her answer then.'

Cyrus stopped his pacing. 'You did! Why didn't you say so earlier?

'Because . . . because I never, that's all.'

Cyrus narrowed his eyes. 'Well, you just make sure her answer's yes, or I'll wanna know why. And get a bloody move on and fix a date before summat happens to stop yer. There's still time for that drip Wilfred to come back on the scene.'

He turned away from Reginald and stared across the room. Cyrus didn't like it when any of his schemes failed, it made him angry, very angry. He was more determined than ever now to get Billy Cartwright off the scene. Without him around to help with the heavy lifting Septimus surely wouldn't manage the business on his own. Then things could get back to normal. He would get his passengers and deliveries back, he would be able to hold his own in the village once again. He knew they all sniggered and sneered behind his back. He knew they were all glad to see his gradual demise.

He slyly smiled. Well, they hadn't seen the last of Cyrus Crabbe just yet. He still had an ace up his sleeve and the time was about right to play it.

After extensive enquiries, Billy caught up with Mick Matterson two days later as the latter skulked in a far corner of the Three Tuns supping distractedly at a pint of brown ale.

He jumped in alarm when Billy pounced on him. 'You've some explaining to do,' he seethed, sitting down opposite. 'And it better be good.'

'About what?' said Mick cautiously.

'About how I nearly ended up in jail, that's what. How did the police know about our dealings?'

'I dunno, Billy, 'onest I don't. I don't know what yer talking about.'

'Yes you do. How else would Jesson have got his information if you hadn't blabbed to him?'

Mick shrugged his shoulders. 'Search me. But it weren't me, Billy. I didn't know that he knew anything.'

Billy stared at him, unable to ascertain at this precise moment whether Mick was telling the truth or not. 'Has he been to question you?'

Mick shook his head. 'No. I ain't seen 'ide nor 'air of 'im. But that settles it.'

'Settles what?'

'I'm getting outta 'ere. I've bin thinking for a while about trying me luck down south. I've a cousin that lives in Bethnal Green, runs some sort of posh jazz club. He's bin asking me for a while to go and work for him. Sez he'll show me all the ropes.'

Billy nodded. 'Sounds like a good idea, considering. But I still don't like this business, Mick. Someone put the finger on me and I'll break their bloody neck when I find out who it was. What I can't understand is why you weren't pulled in as well?'

Mick cringed. Should he inform Billy that Cyrus Crabbe was his man? Was it worth the risk? No. Best to leave well alone. He liked Billy. He had always treated him fairly. He didn't want to see him hanged for murder.

He hadn't slept since the night of the summons to Cyrus's house. He hadn't willingly divulged the information that Cyrus had demanded, even though he had been assured his name wouldn't be mentioned. But he had found he had no choice. Mick, used to dealing with the hardest of men, knew Cyrus was one of the worst kind. His threats were not idle, he would have no desire to listen to reason. He would just act without further thought.

Getting well away was his only option, he had already hung around for far too long. The consequence of staying was doing all future business with Cyrus, and he knew before long Cyrus would want to know the full extent of his operation. When he had discovered all, he would take over. Mick himself would not be useful any more. Ashen-faced, he rose abruptly. 'I'm off, Billy. I'm gonna take the opportunity to get out of this place while I can.'

'Er . . . yeah,' Billy responded as he watched Mick rush for the door.

He frowned deeply. He had never seen Mick so jumpy. What had got into the man? Why was he so desperate to get away when he had such a good thing going which had taken him years to build up? He finished his drink and left, wholly thankful for the fact he was still free to do so.

One thing was for sure, this business had taught him a severe lesson. There were many ways of making money and this one was not for him. At the end of the day he hadn't the stomach. He didn't want to be peering over his shoulder every two minutes, worried he was going to be caught. He wasn't like Mick. He hadn't a cousin in London to run to.

During the last couple of months he had had two narrow escapes and that was enough to last him a lifetime. From now on it was the straight and narrow for him, regardless of how strapped for money he was. He was going to throw himself whole-heartedly into

153

helping the family business prosper.

As Billy made his way back he would have been devastated and bewildered had he known that another plan was afoot to bring his downfall.

Chapter Fourteen

Sep tightened the last of the bolts, laid down the spanner and yawned loudly. 'Well, I don't know about you, son, but I've had enough for the day.'

He scanned his eyes quickly over the bus and smiled. Now they had reinstalled the seating she was all ready for business first thing Monday morning. Tomorrow afternoon they could concentrate on fully finishing the overhaul on their new acquisition. He turned to Billy, who was half hidden under the bonnet of their second Model T.

The next day, after the visit from Constable Jesson, true to his word, Sep had sat down and worked out how much money was available for another vehicle. This information to hand, and after telling Billy to give notice at the mine, he had travelled into Leicester and scoured the garages for an affordable lorry. After viewing several different models in all states of repair, Sep decided to stick with a make they were already familiar with. Several days later, after travelling into town on the draycart, he clambered into the driving seat and began the journey home.

Arriving in Desford, Winny came to mind and he used the opportunity to pay her a call. She was delighted to see him and even more delighted to hear of the astounding progress of the business. Replenished with several cups of her strong brewed tea and slices of home-made cake, he re-embarked on his journey, worried that the lorry could break down en route. Happily it didn't and both arrived home in one piece.

The family were delighted and eagerly agreed to help as much as they could in bringing this new vehicle up to the Cartwright standard. Sep told them of his idea to use this lorry for haulage and keep the other for permanent passenger services. That way would cut down the time and effort needed in the required conversion.

Sep wiped his oily hands on an even oilier cloth. Despite his misgivings, he couldn't help but feel proud as he watched his son beavering away. The Cartwrights were now the proud owners of a small but thriving business, something he would never have envisaged this time last year. And they all deserved praise for the part they were playing, even lazy Primrose and the preoccupied Letty.

'How's it going?' he asked, walking over to join him.

Billy straightened up and pulled forth a metal spring. 'I think this is knackered, Dad. We'll need a new 'un.'

155

Sep inspected it thoroughly. 'Mmm, I agree. We'll see Blackie. He'll make us a new one.'

Billy nodded. 'I'll take it round first thing Monday. It's too late now. Pity we can't do things like this ourselves. Save us a fortune in the long run.'

Sep laughed. 'I can fix most things, but blacksmith I ain't. And I shouldn't let Blackie hear you talk like that. He'll clobber you with his anvil if he thinks his livelihood looks threatened.' Sep yawned again. 'Come on, Billy. Down tools and call it a day. You'll need to get a move on if you're going to the village dance. I bet the girls have been at it all afternoon.'

'At what?'

'Doing themselves up, that's what. And I bet they look a picture.'

Billy pulled down the bonnet and began to pack away his tools. 'Why don't you and Mam come to the dance?'

'Me and your mother? Oh, I don't think so, Billy. We're too old for things like that. 'Sides, all I want to do is put my feet up and read the paper. That's all I feel fit for these days. So we'll leave the jigging to you youngsters.' Sep looked around him. 'You just about finished?'

'Yeah,' Billy answered. 'If you want to get off, I'll shut up.'

'Fine. Thanks, son,' he said, heading for the door. 'I'll see you in a couple of minutes. I'll tell your mother to put your dinner out.'

Fifteen minutes later Billy looked around him and extinguished the oil lamp. Fastening the two large wooden doors of the shed, he walked down the cinder path towards the back of their cottage. He was looking forward to tonight. It would feel good to get out of his dirty dungarees and smarten up.

The annual village dance had been abandoned during the war years. The villagers hadn't thought it right to be seen acting frivolously with so much suffering going on around them. But now things were gradually getting back to normal the dance had been reinstated and all were anxious for the allotted time to arrive when, for a few hours at least, problems and hardships could be cast aside.

Billy himself was looking forward to a few pints, a crack with his mates and maybe a couple of dances with some attractive females who were attending from neighbouring villages.

He was met outside the back gate by Primrose.

'Mam sent me to tell you to get a hurry on. Yer dinner's on the table and the water heated for yer wash.'

He ruffled her hair. 'Thanks, Rosie.'

Primrose beamed. She loved her big brother. Looked up to him in awe, she did. And Billy was the only one she allowed to call her Rosie. She made to skip ahead of him but stopped. 'Oh, this is for you,' she said, handing him an envelope which she had fished from the pocket of her pinafore. 'It was pushed under the door about an hour ago.'

Billy frowned. Why would anyone be writing to him? He ripped the envelope open, extracted the paper inside, and, with difficulty, read it by the light from the moon.

'Deer Billy, Please come to my ouse at 12 to nit. I nede to cee you. Its desporatly inportant. Make sure its 12 and not befor. Yors ever. Alice.'

Billy groaned and stuffed the letter inside his pocket. He had so far managed to avoid Alice, but as she had taken the trouble to write, stressing the importance, he had no option but to go. The time fitted in with his plans. The dance would be just about finished by then. He could keep the appointment on his way home. He rubbed his hand across his unshaven chin. He would have to tell her. She would be hurt, but he would have to make her believe it was all over between them. It had been good while it lasted but now it was time it finished. He just hoped he could make her see it that way.

Peggie, dressed in her underwear, scrutinised herself in the piece of mirror propped up against the washstand. 'I wish I'd had my hair cut. It drives me mad. Considering there's five of us, how come I got all the curls?' She gave up trying to catch all the tendrils of her hair and, gathering what she could, tied the bow at the nape of her neck, spreading the wide piece of red ribbon out with her fingers. She turned to face her sister sitting on the bed. 'Letty, a' you listening to me?'

Letty raised her head absently. 'Eh! Yes, 'course I am. You're moaning about your hair as usual. Well, it looks fine to me.'

Peggie frowned, walked over and joined her. 'What's up, Letty? I thought you were looking forward to the dance?'

'I am. I'd have just liked a new dress, that's all. I don't wanna go in my old skirt and blouse. Why couldn't Dad have spared some money for material for us instead of spending it all on that blasted new lorry of his? That's all he thinks of these days.'

Peggie sighed. 'Because that blasted vehicle of his is going to make our fortunes in the long run. Surely it's worth going without a new dress for that?' In Peggie's case she had still to pay Billy back the thirty shillings she owed him, plus the fact she was still trying to save the money to collect her locket and time was quickly running out. New clothes were way down her list.

'I'm not so sure it is,' Letty sulked. 'I wanted to look nice for once, Peggie. I wanted one of those new Charleston style dresses I saw in *Woman's Realm*. They look ever so easy to make.'

'Yes, but material costs money and what with our Billy nearly getting arrested . . .'

'Yeah, well, he knew what could happen. He knew that the stuff he was selling was illegal, even though he says he didn't. We both know our Billy ain't daft. Anyway, I still don't think it would have hurt to have given us a few bob towards some material . . .'

'Stop it, Letty. You're just being selfish. Don't you think I would have liked a new dress? Don't you think Mam'd like a few nice things instead of having to make do and mend? And what about the

157

likes of Aggie? She ain't got a dad no more to moan about. They have enough worry wondering how they're gonna pay the rent and eat to bother about new dresses. Now either get your clothes on or I'll go without you. 'Cos to be honest, I don't give a damn either way. I'm only going myself 'cos I promised Aggie and that woman needs to get out of the house for a few hours and enjoy herself. Her and Brenda will be around here in a minute all raring to go.'

'All right, all right,' Letty snapped. 'You don't half go on, our Peggie. It wouldn't surprise me in the least if Harry got himself killed just to get away from your nagging.'

Peggie froze. 'How dare you say that?' she uttered, shocked. 'Letty, how could you?'

Letty reddened. 'I'm sorry, Peggie. Really I am. I didn't mean it. It's just you get me so mad sometimes.' She jumped up and started to pull on her clothes, feeling dreadful remorse for what she had said. What was really upsetting her was the fact that Reginald would be at the dance and possibly Wilfred, and if Wilfred did happen to go she wanted to make full use of the opportunity to try and put matters right. But secretly she was afraid it was already too late.

She tucked in her blouse, buttoned her skirt and stared over at her sister, biting her bottom lip in anxiety. 'I said I was sorry, Peggie. You're always saying things you don't mean, so you can't hold it against me.'

Just then Primrose came through the door. 'Aggie and Brenda are downstairs and they said to tell you to hurry up.' She looked quizzically at her eldest sister. 'What's up wi' you?'

Peggie inhaled deeply and raised her head. 'Nothing that getting rid of a sister wouldn't cure,' she said harshly. 'Tell the girls we won't be a minute. In fact, tell 'em to come up. I could do with some light relief.' Without looking at Letty she rose and began to dress.

Aggie and Brenda burst excitedly through the door, kicking it shut behind them. Brenda pulled up her skirt. Down the top of her best cotton stockings was stuffed a half bottle of cheap sherry. 'Look what I've got,' she laughed in glee. 'Who fancies a swig?'

Letty pounced on her. It was just the thing she needed to calm her nerves. 'I do,' she said, wrenching the bottle out. She uncorked the top and took a mouthful. 'Ugh,' she grimaced. 'Where the hell did you get this from? It's disgusting.'

'It might be,' Brenda replied, hurt. 'But it was all I could afford. I bought it off me brother.'

'Keep your voice down,' Peggie hissed. 'If Mother finds we have drink up here she'll scalp us all and we won't be going anywhere, let alone to the dance.'

Brenda and Letty looked at each other. 'Sorry,' they giggled.

Finally, after much titivation, rearrangement and lots of laughter, they departed into the warm night air towards the village hall, Nell's warnings to behave themselves and to make sure they were home before twelve ringing in their ears.

When they arrived, the dance was already in full swing. They handed over their tickets and made their way towards the beverage table.

'What can I tempt you with, ladies?' Freda Smith asked as she collected several dirty glasses and put them on a tray. She put the full tray on the ledge of the hatch at the back of her ready for washing by several ladies who had volunteered and turned her attention back to the girls. 'Orange juice, lemonade, ginger beer or what about some fruit punch? Made it meself I did. It's ever so quenching.'

Letty eyed the barrel of beer and bottles of stout by the jugs of lemonade and juices. 'I'll have one of those.'

Peggie nudged her hard in the ribs. 'We'll try the punch, thank you, Mrs Smith.'

Armed with their glasses of punch, the four girls gazed around the crowded hall.

'It looks as though most of the village is here, and more besides,' Aggie said. 'Isn't that Basil Hall and his mates from Barton?'

They all peered over. 'Yeah, it sure is,' Brenda said matter-of-factly. 'If he's here, you can be sure the night will end in a fight.'

'I don't think much to the music,' Letty grumbled. 'I don't fancy waltzing all night. I hope they've got some of those new jazz records or the tango . . .'

'The tango?' Brenda interrupted. 'What's that?'

'The new dance craze. I read about it.'

Aggie blew out her cheeks. 'I can't see Major Allot having anything modern. I suppose we're fortunate he was persuaded to loan the gramophone in the first place. He wasn't keen. Miserable old bugger.'

They all looked through the crowd and eyed Major Allot presiding over his precious gramophone.

'They should have asked Mrs Pegg,' Peggie said. 'My mother says she's got a good collection of gramophone records. Still never mind. We'll just have to make do with what's on offer and make the best of it like the rest of the crowd.' She grinned broadly. 'I see Wally is getting ready to play his fiddle later.'

Letty grimaced. 'I'm not doing the Gay Gordons or the barn dance, so you can count me out. And anyway, considering the way he's knocking back that whisky he's got hidden inside his flask, I doubt he'll be in any fit state to play.'

They all laughingly agreed.

Brenda spoke excitedly. 'I hope we get asked to dance.' She looked across the room to where a row of chairs were placed against the wall. All were filled with an assortment of expectant-looking women. 'I ain't sitting with that lot all night. Oh, look, your Billy's just come in. I'm off to ask him for a dance before all the other females snap him up.'

An hour or so later a breathless Aggie plonked herself down on the chair beside Peggie, her face flushed with excitement, her feet tapping to the music. 'It's good, ain't it, Peggie? I ain't half enjoying meself.'

Peggie smiled. It was good to see her friend having so much fun.

'That chap over there,' she continued, inclining her head towards a tubby, balding man, who was at least a foot shorter than herself, standing with several other men by the beverage table, 'keeps looking over here.' As she spoke the man turned and grinned shyly at her. 'D'you think he fancies me?'

Peggie discreetly gazed over. 'Yes, I think he does.'

'Oh, er . . . what do I do? What do I do?' she asked, flustered.

'Pretend you're not interested. That's what you do.'

'Oh, all right.' Aggie twisted in her seat giving her full attention to Peggie. 'Seen anybody you fancy?'

'Aggie!'

'Well, I only asked. You seemed to be getting on with Sam Harkins very well earlier.'

Peggie smiled. 'You don't miss much, do you, Aggie? We had a couple of dances that's all.' She gazed around and frowned. 'Where's our Letty got to?'

Aggie pulled a face. 'Dunno. Last time I saw her, her and Brenda were chatting to Eunice Eversley and her friends. She paused abruptly, her face paling. 'That man's coming this way, Peggie, and he's a friend in tow. You will dance with him, won't yer?' she pleaded.

Peggie tutted and quickly eyed the two men making their way over. The 'friend' didn't appeal to her one little bit. Suddenly an image of Harry rose up, a smile, his special smile kept just for her, spread across his handsome face.

Harry had loved dancing, had loved life in fact, and if he was here now would be twirling her around the dance floor, his strong arms wrapped tightly about her, both blissfully unaware of anybody or of any other goings on. She mentally scolded herself and forced away the picture. 'Anything to please you, Aggie,' she said reluctantly.

On the other side of the hall, Letty stood with her back against a wall, sipping at a glass of lemonade – or what others might think was lemonade but was in actual fact topped with a generous amount of gin smuggled in by Eunice Eversley. Her eyes darted around. So far she had managed to avoid Reginald whom she had spotted several times as he had prowled around on the look out for her. But he was not the one she was hoping to bump into. Her heart thumped as she suddenly spied the one person she was hoping to see.

'Wilfred,' she sighed. 'Oh, Wilfred.'

He stood uneasily by the door fingering his cap and for a moment she was unsure whether he had just arrived or was contemplating leaving. Either way she wasn't going to stand around and hope he might approach her. Peggie was always telling her you

160

had to create your own opportunities. If you waited for others it might never happen. As she pushed her way towards him through the crowd, she hoped her sister was right.

'Letty,' he said, stepping backwards, his face reddening.

'Hello, Wilfred,' she said boldly. 'Don't look so surprised, you must have known I'd be here.'

'Er . . . yes. Er . . . I was hoping to see . . .'

'Wilfred,' a voice boomed. It was Effie Dage and the sight of Letty Cartwright talking to her son as she entered the hall sent a scowl of disapproval across her face.

Letty smiled sweetly, glad of the gin and the courage it was giving her. 'Hello, Mrs Dage. How nice to see you,' she lied.

'Is it?' Effie snapped. She grabbed her son's arm. 'Come along, Wilfred. Mrs Crabbit and her daughter will be waiting for us.' She turned to Letty, her eyes malicious. 'Wilfred is stepping out with Jessica Crabbit.' She raised her eyes to her son's. 'Aren't you, Wilfred? It wouldn't surprise me if there's a wedding in the air. Such a nice girl is Jessica.' She turned to face Letty, her beady eyes narrowing. 'Treats her mother and me with such respect.'

'Mother!' Wilfred said, his voice rising. 'I'm not . . .'

'Letty. Here you are. I've bin looking all over.'

She turned abruptly to find Reginald at her side.

'Evening, Mrs Dage. Wilfred,' he said, dropping his cigarette end on the wooden floor and crushing it beneath his boot. He grabbed hold of Letty's arm and propelled her round. 'Come on, me dad's waiting for us.' He grinned slyly at Wilfred. 'Thanks for keeping an eye on me fiancée.'

Before Letty could protest he dragged her away. Effie Dage stared after them. She turned to Wilfred, a satisfied smile on her face.

'Well, fancy that! She didn't waste much time, did she? Engaged to one of the Crabbes. Well, I never.' She filled her lungs. 'I told you, didn't I? For years I told you all she was after was our money and this proves it. Reginald Crabbe is just about her barrow . . .'

Wilfred wasn't listening. Letty couldn't possibly be engaged to Reginald Crabbe. Not his Letty. His body sagged. She wasn't his Letty any more, she belonged to Reginald. His mother's callous droning began to register above the din of the crowd and the blare from the gramophone. He spun round on his heel, his face uncharacteristically angry. 'Stop it, Mother. In all the years I was seeing Letty, you never had a good word to say about her. In fact you never have a good word to say about anybody unless it's for your own ends. And you'd no right to tell Letty I was engaged to Jessica Crabbit. I've never so much as taken the woman out.'

'Wilfred, how dare you . . .'

'Don't, Mother. Stop treating me like I don't know my own mind.' He bent towards her. 'Remember Father left. D'you want me to do the same? Now you go and find your friends, I'm going home.'

He turned and strode back through the door, leaving his mother staring after him. She jumped as Mrs Crabbit and her daughter approached.

'Mrs Crabbit,' she said, planting a smile on her face, 'Wilfred's taken sick, I'm afraid, and gone home to bed.' She turned to Jessica. 'But he'll be all right tomorrow and he's asked me to invite you to tea. Now won't that be nice? You two have such a lot in common. I'm sure you'll find plenty to talk about.'

Before she had had time to collect her thoughts, Letty found herself face to face with Cyrus Crabbe. He put down his glass of beer and held out his hand.

'Nice ter meet you at long last. Let's find a seat,' he said, directing an icy glare at a couple seated at a table to the side of him. They quickly departed. 'I believe we've a lot to discuss about the wedding.'

As they sat down Letty turned to Reginald. 'Wedding?'

He smiled at her sheepishly. Before he had time to speak Cyrus interrupted.

'You've done well for yourself, Letty. Reginald'll make you a good husband. Won't yer, Reginald?'

'Eh! Oh, yeah. Yeah, I will, Letty.'

Her mouth dropped open even further. 'Husband! But I . . .'

He quickly interrupted. 'Dad says we can live with him 'til we get a place of our own.'

She turned to him. 'Eh?'

Cyrus eyed them both as it dawned on him that this was the first Letty knew of her impending wedding. He hid a smile. 'Place of yer own? I'll have no talk of that. My house is big enough for all of us. You'll have the kitchen to yerself, Letty. No interfering in-laws poking their nose in, eh?' He laughed loudly and slapped her playfully on her knee.

She cringed and stared at him. 'I think there's been some mistake. I never agreed . . .'

'It's no good protesting, Letty,' Reginald cut in. 'Dad's insisting we live with him. Ain't yer, Dad?'

'I am that. You'll be in your element, Letty, with just us two to look after. It'll be nice having a woman around the place again.'

Reginald, getting hot under the collar, jumped up. 'Fancy another drink anyone?'

'Yeah, I'll have a pint. What about you, Letty?' Cyrus asked.

She shook her head. 'No. Nothing, thank you.'

Reginald rushed off. Letty turned to Cyrus.

'Mr Crabbe . . .'

'Oh, Cyrus, please. I can't have my future daughter-in-law calling me Mister.'

Letty reddened. 'But that's just it, Mr Crabbe. I won't be your daughter-in-law. I have no intention of marrying Reginald.'

Cyrus narrowed his eyes. 'Oh? And why not?'

Letty gulped at the harshness of his tone. 'Well, for a start he never asked me. And if he had, I would have refused.'

Cyrus' face darkened. 'Oh, you would have, would you? My son's not good enough for you, is that it?'

She shook her head. 'No, no, it's not that. It's . . . well, I don't love him.'

'Oh, I see. Well, give it time and he'll grow on you.'

Letty's temper rose. 'I don't intend to let him grow on me or give it time for that matter. I'm not marrying your son, Mr Crabbe, and you can't make me!'

She made to rise. Cyrus grabbed her arm, nipping her flesh, and pulled her back down. He thrust his face within inches of hers.

'I'll not make you do anything, Letty. You'll marry my son voluntary. You'll walk down the aisle with a smile on yer face like any radiant bride. No Cartwright is going to make a fool of a Crabbe. The villagers would love that.'

'I'm not making a fool of him,' she said defensively. 'He's done that to himself by reading things that ain't there. I've never led him to believe I wanted anything else but friendship.'

'Didn't you? You forget, little lady, I've seen how you've drooled over my son and I'll stand up in court and testify as much.'

'Court?'

'Yes, court. 'Cos if you don't go through with this wedding, I'll take you to court for breach of contract. I'll sue your family for every penny you possess and more besides.' A smile played on his lips. 'Your father can kiss goodbye to that business of his for a start.'

She stared at him. 'You . . . you wouldn't?'

Cyrus laughed. 'Oh, wouldn't I just? So I'd think hard if I were you. It's marriage to Reginald or I'll ruin your family. Now what is it to be?'

Letty froze. She couldn't believe what she was hearing. Oh, God, how had she got herself into this awful mess?

'Well?' he hissed.

She gasped, knowing she had no choice. Slowly she nodded.

'Wise, Letty. Very wise.'

Reginald came back with the drinks and Cyrus raised his glass of beer.

'Here's to the happy couple,' he said, smiling broadly.

Billy guided Brenda to the side of the floor. She was gazing up at him in adoration.

'Thanks for the dance, Brenda,' he said, preparing to leave her.

'Oh!' she uttered, dismayed. 'What about one later?' she asked hopefully.

'If you're not already spoken for. There's a bloke over there eyeing you up.'

Brenda looked over and he took the opportunity to leave her and rejoin his mates who were already the worse for wear after a few pints too many. Fred Noble slapped him on the back. 'Never short

163

of the ladies, a' yer, Cartwright? Leave some for us, there's a pal.'

'I can't help being good-looking,' Billy bantered. 'Anyway, has anybody got the time?'

'Just after eleven thirty,' one of the men piped up. 'Why?'

'No reason. Just wondered that's all.'

Twenty minutes later, Billy reluctantly left his friends all securing a female for the last slow dance and slipped out of the door. He would have liked to have stayed. In the final few minutes he had spotted a very pretty, fair-haired woman whom he understood to be the new teacher at Primrose's school and he would have liked to have made her acquaintance while he had the chance. Still, he had to get the matter with Alice sorted, the pretty teacher could wait.

He trod down her path, the crunching of the cinders echoing loudly beneath his boots. The cottage was in darkness. Alice would be sitting by the fire, waiting for him as she had always done. He tapped on the door and let himself in.

'Alice,' he called softly, mindful not to wake her children, 'it's me, Billy. I got your letter. Now what's so urgent?'

The door slammed behind him and before he could gather his wits he had been grabbed from behind, his head forced back and a strong arm clamped round his throat. He struggled for breath as the pressure tightened. In the distance he heard a muffled scream.

'Mess wi' my wife, eh, Cartwright?' Bull Hammond's drunken voice boomed. 'Well, by the time I've finished wi' you, you'll wish you hadn't.'

'No, Bull, no,' Alice screamed. She leapt at her husband who raised his booted foot and kicked her away. 'Stay outta this, you whore,' he bellowed. 'It's your turn when I've finished wi' 'im.'

Upstairs several children cried hysterically. 'Mammy, Mammy!' they wailed.

Billy brought his elbow back hard in Bull's ribs and for a second the grip on his throat eased. He wrenched himself free and spun round, his fists clenched ready to punch. 'You're wrong, Bull. Tell him, Alice? Tell him?' he croaked, frantically fighting for breath.

Bull grabbed at a bottle on the table and smashed it, brandishing the jagged neck towards him.

'Wrong am I? You bloody liar! You're gonna get what's comin' ter yer, Cartwright. Nobody meks a fool of Bull Hammond and gets away wi' it.'

He lunged forward and Billy jumped to the side, but not before a jagged edge of the bottle had caught him on the cheek. For a split second Billy froze. Blood from the cut dripped on to his collar. Outraged, he threw himself at Bull, grabbing the arm which held the bottle. They struggled ferociously in the dim light cast from the dying embers of the fire. Alice cowered in fright in the far corner of the room, her body bruised and battered from the beating she had received earlier.

Billy quickly realised he was no match for Bull. Pounding blows rained relentlessly down and he was weakening rapidly. He tried to punch back but Bull avoided most of his efforts, the ones that did strike home having little or no effect. A smash from Bull's fist caught him under his chin and he fell back across the table which disintegrated beneath him. Bull's steel-capped boot caught him in his chest and he cried out in agonising pain. The boot found his legs, then his back near his kidneys. Then everything blackened.

Long after Billy passed out Bull continued to kick relentlessly into his limp body. Finally, exhaustion overtook him. He stood for several moments, panting heavily as he stared down at the broken body below him. He backed away towards the door, sank to his knees then collapsed in a heap.

Shaking uncontrollably, Alice dragged herself up and raced out into the street.

She collided with Peggie strolling home from the dance, preoccupied with wondering where her sister had got to. Alice fell on her, screaming hysterically. 'He's killed him! He killed him!'

Peggie stared at her in shock. 'Killed?' she uttered. 'Who's been killed?' She slapped Alice hard around the face. 'Alice, who's been killed?' she demanded.

Alice's hand shot to her cheek and she stared back toward the cottage. 'Your Billy,' she whimpered. 'Bull's killed your Billy.'

Peggie pushed Alice aside and raced into the cottage. She gasped at the sight that met her. The cottage was a mess of broken furniture and crockery. Bull was slumped on the floor by the door in a drunken stupor, blood from a deep gash on his lip trickling on to the stone slabs. Peggie stepped over him and frantically searched around the darkened room. She clutched her hand to her chest in horror. Lying on the floor, broken bits of table protruding from beneath him, was her brother.

'Billy, Billy!' she cried, stepping quickly towards him. She knelt down beside him, tears of anguish filling her eyes.

'Is he dead?' Alice whispered hovering on the doorstep.

Peggie raised her head. 'Get my father,' she shouted. 'Now, Alice. Fetch my father.'

Doctor Ripon finished wiping his hands and looked across at the anguished gathering staring back at him.

He sighed deeply. 'I'm sorry I haven't better news to tell you. I can only assure you I've done all I can.'

Nell's sorrowful eyes met his. 'He ain't going to die, is he, Doctor?'

Doctor Ripon pursed his lips. 'I won't lie to you, Nell. I don't honestly know. He's in a bad way and it's difficult to tell what internal injuries he's got. But I daren't risk the journey into Leicester to the Royal Infirmary. Not at this stage, at any rate.'

'Not even in the bus?' Sep asked hopefully.

'No,' he replied firmly. He took a breath and picked up his bag. 'I'll be in after surgery tomorrow morning to have another look at his legs. I can't set them properly until the swelling goes down.' He was building their hopes up, he knew. If Billy made it through the night it would be a miracle. By rights he should stay longer, but he couldn't. Two births were imminent and he had several more patients to see to before he returned home where if he was lucky he might snatch an hour's sleep. He sighed deeply. An educated man like himself would never understand why one human being could inflict such damage upon another for whatever reason. Surely there were other ways to resolve grievances?

Sep made to rise. 'Doctor, your fee.'

He waved him aside. 'We'll sort that out later.'

Nell accompanied him to the door and walked the short way with him down the path, glad of the feel of the cool night air.

He stopped at the gate. 'Try and get some sleep, Nell. Do as I say and take it in turns to sit with him. You'll be no good to him exhausted.'

'All right, Doctor,' she whispered.

'Nell?'

She raised her eyes. 'Yes?'

'I'd like to see you about those legs of yours. They trouble you, don't they?'

'Not now, Doctor. When our Billy's better.'

He smiled and patted her arm. 'As you wish.'

She watched him climb into his trap, gee up his horse and trot off.

'Why?' Sep uttered as she re-entered the cottage, closing the door behind her. 'Why did Bull set on Billy like that?' His eyes grew troubled. 'And why was Billy in his house in the first place?' He looked towards Peggie for an answer.

She shrugged her shoulders. 'I dunno, Dad.' How could she tell her father that she had grave suspicions that Bull had somehow found out about her brother and Alice and that's what had provoked him?

Sep rose. 'Well, I can't sit here and wonder. I'm going around to see Alice now and find out. She must know.'

'Sep, you can't,' Nell cried. 'Leave it 'til morning. She's enough on her plate having her husband carted off to jail, let alone 'ote else.'

'I'm sorry, I can't, Nell. I can't wait 'til morning. I want to know why her husband beat my son to within an inch of his life and I'll not rest 'til I get the truth.'

Before she could stop him he had reached the door.

Peggie ran to join him. 'I'll go with him, Mam.'

'No, you stay here with your mother,' he commanded.

He found Alice crouched by the wall in the front room of her cottage, her six children huddled closely by her side. The frightened children stared up at him wide-eyed as he approached, the remains of dried tears still evident upon their little faces. On seeing him they inched closer to their mother.

Stepping across the debris he approached Alice and gasped,

166

horrified, at the sight of her battered face. 'Oh, Alice,' he whispered, shaking his head. 'I'm sorry but I've got to know. Why did Bull do it?'

She stared up at him blankly.

'Alice, please, tell me what happened to cause this?' He squatted down on his haunches and laid a hand gently on her arm.

She absently stroked the top of the baby's head. 'It was Cyrus,' she said distantly. 'It was him who told Bull.'

Sep frowned hard in confusion. 'Cyrus!' He shook his head. 'Cyrus told Bull what?'

She raised her eyes. 'He knew, you see. He'd seen Billy come into the 'ouse when Bull wa' out. He must 'ave bin spying on us.'

Sep gawped. 'Our Billy and you? But you're a married woman!'

'But we love each other, you see. We're going to run away together.' Her eyes travelled down again to the baby and she bent her head and kissed him gently. 'Cyrus told Bull. Said he'd got a right to know. Bull went crazy and made me write Billy a letter.' Her eyes filled with tears and she began to shake. 'I couldn't warn him,' she cried. 'I tried but I couldn't.' Her voice softened and her eyes grew misty. 'But it's all right now, isn't it? Now Bull knows everything, me and Billy can be together.'

Sep clasped his hand to his forehead and closed his eyes tightly. Why had Cyrus instigated all this? What had he hoped to achieve by interfering in people's lives on matters that were none of his business? Maybe his son had been wrong in seeing Alice behind her husband's back but it was not Cyrus's place to inform on them.

An uncontrollable rage built within him. Cyrus had gone too far this time. By his spiteful actions people had been hurt, possibly beyond repair. His own son would be lucky if he made it through the night and this poor woman and her children now had to survive without a husband and father. Crabbe had to be stopped. Stopped once and for all, and Sep himself was going to see that he was.

He stumbled out of the cottage and turned in the direction of Crabbe's house.

So preoccupied was he that he didn't see Letty hiding behind a bush as he passed by her. She stared at him bewildered, worried sick because she was so terribly late, wondering if her father was on his way to find her. But the look on his face . . . She had never seen her father look so upset. Her own face clouded over. An inquisition on her lateness was something she could not face, not tonight, she had enough on her mind coping with her enforced forthcoming marriage. She darted from behind the bush and headed home, hoping she could get inside undetected.

Arriving at the forbidding ivy-covered house at the end of the village, Sep hammered on the door.

'Cyrus Crabbe,' he shouted. 'I want to speak to you, Cyrus Crabbe.'

The door flew open. Cyrus stood on the threshold. 'Well, well,

Septimus Cartwright!' he exclaimed. 'What a pleasant surprise . . .'

Sep pushed him back inside. 'Don't you play games with me. This ain't a social visit.' He flattened Cyrus against the wall, thrusting his face to within an inch of his. 'A' you satisfied now?' he hissed. 'A' you happy you've near got my son killed?'

Cyrus smirked. 'Me? Now how am I supposed to have done that?'

'By causing trouble, like you're always doing, only this time you've gone too far. My lad's lying on his death bed 'cos of you, and Bull Hammond's in jail.'

He pushed Sep forcibly away. 'Are they? Well, it's the first I've heard of it.'

'Don't lie. You're behind all this.'

'Am I? You should be careful what you say. I could have you for slander.'

'Slander! I doubt you know the meaning of the word. Well, I've proof that you're behind all this and I'm going to put a stop to you, Cyrus Crabbe, once and for all.'

Cyrus' face darkened. 'What proof?' he asked, worried.

'Alice. She told me herself . . .'

Cyrus laughed harshly. 'I would have thought a God-fearing man like yourself would know better than to take the word of a slut . . .'

'What's going on, Dad?' Reginald shouted from the top of the stairs.

Cyrus spun round and glared up at him. 'Keep your nose out. I can handle this.' He turned back to Sep. 'You've got the wrong man, Cartwright. Why should I put my business dealings in jeopardy by getting Billy done over?'

Sep stepped back, confused. 'What d'you mean? What business dealings?'

'The business I put your Billy's way, that's what.'

Sep stared. 'You! It was you who enticed Billy to sell stolen goods?'

'Eh, just a minute. Who said anything about stolen goods? If your Billy's been doing that, it's nothing to do with me.' Cyrus stopped and smiled charmingly. He was beginning to enjoy himself. He had Septimus Cartwright just where he wanted him. 'Seems to me for such a family man you know very little of just what that family of yours gets up to. I suppose you're gonna tell me you had no idea Billy's took over where Matterson left off when he scarpered?'

Sep frowned deeply. 'What d'you mean?'

'You know exactly what I mean. You've just told me yerself you know everything your family is doing. In fact, it wouldn't surprise me in the least if you weren't behind it all.'

'Behind what?'

Cyrus clapped his hands together, his eyes sparkling wickedly. 'Of course. Why, that's it. It's a wonder I didn't think of it before. It's your bus that's being used to transport all the contraband that comes into the county via the canal from Manchester and Liverpool. The passenger service is just a ruse to foil the coppers.'

'Oh, that's it. I've had enough.' Sep leapt forward and made a lunge at him, but Cyrus was too quick and darted out of the way.

'You know, we shouldn't be fighting like this. Not when we're about to become family.'

'Family?'

'Oh, Septimus,' he said patronisingly, 'don't yer know about Letty and Reginald? Don't your children tell you anything? Why, our two youngsters are in love, they're getting married.'

He watched in delight as a look of horror settled on Sep's face.

'You're lying. No daughter of mine would ever consider marrying a Crabbe.'

'Wouldn't she? Well, I shouldn't let my son hear yer say that, he'll be right upset. And I don't suppose your Letty will take kindly to you speaking ill of her fiancé.'

Sep clenched his fists, the knuckles showing white. 'I don't believe a word of any of this. No Cartwright would ever voluntarily have any association with a Crabbe.'

Cyrus's face darkened in anger. He walked towards Sep and stood before him. 'No Cartwright would have any association with a Crabbe, eh? Is that right!' His eyes narrowed icily. 'Well, you just ask that precious wife of yours what she was getting up to while you were away during the war.'

Sep froze. 'What . . . what d'you mean?'

'Just what I said. Ask her who was keeping her warm at night? Ask her who satisfied her needs? And believe me, your wife takes a lot of satisfying.'

Sep stared at him wildly. 'Liar!' he spat. 'You liar. My Nell wouldn't.'

'Wouldn't she? Well, you just ask her. Go on, ask her. And if she denies it, then she's the liar.'

Blind rage flared up. A rage so intense it filled his being, a feeling so alien he was powerless to control it. Sep brought back his arm and smashed his fist in the middle of Cyrus's face.

He fell back against the wall. 'You bastard! You've broke my nose. I'll have you for this,' he shouted, wiping a stream of blood from his face.

'You'll have me for murder,' Sep erupted, lunging forward. 'My wife would never have anything to do with you.'

Cyrus stepped quickly out of reach. 'Wouldn't she? Well, let me tell you, she practically dragged me into her bed. And if yer don't believe me, just ask her how her legs are. How would I know about them if I hadn't seen 'em with me own eyes? Why don't yer face it, Septimus? Your precious family's so thick with the Crabbes you could spread it on bread.' He laughed harshly. 'And you so righteous, so well respected, when all the time your Billy's a thief, your wife's an adulteress and . . .'

But Sep could take no more. He rushed blindly from the house,

Cyrus's laughter echoing in his ears. The only thing he'd lived for, worked for, believed in – his wife and children – were a living lie. He didn't know them, had never known them. How could he have done if all this had been happening behind his back?

He found himself at the bridge and stared blindly down into the dark running water. 'Oh, God,' he groaned in despair. How could he have been so blind as to have all this happening and himself not aware of any of it? But worse, far worse than Billy's thieving or Letty's relationship with Reginald, was the very idea of Nell, his beloved Nell, with that . . . that dreadful specimen of a man. The thought of them intimately together sickened him more than anything had ever done before.

'Oh, Nell, Nell, how could you?' he cried distraught. 'How could you do this to me when you know I love you so much? And with him, of all people.'

He placed his hand on the edge of the bridge and leaned over.

Peggie was roused several hours later as daylight began to seep through the tiny windows of her parents' bedroom. Memories of the previous night flooded back. Still stunned about the happenings she looked down at her brother and sighed in relief. He was still breathing.

He moved just a fraction but the effort was enough to make him groan in agony.

'It's all right, Billy,' she soothed, her hand hovering, not daring to touch in case it caused him further pain. 'It's me, Peggie. You're going to be all right. We're all here with you. Now just try to sleep. The doctor's coming back shortly.'

She fought back the tears as she scanned his body. A body once so handsome, so filled with life. What lay in her parents' bed was a broken man, covered in black bruises and deep abrasions. She just prayed he would heal, that her Billy, her lovely, lovely brother, would be returned to her whole. But at this moment at least they could be thankful he was still alive. That in itself brought hope.

Stiff with fatigue she made her way into the kitchen, finding her mother huddled in the chair by the dead fire. There was no sign of her father and Peggie frowned as she knelt down and began to rake the ashes.

Nell opened her eyes. 'Billy?'

'It's all right, Mam. He's sleeping.'

Nell groaned in relief. She gazed around her. 'Where's your dad?'

Peggie shook her head. 'I don't know,' she said worriedly. 'He never came back last night.'

Chapter Fifteen

Nell's eyes flew towards Peggie the moment she entered the door but she knew immediately by her daughter's grave expression that she had been unsuccessful.

'Oh, Peggie. Where is he?' she said, slumping down in a chair.

She shook her head. 'I don't know, Mam. I've searched all over, so have Primrose and Letty, and no one has seen hide nor hair of him.'

Nell bent her head in despair, wringing her hands tightly. 'Oh, Peggie, I can't cope with this, not on top of our Billy, I can't. What the hell are we going to do?'

Peggie rushed forward and knelt before her, grasping her hands in hers. 'We have to cope, Mam. Billy needs us and Dad'll turn up when he's ready. Going off is probably his way of coping with the shock.'

Nell slowly nodded. 'I hope you're right, 'cos if anything should happen to him . . .'

'I know, Mam. I know. But I'm sure he'll be fine and come back when he's ready,' she said with conviction.

Peggie knew it wouldn't do to let her mother see how worried she actually was. Her father's disappearance was most unusual. Any Cartwright catastrophes in the past had been dealt with and seen through together. So why had her father turned away from them now?

She looked at her mother searchingly. 'Mam, it's just a thought. But you don't think he's gone to Aunty Cissie's?'

Nell shook her head. 'My sister has never spoken to me since the day our mother died and she found out I'd been left her wedding ring. She were eaten up with jealousy and said some dreadful things to me. We ain't seen each other since. No, he wouldn't go there.' She sighed in sorrow and raised pitiful eyes. 'He's no family left to turn to apart from us, so where's he gone, Peggie? Where's he gone? He left with nothing, not even his coat. How's he going to manage?'

Peggie shrugged her shoulders helplessly, slowly rose, shook the kettle and put it back on the hob. She frowned. Her father was not the only one who had disappeared. Alice and her six children were nowhere to be found either and she worried for a fleeting moment that for whatever the reason they had departed together. No, that thought was silly. Her father was hiding somewhere whilst he came to terms with the shock he had received and in the meantime it was up to her, as the eldest, to keep things going until he returned, which she prayed would not be long.

She turned to her mother. 'I'll just pop and see Billy, then get some food on the go. Letty and Primrose will be home in a minute. They've gone to check up the shed again, just in case.'

Nell inclined her head absently towards the table. 'Mrs Hubbard dropped round earlier and brought us a pie. I don't know what's in it, but it were good of her all the same. You could heat that up if you fancy. I can't manage 'ote. Food'd choke me at the moment.' She sniffed back a tear. 'Saddie Adkins and Aggie, and Jenny Pegg came by to offer their help. But I said we could manage.'

Peggie smiled. 'That were good of 'em,' she said sincerely.

She found Billy no different from when she had left early that morning with her sisters to scour the village. The doctor had been and Peggie could see where he had applied fresh bandages. The swelling on Billy's legs had not abated sufficiently enough for his legs to be set and they had been secured as best as possible so that he, in his delirium, did not inflict any further damage on himself.

She picked up a piece of clean flannel, dipped it in a bowl of cold water and moistened his lips, careful not to reopen any of the cuts.

She gasped as she saw one eye flicker and partially open. 'Billy, Billy, it's me, Peggie,' she whispered, full of emotion. 'You're going to be fine, just fine. Try to keep still, there's a good lad.'

His cracked lips, still congealed with dried blood, parted slightly. 'Am I gonna die, Peggie? Am I gonna die?' he whispered urgently.

His words, barely audible, cut her to the core.

'No. No,' she cried. 'You're in a bad way, but you're not going to die. Now please, please, don't try to move or you'll damage yourself further.' She grabbed the bottle of medicine the doctor had left. 'Try to take some of this,' she soothed, spooning a little into his mouth. 'It'll help you sleep.'

He gurgled, spluttered and began to choke, his body shuddering in excruciating pain. She watched in helplessness, hoping the medicine quickly did its job.

When the spasm was over, his eyes flickered again. 'Oh, Peggie,' he murmured. 'A' you still there, Peggie?'

'I'm here, Billy,' she said, kneeling down next to him.

He swallowed with great difficulty. 'I feel like a herd of elephants has jumped all over me.'

'You will for a while. But we're all here with you. We'll all help make you better,' she said, desperately fighting an urge to embrace him in comfort.

'It were Bull. He did this to me.'

She nodded her head. 'We know.'

He tried to turn his head towards her. 'It were no more than I deserve.'

'No, you're wrong, Billy, wrong,' she cried. 'A thumping probably, but you didn't deserve this.'

Silence prevailed for a while before he uttered, 'How's Alice?'

Peggie gulped. Billy was in no fit state to hear any bad news about their father or Alice's disappearance. 'Er . . . she's fine, just fine. And the children.' She paused momentarily. 'Bull can't hurt you no more, Billy, nor can he Alice. He's in jail and he'll be there a long time.' She heard him sigh in relief. 'Now please try and get some sleep.'

He tried to raise his arm but failed. 'Peggie, promise me. If 'ote should happen to me, make sure Alice gets any money I'm due. Make sure she's taken care of.'

Tears rushed to her eyes and frustrated anger rose up. 'Billy Cartwright, you're not going to die. D'you hear me? You're not going to die. We've a bus company to run and we can't manage without you.' She swallowed hard to rid the lump in her throat. 'Besides, you daft ha'porth, we all love you.'

She watched as he tried to smile. 'You're a bossy bugger, Peggie Cartwright.' He spoke slowly, fighting for each word. 'No, you're right, I can't die, can I? You still owe me thirty shilling.' His eye closed, he groaned and appeared to fall asleep.

Awkwardly rising, she stared down at him for several moments. She shuddered at the sight of the ugly gash on his face closed tight with several large stitches surrounded by swelling and nasty bruising. Billy would always bear the scars of his ordeal no matter how well his other injuries healed. She turned as her mother came through the door and managed a reassuring smile.

'He spoke to me, Mam,' she whispered lightly. 'He asked if you were all right. I gave him some medicine and he's gone back to sleep.'

Nell's face lit up as a surge of hope flooded through her. 'He spoke to you? Oh, Peggie, that's a good sign, ain't it? Doctor Ripon said he could be unconscious for ages. Well, if he spoke then he's on the mend. That must mean he's going to be all right.'

Peggie placed her arm around her shoulder. ''Course he is, Mam. He's got us to look after him, ain't he?'

Nell nodded. 'I'll sit with him while you get something to eat.'

She looked at her mother in concern. 'What about you? You need to keep your strength up.'

'Later,' Nell replied, patting her arm.

Knowing it was useless to argue, Peggie left her settling herself in the chair by the bed, the cold compress cloth in her hand in readiness, and returned to the kitchen. Letty and Primrose stared up at her worriedly. She quickly told them about Billy and they both sighed deeply in relief. Primrose started to cry.

'Oh, Peggie,' she wailed. 'I miss me dad. Where is he?'

Letty moved her chair closer, placed her arm around Primrose's shoulder and pulled her close. She looked across at Peggie, her face deeply concerned.

'People are saying that Bull beat our Billy up 'cos he was knocking off Alice. Is that true, Peggie? Is it true?'

Peggie inhaled sharply. 'Knocking off! I'll give 'em knocking off.

Our Billy went to help Alice, that's how he got beat up,' she lied. 'And you make sure you tell them that. Bloody gossips. You can't do a good turn round here without people twisting it round.'

Primrose's sobs grew louder. 'Dad. Oh, Dad, where are you?' She suddenly stopped, then asked the question that had crossed all their minds. 'He ain't dead, Peggie, is he? He ain't dead?'

'Dead!' Peggie erupted. 'If he was dead we'd have a body to bury, wouldn't we?' She stopped abruptly and her body sagged. 'I'm sorry, I'm sorry,' she said, lowering herself down in a chair opposite. 'I shouldn't have shouted.'

'What about our Ronnie? Shouldn't he be told about all this?' Letty asked.

Peggie shook her head. 'No. He's got enough with his job. It's not as though he can do anything. So unless absolutely necessary, we say nothing when we write.'

Letty nodded. 'Okay, if you think that's best.'

Peggie folded her arms, her face set firmly. 'Look, girls, I know this is going to be hard, but we're going to have to be strong for Mam's sake. She's enough on her plate without trying to comfort us as well. We've got to try and keep things going.'

'Going?' Letty asked. 'How?'

'I don't know.' She shook her head. 'I really don't know. But we've got to try.' She rose, walked across to the door and took her coat off the hook. 'I'm going for a walk. I'm gonna try and sort some things out in my mind. In the meantime, try and be cheerful and act normal for Mam's sake.'

They both stared across at her and nodded, glad that someone was taking charge. Letty let go of Primrose and rushed over to join Peggie by the door. She pulled her aside.

'I really need to talk to you, Peggie.'

Peggie sighed. 'Not now, Letty. I've too much on me mind to waste time gossiping. We'll chat later, eh?'

Letty sighed. 'All right. It'll keep.'

As Peggie departed Nell plodded heavily through carrying a bowl of water and a wet towel. Silently, her face lined in worry and grief, she made her way over to the sink, washed out the bowl and refilled it with clean water, seemingly unaware of anyone else in the room.

Letty stared after her. She so desperately needed to unburden her troubles. She knew she shouldn't bother her mother at a time like this but her problem could not wait.

'Mam, can I speak to you for a minute, please?'

Nell looked across at her blankly. 'Eh? Oh, not now, er . . . er . . . Letty. I must concentrate on Billy. He's the one that needs me now.'

'But, Mam, I have a problem . . .'

'Oh, you've always got problems, Letty. This problem of yours can't be as important as our Bill's welfare, now can it?' She turned away from Letty and headed for the bedroom, not noticing the

174

water she was slopping on to the floor. 'Go out and play or something, Letty, and stop being selfish,' she added as she left the room.

'Play!' Letty exclaimed in disbelief. Had her mother forgotten she was twenty-five years of age? She slumped down into her mother's rocking chair and stared transfixed into the fire, an overwhelming feeling of foreboding settling upon her.

Peggie let herself into the shed and stared hard at the two vehicles facing her. For the last hour, pacing up and down the isolated edge of a field, wearing a deep groove in the mud, she had mulled over and over their immediate problems until her head ached. And the answer to it all was here.

The business her father had built up must not be allowed to slide in his absence. Keeping it running would help pay the bills and for Billy's medical care, and also make sure her father had something to return to. It was going to be hard, she wasn't sure even if she could manage, but she was determined to try. Besides, she thought ruefully, despite last night's events, people would still be expecting the bus to appear in the morning to take them to work. Well, that's what they would have and she would be driving it.

To be prepared for the morning she would need to take it out for a practice run, before now she had only driven it with her father present, and it would have to be now before the evening drew in.

Stripping off her coat, she pulled on a pair of her father's old dungarees over her skirt, gathered her hair as best she could in a ball and shoved it underneath his cap which he had forgotten to take home the previous night. Grabbing the starting handle, she slotted it into place, then stood back.

'Now you'd better start,' she said, wagging a finger severely at the bus. 'Else I'm warning you.'

Bending down, she took hold of the crank handle with both hands and, using all her strength, yanked it round. The bus must have heard her warning. It roared deafeningly into life.

Peggie exhaled in relief. 'Thank you,' she said gratefully.

She propped open the wooden doors of the shed and clambered aboard. The hand brake was stiff and it took several attempts to release it. That done, she selected the gear and, holding her breath, her hands gripping the steering wheel tightly, gently pressed her foot against the gas pedal. The bus inched forward. Slowly and carefully she eased it out of the shed and down the yard.

Once out of the village, she faced a deserted dirt road and felt brave enough to increase her speed to the maximum fifteen miles an hour. Exhilaration filled her as the hedgerows sped by.

'I'm doing it. I'm actually doing it by myself,' she spoke proudly aloud, her mind so filled with the difficult task in hand, her problems were temporarily forgotten.

She relaxed back a little in her seat and dared to look around her. The night was drawing in and in the distance the trees looked eerie as they swayed in the chilly autumnal wind. Golden yellow and orange leaves fluttered down and were filling the ditches and lining the roads. Winter would soon be upon them and she sincerely hoped it would not be a harsh one.

She realised she would have to make tracks home before it got too dark, not wanting to become lost on unfamiliar roads, and looked for a place to turn the bus around. Suddenly she frowned, her attention drawn back to the bus. It was slowing down. She increased the pressure on the gas pedal but to no avail. The bus crawled to a halt and the engine died.

She stared, confused, wondering what was wrong. Jumping down, she ran around to the front and pushed up the bonnet, standing on tip toes to peer inside, not really understanding what she was looking for. Nothing looked wrong, nothing seemed loose. She twiddled with several parts as she had seen her father and Billy do, then tried the crank handle again. But still nothing happened.

She stepped back and stared helplessly up and down the deserted road.

Suddenly from out of nowhere a figure loomed in the darkness. 'Can I help you, sonny?' a firm male voice asked.

Peggie jumped in surprise and her hat fell off. 'Sonny?' she said indignantly. 'I'll thank you to note I'm a woman, not a sonny!'

The man gasped at the sight of her golden mane tumbling past her shoulders, tendrils catching in the wind. 'No,' he agreed, 'you're not. I'm sorry for the mistake. Well, can I help or not?'

'Not if you can't fix that, you can't,' she replied sharply, turning towards the bus.

Without a word the man stuck his head under the bonnet, quickly surveying what he could in the darkness. He poked a few things and prodded others. Bending down, he tried the crank handle. When nothing happened but a loud grating noise and a splutter, he strode round and climbed aboard, peering down at the gauges. He jumped down and rejoined her.

He shook his head gravely. 'Well, it's pretty serious, but . . .'

'Oh, no!' Peggie cried.

Suddenly everything was too much. All the events of the previous night and now this final blow was more than she could bear. Tears of anguish filled her eyes and flowed down her cheeks. She crumpled to the hard ground and doubled over, sobbing loudly.

Bemused, he knelt down beside her and placed his arms around her. 'I'm a good listener if you want to tell me about it.'

Peggie made to pull free but her grief was too strong, the comfort his arms gave so welcome, and despite herself, and still sobbing uncontrollably, she told the stranger all. About Billy; about her father's bewildering disappearance; about how it was up to her to keep the business going until things got back to normal; and lastly of Harry and how she still missed him so terribly. As she finished, she realised just what she had done. She had bared her soul, spilling all the family problems and more, leaving nothing unsaid, to a man she had never seen before in her life. Embarrassment and remorse filled her. Her family would be horrified if they knew.

'I'm so sorry,' she apologised abruptly, struggling to her feet. 'I shouldn't burden you with my problems. Especially with you being a stranger.' She turned towards the bus and stared worriedly at it. 'Oh, God, I don't know what I'm going to do,' she uttered helplessly.

'I can fix it for you.'

She spun round on her heel to face him. 'You can?' she cried, her face lighting up with delight. 'Oh, thank you. Thank you,' she added in gratitude.

He turned from her, bent down and scanned his eyes around the vehicle. His object located, he walked towards it, unhooked it from the tail board and unscrewed the top.

She stared at him. 'That's the spare petrol can,' she said, confused.

'I know,' he replied sheepishly. 'I was having a bit of fun when I said the damage was serious but you interrupted before I could finish.'

'Fun!' she exclaimed as humiliation rose up in her. 'How dare you have fun at my expense?' She reddened painfully. How could she have been so stupid as to have run out of petrol? This man must think her an idiot.

She leapt forward and grabbed the can from him, slopping some of the petrol on the ground. 'I can manage, thank you.'

'It's no trouble . . .'

'I said, I can manage, thank you,' she insisted, trying to salvage some of her pride.

'If you're sure.' He turned from her and walked away, soon to be lost in the darkness.

Seated once more behind the wheel, the engine ticking over, her mind returned to the man. Where had he come from? And where had he gone to? He seemed to have vanished into thin air. And fancy her baring her soul like that! She smiled wanly. She did feel better though, so maybe that was something. But how rude she had been, how ungrateful. Not once had she thanked him for his help. She shrugged her shoulders. Still he was gone now and it was too late for remorse. It was no good worrying about someone she would never see again.

She raised her head and stared out into the darkness. She knew one thing for sure. She knew without a doubt she would never be able to operate the bus service on her own. It was one thing taking the vehicle for a drive, even with passengers on board, but another coping with the repairs and endless other things involved. She needed help – a man's help. Someone who could do the things she couldn't. But where would she find someone with mechanical knowledge at short notice? And, more importantly, one who wouldn't want paying.

She had to get home, she needed to re-think her plans, needed to feel what was left of her family around her. Her spirits lifted. Maybe her father had returned. Then everything would be all right. She released the brake and pressed her foot down on the gas pedal.

It began to drizzle and this turned into a downpour. The canopy overhead did not stop the rain from coming in through the sides of the driving cab and by the time she got back it was very late and she was soaked to the skin. It was a hopeless task attempting to manoeuvre the bus inside the shed in the pitch darkness with the rain lashing down, so she left it outside in the yard, hoping Mr Brotherhood would not be too put out.

The cottage appeared deserted when she entered, the only light coming from the remains of the fire. Frantically she checked around, gratefully finding Letty and Primrose huddled together asleep in their bed. There was still no sign of her father. She poked her head around her mother's bedroom door. Billy was asleep; her mother huddled in the chair by the bed still clutching a damp cloth with which to wipe his brow.

On hearing the door her eyes fluttered open. 'That you, Sep?' she muttered.

'It's me, Mam,' Peggie spoke softly.

'Oh,' Nell muttered forlornly. Her body sagged and her eyes drooped shut again.

Peggie was distressed at the exhausted state her mother was in. She sighed heavily, pulled shut the door and made her way back into the kitchen.

She thankfully stripped off her wet clothes, hung them over the drying cradle and wrapped herself inside her father's old army grey coat that was hanging on the back of the door. Making herself a mug of tea, she sank gratefully into the armchair and closed her eyes.

She was woken several hours later by a persistent tapping on the window. She jolted upright, trying to focus in the darkness, then stared terrified at the face pressed against the glass pane. The grotesque apparition seemed to be grinning at her and a finger was pointing towards the door.

She inched herself up, pulled the coat firmly round herself and walked gingerly over, opening the door just a crack.

'Who's there?' she demanded.

'Is this the Cartwrights' residence?'

'Er . . . yes?'

'Good, then I'm reporting for work.'

'Pardon?' she uttered, confused, opening the door just a fraction wider.

There was a pause. 'Look, I'm freezing out here, can I come in?'

Peggie hesitated. 'Just a moment. Let me light the lamp.'

That done she returned to the door and pulled it open.

A man entered, dropping a large canvas navvy's holdall on the floor.

'Brrr,' he said, shuddering, rubbing his hands together. 'That's better.'

178

'You're . . . you're the man who helped me last night,' she said, her brow crinkling in surprise as for the first time she looked at him properly.

He was tall and broad-shouldered, but not nearly as handsome as Harry had been and his shock of thick brown hair was in need of a cut and brush. His clothes looked oddly out of place, as though they had been plucked from a washing line in the hope that they fit. The trousers too short, the jacket too tight and his shirt was straining across his chest. There was something wrong about him, something that didn't quite fit. She felt sure he'd looked better dressed the night before, but couldn't be sure, it had been dark. But the brown eyes twinkling down at her were warm and the fear she had felt, the hesitation she had shown a moment before, flew from her.

He grinned mischievously, showing slightly crooked but very white teeth. 'Dan . . . er . . . Dickinson, at your service.'

'But what are you doing here? And how did you find us?'

'Oh, that was easy. I just asked for the family who owned the motorbus from a woman pumping water at the other end of the village and she pointed me here. And you need help, don't you? You told me that last night. So here I am.'

'Shush!' Peggie whispered sharply. 'Don't ever let on to my family that you know our business. I was upset last night. I didn't know what I was saying. And you didn't help, kidding me on like that.'

Dan's face fell. 'And you don't need any help now?'

'Oh, yes, yes I do. But I don't know whether you can. Not the kind of help we need at any rate.' She looked at him quizzically. 'Although you did seem to know about engines . . .'

He nodded. 'A fair bit. And I can drive,' he added.

'You can drive?'

He nodded.

'Oh!' exclaimed Peggie. She couldn't believe her luck. She had prayed for this and it seemed her prayers had been answered. She pursed her lips. 'But I don't know anything about you.'

He held out his hands. 'What do you need to know? I'm twenty-nine years old, honest, reliable, I don't mind hard work. I've travelled a fair bit and have been lucky to get work with the kind of people who can afford motors so I learned all I could about them. 'Course, I can't prove any of this so you'll have to take my word for it.'

She eyed him searchingly. He did seem nice enough and he looked honest, but then their Billy had looked honest, as though butter wouldn't melt in his mouth, and look what he used to get up to and what subsequently happened because of that. But she needed somebody, so she would have to take a chance.

She took a breath and folded her arms. 'I need someone to help with the deliveries and the maintenance of the vehicles. Just until my father returns and my brother gets better. That means heavy

179

lifting and long hours.' She paused thoughtfully. 'I'm not sure whether the other lorry is in full working order yet.'

'I could have a look at it for you.'

'Could you?' She scratched her chin. 'But there's one big problem.'

'Oh?'

'I can't offer you much in wages, if anything in fact. I have my brother's medical bills to pay and . . . and . . .'

He smiled, walked towards her and placed his hand on her arm. 'Board and lodging will do for now and we'll see how it works out, eh?'

She averted her eyes, conscious of the effect his presence was having on her. She felt feelings beginning to stir that she had long forgotten. She pushed them away. 'Well, I don't know where we're going to put you.' She thought for a moment. He could use her brothers' room. At the moment it was empty and she couldn't see Billy moving rooms for a long time yet. But her mother would need to use that once she could be prised away from his side. Her eyes settled on the recess by the welsh dresser. 'Would a mattress do for now in the corner? It's not much but it's the best I can offer.'

Dan nodded. 'That'd be fine.'

'Well, if you're sure . , er . . .'

'Dan.'

'Dan,' she repeated, raising her eyes to his and smiling. 'But why? Why are you willing to do all this for us?'

Dan exhaled loudly. 'My word, woman, you do ask a lot of questions. If I was in your shoes I'd just accept my help before I change my mind. Will you settle for the fact that I need a roof over my head and food in my stomach and I'm willing to exchange that for my services?'

Peggie stared at him. That seemed a reasonable explanation to her. And he was right, she was in no position to refuse. 'Well, yes, I'll accept that.'

'Good, I'm glad that's settled. Now just one other thing?'

'Oh?'

Dan smiled. 'What do I call you?'

'Call me? Oh, I see. Miss Cartwright – Peggie.' She grinned. 'Peggie will do. But don't think that gives you the right to be familiar.'

'I wouldn't dream of it,' he replied gravely and held out his hand which she accepted. 'Pleased to meet you, Peggie. Now I wouldn't say no to a cup of tea before I start. Would you like me to make the fire,' his eyes twinkled at her, 'while you get dressed?'

Her eyes travelled down to her father's coat and she blushed, realising that she had not one stitch on underneath. Her clothes were hanging above them on the washing cradle but she was not going to face the embarrassment of getting them down in front of him. Letting him see what she wore underneath.

'You'll find the sticks and the coal in the yard,' she said

180

abruptly, rushing from the room.

Arriving in the bedroom she shook Letty hard. 'Get up, Letty, get up. We have a man downstairs. Dan his name is and I want you to be civil to him.'

Letty forced her eyes open. 'Eh! What? Has he come with news about Dad?'

'No, no. He's going to help us – work for us. Just 'til Dad comes home and Billy gets better. He's a Godsend, Letty, an absolute Godsend. So you make sure you treat him right while he's with us.' She leaned over Letty and shook Primrose. 'Get up,' she said firmly. 'I need some fresh water from the pump and some milk fetching.'

Primrose groaned and turned over and Peggie shook her again. 'What time is it?' she moaned.

'Six o'clock, and I've a bus to get out in half an hour.'

She turned to Letty who had reluctantly risen and was sitting with her legs over the edge of the bed. 'Leave Mam to sleep, she looks fair whacked out. You can explain what's happening after I've gone.'

Letty grunted, rubbing the sleep from her eyes. 'And what about my work?'

Peggie stopped abruptly. She had forgotten about that, and her own. She thought rapidly then took a breath. 'I'm sorry, Letty,' she said firmly, 'but we've stopped working at the factory from now. We wanted to leave anyway. Your job is to stay at home and help Mam by running things from this end. And while she looks after Billy, you can do her job at Mrs Pegg's.'

Letty sniffed. 'That's all right with me. I'd have been leaving the factory soon anyway.'

'Why? What d'you mean?'

'Nothing. I'll tell you later,' she replied flatly. Now was not the right time to discuss her problem with Primrose in the room.

'And what about me? What job will I be doing?' she asked.

Peggie frowned at her. 'Going to school.'

'Ah, Peggie . . .'

'School. And I don't want to find out you haven't been else you'll get a thick ear from me.' Her voice softened. 'If you behave yourself, I might let you come conductressing sometimes.'

She turned on her heel and entered her brothers' room, rummaging through Billy's clothes. Having selected what she wanted, she dressed and returned to the kitchen.

Primrose had already fetched the water and gone off to get the milk. Peggie was surprised. For once her little sister hadn't needed telling twice. Letty was cooking porridge.

She turned and stared at Peggie just as Dan came through the back door, carrying a bucket of coal.

'I filled this up for you for later.'

'Thanks,' Letty said, smiling graciously at him.

He put the bucket down then noticed Peggie. He began to laugh.

181

'What's wrong?' she snapped.

'What's wrong? It's you that's all wrong. You told me yesterday you were a woman.'

'And so I am.'

'Well, why are you dressed like that?' he guffawed.

She stared down at her attire. She had on Billy's best Sunday shirt, that strained across her chest, his trousers, which bunched at her ankles, and his jacket which hid her hands.

'I thought I looked more like a driver.' Her face set firmly. 'I just thought I'd be taken more seriously if I dressed like a man,' she said crossly.

Dan shook his head. 'You look like a clown. Peggie, wear your own clothes. People will be too glad you've turned up to bother about what you're wearing, and if they're that bothered they can walk.'

She stared at him, unsure what to do. But she knew he was right, that she looked ridiculous. But still she felt annoyed that he had dared to talk to her that way.

'I suppose you're right. But I'll thank you not to get familiar with me. You being an employee,' she added haughtily.

Letty raised her eyebrows and fought to restrain her mouth. Her sister did look a sight. But another thing was apparent. Peggie liked this Dan whether she realised it or not.

'Porridge anyone?' Letty asked casually.

Peggie dressed in her own clothes of a brown woollen calf-length skirt, high-necked cream blouse and green jacket which flared out from the waist finishing just short of her hips. After giving instructions to Dan to check over the other lorry and assess what still needed doing, she left the cottage.

She drew the bus carefully to a halt just as several passengers were beginning to gather. There was no sign of Crabbe's brake and she was grateful for that. She jumped down and walked round to join them. They looked at her sympathetically.

'Is it true what we've 'eard?' a woman asked.

Peggie nodded.

The woman turned to a fellow traveller and tightened her lips. 'Madman. I always said that Bull Hammond 'ud go too far one day. 'E deserves jail, 'e does. 'Ope he rots there,' she spat. She turned back to Peggie. 'Tell yer mam, if there's 'ote we can do.'

Several other people mumbled in agreement and Peggie smiled wanly in gratitude.

A man frowned at her. 'Where's yer dad, Peggie?'

'Oh,' she spoke lightly, 'he's . . . er . . . had to go and visit a dying relative. In Scotland,' she added before she had time to think. 'He's gone on the train.'

'Scotland! Scotland, eh? Never knew he had people in Scotland.'

Several other people arrived and they all whispered between themselves.

Peggie took a deep breath. 'Well, if you'd all like to get aboard, we can be off.'

Just then Reginald Crabbe arrived on the brake. He pulled to a halt, glared at Peggie, then at the bus, and quickly sized up the situation.

'Doing a man's job now, a' yer, Peggie Cartwright?'

She scowled deeply. 'And what if I am? There's n'ote in the rule book that says driving's just for men.'

Several people looked at her nervously and began to move towards Crabbe's brake. The others milled around, unsure what to do.

'I wouldn't trust a woman,' he shouted across. 'What if yer broke down? What happens then?' he said, eyeing her mockingly.

Her temper rose sharply and she turned to the crowd. 'Has this bus ever broken down while you've been travelling on it?'

'No,' they all mumbled.

'Have we ever left you stranded like Crabbe's do in the pouring rain?'

'No,' they all answered, shaking their heads.

'Well, how d'yer know she can drive?' Reginald demanded.

The crowd looked at Peggie, unsure, then at Reginald, then back to Peggie.

'That's right, we don't know she can drive, do we?' someone said loudly.

Peggie fought to control her rising temper. 'For your information I was taught by the best – me dad. And us women can drive better than a man any day. We're more careful for a start.' She reared back her head, unable to control herself any longer. 'And you can talk, Reginald Crabbe. You drive that brake like a madman. Anyone travelling with you risks their life!'

'She's right, he does,' Hannah Willett said, nudging her friend Lilly in the ribs. 'I nearly fell off the other week when he took that corner too sharp. Remember, Lilly? You grabbed me coat and saved me.'

'That's right, I did. Oh, I'm fed up with this, we'll be late for work,' Lilly grumbled loudly. 'Follow me, gels. I going wi' Cartwrights. You blokes can please yerselves.' She grabbed her husband's arm. ''Cept you, you're coming wi' me.'

Peggie exhaled slowly in relief as all but a handful clambered aboard, following Lilly's lead. She turned towards Reginald who was still perched in his seat, his face thunderous. She nodded her head and smiled before turning back towards the bus.

She had collected the fares and was just about to move off when she saw Aggie racing towards her.

'Oh, I thought I'd missed yer,' she said breathlessly. Then her mouth gaped as she realised it was Peggie in the driving seat.

'What the . . .'

'Don't ask,' Peggie commanded. 'I'll explain it all later.'

* * *

183

The following Saturday night Peggie sat at the kitchen table dividing the weekly takings into neat piles. One for rent, food and so on, until all the money was accounted for. A small collection of coins lay in front of her. She smiled in pleasure. Profit. Not much but still a profit. She gathered the coins in her hand and put them in a tin.

'Not bad for the first week,' she said, addressing Letty who was standing by the table folding clean washing ready for ironing.

Primrose came through the door struggling with a heavy bucket. She plonked it on the floor by the sink, slopping some of the water on to the floor, straightened up and blew out her cheeks.

'Right,' she said, addressing Peggie sullenly, 'I've swept the floor, shook the rugs and got the water in. Can I read my comic now?'

'No, go and see if Mam and Billy want a drink, then you can,' Peggie said, without raising her eyes.

Primrose scowled. 'Why is it always me?' she grumbled.

'Well, I can't very well do it, can I?' Letty spoke sharply. 'I'm doing the ironing,' she said, as she picked up the hot iron from the fire and spat on it. 'You can do the ironing if you want?' she offered. 'And I'll make the tea.'

Peggie made to scold them both but stopped as Dan came through the back door.

'All finished?' she asked, smiling.

He nodded. 'I've jacked them both up and put oil lamps underneath.'

She frowned. 'Oh? Why?'

He grinned. 'To keep them warm, Peggie. It's going to be cold tonight and if an engine is started from cold you're asking for trouble. Jacking up the wheels overcomes the resistance of the transmission and epicyclic gearbox and allows the engine to turn more freely.'

'Pardon!' she exclaimed, then sniffed haughtily. 'Oh, I see. Good thinking.' She shot Letty a warning glance, then turned her attentions back to Dan. She smiled and pushed several silver coins towards him. 'It's not much, Dan . . .'

He waved it away. 'Our bargain was for food and board. You still have medical bills to pay.'

'But it's the least I can do. You've worked so hard . . .'

'Peggie, please, stop going on. A bargain is a bargain. Now if it's all right with you, I'll get cleaned up and be off.'

'Off?'

'Yes, I'm going to the pub for a pint. I'm, er . . . meeting a friend and staying the night. I won't be back until late tomorrow.'

Peggie looked at him closely. She hadn't realised he knew anyone round these parts.

'That's all right with you, isn't it?' he asked out of courtesy.

'Yes, why shouldn't it be?' she replied curtly. 'Your free time's your own.'

184

He smiled. 'May I use Billy's room to wash and change?'

'Yes, of course. Use that jug for the water, the kettle should be hot. There's soap and a towel by the washstand.'

When he had gathered his things and left, Letty leaned across the table. 'I wonder if it's a lady friend?' she whispered.

'I wouldn't know and I don't care,' Peggie bristled, gathering the coins together and putting them in another tin.

'Don't you? Doesn't look that way to me,' she said, returning her attention to the task in hand.

Peggie's eyes flashed. 'I happen to be in mourning, for your information, and don't you forget that.'

Letty tutted loudly. 'For three years? Oh, for goodness' sake, Peggie, it's about time you faced facts. Harry's dead and you fancy Dan like crazy.' She folded an ironed sheet and picked up a blouse.

'I do not,' her sister snapped coldly. 'I know nothing about him, not even where he comes from, and whenever I approach him he changes the subject.'

'Yes, I noticed. Very fishy that. But it still doesn't stop you fancying him, does it?'

'Oh, shut up, Letty. For all we know he could already be married?'

Letty frowned thoughtfully. 'D'you think he is?'

'How should I know? I employed him for his skills not his marital status.'

'Well, you should know. As you said, it was you who employed him.'

'I had no choice but to take him on, he was the only one available.' Peggie eyed her sharply. '`A' you saying I shouldn't have?'

'I'm not saying 'ote of the kind. I'm just making a point that he could be anyone. He could be a murderer for all you know.'

'A murderer!' Peggie exclaimed in alarm. 'Why d'you say that?'

'No reason. I happen to think he's rather nice, actually. I'm just saying if it'd been me, I'd have checked him out first, just to be sure.'

Peggie's temper rose. She jumped up and placed her hand flat on the table. 'Oh, you would have, would you? Well, I tell you what, Letty, in future if we have to hire anybody else, *you* can do it. In fact from now on you can take over the running of the business, 'cos I've had enough.'

Letty blew out her cheeks in horror. 'Oh, our Maggie, you know I can't,' she cried. 'I can't drive for a start.'

'Well, you should have thought about that before you shot your big mouth off. And fancy insinuating Dan was a murderer.'

They both froze as they heard footsteps on the stairs and Dan appeared carrying his bag. He eyed them both.

'Everything all right?' he asked, advancing into the room. 'Only I heard raised voices.'

They looked at each other.

185

'Er . . . yes, yes,' Peggie replied, reddening. 'We were just discussing a few things, that's all. Weren't we, Letty?'

Letty banged the iron down on one of Peggie's blouses and smoothed it vigorously. 'Yes, that's right,' she said hurriedly. 'Just having a discussion.'

'Oh, right,' he said, smiling. 'I'll say goodnight then and I'll see you both on Sunday.'

'Goodnight,' they both said in unison.

When he had left Letty stared at Peggie worriedly. 'Oh, you don't think he heard us, do you?'

Peggie grimaced hard. 'I hope not. He could have us for slander. Anyway, we'll soon know.'

'How?' asked Letty, horrified.

Peggie erupted into laughter. 'When we're both found dead in our beds, that's when.'

Primrose came through. 'When who's found dead in their bed?' she asked.

'Oh, shut up, Primrose,' they both snapped.

'Well?' Peggie asked.

'Well, what?' Primrose replied.

'Do they want a drink or not?'

'Oh, yeah. They both want some tea.'

'Well, make it then,' Letty ordered. She folded her arms and took a deep breath. 'And hurry up about it. I need to talk to Peggie. In private, if you don't mind.'

Peggie exhaled sharply. 'Not now, eh, Letty? I've a million things to do. Then I'm going to relieve Mam. I'm right worried about her. She won't leave Billy's side for a minute, even though he's showing signs of improvement. I know she's fretting over Dad and she's hardly eating. To be honest, I don't know what to do.'

Just then Nell shuffled through and three pairs of eyes stared at her. Letty rushed forward and took her arm. 'Mam, come and sit down. I'll get you something to eat,' she offered.

Nell shook her arm free. 'Get off,' she muttered, annoyed. 'Can't you see I'm seeing to Billy? I'm going to make him a cuppa.'

'I was gonna do that, Mam,' Primrose said.

'I can do it, thank you,' her mother snapped. 'I'm quite capable of looking after me own son.' She clumsily picked up a mug which slipped out of her fingers and smashed on the floor. She stared down at it, bewildered. Tears sprang to her eyes and rolled down her cheeks. Peggie rushed forward and placed a protective arm around her. 'Come on, Mam. You're going to go up to our Billy's room and have a rest on his bed. I'll not take no for an answer. Now come on.'

As she guided her mother, she turned her head towards Letty and Primrose. 'Sweep that mess up and mash a cuppa for Mam and Billy,' she ordered.

As Primrose grabbed the brush and pan, Letty sank heavily into a chair and sighed. She was so worried about her mother, but not as worried as about the news she had to impart to them all. News that if she didn't tell soon would be too late. When the banns went up all the village would know, then there would be trouble.

She did not want to marry Reginald, she hated the very thought. But what could she do? Cyrus had meant every word of his threat to sue if she backed out, so she had no alternative but to go through with it.

Suddenly she hated her family for not being there when she needed them. They should be helping her sort out this mess, not all cocooned in their own little worlds without a thought for anyone else. Tears sprang to her eyes. She was being selfish, she knew she was. This predicament she found herself in was of her own doing. It wasn't any of her family's fault that events prohibited their being there for her. It was just unfortunate that everything had coincided.

She gulped back a lump in her throat. How was she going to tell them that a date had been set for her wedding in early January, just a few short weeks away? Would they understand that she had done everything she could to get out of it? But more to the point, what was going to happen to her once she committed herself for life to Reginald Crabbe? For committed was what it felt like. It certainly wasn't love or even affection. What was her life going to be like once she was under their roof? She shuddered, dreading to think.

A feeling of doom settled upon her as she raised her eyes to the old clock on the mantle and realised she should have been at the Crabbe house over half an hour ago. She did not want to go. But she would have to or face both the Crabbes' wrath. She decided to fake a headache. That way she could get home early and try to catch Peggie on her own. She prayed with all her might that her sister would think of or be able to do something that would save her.

She rose, put away the ironing and grabbed her coat from the back door, pulling it on.

Primrose, armed with the tea tray, eyed her keenly. 'Where you going?'

'Mind your own business,' she snapped.

When she arrived at the Crabbe household Cyrus opened the door to her.

'Come in,' he said, smiling broadly. 'You're late. Reginald's had to go out on an errand.'

Letty's heart lightened. 'Has he? Oh, never mind. I'll come back tomorrow.'

Cyrus grabbed her arm and pulled her inside. 'I've got the kettle on. Surely you can take the time for a cuppa with your future father-in-law?' He eyed her sharply.

Letty gulped. 'Yes, yes, 'course I can.'

'That's a good girl.'

He pushed her gently forward. 'Give me your coat and make yourself at home.'

187

Unnerved she perched on the edge of her seat and looked warily at him as he busied himself mashing the tea. She accepted the cup from him.

'Thank you,' she whispered.

Cyrus sat down opposite. 'So, how are you all managing?'

'Pardon? Oh, er . . . quite well, thank you.'

'Good. It must have been some shock?'

'Shock?'

'Your Billy getting beaten up like that. Hammond's a madman. It was only a matter of time before he did someone a damage. Shame it had to be your brother. He's a nice lad. And your father going off like that. Where did you say he had gone?'

Cyrus looked keenly at her, expertly hiding a smug look of pleasure.

'Gone?' Letty squirmed in her seat. 'Oh, er . . . London. He's gone to London to visit a sick relative.'

'London, eh? Funny that. I heard that your sister Peggie reckoned he'd gone to Scotland. Still never mind, as long as he's back in time to give you away.' He leaned forward and stared at her coldly. 'But if by chance he's not, I'll do it.'

'You! Oh, I couldn't possibly . . .'

'No need to thank me, Letty. It'd be my pleasure. In fact I'll mention it to Reverend Forest the next time I see him. Put him in the picture like. Well, what with your brother incapacitated and your father absent, and as far as I know you've no other male relatives hereabouts, well, I'm the obvious choice.' He leaned even further forward. 'No excuse, eh?'

Letty stared at him, the full meaning of his question hitting home. 'No,' she uttered. 'No, no excuse.'

By the time she was allowed to leave her heart felt even heavier than when she had arrived. Peggie was already in bed fast asleep. But that was no problem. The time for asking Peggie for a plan of escape had passed. After tonight Cyrus had left her in no doubt that he meant her to become Mrs Reginald Crabbe and woe betide her if she defied him.

She stripped off her clothes, climbed in beside her sisters and stared up at the ceiling. Suddenly she saw her life as a deep dark void stretching endlessly into the future gripped in the clutches of the Crabbes.

Tears spurted from her eyes and ran down the sides of her face and on to her pillow. Never had she felt so desolate, so alone. She felt sudden remorse for taking her loving, supportive family so much for granted. What she would give to turn back the clock and be the carefree happy Letty Cartwright of a few weeks previous. She felt at this moment she would give anything for that to happen. But miracles were only fiction. In a few short weeks she would walk up the aisle and her life would be ended and there was nothing, nothing at all, she could do to change that fact.

Chapter Sixteen

Three weeks later Peggie drew the empty bus to a halt at a turning in the road. In other circumstances life would have been grand. She was doing something she loved, and as the days passed her confidence had grown. Folk were getting used to her now and liked the way she helped them with their shopping and went out of her way to drop them at an isolated spot which she felt enhanced the service she provided.

Her thoughts dwelled on her father. What would he have done about the other operators encroaching on their routes? What would he have done if he had turned up one morning to find all the passengers gone because another bus had arrived earlier? Seen how other buses had raced each other dangerously along the narrow roads, hoping to arrive ahead. She hoped he would have acted as she had, deciding not to race for passengers, turning up at any old time to secure a load. She had stuck to her timetable and it had paid off. Reliability. People wanted to know where they stood. Wanted to know that the bus would arrive when the timetable stated it would.

'Oh, Dad,' she sighed forlornly. 'Where are you? What are you doing?' She scanned her eyes across the forbidding fields, lying fallow for the winter. Was he lying in some ditch somewhere? Had they somehow missed him? She thumped the wheel in frustration. How could he just abandon them like this? Just walk out into the night and not return. She took a deep breath, the chill in the air nipping her lungs. They had made every effort to find him. Had called at farms, searched isolated buildings, stopped people in the street. Dan also, whilst making his deliveries, had made extensive enquiries, but no one had seen him. So all they could do was be patient and wait for news. But patient was something she was not and the not knowing was driving her to despair.

Still, she had to be grateful. At least Ronnie seemed settled. His first letter, received that very morning, scant though it was, was filled with glowing reports on his job and his lodgings. He seemed so happy in fact there was no mention of a visit home. It was best that way, that he stayed oblivious to the troubles at home. She had enough problems coping with the rest of the family without having Ronnie adding to her problems. She lifted her eyes and smiled. Though what she would have done without Dan around she dreaded to think.

The unfamiliar road to her right looked inviting. She stared down it, wondering what was round the corner, and her curiosity grew. She had spare time before her next pick up – time for a diversion – and without further ado she pressed her foot on the pedal and turned the wheel.

The view was enchanting. From her seat in the cab she could see in the distance a small hamlet nestling between the trees, smoke spiralling from chimneys. A farmer was ploughing a field, struggling with his team of horses against the hard earth. A dog ran ahead, yapping at the birds as they swooped down on the worms. A brook ran swiftly to the side of her and just ahead a hump-back bridge crossed it.

She turned the wheel expertly to negotiate the bridge and glanced down in delight, gazing along the length of the water as it wove through the fields, its banks covered in grasses and reeds. She remembered days long past when she had ran with her brother and sister in the long grasses by the river near her home, throwing themselves down to eat the dripping sandwiches their mother had prepared, scattering the crusts for the ducks.

Suddenly, without warning, the bus abruptly stopped, a horrendous grating noise hitting the air. The force threw her forward. She gathered her wits and stared around, wondering what had happened. She looked down and gasped in alarm. The bus was jammed, packed tight against the sides of the bridge. She clenched her fists. How could she have been so stupid? It was obvious that the vehicle was too wide for such a narrow bridge, but she had been so taken with the countryside, so intent on having a few moments to herself, that the glaring fact had not registered.

On hearing the loud noise the farmer ran across the field and stood by the front of the bus. He lifted his cap and scratched his head.

'You're stuck, gel,' he said, grinning up at her.

'I know that,' she said hopelessly. 'Can you help me? Is there anything you can do? Please?' she added.

The farmer pursed his lips and sighed gravely, surveying the situation. 'Well, it's on lunchtime, you see. And it's Thursday today.'

'Thursday?'

'Thursday's steak and kidney puddin'. Makes a right tasty steak and kidney puddin' does my Iris. Lovely thick gravy,' he added, smacking his lips. 'She don't like it to go cold. Plays merry 'ell, she does, if I'm late.'

'Oh, I see,' Peggie replied, frowning.

He shook his head slowly. 'But then old 'Enry will be comin' shortly.'

'Old 'Enry?' she enquired, frowning.

'Yeah, with 'is cows. And 'e'll need the bridge. 'E can't milk 'is cows wi' out crossin' the bridge, now can 'e?'

Peggie sighed, frustrated. 'Well, can you help or not? Or do you know anyone else who can?' She quickly looked around her. There was no means of escape unless she wanted to jump into the icy waters below and she didn't fancy that. So this farmer was her only hope. She eyed him sharply. He was certainly hard work and getting on her nerves.

He scratched his head again, deep in thought. 'Well, I suppose I could get Sadie and Sally,' he drawled slowly.

'Sadie and Sally?' she asked, bewildered.

'Me 'orses.'

'Oh, horses.' She took a breath and planted a smile on her face. 'Oh, could you? I'd be ever so grateful. So will my passengers. They'll be waiting, you see. They're all old ladies wanting to go shopping.'

'Old ladies. Oh, in that case Sadie and Sally be glad to 'elp. We can't 'ave old ladies kept waitin'. A merry stink they'll cause. Me dinner'll just 'ave to go cold,' he added forlornly.

Half an hour later, two magnificent shire horses had been led across the field and the tackle hitched to the back axle of the bus. Slowly, with much grating of metal, the bus moved backwards, thankfully taking none of the bridge with it. The task complete, Peggie sighed in relief. She had learned her lesson. Never again would she take the bus anywhere that had not been checked out first.

She thanked the farmer profusely, telling him she hoped his dinner was not ruined, and offered him payment which he flatly refused. As she drove home that night she frantically thought of an excuse for the damage, dreading telling Dan how it had happened, especially since not so long ago she had run out of petrol and he had delighted in the fact.

On seeing the damage, he stared at her quizzically and she had no option but to tell the truth. Much to her embarrassment, he guffawed loudly and she stalked off angrily into the cottage. But not without telling him first that he was the employee and just to get on and carry out the necessary repairs.

It was a week later when Peggie, dreadfully fatigued after a long arduous day, decided to go to bed early. A simple decision but one she had contemplated for over half an hour. She would not admit to herself that she enjoyed Dan's company.

She had begun to notice the tilt of his head when he smiled; the way he held his mug and did not bolt his food; the way his eyes twinkled when he looked at her. The way he had fitted into their lives as though he'd always belonged, doing far more than he should do to help ease their burdens, still accepting little remuneration in return.

But for all this there was something about him that niggled her, something that did not quite ring true. Her mind was always too full of daily business to dwell for long, but it remained all the same. Not that it really mattered, she kept reminding herself. His stay was not permanent. Could not be permanent once her father returned and

Billy was fully recovered and able to take over.

She forced herself to rise. Letty and Primrose were already upstairs and she knew the bed would be nice and warm. Her mother was bedded down next to Billy. She wished Dan goodnight and made for the stairs.

'Oh, Peggy,' he said, raising his eyes from the newspaper.

She stopped and turned. 'Yes?'

'Cyrus Crabbe? Is he the man you told me about? The one who stole your father's brake?'

Peggie turned and retraced her steps. 'Yes, he is,' she replied quizzically. 'But please, Dan. I asked you not to talk like you know our business. If my mother heard . . .'

'I'm sorry. I forgot.'

'Well, why do you ask?'

'He stopped me today when I was delivering some wood. Pulled his carrier cart right across the road. Wanted to know who I was and what I was doing.'

Peggie's eyes flashed. 'And did you tell him?' she demanded.

Dan grinned. 'Not exactly. I told him if he had any questions to ask you himself. He wasn't pleased. He wasn't pleased at all.'

Peggie sighed, relieved. 'Thanks, Dan. The less he knows the better. He's bad news is Cyrus Crabbe. I'd try and keep out of his way if I were you. I wouldn't want him doing something to you 'cos you work for us.'

'Don't worry, Peggie,' he smiled. 'I can take care of myself.'

She looked at him searchingly. 'Yes, I'm sure you can,' she said flatly.

Dan lay on his mattress unable to sleep, a picture of Peggie stuck firmly in his mind. He had only known of her existence for a few short weeks but in that little time he had fallen in love. Fallen in love with a woman who would drive many men to distraction. He had never before met one like her. Apart from her physical attractions, she was spirited, determined, and he so admired the way she was striving to keep things running despite the misfortunes that had befallen her and her family. Many women in her position would have crumbled, but not Peggie. She had risen to the challenge, put personal feelings aside and got on with it against all the odds.

But falling in love was something he'd never thought would happen to him again. It frightened him but he knew he could not leave. To leave would mean not seeing her again. It also meant abandoning this endearing family when they needed his help so much, leaving them to cope on their own and he couldn't do that. His conscience would not allow it.

He sighed deeply, envisaging the feel of her body next to his, his face buried deep inside her golden mane of hair, his arms encircling her against the harsh realities of the outside world – something which in actual fact she was handling quite admirably. But he dare not risk telling her of his feelings, not while she was still carrying a torch for her dead fiancé. He could not risk her rebuff.

Absently he traced his eyes across the cracked ceiling visible through the cradles of drying washing, listening to the wind howling through the gaps in the windows. Should he tell her the truth about himself? Could he dare hope she would understand why he had lied to her? Would she still allow him to work for her once she knew the truth? He closed his eyes. Not with that temper of hers. She would have his bags packed and thrown out of the door before he had proper chance to explain his motives.

He drew the blankets further round him for warmth, moving his body to a more comfortable position on the lumpy horsehair mattress that had been borrowed from a neighbour. He would leave things alone. At the moment he was quite happy with the situation, quite content to play the part. He blanked his mind and tried to sleep.

Chapter Seventeen

'Mam?'

Nell jerked from her doze and peered down at her son. 'Yes, Billy?'

'Can I have a cuppa tea, please, I'm parched?'

She awkwardly rose, her joints stiff with sitting by the bed for the last few weeks. The only consolation was that the swelling of her legs had gone down considerably through all the rest she was getting. ''Course, son, 'course. And something to eat? I think there's some soup left or I could do you an egg?'

'No, Mam, ta. Just tea.'

She looked down at him. 'You look better today. The bruises on your face have just about gone and your stitches are healing nicely. How's the pain in your legs? Need any medicine just now?'

Billy sighed, frustratedly. 'No, Mam. Just tea.'

'Okay, son. I won't be a tick.'

'Mam?'

She stopped and turned. 'Yes?'

'Where's me dad?'

Nell froze. She had been dreading this question. So far they had managed to fob him off, but by the tone of his voice she knew he would not be satisfied by her feeble explanations any longer. But she worried he wasn't strong enough to take the truth.

'He's at work,' she lied. 'He popped in before he went but you were sleeping.'

Billy tried to sit up against the pillows but failed. He sighed in frustration, ignoring the pain movement still caused. If he let his mother see she would start fussing again and he couldn't stand that. She was beginning to get on his nerves. She never left his side for a moment. But how could he hurt her when he knew how worried she was about him, and him feeling so guilty for the trouble he had caused?

'Mam, don't lie to me. What's going on? What's happened to Dad?'

Nell sighed deeply. 'We don't know, son.'

'Don't know! I don't understand.'

'He disappeared the night of your accident and we ain't heard a word since.' Tears welled up in her eyes. 'I'm worried sick, Billy,' she said, unable to control her pain and anguish. 'I just pray he's all right. That he'll come back soon. I don't know how much longer I can bear not having news.' She sniffed loudly and wiped her hand under her nose. 'I'll just make your tea.'

Billy closed his eyes and groaned. 'Oh, Dad, Dad,' he whispered sadly.

Nell sat at the kitchen table, her head buried in her arms, crying softly. Having to answer Billy's questions had brought everything flooding back. Life was unbearable without Sep around. She missed him so terribly. But the worst fear she faced was that he was dead. How would she cope if that were true? How would she ever get through the rest of her life without him? The longer his absence continued the more worried she became, despite Peggie's continual reassurances.

The tap on the door shook her rigid. She couldn't answer it. She could not face whoever was behind it, even if she knew them she couldn't. The tap came again and she stared shaking. She saw the latch go up and the door began to open.

She held her breath in terror that whoever was there would tell her news that she didn't want to hear. Where was Letty? Why wasn't she here? These days her daughter was never where she said she would be. Then she remembered she would still be at Jenny Pegg's, covering her mother's work.

The door opened wider and a woman entered, one Nell had never seen before; a plump, jolly-looking woman with kindly eyes. Nell stared at her blankly.

The woman's gaze came to rest on her and she smiled.

'Mrs Cartwright?' she asked hesitantly. 'Mrs Nell Cartwright?'

Nell slowly nodded and the woman closed the door and advanced.

'I'm sorry to barge in,' she began, 'but I do need to see you. I was so frightened you wouldn't be in. I should have come before, but I made him a promise, you see.' She shook her head gravely. 'But, well, I feel I cannot keep this promise, not with Christmas round the corner. And not when I know how worried you must be.'

'Is it . . . Is it about Sep?' Nell whispered hesitantly.

The woman nodded. 'Yes, it is.' She held out her hand. 'I'm Winny Freeman. A friend of your husband's.'

Nell's eyes opened wide. 'A friend?'

Winny looked around her. 'May I sit down?'

Nell nodded, wringing her hands in worry for the words that had yet to be spoken. She suddenly became conscious of her unkempt appearance. She hadn't bothered with herself much lately. She hadn't felt the need or inclination to do more than have a quick wash down, and even that simple task was getting to be more and more of an effort. Her hair was greasy, scraped back in an untidy bun, and her clothes needed changing. 'I'm sorry, I'm forgetting me manners,' she said apologetically. 'Would you like a cup of tea?'

Winny smiled warmly. 'That would be welcome.' She hurriedly rose, Nell's distressed state not lost on her. 'Here, let me make it.'

Nell did not answer, just watched Winny bustling round her cluttered kitchen, searching under things for clean crockery.

The tea finally made, she sat down and pushed a mug towards

her. 'Drink this whilst it's hot,' she ordered.

Just then the door opened and Peggie came through. She stopped abruptly on spotting the strange woman and quickly eyed her mother.

'I just popped in for my gloves. It's freezing out there today.'

'Oh, Peggie, Peggie,' Nell uttered thankfully at her daughter's appearance. 'This lady – Winny – has news of your father.'

Peggie's eyes opened wide. 'You have?' she said, rushing towards the table and sitting next to her mother. 'What news? Please tell us.'

Winny sat back in her chair and loosened her coat. 'We found Sep, your father, in our barn,' she began.

Nell sat bolt upright. 'In your barn? He's not dead then?'

Winny smiled kindly. 'No. He's not dead. But when we found him he was as near as damn it. Right poorly he was. Been sleeping rough for many nights.'

'Sleeping rough?' Peggie repeated, alarmed. 'Why?'

Winny shook her head. 'We never could get the reason out of him. But we – that's my husband Jess and meself – suspected he must have had something dreadful happen, some horrible shock, to make him act the way he had.' She looked at Peggie and Nell expectantly. When nothing was forthcoming she leaned heavily on the table. 'When I first met Sep, when he came to ask after our old motor, he was such an upright man, such a family man, so excited about providing a proper living for you all. And to be reduced to such a state in such a short time . . . Well, something awful must have happened, mustn't it?' She raised her eyes enquiringly.

Peggie, not willing to divulge family business and anxious for the rest of the news, rushed her on. 'And?' she asked, irritated.

Winny puffed out her chest. 'Well, I told him. Said I felt it weren't fair, not letting you have news, knowing how worried you all must be. Jess agreed and told him straight, we didn't mind how long he stayed with us as long as he squared matters with his family.'

Nell's face lit up. 'He's on his way home. Sep's coming home.' She made to rise. She had things to do, things to get ready.

Winny held up her hand. 'No. No, he's not.'

Nell sank down. 'He's not?'

She shook her head. 'When I rose this morning he had gone. Left a note to thank us for our help and said he was going to try to find work and lodgings in Leicester. Very nicely he put it but he was telling us in no uncertain terms to please keep our noses out of his business.' She bit her lip. 'But I couldn't, could I? Me and Jess talked it over and felt it only fair that I come and tell you what we knew.'

Peggie sighed deeply. 'And we're grateful you did.'

Winny smiled and gathered her bag. 'Well, that's all right then.' She smiled. 'I feel sure that given time he'll come back.'

Peggie nodded, rose and walked with her to the door. Winny looked over at Nell who was staring blankly towards the fire.

'She's took it bad, ain't she, poor woman?'

Peggie smiled wanly. 'Yes, she has. But thanks, Winny, for coming. At least we know something now. If you hear anything else, will you please tell us?'

Winny patted her arm. ''Course, me dear. Anything I can do, just ask. I grew quite fond of your father. Such a nice man. I hate to see what he's reduced himself to. But I'm sure it'll come right in the end.' She walked through the door, then stopped and turned. 'Oh, there is just one thing. I don't know whether it's worth mentioning.'

Peggie stepped through the door and joined her. 'Oh, what's that?'

'Well, when he was delirious he was calling a name. Sounded something like Crab. I feel sure it was Crab 'cos it made me think of the seaside. Not that I've ever been to the seaside but I've seen pictures. Anyway, shouting out he was, night after night. "I'll kill you, Crabbe, for what you've done."'

'My dad was shouting that?'

'Oh, yes,' Winny said with conviction. 'Jess heard an' all. So I know I'm right.'

Peggie's face darkened. She should have known. She should have known all along that Cyrus Crabbe had something to do with this, if not everything in fact.

'Thanks again, Winny,' she managed, and remembered her manners. 'How are you getting home? I could take you in the bus.'

'Oh, no, that's all right, me duck. My Jess bought me up in the pig. He's waiting in the Jolly Toper. I've never been to Barlestone before and it looks a nice place from what I have seen. I'm going to have a quick gander round the village before we set off. But thanks all the same.'

As she walked away, Peggie watched, deep in thought, torn between her customers and her father. There was no real need for her to ponder, her father was more important than anything. She was going into Leicester to search for him. The customers would have to do without Cartwright's for one afternoon. She hoped they would understand.

Without a word to her mother of her plans, not wanting to raise any hopes, she boarded the bus. It was then she decided that she would commandeer Dan to help. Two making enquiries would be better than one. She found him loading a stack of bricks on the back of the lorry at the local brick yard. She quickly told him what had happened, asked him to explain, using any excuse but the truth, to the brick yard foreman and to join her.

He readily agreed and together they set off.

Arriving in Applegate Street, she parked and they both made extensive enquiries from locals in areas where a man like her father, with not much in his pocket, might have gone. They went their separate ways, arranging to meet later.

She walked for miles, losing herself down grimy streets, knocking on shabby doors answered by workworn women with pale-looking children. All her enquiries resulted in the same shake of the head and advice to try up the street. Mrs So and So took in lodgers, she might know something.

Several hours later, weary and hungry, Peggie slumped down on a bench in a tiny park at the end of a row of terraced houses and took from her pocket the packet of sandwiches she had put there early that morning for her lunch.

She bit into one absently, searching her mind for anything else she could do, and hoped that Dan had fared better than she. Several shoeless children were playing on the roundabout, some girls skipping with a length of washing rope, a group of boys playing snobs with stones. A child on a swing caught her attention and she watched him for several moments as he swung back and forth.

She heard a name being called and turned her head to see a man standing in the doorway of a house further up the street. She looked across at the young boy still happily swinging. 'I think your father's calling you,' she said.

The boy ignored her and carried on.

The man appeared at the park gates and strode across to the boy, pulling the swing to a halt. He clipped the boy around the ear and dragged him off. 'Don't you ignore me when I call, you little bugger,' he grumbled, shaking him hard. 'Your dinner's on the table and your mother ain't 'appy.'

He turned to march him back across the road when he spotted Peggie. He inclined his head in her direction. 'I dunno,' he said, grinning. 'Kids. Who'd have 'em?'

Me, she thought sadly. For a fleeting moment she envisaged the children she would have had with Harry. She forced the picture from her mind, rose and made her way towards the park gates. It must be nearly time to meet Dan.

She stood in Grandy Street by Nelson's the tobacconist's and sheltered under the green canopy as the heavens opened and a deluge poured down.

A man carrying a suitcase ran under for shelter, instantly spotting Peggie from the corner of his eye. A possible customer, he thought. Not a chance to be missed.

She casually scanned him, thinking he looked like a toff on a Sunday afternoon jaunt in the park only instead of the fashionable lady hanging on his arm he was carrying the suitcase. She thought he looked out of place in his loud purple and gold striped jacket, off white flannels and a white trilby hat trimmed round with a broad purple band.

'Can I interest you?' he began as he expertly flicked open a tripod which he placed on the wet pavement. He opened out the suitcase and put it on the metal bars of the tripod. 'I have a selection of brushes, something for all needs.' He pushed back his trilby and smiled at her winningly. His smile froze, then his face fell in shock. 'Peggie,' he uttered.

She raised her eyes from the contents of the case and stared up at him. It was several long moments before she found her voice. 'Harry!' she gasped. 'Harry? But . . . but you're dead!' she exclaimed in horror.

He laughed uneasily. 'Er . . . not quite, but I had a couple of near misses.' He wiped away the sweat of acute embarrassment forming on his brow then dug his hands deep down inside his trouser pockets. 'Look, Peggie, I know what it seems like . . .'

'You know what it seems like?' she cried, and jabbed him in the chest with her finger, unaware of passersby looking on. 'You left me mourning you for three damned years when all the time you were too bloody chicken to face me! You've been in Leicester all this time and I've been desolate because I thought you were dead. How could you?' she cried. 'Harry, how could you do that to me? You . . . you . . . Oh, bloody, bloody hell!'

Harry gawped at her, shocked. 'It's not like you to swear . . .'

'Swear? You ain't heard nothing.'

He lowered his head, ashamed, and studied his feet. 'I didn't mean to hurt you, Peggie. Things just kinda happened.'

She clenched her fists in anger. 'Well, what did you expect? What did you think I would feel when you didn't come home? I thought you were rotting on the battle fields. I thought . . . I thought you loved me.'

'I did. I do . . . Look, Peggie, I'm sorry. I couldn't help it. I got stranded behind enemy lines. It was terrible, Peggie, I've never been so frightened in all my life, playing cat and mouse with the Germans. By the time I managed to rejoin my unit, I'd long been posted missing,' he lowered his gaze, 'and me mam had died.' He paused. 'Then I got shot in the foot.'

'Shot in the foot?'

Harry smiled weakly. 'It was an accident. I was cleaning my gun. I was in hospital for weeks. I still have a limp. I was invalided out of the army and sent home in early 'eighteen.' He shrugged his shoulders apologetically. 'I arrived back in Leicester with a mate who put me up for the night and . . . well . . . he told me how I could make a fortune selling door to door.'

'And have you?' she snapped.

'Well, no, not a fortune exactly.'

'And you came back in early 'eighteen?'

He nodded.

'And you told no one?'

'Well, I meant to, but I never quite got round to it.'

She stared at him, horrified. 'And I was still knitting you socks. Thick ones to keep you warm. And all the time you were here.' Her eyes went to the case. 'Selling brushes.' She clasped her hands to her forehead, humiliation racing through her. 'But your mother, your poor mother . . .'

'Yes,' he said, ashamed. 'It was a pity about her.'

'A pity! She died, Harry, with a broken heart, thinking you were dead.' She stopped herself from adding like she nearly had herself.

Her eyes flashed. 'And did you think of me at all? Did you think of what I would be feeling?'

'Yes, 'course I did,' he said with conviction. 'I was coming to see you.'

'Were you? When? It's been three years, Harry. Three bloody years.'

He took a breath and smiled at her fondly. 'Well, now you're here maybe we can . . .'

'We can what?' she exploded. 'Carry on where we left off? After what you've done to me? You must think I'm stupid.'

She stopped abruptly, seeing Dan approaching in the distance, his head just visible above the crowd. Her mind raced frantically. The last thing she wanted was for him of all people to see her in this dreadful predicament. But his arrival was imminent and there was nothing she could do. Or was there? she thought as an idea struck. It might be too late to stop Dan finding out about Harry, but not to do something that would salvage at least some of her pride.

'Dan,' she cried in greeting, planting a smile on her face. As he joined them she hooked her arm in his, gazing up at him adoringly. He looked at her, confused.

She stared boldly at Harry. 'This is my husband, Dan,' she announced. 'Meet Harry, Dan. Remember the friend I told you about, the one who went to war?'

'Oh, er . . . yes,' he said, holding out his hand. 'Peggie's told me all about you,' he said flatly, a harsh glint in his eye.

Harry reluctantly accepted his hand and shook it limply. 'Your husband?'

'My husband,' she reaffirmed. 'We have our own business. In transport. Doing ever so well, isn't it, darling?' she said, nudging Dan in the ribs.

'Er . . . yes, yes. Ever so,' he said with conviction. 'In fact we're just about to expand.'

Peggie stared up at him. 'Are we? Oh, yes, that's right, we are. Expanding in a really big way.'

Harry gawped. 'Oh! Oh, I'm pleased for you, Peggie. Very pleased,' he muttered.

She breathed deeply. 'Right, we must be off,' she spoke jauntily. 'Things to do, you know.' She unhooked her arm and shook Harry's hand. 'It's so nice to have seen you again. And if you're ever in Barlestone, please look us up. We wouldn't like you to pass our door. Would we, Dan?' She looked up at him. 'Would we?'

'No. No, definitely not. Any friend of Peggie's is welcome.'

She grabbed Dan's arm again and made to walk away. As she did so she kicked back her leg, her foot catching the tripod. The case tipped over, spilling its contents into a large puddle.

'Oh, I'm so sorry,' she spluttered, fighting back mirth at Harry's horrified expression.

She gripped Dan's arm tighter and together they ran off down the street.

201

Out of sight of Harry, he pulled her to a halt.

'Was that your fiancé? The one you thought was . . .'

'Don't, Dan. Please don't say anything,' she snapped coldly, letting go of his arm.

He stared at her helplessly. 'Look, Peggie, I'm . . . I'm so sorry you found out about him this way,' he said sincerely.

'Sorry!' she exclaimed. 'Please don't feel sorry for me. I feel bad enough you had to witness all this in the first place without further humiliation.' She inhaled deeply. 'Let me just say that I know I've been stupid mourning a man who wasn't worth tuppence. I was daft to have believed his promises in the first place.'

She fought back the tears that threatened. Tears of humiliation, rejection and hurt pride. 'I'll never be so daft again,' she said with deep emotion. 'I've learned my lesson, believe me. I've spent three years mourning that man. Moping round the house, crying myself to sleep, thinking my life had ended. When all the time he was alive!' She lowered her head, her eyelashes glistening wet, and ran her fingers over her bare neck where the locket used to sit. 'He never gave me a second thought. Well, I'll never be that stupid again.' And as for the locket, she thought, well, that could stay where it was. At least she would not have to worry about raising the money to redeem it.

Dan gently laid his hand on her arm, his eyes filled with concern. 'I don't think you're stupid, Peggie. It's him who's the stupid one, letting someone like you go.'

'Is he?' she snapped, fighting anger. 'That's not how I see it. And obviously not the way he saw it either. I'm beginning to think all men are a law unto themselves. You all do just what you want, regardless of how much hurt you might cause.'

'No, Peggie, that's not quite true. We're maybe a little thoughtless sometimes.'

'Only a little?' she cried, raising her eyes. 'Well, what about Wilfred and how he treated Letty? And look at my dad just walking out on us without any explanation. And now this with Harry, and that's not to mention the Crabbes. They're the worst of the lot.' She took a deep breath and looked at him, ashamed. 'I'm sorry to pour all this out to you. This is the second time you've listened to my troubles.'

'It's no problem to me, Peggie. You pour as much as you want.' He laughed wryly. 'I just feel like punching him in the face.'

'That's enough of that,' she said coldly. 'There's been enough violence around me just lately to last a lifetime.'

'Yes, I agree. But it would certainly make me feel better.'

'Make you feel better? I can't think why.' She suddenly became conscious of people staring as they passed by. One woman had even stopped and was listening to the proceedings with great interest. Peggie glared at her, then turned back to Dan. 'Let's go, please. I want to get home.'

They began to walk. After a while she glanced at him cautiously.

'Dan?'

'Yes.'

'I, er . . . trust you'll not tell anyone of this?' she asked worriedly. 'I couldn't stand the thought of anyone finding out, especially the villagers.'

'Don't worry, Peggie. I won't say a word.'

She sighed in relief. 'Thanks.' She smiled shyly. 'Thanks too for going along with the charade. I don't know whether Harry believed it all.' She paused thoughtfully. 'But for that matter,' she said lightly, 'I don't really care. I don't care what he thought.'

He laughed. 'I'm glad. And it was my pleasure. To be honest, I quite enjoyed it.' A warm glow rushed through him. 'I enjoyed it enormously in fact.'

It wasn't until Dan had driven halfway home that Peggie suddenly remembered the point of their visit into Leicester.

'Oh, Dan. Any news of my father?' she asked.

He turned to face her and shook his head. 'Not a sign. But,' he added hurriedly, not wanting to dash her hopes, 'there's still plenty of places left to look. And I'll help you.'

She smiled in gratitude. 'I'd appreciate that.' She sighed forlornly. 'I have to find him, Dan. I just have to. Even if it's just to check he's all right. I'm afraid for my mother else. I don't think she can go on for much longer without more news. You should have seen her face when she thought Winny was telling her he was coming home, only to have her hopes dashed like that. It breaks my heart to think about it.'

'Peggie, we'll find him. Don't worry. He's got to be living somewhere. Someone must have seen him. It's just a case of narrowing things down.'

'Yes, you're right. We'll just keep trying, eh? It's all we can do.'

They lapsed into silence. Dan glanced discreetly at her and became concerned when he saw she was wringing her hands in her lap, staring blankly ahead into the darkening night sky.

'Are you all right?'

'Eh? Oh, yes, of course I am,' she said. 'I was just thinking, that's all.'

'May I ask about what?'

She took a deep breath. 'Cyrus Crabbe. That's what. I don't like it, Dan. I feel uneasy.'

'Why?'

'Because it's not like him to sit back and do nothing. What I mean is we're managing to keep the business running, despite me dad's absence. We've picked up lots of work that used to be Crabbe's and more besides, and he ain't done anything about it. I'd have thought he would've somehow got himself a bus – a lorry – or even both, in competition. And tried to force us out by now. Which is the usual way he goes about things.'

'Oh, I see what you mean. Well, maybe he's had enough? Maybe he's given up the fight? To be honest, Peggie, I can't for the life of me see why he's so against your family in the first place.'

'You're not the only one. But all the same, it's not like him and despite what you say, I don't feel somehow he's quite finished yet.'

Dan exhaled slowly. 'Well, let's just say he'd better not start anything while I'm around.'

Peggie turned on him. 'Oh, thump him, would you, to near an inch of his life to frighten him off? Is that what you'd do?'

He shook his head. 'Oh, no, Peggie. Nothing like that. I'm not a violent man really. No, no, there's other ways to deal with the likes of him.'

She stared at him in awe. And that niggle, that tiny doubt she had about him, returned.

Later that night she stared out of her bedroom window and mulled over the events of the day. Anger rose within her and she clutched the edge of the curtains, wringing the material between her hands. How could Harry have done that to her? Cast her aside without a thought or care for her feelings? After all they had meant to each other, after they had promised themselves to each other for ever.

The man who had gone away to war, the man who had kissed her longingly and made all those promises, was not the man she had encountered earlier that afternoon. And if she was truly honest with herself she was glad this had all happened, glad she had seen how he had changed. He resembled nothing of the man she had fallen in love with. For a moment sadness enveloped her. Sadness for what she had lost and mourned for for over three years. But all things happened for a reason. Harry and she were just not meant to be. She felt relieved that she could finally put his memory to the back of her mind, remember him as he used to be, and get on with living. During the last three years she had learned gradually to manage without him, so today's revelations were not such a lasting shock as they could have been.

Letty broke into her thoughts as she tossed and turned and mumbled inaudibly in her sleep. Peggie stared across at her in the gloom of the late-evening. What was the matter with the girl? For weeks now she had been withdrawn and when she did speak she snapped without reason. She sighed, annoyed. She had enough to cope with without worrying about Letty, whose only problem was how she was going to put matters right between herself and Wilfred. Well, for once she would have to sort things out for herself. Peggie had enough to cope with.

Chapter Eighteen

Sep stared down at the pale-looking substance that had been plonked unceremoniously down in front of him and smiled wanly. 'Thanks, Mrs Scroggins,' he said politely.

He studied the substance, wondering what it was, realising that he was paying over half of his wages as an odd job man in the factory for this, plus his room of course. He must not forget the room he shared with Archie Harrop sitting opposite.

Mrs Scroggins bustled back from the kitchen with a dish in her hand. 'Greens, anyone?' she asked, placing the dish down and sitting at the head of the table. The greens in the dish looked anything but green and they all looked at them apprehensively.

Then all four of her boarders dug in. After all, this was all that would be offered until breakfast and that was only toast, and cold toast at that, scraped sparingly with marg. Still, he must not grumble, he supposed. He had been lucky as it was in getting the lodgings in the first place, looking like the tramp he had been when he'd first stood on her doorstep and enquired after the room.

She wasn't a bad woman, wasn't Mrs Scroggins, she did her best, he supposed, in the circumstances. She'd had it hard in the war. Lost her husband and two sons and now made ends meet by taking in lodgers. Which she must find hard. Not many people enjoyed turning their home over to strangers.

She was addressing the table as usual. Having been starved of company all day, she attacked her lodgers verbally when they came in of an evening whether they liked it or not.

'A young woman knocked on the door today,' she was saying. 'Asked if I knew of a Septimus Cartwright.'

Sep's ears pricked up.

''Course, I thought of you straight away, Mr Carter. You being a Septimus an' all. But you're nothing like she described. She said the man she was after was muscly, well made, and you're not, are you, Mr Carter?'

Sep shook his head. Having lost so much weight he could not be described as muscly.

'Anyway, your name's Carter not Cartwright,' she continued, 'so I sent her up the road to Mrs Bingham's. Any more spuds, anyone?'

Sep swallowed hard and cleared his throat. 'What did she look like, this woman?' he asked casually.

'Oh,' Mrs Scroggins frowned and thought hard as she tried to recall. 'Smallish, pretty, with a mass of golden hair. Very curly. And a chest. I noticed the chest.' She looked down at her own flat offering. 'I'd have liked a chest like that,' she muttered under her breath. She raised her head and looked across at Sep curiously. 'Why do you ask?'

'Oh, no reason. Just outta interest, that's all.'

'Oh, I see,' she said, not quite satisfied with his answer. She rose. 'Well, if you're all finished I'll clear away.'

Later that night Sep sat on the edge of his bed. 'Archie?' he said, addressing the man opposite lying in his bed reading a western comic.

'Mmm,' he replied absently.

'You were married, weren't you?'

'For twenty years I was, 'til she ran off with the coalman and left me in debt up to me eyeballs. And he weren't the first by no means. Why?'

'Did you know her? I mean, really know her?'

Archie put down his comic, turned his head and looked across at Sep. 'As well as a man ever knows his wife. Why?' He raised himself up and leaned on his elbow. 'If you mean, did I always know she had a wandering eye, then yes. But I thought she'd settle down after we married. I was wrong, wasn't I? Lost everything, I did, 'cos of that bitch.'

Sep frowned thoughtfully. 'D'you think you can live with someone for nearly thirty years then find out they were completely different? That they were nothing like the person you thought they were?'

Archie frowned. 'Eh?' He paused thoughtfully. 'Not unless you were completely blind, you couldn't. Anyone would make slips sometimes. It's human nature.' He stared across at Sep in interest. 'Why? Is your wife a murderer or summat and you've only just found out?'

'No,' he snapped. 'Nothing like that.'

'Well, what then?'

Sep laid back on his uncomfortable bed and stared up at the ceiling. Yellow stains where water had leaked through the roof formed patterns. They were like faces laughing down at him, mocking him. Could it possibly be that he had been a fool? Could he dare hope?

Oh, Nell, Nell, he cried inwardly. He missed her so much. Missed all his family, but not in quite the same way as his wife. The pain of her memory had caused him many sleepless nights. What were his family all doing? Had they missed him at all? Were they coping without him?

His mind flew back to the nightmare of that night when he had stared down into the dark waters prepared to end it all. Had he been fair in not affording them the right to an explanation? Had he been temporarily insane to take Cyrus completely at his word when he knew him to be an accomplished liar?

Sep closed his eyes tightly, trying to shut out the terrible memories of that harrowing night when the world as he knew it had gone mad – been turned upside down – and he had lost everything he cared for. He had temporarily lost his sanity. He must have, or why had he chosen to take Cyrus's word against those of the people he loved and trusted?

He opened his eyes and again studied the ceiling. For all his profound thoughts, for all his remorse for the way he had mishandled matters, there still remained the one question that he would never be able to answer. How had Cyrus known about Nell's bad legs if he hadn't seen them with his own eyes? She had never allowed anyone, let alone himself, to see her legs since they had started to give her trouble. She had striven to keep prying eyes off them. So how come Cyrus had? He must be telling the truth. All the other accusations of Cyrus's he had managed to disregard, but not this one. However much he loved her, the thought of Nell with Cyrus was far too much even for him to come to terms with, let alone try to forgive.

He climbed under the thin grey blanket and none too clean sheet, pulling them up around his ears.

''Night, Archie,' he muttered.

'Eh? Oh, night, Sep. Sleep tight.'

Sep grunted. He'd never sleep tight again.

Chapter Nineteen

Three nights before Christmas two men sat facing each other across a table in a smoke-filled room, a pile of empty bottles that had held brown ale strewn across the floor.

A man sat in the recess at the back of the room watching the proceedings, hardly daring to breathe. Even though the fire had burned low, sweat glistened on his brow. He grew more anxious as the minutes ticked by.

One man suddenly grinned broadly and laid the cards he was holding flat.

'Beat that?' he said triumphantly.

Cyrus gulped and stared at the royal flush, then at his own of two kings and an ace, a six and a four. Two kings and an ace that he would have sworn would have won. He saw all hopes of the vehicle he had hoped to buy with his winnings evaporate. His hope of beating the Cartwrights cruelly vanish. He hadn't even his house left to raise money on.

'You fucking bastard! Where did that king come from?' he spat, rising up and leaning heavily on the table, his eyes narrowing in malice.

'You dealt the cards, Crabbe. Yer sayin' I cheated?'

Cyrus made a grab for the deeds lying on the table but the man was too quick for him.

'I'll have those if yer don't mind. After all, I won 'em fair and square,' he said, stuffing them into the inside pocket of his jacket, along with the declaration of ownership he had made Cyrus sign before he would allow him to pledge the house. He also swept the pile of coins and notes into his hands then his pockets, mindful that Cyrus was watching his every move.

''Nother 'and?' he asked.

'You bastard. You know I can't.'

'Just asked. Thought you might like one last chance at winnin' it back.'

The man stood, all six foot three and nearly as wide, and moved over to the door. He stopped and turned. 'I'll be fair, give yer a fortnight to come up wi' the money. Only 'cos it's Christmas. I wouldn't turn a dog out at Christmas. Then I come and collect. And in case you have any ideas, I won't be alone.'

Cyrus reddened in anger. 'You're not having me house! You've got everything else. You're not having me house. I'll kill you first.'

The man laughed loudly. 'Threats, eh?' He shook his head. 'You asked me to play. Begged in fact when you saw the wad I was carryin'. Thought I was easy, didn't you, Crabbe? Thought you had a right one 'ere? Well, I'm sorry to disappoint yer. As far as I'm concerned a debt is a debt. I think I'm being rather generous as it is. I could make you leave now.' He glanced across at Reginald. 'The both of yer. So I'd count meself lucky.' He opened the door, then paused. 'I tell yer what, I'll let you rent it from me. How's that? I'm a generous man really. Besides, I don't really have need for a place like this.'

'Rent!' Cyrus erupted in anger. 'You're asking me to rent me own house?'

'It ain't your house no longer. It's mine. So take it or leave it. I'll be back two weeks from now and you either leave or pay rent. It's up to you.'

Laughing loudly, he turned and walked out of the door.

Cyrus grabbed a bottle from the floor and made to follow. He stopped, dropped the bottle and froze. He knew it was useless, a man built like that would flatten him with one blow. For once he had met more than his match. For once he had come off the loser and he wasn't happy. Not happy at all. He turned on Reginald cowering in the corner.

'What you looking at?' he spat. 'Clean this mess up.'

Reginald slowly rose. 'What we gonna do, Dad? What we gonna do? We'll be out on the streets.'

'Shuddup. I'm thinking.'

Reginald crept slowly round, gathering the debris, glancing now and again at his father out of the corner of his eye. It seemed like an age before he noticed Cyrus's eyes light up. An age in which he sweated profusely at the thought of the beating he might receive.

'I've got it. That's it!'

'Got what, Dad? Got what?' Reginald asked hesitantly.

'He can have the bloody house. Have the lot. It won't matter to us, we'll have a bus business to run.'

'Will we?' Reginald gawped.

'We will.'

'How, Dad?'

'By your marriage to Letty, that's how. In just over a week you marry the silly bitch and then we can move in.'

'Move in? What, with the Cartwrights, you mean?'

Cyrus nodded, his eyes glinting with wickedness. 'The Cartwrights can't turn their daughter out into the street. Even they couldn't do that. And with her come the in-laws. Simple, ain't it? Once in, we get rid of that bloke that's helping out and take over the business.'

'Oh! Oh, I see.' Reginald smiled at the simplicity of it all. His father was a genius. A ready made thriving business just ripe for the taking. When it was in their hands, he could get rid of Letty. He eyed his father. Cyrus would get rid of all of them, he had no doubt of that. He would wheedle the business from them before they knew what had happened and had time to stop it. His face clouded as a thought struck.

'But what about Billy?'

'What about him? What's a cripple gonna do to stop us?'

'Yes, yer right, Dad. What can a cripple do to stop us? It's us against them women and they ain't got a chance.'

Walking down the road, chuckling with mirth, the huge man tapped his bulging pocket. He stopped at a corner and leaned against the wall, looking up and down the dark road. He yawned loudly. It had been a long arduous night. He had come across many ruthless men in his time, but Cyrus Crabbe beat all of them. He smiled to himself. He was glad he had taken him for every penny. By Crabbe's greed and conceit he had deserved to lose the lot. And that greed had been his own good fortune. Hadn't his boss told him that whatever he gained he could keep? Well, he felt no guilt in keeping what sat snugly inside his pocket. Though what on earth he was going to do with a house was anybody's business, him being a single man with no thoughts of marriage.

He laughed as he remembered the look on Crabbe's face when he had offered to rent his own house back to him. If looks could kill he would be resting now in his coffin. He grimaced. He hoped he wasn't taken up on his offer. His boss wanted rid of Crabbe for good. Still, it was too late now for retraction.

He yawned again. He had a long journey ahead of him and had better make a move if he was ever going to make it back in time to start his day's work.

Chapter Twenty

Peggie rested her back against the pot sink and gazed across the room, her eyes settling momentarily on the two other occupants. It had been the worst Christmas she had ever spent and she knew without doubt that the same was felt by the rest of them.

She dwelled for a moment on all the other Christmases she had shared with her family, each filled with excitement and joy. But for all the joy in this household today it might just as well have been any ordinary day.

The days previous had been a whirlwind of continuous hard work, flopping into bed at the end near exhaustion, and Peggie had been longing for her two days of rest. Restful compared to running the business it had been, but not enjoyable. And the reason was simple. The head of the family was still absent and they were all missing him dreadfully.

The mountain of food half heartedly prepared by herself and Letty; mince pies, a small goose, plum pudding, trifle, oranges and nuts, remained hardly touched on the table. The holly and mistletoe collected by Primrose for decorations was still in a bundle outside in the yard. The Carol Service normally attended by all of them was given a miss, and so were visits to friends.

To make matters worse, if that were possible, a short letter arrived from Ronnie saying he could not manage to come home. His shifts coincided with the holiday period and except for the holy day he would be working. But they were not to worry, Mrs Piddlesworth was quite happy to have him there. After receiving the letter, an even blacker cloud of doom settled over the remaining Cartwrights and try as they might no one could muster anything like a Christmas spirit.

For Peggie her worst moment had come several days previously when Dan had announced that he would not be with them for Christmas. She tried her hardest to hide her disappointment. She had taken it for granted that he would be spending the time with them. It came as even more of a surprise to her that she had been upset by the news and she had spent the time since filled with thoughts of where he had gone, and more importantly, with whom?

She sighed loudly as she picked up the water jug and filled up the kettle, walked over and placed it on the hob.

'I'll go and sit with Mam and Billy for a while.'

Letty raised her eyes and nodded absently. 'Okay. I'm off up to bed in a minute.'

'What, so soon? It's hardly eight o'clock. I thought we might have a game of charades or something.'

'No, I don't think so, Peggie. I'm tired.'

'I think I'll go as well,' Primrose said, rising to join her.

Primrose going voluntarily to bed, Peggie thought ruefully. Things must be bad.

She wished them good night, knowing that like her they would be glad to see the back of the festive season, be glad to see the back of the year in fact, and she hoped wholeheartedly that the heralding of 1921 would treat them better in some respects that 1920 had done.

'How you doing, Billy?' she asked as she walked through into her parents' bedroom. She eyed her mother fast asleep in the chair, then walked round to the other side of the bed and sat on the edge, handing Billy the mug of tea she had mashed for him.

'Some Christmas, eh, Peggie?' he said, inching himself up and accepting the mug. He looked at it and sighed. 'What I'd do for a pint of best bitter.'

'Bitter's off, I'm afraid,' she said sharply. 'You'll have to make do with that.' Her eyes twinkled. 'But if you behave yourself I might consider sending for a jug from the pub at New Year.' She looked across at her mother. 'How long has she been asleep?'

'About an hour.'

Peggie tutted. 'She'd be better off in bed.'

'Well, I've tried telling her . . .'

'I know, I know,' she cut in. 'But she takes no notice. I think she worries something might happen to you if she did that.'

'I don't know why. What can happen to me whist I'm stuck here?' Billy sighed forlornly. 'I can't stand it much longer, Peggie. It's driving me mad being stuck inside these four walls. It wouldn't be so bad if I could get up the stairs. I'd feel better in my own room.'

'Stop moaning and just be grateful because by the state you were in when we got you home that night, we didn't think you'd make it through the night let alone 'ote else. Anyway, you're well on the mend so you shouldn't be bedridden for much longer.'

'I bloody hope not.'

Peggie glared at him. 'Don't swear whilst Mam's in the room, she'll paste you,' she whispered crossly.

Billy glanced across at her. 'I doubt it, Peggie. She ain't got the heart to raise her voice at the moment, let alone her hand. Oh, God, I just wish I could walk. I could help you and Dan in the search for Dad. I feel so helpless.' He shook his head. 'Just look at her, Peggie. She's wasting away before our eyes.'

'I know, but we're doing all we can. Anyway, you just concentrate on getting better and for the moment leave the searching to me and Dan.'

Billy stared thoughtfully at her. 'He's been a Godsend in more ways than one.'

'Who has?'

'Dan. And don't play coy with me. You knew fine well who I was talking about.' His eyes glinted with mischief. 'I've a notion you kinda like him.'

'He's all right, I suppose,' she replied lightly. 'Anyway, a man of his age is probably married. He told me he's travelled around for work. Probably sends all his earnings back to his wife.'

Billy laughed. 'We aren't paying him enough to send any back home. Anyway, he's not married.'

'He's not? How d'you know?' she asked cagily.

'Because I asked him, that's how.'

'And he said he wasn't?'

'He's not married, Peggie, and never has been,' he said firmly, and eyed her keenly. 'So you do like him then? You must do or you wouldn't be asking these questions.'

'He's all right, I suppose.' Her voice rose sharply. 'At any rate, I'm asking these questions out of interest as his employer, that's all.'

'And I'm your brother, Peggie. I ain't daft. Anyway, he's more than all right. He a good man is Dan, and he's educated an' all.'

'Is he?'

'Don't tell me you haven't noticed?'

'Well . . . I suppose I have. But I wouldn't have said he was educated.'

'I would. You should sit here and listen in on some of the conversations we have. He gets carried away sometimes and drops his guard. Then he talks knowledgeably about all sorts of things. It puts me to shame, I can tell you.'

Peggie frowned. 'Drops his guard? What d'you mean?'

Billy took a gulp of his tea. 'Come on, Peggie, stop acting thick. It's obvious Dan's playing a part. I don't know what part and why, but he's playing a part all the same.'

Her eyes opened wide in alarm. 'D'you think he's a bad 'un, Billy?' she asked hesitantly.

'I ain't sure what he is, Peggie. But I shouldn't worry. If he had wanted something from us or had come here for a reason, it would have come out by now. No, I think he's hiding from something or someone.'

'You do? Oh!' Peggie's stomach knotted. Suddenly she realised that she couldn't bear the thought of Dan being something other than he gave the impression of being – a hard-working man who like many others moved around in search of work. And it had been her good fortune that he had happened upon her the night she broke down. Her hand shot to her mouth as a thought struck her. 'Oh, Billy, you don't think he's hiding from the law, do you? Or that maybe he's a deserter from the army?'

Billy shrugged his shoulders. 'The thought had struck me. But to be honest, I don't really care what he's done. I like the bloke. He's done more than pull his weight round here and I shall be sorry to see him go.'

215

'Go? Is he leaving then?' she asked, dismayed.

'Not as far as I know. But let's face it, Peggie, he'll have to be moving on some time. He won't stay here for ever.'

Peggie bit her lip. 'No. No, I don't suppose he will.' But more to the point, why do I care? she thought worriedly. She tightened her lips. After being so harshly treated by Harry it would take a great deal to learn to trust another man with her affections. Besides, she hadn't a clue as to whether Dan wanted them.

Billy interrupted her thoughts. 'What's the matter with Letty?'

'Eh?'

'I said, what's with Letty? I might be bedridden but I ain't blind. That sister of mine has something on her mind. And summat big by the looks on it. I've tried asking her but she clams up. Tries to tell me I'm imagining things. But I know I'm not. I do know me own sister.'

Peggie stared at him blankly, then sighed deeply. 'Oh, Billy, I've been so busy just lately I haven't had time to notice anything.'

'That ain't your fault. I think you've done marvellous as it is. Not many women would do what you have.'

'Oh,' she smiled gratefully, 'it's only my duty. I'm only trying to keep things going 'til you get better and,' she added softly, 'Dad comes back.'

Their mother began to stir. She opened her eyes and peered over at them both. 'Oh, I must have dozed off. What day is it?'

Peggie and Billy looked at each other. Nell was declining rapidly. Without Sep her life was meaningless. She was withering before their eyes and they both felt powerless to stop it. The cuddly, sharp-tongued mother they all knew and loved no longer existed, and if something didn't happen soon all hope for any recovery would be lost.

Dan returned late on Boxing Day. Under his arm he carried a pair of crutches, flatly refusing to divulge how he'd acquired them. Billy was ecstatic and couldn't wait for the day to arrive when he could try them out.

Peggie tried her hardest to hide her delight. She would not admit to herself that she had missed Dan though unwittingly welcomed him back like a long lost soul, plying him with mugs of tea and foodstuffs left over from Christmas Day.

Dan took it all in his stride. Peggie's attentiveness, though, was not lost on him.

Peggie did not make any special plans to celebrate the coming of the New Year. She had failed dismally over her ones for a happy Christmas, so New Year's Eve was left to its own device. She did however fetch a jug of best bitter for Billy, hoping that Dan might share it with him. But it seemed he had other plans for the evening and she forced herself not to dwell on this.

She was sitting by the fire feeling quite lonely when a knock sounded on the door. She looked over at it apprehensively. She wasn't expecting anyone. Cautiously she walked over and as she got nearer heard giggling coming from outside. She wrenched the door open. Aggie and Brenda were standing on the doorstep, a bottle of port nestling in the crook of Brenda's arm. Before she had chance to say anything, they both pushed past her.

'We thought you'd be sitting here by yerself,' Brenda spoke firmly, 'so we're come to cheer you up. Didn't we, Aggie?' She nodded. 'So you needn't bother saying anything, just get the mugs. And yer mam can have a drop as well. Might do her good.'

Peggie smiled. It was so good to see her friends. Suddenly the evening didn't seem so daunting. She fetched some mugs and they all sat down at the table.

Peggie looked hard at Brenda. 'Where's Letty?'

'Letty? How should I know?'

'Well, she said she was going round to yours for the night.'

'Did she? Well, she never turned up and we had no plans to see her, did we, Aggie?'

She shook her head.

'Oh, I'm sure that's what she said when she went out. "I'll see Primrose safely to Violet's house, then I'm off to Brenda's and don't wait up, I'll probably be late."' Peggie scratched her chin. 'That's strange.'

'Oh, never mind her,' Brenda said flatly. 'She's been acting strange for a while now so tonight ain't n'ote different.'

'So come on then?' Aggie cut in as she poured out the port. 'We ain't seen much of you just lately. Well, to talk to proper, that is. So what's been happening?'

Peggie took a sip of her drink. It wasn't bad. Better than the sherry Brenda had procured for the dance. 'Not much,' she answered. 'All I seem to do at the moment is work.'

'Yeah, with that lodger of yours,' Brenda interjected.

'Lodger? Oh, you mean Dan. He's not a lodger, he works for us.'

'Lodger, employee, what's the difference?' She grinned and leaned on the table. 'Anyway, he's ever so good-looking, don't you think?' she asked, watching Peggie's reaction closely.

Her back stiffened. 'He's all right, I suppose. To be honest I hadn't noticed,' she lied. 'And I tell you this now, if it's him you were hoping to catch in tonight, well, you're gonna be disappointed, 'cos he's gone out.'

'We know that,' Aggie said. 'We saw him earlier, when we went to see about the port.'

Peggie frowned. 'You saw him? Where?'

'He was in Washpit Lane.'

'Washpit Lane? What was he doing there? And what were you doing there for that matter? It's as black as a coal mine down that lane, 'specially at this time a' night.'

Brenda grinned. 'Oh, I'd arranged to meet me brother. We

didn't want anyone seeing what we were buying, did we, Aggie? If it got back to me mother she'd give me a leathering to be sure.'

'Yeah, and me,' Aggie said ruefully.

'Anyway,' Brenda continued, 'we were standing behind Cobbit's lean-to when we hears this motor. Bit like your bus only not half so loud. Anyway, we peeps out and who should be standing quite near us but him – your lodg . . . employee, Dan.'

'Was he? A' you sure?'

'Is she sure?' Aggie laughed. 'When it comes to a good-looking man, Brenda could tell you exactly who it was blindfolded.'

'Yeah, I could an' all,' Brenda replied with conviction.

'And what about the motor?'

'Oh, the motor?' Brenda grimaced, impressed. 'It weren't half posh, weren't it, Aggie? I hadn't ever seen anything like it before. Dan got inside and it drove off.'

Peggie stared at them blankly. What the girl had told her didn't make sense. What would Dan be doing being driven off in a posh car? Working men like him didn't know the kind of people who could afford such luxuries. Unless, of course, she thought worriedly, it was one of his ex-employers trying to entice him away? She mentally shook herself. The girls must be mistaken. Or, nearer the truth, been drinking before they arrived at her house. Before she could probe any further, Aggie stood up.

'Come on, let's go up and cheer up Billy. I bet he could do wi' a bit of company, him being stuck in bed all this time. It were awful what happened to him, weren't it, Brenda?' She nodded. 'I dunno,' Aggie continued, shaking her head, 'some people treat dogs better than they do humans. Good job that Bull Hammond's in jail or he'd have been lynched by the villagers.'

'They would have an' all,' Brenda agreed. 'And fancy his wife running off like that with all her kids. Too chicken to face the music, I'll bet. Anyway, come on or the New Year will have come in and we'll have missed it.' She picked up the bottle and her mug. She nudged Peggie playfully in the ribs. 'Oh, it's like a party, init? I love parties.'

Starved of what Billy termed proper company for so long, except for the odd mate calling in to see him, he was ecstatic when they all trooped in. There was still plenty of beer left in the jug and before they knew it they were all getting very tiddly, including Nell, who in her confused state of mind drank whatever was handed her. Soon humorous stories were being swopped, several topical issues were argued over, and at one stage they all even sang popular music hall songs.

The New Year arrived and they toasted the air, the drink having been drained long before. Aggie and Brenda reluctantly departed at well past one o'clock. Nell had fallen asleep in the chair and Peggie covered her up and settled down Billy.

'I've enjoyed it tonight,' he said before he closed his eyes in exhaustion.

'Yes,' she smiled. 'So have I.' It had done her good to forget her problems for a few hours.

She had settled down the cottage for the night and was just about to blow out the lamp and go to bed herself when the back door opened and Dan came through.

'Oh,' he said in surprise. 'I didn't expect anyone to be still up.'

She gazed at him and suddenly she was filled with joy at his presence. At this precise moment she didn't care where he had been or who with, the most important thing was that he was here now, standing in her kitchen. 'You're my first foot,' she said unexpectedly.

'Sorry? Your what?'

'My first foot. I've read it's a Scottish tradition. The first person to step into the house after the New Year comes in should be tall, dark and handsome. It's supposed to bring good luck.'

Dan gazed at her. 'And am I, Peggie?' he said slowly, watching her reactions intently.

She tilted her head and smiled up at him, still feeling a glow from the port. 'Mmmm.'

'Does that mean yes?' he asked, advancing.

Standing before her, he gazed down into her eyes. Unexpectedly he bent his head and kissed her lightly on the lips.

'Happy New Year, Peggie,' he murmured.

Suddenly the door flew open and Primrose charged in, still wearing her nightclothes under her coat. The rest of her things were bundled under her arm.

Peggie and Dan sprung apart.

'That's it,' she blurted angrily. 'I ain't staying with her again.'

'What's happened?' Peggie asked worriedly, shivering as a blast of cold air hit her. She hurried over and shut the door.

'What has happened, Primrose?' Dan repeated.

'It's that Violet.'

'What about her?'

'She said my dad's left us. Gone off with another woman. So I hit her. I hit her hard and told her my dad wouldn't do summat like that. She screamed her head off. Said I tried to murder her. I will murder her, the lying . . .'

'Primrose,' Peggie scolded. 'Does Violet's mother know you've come home?'

''Course she does. She chucked me out. Said I was a little ruffian and I wasn't getting to stop ever again.'

'Oh, Primrose,' Peggie groaned.

'Don't you get mad with me, our Peggie,' Primrose said boldly. 'It were her fault for saying things like that.' She sniffed loudly. 'And we'd had such a good time. We sang songs round the piano and her grandad got drunk and took his false teeth out to show us his gums.'

Embarrassed, Peggie leapt over and grabbed her arm. 'Come on,' she said, dragging Primrose towards the stairs. 'You, madam, are going to bed.' She paused and turned, staring over at Dan. 'Goodnight,' she said softly.

'Goodnight, Peggie,' he replied. 'And you, Primrose,' he added as an afterthought.

The memories of Dan's kiss haunted her long after she had got into bed. Try as she might, she could not forget the feeling of his mouth on hers. Had it meant anything to him, she wondered as she tossed and turned, or was it just a gesture because of the occasion? Finally, she convinced herself on the latter, feeling annoyed that if Primrose hadn't made her entrance just when she had then she might have been able to find out. As it was the chance was gone and another New Year's Eve was another long year away. And according to Billy, Dan wouldn't be around that long.

Not long after Peggie fell asleep Letty stole in. She quietly undressed and carefully climbed into bed, but the precious relief of sleep did not come. She lay in the darkness, listening to the gentle sounds coming from her sisters, knowing in a very short space of time she would never again lie in this bed or share the comfort of their presence.

It was three days to her wedding. Three short days after which life as she knew it would be over. How would she cope without her family around her? The enormity of her situation lay heavily as words her mother often said rang loudly in her ears: You made your bed, you lie on it. Whether she liked it or not, that's all she could do. Marry Reginald and face the consequences.

Chapter Twenty-One

'Hello, Mrs Eversly, all set?' Peggie shouted above the noise of the engine as she drew the bus to a halt by the gate.

Mrs Eversly stepped carefully towards the bus, mindful of slipping on the thick mud squelching beneath her boots. 'I can't manage today, Peggie, me duck. I've me sister coming over from Barton. She didn't manage at Christmas or New Year 'cos she likes to spend it with her grandkids so she's condescended to come over today. Good of 'er, ain't it?' she added gruffly, glancing skywards and scowling at the thick grey clouds hanging low. 'That's if the weather holds. It looks like more rain to me. Silly cow won't budge in the rain. Scared of getting wet. Oh, I 'ate winter, I do,' she said, tightening her shawl across her chest. 'I get fed up wi' the cold. If the damp don't get me bones the icy wind does.' She noticed Primrose sitting beside Peggie and gave a toothless smile. ''Ello, Primrose. Looking forward to going back to school?' She was quick to notice her scowl. 'Well, I suppose not,' she said, grinning. 'I wouldn't fancy sitting behind those old wooden desks all day listening to that teacher dronin' on. What yer doing now? Going along for the ride?'

'No, I'm not,' Primrose replied sharply. 'I'm conductressing.'

'Conductressing, eh? Oh.' She puckered her lips, impressed, and turned her attention back to Peggie. 'Anyway, I wondered if you'd do me a favour?'

'If I can,' Peggie smiled.

'Well, I need a few bits picking up. Will you get them for me from Lipton's? Just some butter and tea. Can't give our Ethel marge. She'd have a fit.'

'Yes, of course I will. Have you a list?'

She handed it up plus two half crowns. 'Don't lose the change,' she said jokingly but Peggie knew she was serious. She'd count the last farthing.

'I'll be off then. I'll drop by about four, on my way back.'

'That's if you get there. Looks like fog on its way to me.'

Peggie held her tongue. First it was rain, now fog. She wished Mrs Eversly would make up her mind. She patted the steering wheel. 'A bit of weather doesn't stop Cartwrights' buses, Mrs Eversly.'

'Not like Crabbes' eh? They always have some excuse. It amazes me why they ain't gone out a' business long ago with the way they treat people.' She folded her arms under her dropping bosom and eyed Peggie keenly. 'So you'll be looking forward to the wedding then?'

Peggie stared down at her, wondering if she'd heard right. 'Pardon?'

'The wedding. Tomorrow, ain't it?'

'What wedding?'

'What wedding?' Mrs Eversly huffed haughtily. 'Why, your sister Letty and Reginald Crabbe.'

Peggie stared at her blankly.

'It's all over the village. They're all talking about it. Bella Hubbard reckons someone stuck a notice over the banns so none of us would see 'em. She's mad 'cos she ain't got an invite. Well, 'er being a neighbour she reckons she should have been asked.' She pursed her lips. 'So you'll be looking forward to it then?' she asked nosily.

Peggie shot a glance at Primrose, hoping she could hear none of this over the drone of the engine. Thankfully she hadn't appeared to. She was humming softly to herself, her mind no doubt filled with collecting the fares and ordering the passengers about.

'I'm sorry, Mrs Eversly, but I think you're mistaken.'

She shook her head. 'Oh, I don't think so, me duck. Lettice Cartwright, it said, and Reginald Crabbe. Plain as daylight. Della Hubbard wouldn't mek summat up like that, now would she?'

'I really must be going, Mrs Eversly, else my passengers will all be complaining,' she blurted.

She slammed her foot down on the gas pedal and the bus shot forward. She headed for the pick up point, her mind in a quandary. It just couldn't be true. Mrs Eversly was wrong. Letty couldn't possibly be marrying Reginald Crabbe tomorrow. It all had to be some dreadful mistake.

'What was that Mrs Eversly said about our Letty?' Primrose asked.

'Nothing. Nothing,' she replied. 'Now are you all set? You know what to charge, and be polite else you won't get to do it again,' she said sharply.

Primrose stared at her sister. A few moments ago she had been quite happy and now she looked like someone had died. She wondered for a moment what had made Peggie's mood change so quickly. But the thought didn't last for long. Soon her mind was filled with the job in hand. She was so looking forward to it.

To Peggie the day dragged. All she wanted to do was go home and confront Letty, put her mind at rest that Mrs Eversly, for once, was wrong. But she couldn't, she had commitments.

The journey to Coalville to take the shoppers to the afternoon market was trouble from the beginning. The rain had soaked the mud and the wheels of the bus had a hard job to grip. The vehicle slid several times into deep ruts and twice they were in danger of landing in the ditch. Much to her relief they arrived at the destination in one piece but much later than planned and several of the passengers had the nerve to complain that they would not have much time to do their errands before it would be time to journey back.

Peggie controlled her tongue and settled down to wait. Thankfully Primrose wandered off for a walk around the market and this meant that Peggie would not have to keep up her false front and listen to her chatter.

As the night began to draw in, down came the fog. Both of Mrs Eversly's weather predictions had come true. Soon it was as thick as a bowl of her mother's rib-sticking soup, and as the buildings faded, Peggie's worries rose. She had never driven in fog before, and especially with the bus loaded with weary passengers.

As soon as the last one returned she tentatively set off, but it soon became apparent that it was an impossible task. Her vision was no more than ten yards at the most and she wasn't even sure if she was aiming in the right direction. She stopped the bus, thinking what was best to do. Should she carry on and risk an accident or turn back and somehow find herself and the passengers a bed for the night? She pressed her hands to her temples. This would happen the one night I'm desperate to get home, she silently fumed.

'Excuse me?' a timid voice spoke.

Peggie turned. It was little Mr Abbot.

'Yes, Mr Abbot?' she asked.

'I could guide you if you like.'

'Guide me?'

'Yes. I could walk in front and you could follow.'

Peggie sighed in relief. 'Oh, Mr Abbot, that's a wonderful idea.'

He smiled in delight. Standing several feet in front of the bus, just within her vision, a white handkerchief tied round a stick, he turned and waved. 'You won't run me over, will yer?' he asked worriedly.

Peggie suppressed an hysterical laugh. The very thought tickled her humour and for a split second the seriousness of the situation left her. But it was soon to return. She pressed her foot on the gas pedal and slowly the bus crept forward.

In all her life she would never again experience a journey so bad. It was so frightening that none of the passengers, including Primrose, uttered a word the whole journey. Peggie, acutely aware of the danger they all faced, concentrated so hard on her task that by the time she eventually pulled to a stop outside the Three Tuns her head throbbed violently and she was extremely damp and cold, but no more so than anyone else on the bus.

The passengers breathed deeply and expressed their sincere gratitude.

'I won't ever 'ear a word said against your drivin' again,' Mrs Batterman announced as she came around to the front of the bus and congratulated Peggie on getting them all home safely. 'And that goes for all of us, don't it?'

She smiled as a cheer went up and all twenty people gratefully dispersed to their homes.

Peggie jumped down from the bus and thanked Mr Abbot profusely.

He beamed in pleasure before he walked away.

She was just about to climb aboard again when Primrose jumped down and ran after him, calling his name loudly.

'Where you going, Primrose?' Peggie shouted after her, annoyed. 'We have to get home.'

But Primrose did not answer and Peggie stared into the swirling fog for several minutes before she returned.

'Where on earth did you go?' she scolded.

'To see Mr Abbot.'

'What for?'

'To collect his fare. He never paid it.'

Peggie stared at her horrified. The poor man had just walked eight miles in thick fog in order to guide them home safely and her sister had charged him his bus fare! It was they who should be paying him. Peggie was struck speechless. Of all the nerve. The poor man must think them dreadful to do such a thing. She pushed Primrose hard on the shoulder.

'You'll take that fare money back to him tomorrow. Now get aboard. I want to get home.'

As Peggie guided the bus through the wood yard gates, Dan leapt into view.

'Hi,' Primrose shouted, grinning broadly. 'You should have bin with us. It was awful.'

'Oh, Peggie, Primrose. I've been so worried. We've all been so worried. I was just about to get the lorry out and come looking for you.'

Peggie climbed down from the cab. 'That would have been daft. You could have got lost as well.' She smiled at him gratefully. 'But it was nice of you to be concerned all the same. To be honest it was a nightmare. I never want to go through anything like that again.' She sighed deeply. 'Anyway, could you do me a favour? Could you bed down the bus for the night? I must get home. There's something I need to sort out.'

'Yes, of course I will.' He looked hard at her. 'Is anything wrong?'

'No,' she replied hurriedly. 'I just need to get home, that's all, and get out of these wet things.'

She found Letty in their bedroom, sitting on the edge of the bed, her hands clasped tightly in her lap, her face the picture of misery.

'Letty, is it true? Is it true what they're saying? That you're marrying Reginald Crabbe?'

Letty raised red swollen eyes and nodded. 'Yes, it's true. Tomorrow. I marry him tomorrow.'

Distraught at the confirmation of this devastating news, Peggie closed her eyes and covered her face with her hands. 'Oh, Letty,' she groaned agonised. 'How could you? How could you do such a thing? This will kill Mam. This will end her once and for all. And what it will do to Dad once he finds out, I dread to think.'

Tears sprang to Letty's eyes. 'How do you think I feel?' she sobbed. 'I hate the thought. I cringe when I think of him touching me.' Her voice rose hysterically. 'I don't want to marry him.'

Peggie lowered her hands and walked towards her. 'Well, why is it happening then? Why didn't you put a stop to it before it had gone this far?'

Letty sniffed loudly and wiped the back of her hand under her nose. 'Because I couldn't, Peggie. Once the Crabbes have made up their minds about something, nothing will stop 'em. I used every excuse I could but nothing made any difference. Cyrus wants me married to Reginald and that's that. And if I don't turn up tomorrow, he'll sue us for everything we've got and more besides.'

Peggie sank down next to her and placed her arm around her, pulling her close. 'And you know why? To get back at Dad, that's all. All this is to hurt him, and I wish to God I understood the reason why.' She sighed heavily. 'I did try to warn you, Letty.'

She rested her head on her sister's shoulder. 'I know you did, Peggie, but I was hurting after Wilfred. I was just going with Reginald for spite, to show Wilfred that someone else fancied me. By the time I realised what Reginald was really like it was too late. His father had made up his mind I was going to marry his son and as far as he was concerned, that was that. I really did try to put a stop to it all, but Cyrus is too clever. He has an answer for everything.' She shuddered violently as another wave of misery swept over her. 'They've taken over my life, Peggie. Cyrus even had his dead wife's wedding dress altered by a woman in Hinckley.'

'He never! Why, the nerve of the man! Why didn't you tell me none of this, Letty? Why didn't you come to me? I could have maybe done something.'

'I tried, I really did. But you had so much on your mind and were so busy. And then it was too late. All the arrangements had been made so there was nothing you could do anyway.'

'Oh, isn't there?' Peggie cried savagely. She rose abruptly. 'You just watch me. We'll see if there's nothing I can do.'

Letty looked up at her, horrified. 'Where are you going?'

'To see them, that's what. No sister of mine is being made to marry a bastard like that just 'cos they feel like it.'

Letty jumped up and grabbed her arm. 'Oh, you can't, Peggie. You can't. Please don't do anything. You'll only make matters worse. I have to go through with this. I just have to.'

'But you don't, Letty. I won't let you. We'll suffer the consequences together.'

'No. No. I've seen Cyrus when he's angry. We'll all suffer. Not just me, all of us, and I couldn't bear that, Peggie. I have to go through with this wedding. There's no way out, believe me. I tried everything else.' She choked back a sob. 'Just do me one thing. Please come and see me in church? It will give me so much comfort knowing you're there. Please say you will?' she pleaded.

Peggie lowered her head. 'I don't know whether I can, Letty. I really don't think I could stand by and witness such a terrible thing and hold myself back from putting a stop to it.'

Her body sagged. This was all too much for her to bear. Her poor sister was condemning herself to a life of misery and Letty was right. She had promised herself to Reginald, the banns had been posted and there was no way out. In normal circumstances the wedding could have been cancelled but not when the other party involved was a Crabbe.

Without a word she turned and fled the room, down the stairs and out of the cottage. She arrived at the shed and let herself in where she sank to her knees and sobbed in grief.

'Oh, Letty,' she cried. 'Poor, poor, Letty.'

That was how Dan found her. He quietly approached, knelt down and placed his arm around her.

'Want to talk about it?' he asked tenderly.

'Oh, Dan, Dan. It's awful, just awful.' She shivered. 'Our Letty is marrying Reginald Crabbe tomorrow. Oh, of all people it had to be him. Oh, God, I don't know what to do about it. I just know I can't let her.'

Dan sighed deeply. 'I see.' His face set grimly. 'I don't think there is much you personally can do.'

She raised her tear-streaked face. 'Don't you? Nothing? Maybe if I went to see them . . .'

'No, I wouldn't do that,' he cut in. 'You'll just make trouble.'

'But she wants me to go and see her married. But how can I? How can I just stand there and watch?'

'You'll have to be strong for her sake, Peggie. If you like I'll come with you.'

She stared at him searchingly. 'You will? Oh, Dan, I would appreciate that. But this isn't really your problem. You only work for us and since you've been here I've involved you in all sorts of family troubles.'

'It's no problem to me, Peggie. Really it's not. All I have to do is reschedule that delivery of milk churns to the dairy and my time's my own.' He smiled. 'I'd nothing planned anyway apart from going to watch the football.'

Peggie managed a smile. 'Well, I can't promise you a knees up afterwards. But thanks, Dan.'

'My pleasure. Now go and wash your face and try to compose yourself. Letty will need your support tonight and if your mother sees you looking like that she will know immediately something dreadful has happened.'

'In the frame of mind she's in, I doubt she'd notice but I suppose she'll find out soon enough.'

'Well, we'll see.'

'What do you mean, we'll see?' she asked quizzically.

Dan shrugged his shoulders. He rose and helped her to her feet.

'I didn't mean anything in particular.' He smiled tenderly. 'Sometimes, Peggie, miracles happen when we least expect them. We can always live in hope, can't we?'

'Yes, we can.' She squeezed his arm. 'I'd better get back in before I'm missed and questions are asked. Are you coming?'

Dan shook his head. 'I've an errand to do. I don't know how long I'll be.'

Peggie stopped herself from enquiring what errand. 'Right. I'll maybe see you later.'

He nodded, his eyes following her thoughtfully as she left the shed.

A short while later he knocked smartly on the back door of Dage's general store. It was several moments before it was opened by Effie. Her beady little grey eyes stared at Dan and her mouth set tightly.

'You're that bloke that's up at the Cartwrights'. Drive that contraption for them, don't you?'

'That's right, Mrs Dage. Dan Dickinson.' He held out his hand. 'Pleased to meet you.' He withdrew it when it was ignored.

'Well, Mr Dickinson, what can I do for you? It is rather late, you know.'

'Yes, it is. And I apologise for that. But it's Wilfred I'd really like to see.'

'Wilfred? What d'you need to see him about?'

Dan's back stiffened. 'It's rather personal, Mrs Dage. A matter between me and Wilfred.'

'Oh, is it? Well, you can tell me,' she said, her eyes widening with interest. 'I'm his mother. Me and Wilfred have no secrets between us.'

Dan successfully controlled his temper. What an awful woman. 'Mrs Dage, is Wilfred at home?' he asked.

Just then a voice spoke from inside the room.

'Who is it, Mother?'

Effie's skinny body blocked the doorway. 'Nobody for you.'

Dan stared at her angrily and looked over her shoulder. 'Wilfred? Wilfred Dage? I'm Dan Dickinson. Can I have a few words, please?'

Effie stared at him outraged. 'Well, really,' she spat.

Wilfred appeared behind her. He looked at Dan curiously. 'Yes, what is it?' Then he looked at his mother. 'I'll deal with this, Mother.'

'But . . .'

'Mother!'

Effie, her face thunderous, glared at Wilfred then at Dan, then turned and marched back inside the room. Wilfred joined Dan on the doorstep, shutting the door behind him.

'Well, what is it?' he asked, shivering as the damp dense fog swirled around them.

227

Dan took a deep breath. 'I understand you were once engaged to Letty Cartwright?'

Wilfred's face froze. 'What of it?' he asked flatly.

'I just thought you'd like to know that she's getting married tomorrow.'

Hurt sprang to Wilfred's face. 'I know. My mother took great pains to tell me.'

'And you're not concerned?'

Wilfred's eyes narrowed. 'Why should I be?' he said coldly. 'Letty's made her feelings plain. Very plain.' He stared at Dan quizzically. 'Anyway, what's this got to do with you?'

He shrugged his shoulders. 'Nothing. Nothing whatsoever. Only the fact that Letty is dreadfully unhappy and I don't like to see that.'

Wilfred's face became deeply concerned. 'Unhappy? She's unhappy?'

Dan nodded. 'Yes, she is. She's marrying Reginald because she thinks you don't want her.'

'Don't want her!' he cried gruffly. 'She knows I want her. I love that woman.'

'Do you? In that case why are you letting this happen? Why is she marrying someone else tomorrow?'

'Because she chooses to, that's why. And there's nothing I can do about it.' His face hardened. 'And as you said, it's nothing to do with you.'

Dan shrugged his shoulders. 'Well, I just wanted to satisfy my mind that you knew, that's all.' He began to walk away, then stopped and turned. 'I just know that I couldn't stand by and watch the woman I loved commit herself to someone else, especially when I knew her heart wasn't in it. But then, you're not me, Wilfred. And I haven't got your handicap, have I?'

'Handicap?'

Dan smiled. 'Your mother.'

With that he turned and left Wilfred staring after him.

Peggie spent a restless night. Try as she might she could not empty her mind of harrowing thoughts of the next few hours and the repercussions of the joining of her sister in marriage to Reginald Crabbe. Letty continually tossed and turned. Peggie doubted she was getting much sleep either. Primrose snored on obliviously, unaware of the trauma that her sister was facing.

Finally at five o'clock Peggie got out of bed, rubbed eyes gritty from lack of sleep and wearily made her way down the stairs. It was freezing cold and she shivered as she made up the fire. She placed the kettle on the hob. A cup of strong sweet tea was what she needed. In fact she felt she had never needed one so much in all her life.

In a few short hours the Cartwrights and Crabbes would be united by marriage and the thought filled her with dread.

She went to check Billy, careful not to wake her mother, fast asleep in the chair.

He opened his eyes. 'You're early this morning,' he said, yawning loudly.

'Oh, things to do,' she whispered. 'How are you feeling today?'

'Better, Peggie. I feel I'm improving all the time. When Doctor Ripon comes next, I'm gonna ask him when I can try those crutches out.'

Peggie smiled. 'You'll be driving the lorry before you know it. Fancy some porridge?'

'But I thought that was Letty's job?'

Peggie frowned. 'It was . . . is. I just thought I'd let her have a lie in this morning. She was tossing and turning all night. None of us got much sleep.'

'Oh, that's why you look haggard,' Billy bantered.

She turned on him. 'Thank you for those kind words. Now d'you want some porridge or not?' she snapped.

He looked at her shame-faced. 'Yes, please.'

With head erect, Peggie strode into church and, purposely choosing the middle of a row towards the back, sat down, keeping her eyes fixed firmly ahead. She didn't want to sit near the front. She had no intention of giving the slightest indication she endorsed this marriage in any way.

She was conscious of whispers from several members of the congregation made up of villagers who had come to watch the proceedings out of nosiness. A Cartwright marrying a Crabbe was an event not to be missed. It would fuel gossip for many months ahead.

At the top of the aisle she saw Reginald already in place. Cyrus was nowhere to be seen. Reginald must have sensed her presence. He turned, looked straight at her and smirked. She clenched her fists tightly, fighting a terrible urge to rush up the aisle and confront him, break his neck, anything to stop this charade. But she knew she must not – for her sister's sake.

She breathed deeply and averted her eyes. Dan had promised to attend and was nowhere to be seen. Suddenly she felt a hand touch her arm. She turned. It was Dan. He smiled as he sat down beside her.

'Sorry I'm late,' he whispered apologetically. 'I got side tracked up the shed and forgot the time.'

'No matter,' she whispered back. 'You're here now, that's all that matters.'

She froze as the organist began the Wedding March. The congregation all stood. She struggled to rise, only managing with the aid of Dan's arm for support.

Letty walked slowly by them, her arm resting upon Cyrus's, her face hidden by an old-fashioned veil.

'Oh, no,' Peggie whispered as her legs buckled beneath her.

'He's giving her away. Surely that's not right?' Her eyes hardened angrily. 'He's doing this to make sure Letty goes through with it. Oh, Dan, how could he? How could he?'

'Shush,' he whispered. 'Don't cause a scene, for Letty's sake.'

The organist stopped and they all took their seats.

'Dearly beloved,' Reverend Forest began in a special drone kept especially for just such solemn occasions, 'do you, Reginald Crabbe, take this woman, Lettice Cartwright, to be your . . .' On and on he went, Peggie barely conscious of the words. Finally Reverend Forest raised his eyes to the congregation. 'Does anyone know of any lawful impediment why these two people should not be joined . . .'

I do, I do, Peggie wanted to scream. She felt the pressure of Dan's hand on her arm in warning.

'Don't, Peggie. Leave well alone,' he whispered firmly.

'Speak now,' the Reverend concluded, 'or forever hold thy peace.'

The congregation held their breaths.

The Reverend consulted his hymn book. He opened his mouth to continue the service.

'I do,' a loud voice said firmly.

The whole congregation turned.

Standing at the bottom of the aisle, cap in hand, was Wilfred.

'Oh!' Peggie uttered as mixed emotions overcame her.

Wilfred, aware that all eyes were upon him, advanced forward. 'She can't marry him. She loves me,' he shouted. 'You do, don't you, Letty? You love me!' he shouted.

Cyrus leapt forward and grabbed the Reverend's arm. 'Ignore this man. Just get on with it. Now. Do as I say.'

Reverend Forest indignantly wrenched his arm free and held up his hand. 'He has a right to speak. It's God's law,' he said crossly.

'Stuff God's law,' spat Cyrus.

He noticed Letty had thrown up her veil and had taken several steps down the aisle. He grabbed her arm, pulling her back.

She wriggled free. Before either Cyrus or Reginald could stop her she flew down the aisle and fell into Wilfred's outstretched arms. 'Wilfred! Oh, Wilfred!' she cried ecstatically.

The congregation cheered loudly.

'Oh, Letty, Letty. I love you. Please marry me,' he pleaded. 'I don't care about my mother. I promise I won't let her come between us again. I won't let anything come between us again, ever. Say you'll marry me, Letty? Please say you will?'

'Oh, yes, Wilfred, yes,' she cried in delight.

Peggie closed her eyes tightly in overwhelming relief. She opened them and gazed up at Dan, smiling down at her.

'Oh, thank the Lord. Thank the Lord,' she uttered.

Cyrus turned to Reginald, his face vicious. 'Well, a' you gonna stand there like an idiot and let that . . . that . . . bastard make a fool of you?'

230

Reginald shrugged his shoulders. 'Ah, leave 'em, Dad. As far as I'm concerned they're both welcome to each other. Come on, let's get out of here.'

'Out of here! I came here today to see you married and I'll not leave 'til you are.' He turned and glared down the aisle at Letty and Wilfred hugging each other, villagers clustering around them. 'Nobody makes a fool of Cyrus Crabbe,' he hissed through clenched teeth.

He flew down the aisle, reached Letty and Wilfred and grabbed Letty's arm. 'You promised to marry my son and marry him you will!'

He began to stride back, dragging her behind him. Wilfred leapt after him and grabbed him by the shoulders.

'Oh no you don't. Letty will marry your son over my dead body!'

The crowd cheered.

Cyrus let go of Letty and thrust Wilfred away, his eyes malicious. 'Oh, so that's the way you want it, is it? Mummy's little boy's grown up suddenly, has he? Well, you'll regret this, Dage. I'll make you rue the day you stopped this wedding and made a fool of my son.'

Cyrus felt a pressure on his shoulder. He turned abruptly and found Dan at his side.

'I wouldn't make threats if I were you, Mr Crabbe. You have an audience listening to your every word.'

Cyrus licked his lips as he stared around, suddenly conscious of all the eyes that were upon him. He was beaten and he knew it. This was another occasion when he had lost. 'Have her,' he yelled. 'She's no good anyway. If you ask me my son's had a lucky escape.'

He glared mockingly at Letty then Wilfred before he turned and marched back up the aisle, and out of the side door.

The congregation cheered again.

Chapter Twenty-Two

Nell stared in utter confusion as they all trooped into the kitchen, and especially at Letty, still wearing her wedding dress.

'What the . . . how the . . .' she stuttered.

Peggie quickly took her mother's arm and led her upstairs. She sat her on the bed and tried as best she could to explain what had happened.

At first Nell's muddled mind had difficulty understanding but as the story unfolded she stared at Peggie, horrified.

'Oh, God. Oh, God,' she groaned. 'Cyrus Crabbe was forcing my Letty to marry his son? But this is terrible. And poor Letty was going through with it, to save us from any backlash?'

'Oh, Mam.' Peggie lowered her head ashamed and tears stung the back of her eyes. 'It was my fault, I'm so sorry. I was so busy, so bent on keeping the business running, I didn't notice my sister needed me.'

'Your fault?' Nell's body sagged and she took hold of her daughter's hand. 'Oh, my dear. How can it possibly be your fault? The blame lies with me. I've let you all down so badly.'

Peggie raised her eyes and stared into her mother's haggard face. 'You?'

Nell swallowed hard to remove the lump in her throat. 'It's me who's abandoned you all. From the minute your father left this house my world fell apart. I just couldn't think about anything or anyone but him. Nothing else mattered.'

'But we all understand. You were shocked, Mam. Who wouldn't be after what happened?'

'No, no. You don't see what I mean. Other things did matter, matter a lot. Your father – my husband – is everything to me, but so are my children.' She squeezed Peggie's hand tightly. 'And I abandoned you all when you needed me most.' Her eyes travelled down to her grubby dress and she ran her hand over her untidy greasy hair. 'Oh, Peggie, I feel so ashamed. If your father came back now I would die if he saw me like this. What would he think of me? What must you all think of me?'

'We love you, Mam.'

Tears rushed to Nell's eyes. She fell into Peggie's arms and buried her head in her shoulder, crying softly. 'Please forgive me. Please, please, forgive me. I didn't mean to act like this but I couldn't seem to do anything about it. And as the days passed by I just got worse.' She pulled back and looked Peggie straight in the eye. 'Everything just became such an effort. Without your father around there didn't seem any point in carrying on. And you all seemed to be managing so well without me, I felt no one needed me any more. But I was wrong, Peggie, wasn't I? You all needed me and not just our Billy. I hid behind him. Used his accident as an excuse just to wallow in my own self-pity.'

'But our Billy was very ill. We all thought he'd die. You needed to be with him. We all knew that. If it had been any of us, you'd have done the same.'

'Yes I would have, Peggie.' A hint of a smile touched her lips. 'But I didn't need to be with him all the time, did I? Not after he began to improve. I must have driven the poor boy daft.'

Peggie grinned. 'Yes, I think you did a little. But he understood.'

'Did he? Oh, I hope so.' Nell looked at her sheepishly. 'D'you think you and Dan would do me a favour?'

'Me and Dan? I'm sure we could, Mam. What?'

'D'you think you could carry Billy to the mattress in the kitchen? Dan could move into his and Ronnie's room. And I,' she said, managing a smile, 'can move back into my own bed. Billy'll be much better off. He can see what's going on in the kitchen.'

Peggie smiled broadly. 'I'll see to it straight away.'

Nell sighed loudly and clasped her hands tightly 'You do still all need me, don't you, Peggie?'

'Oh, Mam, you don't know how much. We've all missed you terribly.'

Nell worriedly ran her hand over her forehead. 'It's not going to be easy for me, Peggie.'

'I know that. And we don't expect you just to return to normal overnight. You've had a big shock. We all have. And we've all coped with it in our own way. I did by putting all my energy into keeping the company running.'

Nell raised sad eyes. 'Do you think he'll come back?' she asked tentatively.

Peggie nodded vigorously. ''Course he will, Mam. He loves you. We are looking for him, you know. We didn't tell you because we didn't want to build up your hopes.'

'Oh, Peggie. You've been looking for your father as well as running the business?' Her body sagged. 'And I've done nothing.'

'Yes, you have. You've been nursing Billy.'

Nell smiled. 'Yes, I have, haven't I?'

Peggie smiled at her warmly. 'Look, Mam. Just take a step at a time. Why don't you start by having a good wash and changing your clothes? I'll get some hot water and sort out some clean ones for you. Then whenever you're ready, come down and join us all in the kitchen.' She leaned over and hugged her tightly. 'We need to talk over Wilfred and Letty's future. And to be honest, Mam, your help in this will be most welcome.' She paused, frowning hard. 'Effie Dage has got to be dealt with yet. And I doubt she's going to like this turn up.'

234

'Effie Dage? Oh, we'll soon sort her out. After all, it was her actions that caused most of this situation.'

'That's the spirit, Mam,' said Peggie happily. She gazed at her mother for a moment before rising and walking towards the tall boy. From an old chipped pot vase on the top she shook out her grandmother's ring which she had hidden for safe keeping. She took Nell's hand and placed the ring inside it.

Nell gazed down. 'Oh, Peggie!' she gasped. 'My mother's ring. You redeemed it from the pawn for me.' She raised her eyes. 'Oh, thank you, you don't know how much this means to me.'

Peggie smiled but inwardly hoped that her lies on the matter were never discovered.

'I'll go and get your clothes and organise the moving of our Billy,' she said, heading for the door.

Effie Dage did not like the news one little bit and it was made worse by the fact that she heard it via a customer who took great delight in parting with the gossip. Effie practically threw her bodily out of the door, closed up, raced round to the Cartwrights' cottage and banged loudly on the door.

Primrose answered. The poor girl was pushed aside as Effie burst through. She stood glaring at Wilfred.

'This is a fine way to treat your mother,' she spat. 'I had to hear about what you'd done from a villager. Are you mad? Mad!' she screamed. 'She's a trollop,' she cried, pointing at Letty. 'She was marrying another man. Didn't that prove anything? She just wants your money.'

'Now just a minute,' Billy shouted across from his mattress.

Effie turned on him. 'Don't you start. Your kind is the worst of the lot. You wouldn't be in that state if you hadn't been carrying on with a married woman.'

'We'll have less of that,' Peggie cried, jumping up from her seat.

'It's all right, Peggie. I'll deal with this.'

They all turned and stared open-mouthed as Nell entered the kitchen wearing a clean dress, her hair brushed and neat. Her face set firm, she strode over and stood before Effie, folding her arms under her bosom. 'Who are you calling a trollop, Mrs Dage? I hope it's not my Letty you're referring to. Because if anyone is a trollop, it's you.'

'Me? How dare you.'

'Well, my Letty didn't get herself pregnant then force Wilfred to marry her just to get her hands on his business. She didn't then treat him like dirt, cutting off his conjugal rights so that in desperation he turned to another woman for comfort. Did she?'

Effie turned purple, conscious that all eyes were upon her. 'How dare you? How dare you!' she hissed, outraged.

'Oh, I dare, Mrs Dage, because you're accusing my daughter of being a trollop and there was no bigger one than you. And it's your fault that Letty turned to Reginald in the first place. It was your selfishness that drove her and Wilfred apart and I am not going to stand by and let you do it again. If you care for your son – if you love him – you'll allow him to have some happiness. Happiness that until now you have denied him because of your jealousy.'

'My jealousy?'

'Well, he found what you never did, didn't he? Someone who really loved him.'

'My husband loved me. It was that . . . that woman who stole him. She used her body to entice him away.'

'She never stole him and you know it. Your husband left because you're a cold selfish woman.'

'Oh, is that right?' Effie smiled smugly. 'And is that why your husband's left you?'

Nell reddened. 'For your information, my husband hasn't left me. He's gone away to recover from the shock of what happened to Billy.'

Effie laughed. 'Pull the other one. He's been gone weeks.'

'How long Sep chooses to stay away is none of your business.'

'Then neither is my business any of yours!'

Nell's eyes blazed with anger. 'Oh yes it is. Because my daughter's involved. And I've already told you once, I'll not stand by and watch you interfere again. Now I suggest you give this marriage your blessing, because if you don't you'll lose Wilfred forever. Don't hold the threat of his job or inheritance over him because I'll welcome him into my family. He can live with us.' She turned to Peggie. 'I'm sure we can find him work?'

She nodded.

Nell turned back to Effie. 'It's up to you then. And I suggest you think very carefully on what you say next.'

Effie shook violently with anger. She looked at Wilfred, then back to Nell. She turned on her heel and left.

Peggie rushed over to her mother, grabbed her tightly and grinned. 'Oh, Mam. You were wonderful. Just wonderful. Welcome back.'

'Wonderful? She was bloody marvellous,' Billy chuckled.

Pride swelled within her. 'Yes, I was, wasn't I?' She spun round to face her son. 'And that's enough from you, Billy Cartwright,' she scolded. 'How many times do I have to tell you? I will not have swearing in this house.'

'That's my mam,' he laughed.

Letty jumped up and threw her arms around her mother. 'Thanks, Mam.'

'Yes, and me as well, Mrs Cartwright,' said Wilfred. 'I will look after your Letty, I promise.'

'You'd better, me lad,' she replied sharply. ''Cos if you don't, I'll deal with you far harsher than your mother ever did.'

Later that afternoon, sitting in the chair by the fire, Nell gazed around her family all in deep discussion regarding Wilfred and

Letty's future. How she had missed all of this. It felt so good to be back though she knew it would take a lot of effort on her part not to slip back into depression again. But she was determined. Her children needed their mother more than ever. This knowledge gave her a purpose and a purpose in life was what she needed most of all right now.

For a moment she thought of Sep and wished he were here to witness this family gathering and the happy vein in which it was being held. With an effort of will she pushed those thoughts away. It was one more thing to store up and tell him when he returned.

She looked across at Dan perched on the edge of the armchair that Peggie was sitting in. What a nice man he was. She studied him for a moment and then Peggie. Those two were very fond of each other. She wondered if they knew it themselves.

'What was that?' she said, realising she was being addressed.

'It was me, Mrs Cartwright. I was just saying I don't feel I want to go back to work in the shop. I was thinking about trying my luck in Hinckley or somewhere. My experience should hold me in good stead.'

Nell nodded thoughtfully. 'Yes, it should. If a clean break is what you want?'

'I think it's wise,' said Wilfred softly. 'I love my mother,' he said, smiling at Letty, 'but I love Letty more. And if we are going to stand a chance I have to get away. We can visit her though, can't we, Letty? She's got no one else. I can't abandon her altogether.'

''Course we can. I don't mind visiting. I could just about stand that.' She pulled a face and adjusted her spectacles. 'But not living with her I couldn't.'

'It's just a thought . . .'

All eyes turned to Dan.

'But have you ever considered a mobile shop?'

Wilfred frowned. 'Mobile shop? No, I can't say I have.'

'Well, it's worth thinking about. I mean,' he looked across at Nell, 'your husband has already proved that a lorry can be converted into a bus so why not a shop?'

Wilfred gawped in surprise. 'Oh, I see what you mean.'

'Oh, Wilfred!' Letty spoke keenly. 'That sounds a grand idea. I could help. We could do it together.'

'But I can't drive. And don't lorries cost a lot of money? Not to mention the extras like shelving and such. And we have to find somewhere to live.'

'Don't worry about that. We'll fit you in here,' Nell said.

'Oh, come on, Mam. We're squashed in like sardines as it is,' replied Letty.

'I could move out,' Dan offered.

Peggie's head jerked up. 'Oh, no, Dan. There's no need for that. We'll manage, won't we, Mam?' She blushed a deep red. 'I mean, well, you have to live near because I might need you in an emergency to fix one of the vehicles. You'd have to be on hand like.'

Nell secretly smiled. It was so obvious to her that her daughter did think a lot of Dan. And Dan's face told her he had realised it as well. 'Dan and Wilfred can sleep in my and your dad's room 'cos the bed's bigger, and when Billy's more able he can move in there as well. Me and Primrose will sleep in Billy and Ronnie's room. I dunno,' she said, laughing, 'I haven't even moved back in my own bed before I'm moved out again. Now, enough of this talk of anyone leaving,' she said firmly. 'You can all stop worrying. We'll manage if we have to stack the beds one on top of the other.'

They all giggled at the thought and Nell laughed too.

She rubbed her hands together. For the first time in weeks she was actually feeling hungry. 'Well, I don't know about you lot but I'm starving. Let's get some food on the go and we can finish off this conversation later.'

As the women bustled around the kitchen, Dan pulled Wilfred aside. 'Look, don't take offence,' he began, 'but I'd like to help.'

'Help? In what way?'

'Well, I have some money. You can borrow it if you want.'

Wilfred ran his eyes over Dan's shabby working clothes. 'You have money? How?'

Dan laughed lightly. 'It's not stolen if that's what you're thinking. It's money I've earned honestly.'

'I'm sorry,' Wilfred said hurriedly. 'I didn't think that.'

'You did. Anyway, it's there if you want it. And no one needs to know. You can say your mother gave it to you.'

Wilfred grimaced. 'And you think they'll believe me?'

'They might if you convince them hard enough. Tell them it was your share from your years working in the shop.' He slapped Wilfred on the shoulder. 'Come on, don't let pride stand in the way of your future. Take advantage of my offer. It'll give you and Letty a start and I'm not in a rush for it back.'

'Why? Why are you offering? You don't know me from Adam.'

'Good question. I don't. But I know the Cartwrights. They've been good to me. Gave me a job when I needed it. And took me on trust. Besides, it's Letty's interest I have at heart. I don't want to see her let down again.'

'She won't be,' Wilfred said sharply. 'I nearly lost her once. I won't risk that again.'

'Well, be sensible then. Accept. Offers like this don't come along twice.'

Wilfred frowned thoughtfully, then his eyes lit up. 'You're right and I will. This will be between you and me, you said?'

Dan nodded. 'That's right.'

Wilfred held out his hand which Dan accepted. 'Done,' he said, smiling.

* * *

238

Peggie was itching to ask Wilfred a question and she achieved it just after supper when the others were otherwise occupied.

'Wilfred, I have to ask. Why did you do that? Come to the church, I mean?'

Wilfred laughed. 'Considering I'm a coward, Peggie, is that what you're implying?'

'No, I'm not saying that at all. But, well, you've never done anything like this before, have you? Not that I'm not glad you did it. I am. Truly I am. But, well, it wasn't very you, was it?'

Wilfred scratched his ear in embarrassment. 'I have Dan to thank.'

'Dan?'

'Yes. He came to see me, pointed out what an idiot I was. Said he couldn't stand by and watch a woman he loved go out of his life without a fight.'

'He did? He said that. Oh!'

Peggie stared across at Dan helping Letty with the dishes and a warm glow spread within her. It was then that she knew that she loved him. Loved him like she'd never loved before. She didn't care what had happened in his life before. The Dan she knew was standing in her mother's kitchen now and to her that was all that mattered. She just hoped that he might feel the same about her.

At the other side of the village Reginald cowered in the corner of the room, his face cut and bleeding from the lashing he had received from his father's belt.

'You're a waste of time,' Cyrus spat as he rebuckled his belt. 'Fancy letting a prat like Dage get one over you. How d'you expect us to be able to live here after this with all the villagers sniggering behind our backs? We're a laughing stock, that's what we are.'

He spun round to face Reginald who let out a cry of fright. 'Don't, Dad, please don't hit me again!'

'Don't hit me again,' he mimicked. 'I should kill you, that's what I should do. Through you I'm gonna have to leave this village. I've lost my house and all my plans are in shreds because of you.'

'That's not true, Dad . . .'

'Shuddup,' Cyrus spat.

He strode backwards and forwards across the room, clenching his fists in anger. His eyes narrowed menacingly. 'It's not only you that's caused all this. It's that Peggie Cartwright. I bet the interfering little cow put Wilfred up to that trick. You mark my words, it was her, I know it was. Wilfred ain't got the guts to do something off his own back. Well, before we clear out of this stinking hole I'm gonna make her pay. She'll regret sticking her nose into our business. She did it with Mary. Now she's done it once too often. Get up,' he yelled at his son. 'Go and fetch Jesson.'

Reginald slowly rose. 'Jesson? Why him?'

'Just do as you're told. I've a job for him. And I'm gonna enjoy it. I'm gonna enjoy this more than anything else I've ever done.'

239

Chapter Twenty-Three

Several nights later Peggie picked her way in the darkness across the cinder path towards the shed. The wind had risen sharply and she shivered as an icy blast whipped around her legs. She quickly let herself in and paused by the door, looking tenderly across at Dan. He was lying half exposed under the jacked-up bus, tightening some bolts with a wrench. She smiled as she noticed the oily smudge on his cheek and fought back the desire to kneel down beside him and wipe it off with her handkerchief.

He suddenly sensed a presence, looked up, and seeing it was Peggie, grinned warmly at her. 'Hello, I didn't hear you come in.' He slid out from under the vehicle, stood up and wiped his hands on a cloth. 'What time is it?' he asked.

'Just after eight. I came to tell you the news.'

'News?'

'Yes, about Wilfred, and a right turn up it is as well. His mother's given him some money. Can you believe it after the way she's always acted? Well, I think it was all down to my mother. Her words obviously had an effect. Anyway, he's going to do what you suggested and buy a lorry to convert into a mobile shop. He wants to speak to you about it.' She didn't add that Wilfred had been on his way up to see him himself but she had pushed him out of the way, using it as an excuse to have a few moments in Dan's company. She laughed. 'I don't think he's told his mother what he intends doing with the money. When she finds out she'll have a fit, 'specially since the Co-op has started work on the foundations for their new premises. But all the same, our Letty's really excited and it's so good to see her back to her normal self.'

Dan smiled. 'Good, I'm glad that's settled. That line of business will suit those two down to the ground and I'm sure they'll make a damn good living out of it.' He concealed a yawn and threw the wrench he was holding into the tool box on the floor.

She eyed him searchingly. He looked dreadfully tired, as though he hadn't slept properly in weeks. Deep concern for him rose within her. Maybe she was working him too hard, expecting too much from a man she hardly paid anything to? She knew he had started work before five that morning and it was now well after eight.

'Call it a day, Dan,' she ordered. 'Come and have a rest by the fire and a nice cup of tea. Then an early night might do you good.'

He scratched his neck. Peggie's proposal sounded a wonderful idea but the long day wasn't quite over for him yet. He still had something to do before he finally climbed between the sheets. Not that he slept much. He hadn't slept properly since the day he realised how he felt about her.

He glanced at her out of the corner of his eye. God, but she was lovely. That Harry must have been a mad fool to have passed her up the way he had done. Suddenly her presence was unnerving him. When they were alone, as they were now, he had a dreadful job fighting the urge to gather her in his arms and kiss her long and hard, spilling out all his pent-up feelings. Feelings he never thought he'd feel again for another woman.

'I'm just about done,' he said flatly. 'The bolts on the wheel had worn and I didn't like the look of them so I changed them over. I didn't like the thought of the wheel coming off while you were driving it.'

'Thanks, Dan, that was thoughtful of you.'

He laughed. 'Actually, I was thinking more of the passengers,' he said, meaning it as a joke, but the look on Peggie's face told him it wasn't received as such. He took a deep breath. 'Anyway, I'd better get a move on, I've got to meet someone shortly.'

'Oh? Have you?' She frowned in dismay. Quickly she recovered her composure, spun round and stalked off towards the door. 'Well, I'll leave you to it, then. I don't want to be the one to make you late for your date. Wouldn't do to keep her waiting.' As the words left her mouth she could have bitten out her tongue.

Dan looked across at her quizzically. 'Date? Who said I had a date?'

'Well, haven't you then?' she asked hopefully. 'I just assumed you had if you were going out.'

'Well, you shouldn't presume, Peggie. It could get you into trouble.' He paused thoughtfully. 'But, yes, I suppose I have got a date, in a manner of speaking.' His eyes twinkled wickedly. 'But it's not with a woman like you were thinking.' He studied her for a moment, amused at her probing. 'You weren't feeling jealous by any chance?'

'Jealous?' she snapped. 'Of all the nerve. You're telling me I'm jealous of . . . of an employee?'

'An employee gets paid,' he said, annoyed. He strode towards her and grabbed hold of her arm. 'Go on, admit it. You were jealous, Maggie Cartwright, because you thought I was meeting a woman.'

'I was not,' she cried angrily, wrenching her arm free. She glared at him. 'You called me Maggie,' she said indignantly. 'Who told you about that?'

'Letty. She said you hated that name.' As he spoke his eyes sparkled in amusement.

'And yet you still used it. How dare you?'

She turned and made to storm off. He grabbed her arm again and pulled her forcefully back.

242

'I dare, Maggie Cartwright,' he blurted, 'because . . . because I love you.'

'Oh, is that right?' she spat. She suddenly froze, her mouth clamped shut, staring up at him in astonishment as his declaration struck home. 'What did you say?' she stuttered.

'I said, I love you,' he repeated.

'You do?' Her eyes lit up in delighted surprise. 'Oh, Dan, you do?' she cried.

'Do you mind?' he asked hesitantly.

'Mind! Oh, no. I mean, yes. Oh, I don't know what I mean!' she said, flustered.

He threw his arms around her, picked her up and swung her round. 'Tell me you love me. Tell me you love me,' he pleaded.

'Put me down. Dan, put me down,' she demanded, laughing aloud.

'Not 'til you tell me.'

'Okay, I do, I do!' she cried, burying her head in his neck.

'Say it properly.'

'I love you,' she whispered throatily. 'Oh, Dan, I love you, I love you, I love you. Now put me down.'

He gently lowered her, his eyes full of emotion, circled his arms around her and pulled her close. Then he bent his head and kissed her.

She shuddered as a surge of passion filled her. Never had she been kissed with such urgency, such desire, and she did not want his kiss to end.

Finally they parted and looked at each other longingly.

'Oh, Peggie,' he whispered tenderly. 'You've driven me crazy since the first time we met.'

'Have I? I felt the same too, only I never realised it.'

'Oh, Peggie,' he groaned, his eyes suddenly filled with sadness. 'What the hell am I going to do?' He dropped his arms and turned from her, his face filled with pain.

She stared after him in alarm. 'What is it, Dan? Is it something I've done?'

He spun round on his heel, his face wreathed in anguish. 'You? Oh, no, Peggie. It's nothing you've done. It's me.'

She frowned, deeply worried. 'What is it, Dan? Please tell me.'

'I want to marry you, Peggie. I want that more than anything in the world.'

'Oh, is that all? I thought it was something terrible. 'Yes, I . . .'

'No, no,' he erupted. 'I don't want you to answer. Not yet.' The look of horror that crossed her face was not lost on him. He averted his eyes from her and took a deep breath. 'I've lied to you, Peggie.'

She gazed up at him. 'Lied?'

He wrung his hands. 'Well, I haven't exactly lied. But then I haven't been honest either, and before you give me your answer I want to take you somewhere, I need to tell you a few things, let you

243

see the real me. And then, and only then, I want you to give me your answer.'

Peggie stared at him in anguish. She had always suspected there was something about him, something that didn't ring true. Now that doubt turned to worry. She wanted to run to him, to tell him she didn't care, that nothing mattered but the fact that they loved each other. But the resigned look on his face told her it would be a wasted gesture.

'Are you . . . Oh, Dan, are you in trouble with the police?'

'Peggie, please. Please don't ask me any questions. Just let me explain to you properly.'

'When?'

'Tomorrow.'

'Tomorrow!' she said, aghast. 'Oh, Dan, I couldn't. I couldn't possibly wait 'til tomorrow. I won't be able to sleep tonight.'

'You'll have to, Peggie. We'll go straight after you return from church.'

'Go? Go where?'

'Peggie.'

'I'm sorry.' She fought back tears that stung the back of her eyes. 'I won't be going to church. I couldn't. How could I listen to the Reverend rattling on with all this on me mind?'

'I understand, Peggie. We'll go as soon as it's light.' He noticed her wet lashes, rushed towards her and wiped them gently with his fingers. 'Don't cry, Peggie. Please don't cry. I can't help this. Really I can't.'

She sniffed loudly. 'I'm trying to understand. Really I am.' She sighed deeply. 'Okay, I'll be patient. But you promise, tomorrow?'

He nodded. 'I promise.'

He extinguished the lamp, took her arm and silently they walked the path towards the cottage. So wrapped up in their own thoughts were they that neither of them saw Constable Jesson lurking behind a stack of logs.

He sighed with frustration. For over a week he had been trying to catch her on her own, but to no avail. Whenever she ventured out, there was always someone with her. Cyrus Crabbe would be beside himself when once again he returned empty handed. Jesson sighed worriedly. The man was mad, he had no doubt of that. But to cross him and refuse his demands meant the end for him in more ways than one.

He rose awkwardly and brushed down his uniform. This haphazard approach was useless. Another tactic was called for. But what? He could hang around for weeks to catch her unawares, and time was not on his side. Cyrus was not a patient man. When he wanted something doing it had to be dealt with there and then. He did not understand the word patient. Frowning deeply, Jesson hurriedly skirted the yard, his mind filled with thoughts of how to tackle his problem to Cyrus's satisfaction.

★　★　★

244

An hour later Dan hid behind a tree in Washpit Lane listening out for the sound of the vehicle. Finally he heard it, sprang out from his hiding place and ran down the road to meet it.

'Oh, Cuffy,' he acknowledged the huge man behind the wheel, 'I thought you weren't coming.'

Cuthbert Digby extinguished the lights and grinned across at Dan as he climbed into the passenger seat. 'Sorry, boss, I got held up.'

'Well, never mind that now. What news have you got for me?'

Cuffy shook his head. 'Well, that Crabbe bloke doesn't seem to be doing anything. I can't see any sign of movement.'

Dan frowned. 'Hmm. I would have thought he'd have cleared out by now. What's he playing at, I wonder?'

'Maybe he's just hanging on until the last minute, boss. Maybe he thinks I won't call in the bet.'

Dan nodded. 'Well, if that's what he thinks, he's in for a shock. We'll give him another week. If he's not gone by then, we'll force him out.'

Cuffy smiled. 'It'll give me great pleasure to do that.'

'Now, any other news?' Dan asked.

Cuffy fished in his pocket and pulled out a piece of paper. 'That's the address.'

Dan took it. 'You got it? Good. Well done.'

'Ta, boss,' Cuffy said proudly.

Dan moved across the seat and opened the car door. 'Now best get off, before you're missed. And, more importantly, in this village you never know who's about . . .' He paused. 'How's everyone?' he asked tentatively.

'Well. But they'd be better with a visit from you.'

Dan looked worried. 'Well, I'm going to be making one sooner than anyone thinks. Have a good journey back.'

Cuffy looked at him as he slid out of the car. He'd like to have asked several questions but it wasn't his place. He watched Dan until he disappeared into the darkness. Then he got out of the car, turned the cranking handle, and when the Argyll limousine roared into life, climbed behind the wheel, donned his chauffeur's cap and set off.

245

Chapter Twenty-Four

Peggie arrived in the kitchen early the following morning to find her mother had already beaten her to it. She was busy before the range. A smell of frying sausages, bacon and bread filled the air, but to Peggie it was not appetising at all. In view of her impending visit to God knows where and the fact she had hardly slept a wink all night, the pungent aroma made her feel queasy.

She placed her finger against her lips in a warning to Billy who was sitting up in bed sipping at a mug of tea, forced a smile on her face, tiptoed towards her mother and put her arms around her waist. 'Morning, Mam,' she whispered in her ear. 'You're up early this morning. But I can't deny it's good to see you.'

Peggie released her as Nell turned round, complete with frying pan in her hand. 'Well, I thought I'd start as I mean to go on. I'm cooking you all some breakfast before we go to church.'

'I'll just have tea this morning, Mam, if you don't mind.'

'I do mind and you'll have some breakfast if I have to push it down your throat meself. I dread to think of the last time you all had a decent breakfast.'

'Didn't take you long to recover, did it, Mam?' Billy spluttered, nearly choking on his tea.

'And you can shut up,' she replied. 'You ain't too big to get a thick ear.' She put the pan back on the hob and turned to Peggie. 'Fried bread?' she asked.

She fought back nausea at the thought. 'No thanks, Mam, I just want tea.'

Nell looked at her hard, noticing her ashen pallor. 'A' you ailing for something?'

'No, I'm fine. I just didn't sleep much last night.'

'Why?'

'Oh, Mam . . .'

'Don't "Oh, Mam" me. Why didn't you sleep? A young woman like you needs your sleep, so why didn't you get any?'

Peggie looked at Billy who was listening to the proceedings with great interest, then back at her mother. She felt a desperate need to confide in her, but how could she with her brother present?

'I just couldn't, that's all. Letty was restless. I suppose she was dreaming about Wilfred. And Primrose was snoring as usual. Look, if it'll make you feel better, I'll have a bacon sandwich.'

'Mmm,' Nell muttered, unconvinced at her explanation. 'Well,' she relented, 'that's better than just tea. Sit down, it won't be a moment.'

Peggie did as her mother bade, cut several slices off the loaf of bread already on the table and poured a mug of tea. She took a sip. 'Is Dan up?' she asked casually.

'Yes,' Billy replied. 'He's been up ages. He's gone up to the shed. Summat to do with the bus, he said.'

Peggie addressed her mother. 'I won't be coming to church today.'

Nell turned round. 'You won't? Why?'

'Dan's taking me out.'

Nell's eyes opened wide. 'Is he? Where?'

'Don't know. It's a surprise,' said Peggie lightly.

Nell looked across at Billy, warning him not to make one of his sarcastic quips. 'Oh, that's nice. But I'm sure you could have gone after church.'

'Well, it won't hurt for once.'

'No, well, let's hope the Reverend sees it that way. His beady eyes never miss an absence. Even though he knew I had problems at home, he still managed to make me feel guilty for the times I'd missed.' She placed several slices of bacon on a plate in front of her daughter. 'Well, get that down you. You'll need something substantial in your stomach if you're going out in this weather. It's really wintery out there today. D'you want me to pack a few sandwiches for you?'

Peggie frowned. She wasn't sure. She decided to play it safe. 'I shouldn't bother, Mam, but thanks anyway.'

'Oh, he's taking you out to eat, is he?' Billy said, unable to keep silent any longer.

Peggie looked at him scathingly. 'I wouldn't know. I've already told you, it's a surprise where we're going.'

Just then Dan came in. 'Brrr,' he shuddered as he shut the door. He noticed Peggie and smiled at her tenderly. 'Ah, you're up. Well, I've bought the bus round the front so we'll get off whenever you're ready.' He looked across at Billy. 'When we get back, we'll try out your crutches.' If I'm allowed to come back, he thought worriedly.

Billy grinned. 'Ta, Dan. I can't wait.'

Wrapped up warmly against the cold, Peggie sat in the passenger seat of the bus staring out of the window at the wintery scenery passing by. She restrained herself from asking their destination. As the journey progressed she could not help noticing Dan's face growing grimmer and the sight of that only made her own worries mount about what was facing her.

Finally, after passing through several villages, Dan turned the bus through tall iron gates and after several hundred yards the roof of a huge country house appeared over the tree tops.

Peggie's mind whirled, unable to fathom a reason for such a destination. Dan drew the bus to a halt behind some stabling and turned to face her. Before he could speak a plump old woman appeared carrying a wicker basket full of winter greens.

'Well, well, well,' she cried, her craggy face beaming in delight.

Dan turned his head and looked across at her as she put down the basket and approached them, wiping her gnarled hands on her apron.

'Hello, Ma,' he said, grinning fondly. He opened the door, jumped down and hugged her tightly.

Peggie watched them intently. So Dan had a mother and she worked for the gentry. Why was he ashamed of that?

She climbed down from the bus and walked round to join them.

Dan pulled back, put his arm round Peggie and pulled her close. 'Ma, this is Peggie. Peggie, I'd like you to meet Ma.'

She held out her hand. 'Hello, Mrs Dickinson. I'm so pleased to meet Dan's mother at last.'

The old woman burst into laughter. 'Oh, bless you, my child. But I'm not Master Daniel's mother! God forbid. If I was I'd be up yonder, lounging in luxury, not down here picking vegetables for their dinner.'

Peggie, speechless, looked up at Dan in confusion.

He grinned apologetically. 'I'm sorry, Peggie. Ma here is the cook. Aren't you, Ma? And a better one there isn't this side of London. She should have retired years ago but she's indispensable.'

Ma blushed scarlet. 'Ged away with yer, Master Daniel.' She beamed up at him happily. 'A' yer come back for good? A' yer stopping for dinner? A' yer . . .'

'Ma, I'm just visiting.' He took a deep breath. 'Are they all in?'

She nodded. 'All but Master Roderick. He's visiting friends for luncheon.'

Dan's arm tightened around Peggie's waist. 'I'll see you later then, Ma.'

'You'd better,' she said, wagging an arthritic finger in his direction. 'Don't you dare go away again and not say cheerio to me. You young scally wag!'

Dan laughed loudly. 'I promise I won't.'

He guided Peggie around the side of the stables. She pulled him to a halt.

'She called you Master Daniel. You live here?'

'Yes, I do. Did,' he added.

'Oh, God,' she groaned. 'Why didn't you tell me? Why didn't you prepare me for all this?'

He bowed his head. 'I couldn't. I just couldn't, Peggie. You see, it's not like it looks.'

'Not like it looks? What isn't?' she challenged indignantly. 'Is this your home or not?'

'Yes, it is.'

'Then I'm not moving any further 'til you explain things. If you think I'm going up there to face God knows what, then you're mistaken.' She paused and her voice softened. 'Dan, you told me you loved me. If you do then you'll trust me with whatever's on your mind. At the moment my head is buzzing. I don't know what to think and you're not being fair to me.'

Dan grimaced. 'No, you're right, Peggie, I'm not. But it's too late to stop and explain. Now Ma knows I'm here, it'll be all round the family by now.'

'I don't care, Dan.'

Resigned, he reluctantly agreed. 'All right, all right. I should have told you last night. But I thought if you met my family and talked to them you might understand better.'

'Understand what?'

He took her arm and guided her back towards the stables. He entered and sat her down on a stool before several empty stalls filled with the remains of straw and hay, the pungent smell of horses still lingering. He gazed around.

'This used to be filled with horses before the war,' he said distantly. 'But Father felt it wasn't right to hunt and ride with so many men losing their lives.' He looked down at her and took a breath. 'Peggie, until the war I lived here with my mother and father, three brothers, Gilbert, Henry and Roderick, and my sister Gabrielle. We had a privileged life. This house, all the land you see around and most of the village has been in the family's possession for generations.'

He placed his back against a wooden stall and leaned heavily against it. 'Myself and Gilbert, my eldest brother,' he continued, 'managed the farms and I tinkered in my spare time with the array of vehicles we had then. That's how I picked up most of my knowledge. Father is motor mad and his enthusiasm passed on to me. Henry studied accountancy and works in the City. That's London by the way. And as for Roderick . . .' He sighed. 'Well, Roderick doesn't do anything much. He's a bit of a waster but his heart's in the right place. Gabrielle's married and lives in Norwich.'

He paused and looked at her worriedly. 'Are you all right?'

'Yes, carry on. I'm intrigued to know where this is all leading.'

'Well, the war came and I felt it my duty to do my bit.'

'You went to war? You fought?'

'Oh, yes. I fought all right. On the front, in the trenches.' His eyes glazed over. 'I was an officer in charge of a youthful squad hardly trained in combat. None of them, me included, was prepared for what was facing us. It was terrible, Peggie. The squalor, the stench, the not knowing if we'd ever get out alive. The injuries were appalling. If you were lucky, you were killed. The mud was the worst. It was everywhere. That's how I met Cuffy.'

'Cuffy?'

'Cuthbert Digby. He was my sergeant, and a better one I could never have wished for. He kept me going. It's thanks to him that I'm here now. I was ill with dysentery and he nursed me back to health, though how he managed it defies belief. Unbeknown to me, he used to play cards for other men's rations and with his winnings he forced me back to health.' Dan paused and laughed wryly. 'He always maintained he only did it because I might give him a job in gratitude. And he's right, I did, but not because of his actions. I did it because he's a fine man. You will meet him later. He works here as a chauffeur. Well, really he's more than that, but that's another story.'

He placed one hand on his temple. 'The war changes people, Peggie. It changes them completely. You go away one thing and you come back another.'

She swallowed hard, remembering Harry. 'Yes, you're right, it does. Is that what happened to you?'

He nodded. 'Yes, it was. Before the war I was happy living with the trappings of luxury but when it was time to come back I knew I'd never settle again. It wasn't just guilt at not having died when so many had. It was coming back to all this.' He waved his arm. 'It seemed all wrong, Peggie. I just couldn't come back and carry on where I'd left off. Living my life on the money my ancestors had provided. I wanted to stand on my own two feet.'

'Well, I understand that,' she said sincerely. 'And I admire you for it. I think it's admirable, wanting to make your own way in the world.'

His face lit up in delight. 'Do you, Peggie? Do you really?'

'Yes, very much so,' she said with conviction. 'You're similar to my father in a way. He wanted to make his mark. He was fed up with having his life controlled by others. But 'til we had our . . . windfall, he hadn't the means with which to fulfil his dream.'

Dan smiled. 'Not like me, eh?'

He took a deep breath and walked along to the end of the stable then turned back.

As he did so, Peggie stared after him transfixed. Her heart reached out to him. Her poor Dan, how he had suffered. But that still didn't explain the reason for his secretiveness. A thought suddenly struck her. Unless, of course, he had thought she would fall for the fact he had money if she knew from the beginning? Her temper rose and she jumped up.

'Dan, if you think I'm a gold digger and would have wanted you because I knew you had money, then I'm off!' she cried, insulted.

He grabbed her arm. 'No, I didn't think that. I've never thought that.' He pushed her back down on the stool. 'I haven't finished yet. Afford me that courtesy before you storm off, please.'

She nodded reluctantly.

'Peggie, I was engaged to be married.'

'Engaged?'

'Yes, to a girl called . . .'

'I don't want to know her name,' she erupted. 'Do you still love her, is that it? Then why did you ask me to marry you?'

Dan groaned. 'Peggie, will you please shut up and listen to me? My God, woman, that mouth of yours will run away with you one of these days.'

251

She bit her lip, ashamed. 'I'm sorry. I won't interrupt again.'

'Thank goodness for that. This is very difficult for me, Peggie. I'm trying to explain in the best way I can.'

'All right, all right. Carry on, please.'

He breathed deeply and bowed his head, gazing intently at the ground. 'I thought we were very happy, Peggie. We'd been friends from childhood. She was the daughter of a widowed friend of my mother's. When we grew up, that friendship turned to love. Or so I thought. Everyone assumed we would marry and settle down.' He raked his fingers through his hair as though trying to eradicate a memory. 'Before I was demobbed,' he continued, 'I made my decision. I would give up my interest in the family firm, buy a small house in Leicester and put what money I had left into a business. I wrote to my father and asked his advice. He was delighted. He even offered to help finance me. After all, it wasn't as though I was his direct heir, so I wasn't putting that in jeopardy. And he was only too happy for me to stand on my own two feet. And as he said, if it didn't work out, I could always come home and have my old job back.'

'What kind of business was it going to be?' she asked keenly.

'Selling cars. It seemed the logical thing to do. Motor cars are the thing of the future and it was something I knew about and enjoyed.'

'Sounds a brilliant idea. So why didn't you?'

'Well, when I explained my plans to . . . my fiancée, she was furious. Said I was ungrateful to turn my back on all this. That I'd be blackening the family name. What would happen to my inheritance? You name it, whatever she could come up with she threw at me. I tried to reason with her. Tell her that in the long term this venture would make us a good living. But still she wasn't convinced. I couldn't understand it. It was as though she'd had a personality change. Before all this she had been so kind and gentle, so content with our relationship. I thought it best to let things settle down for a while, let her think properly about the idea. Then I approached her again. She was even worse that time. Flatly refused even to entertain it. Said she hadn't been groomed all these years for living in a poky little house in the middle of town, away from all her friends, whilst I played out the part of the big businessman. She gave me an ultimatum. It was her or the business.'

Peggie's face grew grim. 'And?'

'Well, it was then that I began to have doubts about her. I wondered if she was only marrying me in the first place because she would move to this house and play the lady. I thought if she loved me she'd be happy to consider my plans.'

Peggie nodded. How stupid of the woman not to have given him her support, she thought angrily. She herself would have jumped at the chance of working alongside him. Seeing his dream come alive. To her, just having him come home to her at nights would have been enough.

'I reasoned with myself and thought that maybe she was right.

252

That I should just pick up the pieces where I'd left off. That I wasn't being fair to expect her to fall in with all I wanted, so I tried to come up with ways to keep us both happy.

'And did you?'

'I did, yes. I would have the business and travel backwards and forwards each day. I'd have been very tired but it would have been worth it to keep her happy.'

'And what did she say when you told her?' Peggie asked flatly.

'I didn't get to. It was then I found out.'

Peggie narrowed her eyes. 'Found out what?'

'That she'd been carrying on all the time I was away. Oh, she was very discreet. But it was with someone we both knew very well. And . . . and he was married himself with a young family.'

'Oh, Dan,' she whispered, deeply distressed. Her anger mounted against the unknown fiancée. She felt a desire to claw her eyes out for the pain she had caused this man Peggie now loved.

Dan raised hurt eyes. 'I was distraught, Peggie. I couldn't think straight. I did no more than pack a few things in a bag and walk out. It took me nearly six months to write and explain matters to my parents. I caused them so much suffering and I regret that deeply, but at the time I did not stop to think what I was doing.'

'Where did you go?' she asked.

'Anywhere the road led me. Picking up work as I went along. I didn't care what it was as long as I had enough food and somewhere to sleep. That's how I came across you.'

She smiled at the memory. 'I've often wondered how you appeared out of nowhere like that and disappeared just as quickly.'

'Actually, what had happened was that when I first left, my parents sent Cuffy to find me. It took him quite a while to trace my whereabouts but eventually he caught up with me. He tried to persuade me to go home but I wasn't ready. So Cuffy, the stubborn so and so that he is, wouldn't go back either. The pair of us travelled round together. Cuffy, I know, informed my parents what was happening. Anyway, several months ago, I felt ready to face every-one and we were on the way back when Cuffy stopped to . . .' He smiled. 'Relieve himself behind the hedge. That's when I saw you and came across to help.'

'And all the time Cuffy was in the bushes?'

'That's right. Listening to every word we said.'

'He heard me break down and tell you everything?' she gasped.

Dan nodded. 'But he won't say a word. He's very loyal. Anyway, I decided there and then that you needed me. Needed my help. And that's what you would get. I sent Cuffy home and came to you.'

'Is that it?'

He frowned. 'What do you mean, is that it?'

'Exactly what I said. Is that what all the secrecy was about? Is there anything else you haven't told me?'

Dan shook his head. 'Nothing. I just wanted you to hear it all and

253

to understand that I would never feel comfortable living in this house again. Even though I would be welcomed back with open arms, I wouldn't feel right. And I needed you to understand that before you gave me your answer.'

'Did you ever have any doubt that I would refuse you once I knew I would never get to live in this . . . this mausoleum of a place? Having people wait hand and foot on me?'

Dan looked at her. 'No. That wasn't my worry, Peggie.'

'Well, what was then?'

He tilted his head and grinned at her. 'That you would throw me out on my ear once you knew I'd been engaged before! You know what your temper's like. You would never have allowed me to explain properly before you lost it.'

Peggie stared at him defensively, then smiled. 'Yes, you're right, Dan. I would have gone mad. But I would have regretted it afterwards, believe me.' She clasped her hands together. 'I have to be honest, Dan, I hate the fact that you loved someone before me. But then, I had Harry. So I can't hold it against you, can I?' She smiled up at him, love shining from her eyes. 'If you want my honest opinion she was a bloody fool. And her stupidity has been my gain.'

'So you'll marry me, Peggie?'

She jumped up and ran to him. 'Oh, yes, Dan. Now more than ever. I thought you'd never ask me again.'

Delighted, he threw his arms around her, bent his head and kissed her deeply. 'You'll never regret this, Peggie. I'll make you so happy.'

'And me you,' she replied. 'I'll love you 'til I die.' She gazed up at him adoringly. 'But all this, of course, is on one condition.'

'Oh, what's that?'

'That you carry out your plan for the car business, Daniel Dickinson, and I want to be at your side every step of the way.'

He hugged her so tight she thought her ribs would crack. 'That's fine by me.' He paused, grinning broadly. 'Er . . . there is something I forgot to tell you.'

She pulled back and looked up at him, worried. 'Oh, God, what now?'

'Nothing important, Peggie. But my name's not Dickinson. It's Dixon. I dared not divulge my real name in case the Dixon family was already familiar to you.'

Peggie frowned in surprise as a thought struck her. 'Why, it is. I remember my own father telling me that someone in the Dixon family designed a seating arrangement to go on the back of one of their vehicles. That's where he got his idea from.'

'That was my father,' Dan said proudly. 'And I knew. I knew as soon as I saw your bus.'

They both turned sharply as a commotion came from outside. Dan's name was being called.

He looked at Peggie helplessly. 'Oh, dear, my mother . . .'

He had no time to finish his sentence. A very smart and attractive middle-aged woman strode into the stable. She halted on spotting Dan. Her face broke into a smile of delight and she held out her arms.

'Daniel!' she cried, rushing towards him. 'Oh, darling, you've come home.' She threw her arms around him and hugged him tightly.

Dan responded, kissing her fondly on the cheek.

She raised tear-filled eyes. 'Oh, I've counted the days. I can't believe you're actually here. Your father will be delighted. And the rest of the family.

She pulled away from him and turned her attention to Peggie.

Dan took the lead. 'Mother, I would like you to meet Margaret Cartwright. My future wife,' he added proudly.

She turned back to Dan, her face filled with astonishment. 'Wife? Dan, truly?' She spun back. 'Oh, my dear, welcome, welcome. I can't tell you how happy I am.'

Peggie looked at her. 'You don't mind?'

'Mind? Why should I mind?'

Peggie looked hesitantly at Dan then back to his mother. 'Well, I'm not exactly a . . .'

'Not what, dear? A lady? Was that what you were going to say? Well, let me tell you there are several interpretations of what defines a "lady" and believe me, I have come across all of them in my time. And you can stop those silly thoughts for a start. Any woman who managed to bring my son back is a lady in my book. I owe you a debt of gratitude, my dear. And besides,' she said, smiling broadly, 'with a name the same as mine there can't be much wrong with you, can there?'

'You're called Margaret too?' asked Peggie in surprise.

'Yes, and so were all the first-born females for generations in my family.' She took Peggie's arm and leaned over, whispering in her ear, 'My darling husband calls me Maggie, bless him. Margaret can be such a mouthful for everyday use, don't you think?'

Peggie suppressed a smile. 'Maggie,' she muttered, swallowing her mirth. To her, Dan's mother looked anything but a Maggie. Maggies to her were homely, motherly types with armfuls of screaming babies. They worked behind bars and usually ended up as farmers' wives. This Maggie didn't fit into that category at all, with her coiffured greying hair, stylish country clothes and refined accent. For a moment Peggie wondered if she had misheard her. Then she realised, ashamed, that over the years she had done all the genuine Maggies an injustice.

'Well,' Margaret Dixon said, addressing them both, 'what, may I ask, are we all doing in here? Let's get up to the house. You must both be freezing. And we've so much to talk about. I want to hear all about you, Margaret. And then you must tell me your plans for the wedding. I must meet your parents. Oh, won't that be nice?' she said in genuine delight. 'But first we'll have lunch. You'll both be hungry, I trust?' She smiled at Peggie. 'If that's all right with you, my dear?'

'Yes, very much so,' she replied happily.

Margaret Dixon linked arms with them and all three made their way towards the house.

It was nightfall by the time they were allowed to set off for home, and not until they'd given firm assurances that they would both return soon and that their visits would be regular from now on.

Dan turned to Peggie as he drove out of the gates. 'Happy?' he asked.

She turned to him, her face illuminated by the moonlight, giving it a soft glow. 'Oh, yes. I never been so happy, Dan. Your parents are wonderful people. I've never thought gentry were . . . were . . .'

'Human?'

'Oh, they're more than human, Dan. Your mother and father made me feel so welcome. I was so nervous, 'specially when we all sat down to dinner. Oh, sorry, luncheon. I've never eaten off proper china before. I'm sure I used the wrong cutlery.'

'I shouldn't concern yourself, Peggie. Nobody would have noticed,' he said reassuringly.

'You're right, they never.' She laughed loudly. 'Not even when I dropped my peas on the floor. But your house! Oh, Dan, it's . . . magnificent. That's what it is. Are you sure you've no regrets about leaving it? Are you sure you won't change your mind later?'

'I'm positive, Peggie. Why are you asking? Do you doubt what I say?'

'Oh, no, no. I just wanted to make sure, that's all. After all, you have come from an entirely different life style and our lives once we're married will be more what I'm used to, not the other way round.'

Dan exhaled deeply. 'Peggie, will you please stop worrying? I was very comfortable when I lived with my parents but I can assure you that I feel just as comfortable in your home. Now, please, I don't want to hear any more on that subject. When we're married we'll have our own place and you can do what you like with it, money permitting.'

An excited thrill shot through her at the prospect. A home for herself and Dan. 'I can wait,' she said happily. 'And the first people we'll invite over to tea are your parents. I know me and your mother are going to be real friends.'

Dan smiled warmly. 'I'm glad. I never doubted she would take to you. I just wondered if you would like her.'

'I don't see how anyone couldn't. Her and my mother are going to get on famously.' Peggie sighed deeply. 'Oh, Dan, I was so worried this morning. I never slept a wink last night.'

'I'm sorry I had to put you through that. But you understand why I had to do it? It was for my own peace of mind. I worried that my

256

past might cause a rift later on and I couldn't bear that thought.'

'Dan, I don't know why.'

'No, to be honest neither do I now. But I'm glad the air is clear anyway. I want our marriage to be honest from the start.'

'So do I. That's why I have to ask you two questions.'

Dan pulled the bus to an abrupt halt. 'Oh, what?' he asked, worried.

Peggie gazed at him quizzically. 'Those clothes you turned up in the morning you first came to the cottage. They weren't yours, were they?'

Dan burst into laughter. 'No, they weren't. Cuffy bartered with a man in a public house in the next village we arrived at. He picked on someone who looked more or less my size and it was his clothes for mine, plus a few coppers.'

'Well, he didn't do a very good job, did he? They were far too small.'

'Did I look really dreadful?'

'Yes,' she guffawed. 'Really, really dreadful.'

'Well, I felt if I looked in need you couldn't refuse me. Now I've answered one, what's the other question?'

'Was Cuffy the man you kept meeting when you went out mysteriously some nights?'

'Yes, most times he was. He wanted to keep in touch and if I'd refused he would only have come to the cottage. The nights I stayed out I took a room in a public house and did justice to the local ale. To be honest, Peggie, I fell for you from the beginning and needed to get away. I wasn't prepared to fall in love again, you see. It came as rather a shock.' He smiled warmly at her. 'Now, anything else while we're at it?'

'No, I don't think so for the moment.'

'So we can get home then?'

'Yes, please. 'Cos I'm dying to break the news.'

As they continued the journey Peggie lapsed into silence. Dan was quick to notice.

'You're thinking of your father, aren't you, Peggie?'

She nodded. 'I miss him so much, Dan. Now more than ever. He would be thrilled with this news and I so want to share it with him. And his business. He started it off, Dan. He was so full of hope. So determined to make it succeed. Well, it has and he should be here sharing the benefits.' She turned her head and gazed out into the darkness. 'He's out there somewhere and I keep worrying we've missed him. He needs us, Dan, I know he does. I feel it in my bones.'

He stared straight ahead, wondering if he should tell her what Cuffy had found out. He decided against it. 'Remember not so long ago I told you that sometimes miracles happen?' he said. 'Well, you never know, you might be lucky and another one may happen. Pray, Peggie. Sometimes prayers are answered.'

She turned her head enquiringly. He knew instinctively she was going to question him and he didn't want that. He didn't want to risk building her hopes up.

'I didn't say ask questions, Peggie, I said pray,' he said firmly. As he spoke his eyes glanced down at the gauges. In his preoccupied state of mind that morning he had forgotten to fill the tank. He grimaced. 'And while you're praying, say one for the bus. I've a feeling we're about to run out of petrol.'

They both looked at each other and burst into laughter.

'Well, you can be assured of one thing,' she spluttered, 'if we do run out, I'm not pushing. I draw the line at that.'

The family, of course, were delighted with the news. It was only what they had all secretly expected anyway. Shocked surprise though was shown at Dan's parentage. Wilfred and Letty were struck speechless. Billy had suspected many things but never that. Nell had to stop herself from curtseying and was horrified at the thought of a visit to the Dixons. Dan and Peggie soon put her fears at rest on that score.

Primrose took to calling Dan 'his lordship', much to the amusement of everyone else. But Dan took it all in good part, much to Peggie's relief, and soon the talk got around to weddings and the possibility of a double one. But Peggie wasn't having it. When she married Dan, she was adamant that she would be the only bride walking up the aisle.

Peggie and Letty were both agreed on one thing. Neither of them would consider any ceremony until their father was safely back amongst them.

Chapter Twenty-Five

Just after nine the next day Dan walked through the cottage door and glanced round. As usual the room was full to overflowing. Steaming washing hung from the cradles suspended from the ceiling; the welsh dresser was even more cluttered by bits and pieces; the shelf above the range would have difficulty housing even a sewing needle; and now that a mattress had been wedged in the recess in the corner, accommodating first himself, now Billy, the room looked even more congested, if that were possible.

Dan smiled to himself. He loved this room, this cottage and all the people in it, and by God, should an outsider do the slightest thing to harm any one of them they would have him to answer to now.

He sniffed appreciatively. Nell was standing over the kitchen table preparing the evening meal and the smell made his mouth water. Ma, his mother's housekeeper, was a very capable cook but Nell Cartwright surpassed even her.

'Is Letty about, Mrs Cartwright?' he asked. He suddenly spotted Billy manoeuvring his crutches and rushed over. 'Here let me help you with those. I thought I told you to wait until tonight so I'd be here in case you have trouble with them.'

'Oh, he couldn't wait,' Nell said matter-of-factly, glancing disapprovingly at her son from the corner of her eye. 'Once Doctor Ripon gave him the go ahead there was no stopping him.' She slapped the pastry over and vigorously rolled the other side. 'I've told him he'll end up back in bed, but with a broken neck this time. You mark my words.'

'Stop fussing,' Billy scolded, frustrated. 'I'm just a bit wobbly after being in bed for so long, that's all. But it won't take me long to master them,' he added determinedly.

Dan scratched his chin. 'Well, if you're sure. But just take things a stage at a time.'

'What, you mean I can't go down the pub tonight?' Billy asked seriously.

Dan chuckled. 'Well, I suppose I could always walk down with you. Just for support.'

'Hey, we'll have less of that, you two. The doctor said you could try them out, not take a hike.' Nell threw the pastry over a dish of beef skirt and kidney and began to edge it around with a knife. 'In answer to your question, Dan, Letty's up at Jenny Pegg's. Wilfred's gone with her to look at some furniture Jenny said they could have

259

if they wanted. Neither of 'em will be back for a few hours yet.'

Dan, who already knew this, groaned loudly. 'Oh. Oh, dear. That's torn it.'

Nell raised her head. 'Torn what?'

'Oh, it's nothing,' he replied distantly. 'I'll just have to hope I can manage by myself, that's all.'

'Can I do anything?' Billy asked, balancing precariously on his crutches.

Dan grabbed him just in time to stop him from falling over. He laughed. 'I need someone with two good legs, Billy. But thanks for the offer.'

Nell wiped the table clean and collected ingredients together in order to make bread. 'What did you want Letty to do anyway?' she asked, tipping flour into a bowl.

'Well, I've been asked to deliver a bed to an address in Leicester. It's a last minute job and wants doing as a matter of urgency. Only I'm not sure exactly where the address is. So whilst I ask around I need someone to sit in the lorry and guard it in case someone helps themselves.'

'A bed!' Nell exclaimed.

'Yes. Er   it's a wedding present from Major Allot to his niece. And for some reason it's got to be delivered today.'

Nell frowned. 'Major Allot giving a present? I've never known that man give so much as a pea from one of his pods before now.' She looked thoughtful. 'You'll be wanting someone to help lift it then.'

'No, no. There's men all ready at the other end to do that. Only I said I'd do it today and I hate to let them down. I negotiated a good price,' he added casually.

'Oh, seems a shame to lose the money. Would I be of any use?'

Dan clapped his hands in delight. 'Mrs C, you're a wonder. And you'll get a trip out into the bargain.'

'Oh, well, in that case I'll get me coat.' She turned to Billy. 'If I'm not back in time put that pie in the oven about half-past four. If you forget, you'll be for it. And tell our Primrose to get the vegetables peeled when she comes home from school. And the water. We need some more water fetching. Oh, Wilfred might do that. Ask him.'

'Yes, Mam,' he replied. 'Just go with Dan and enjoy the ride. You ain't been outside this house for weeks. It'll do you good.'

Dressed warmly against the wintry wind, and with the aid of a shove up from Dan, Nell settled herself into the passenger seat. She tucked a thick knitted blanket over her legs and turned hesitantly towards him.

'You can drive this thing all right?'

'Yes. Don't worry,' he replied firmly.

'And you won't go too fast, will you?'

Dan grinned. 'Trust me, Mrs C. I wouldn't harm a hair on your head.'

She sniffed haughtily. 'I think it's in order for you to call me Nell. After all, we'll be related sometime, won't we?'

They arrived in Leicester two hours later and he stopped the lorry in the middle of the Humberstone Lane opposite rows and rows of grimy-looking terraced houses. Nell wouldn't admit that she had enjoyed every minute of the journey. She just stared down the streets thankful she didn't live in such dismal, rundown surroundings. But even more surprising was the fact that a niece of Major Allot's lived around here. Everything looked so drab and decaying. The never ending rows of houses; the people spilling out from the factory gates on the other side of the road, heading home for their lunch; the factory chimneys still belching thick black smoke. Even the grass in the tiny park further down looked dirty and uninviting.

'Time's getting on,' she grumbled, shivering with cold. 'I never realised it would take this long. If I'm not back the dinner'll be ruined and I won't be there to dish it up.'

'Don't worry, Mrs C . . . Nell. Billy and the others are quite capable of taking over. Now, will you wait here while I go and check out the address? It's one of these streets but I'm not sure which.'

Nell reluctantly nodded and Dan set off, the address that Cuffy had given him in his hand. Nell looked around her and her eyes settled on the back of the lorry. She frowned. Although it was covered in a sheet of thick grey tarpaulin, it didn't appear to her to be covering anything up. It was too flat.

She shrugged her shoulders and turned back, settling her attention on a group of ragged children loitering by a shop doorway on a corner.

Suddenly a shout rent the air and all the children scattered. A shop keeper rushed out of the shop waving his fist in the air.

'You thieving buggers!' he cried angrily. He spotted Nell. 'Did you see that? They were pinching me apples.' Without waiting for a reply he waved his fist again, shook his head angrily and disappeared back inside.

Dan meanwhile was knocking on a door. He quickly noticed that the doorstep was scrubbed and the nets hanging at the windows looked clean. Not so in several of the adjoining houses. A fat grubby woman, her arms folded, giving the appearance of holding up her enormous chest, was leaning on the door frame of a house further down. She was glaring at him suspiciously. So were several children who had abandoned their game of football and were gazing over at him. Dan ignored them all.

Eventually his knocking was answered by a tall thin woman. She looked at him enquiringly.

'Yes?'

'Does a Mr Carter live here?'

'And who's asking?' Mrs Scroggins replied cagily.

'Me. I'm asking,' Dan said firmly. Time was running out and he could not afford to waste precious minutes making polite conversation to this woman. If he did, Sep would be upon them, then all his careful planning would have been in vain. 'Does he live here or not? It's important and I haven't got time to mess around.'

Mrs Scroggins folded her arms under her flat bosom, glanced up and down the street and back at Dan. 'He might do. What do you want him for?'

Dan held out an envelope, inside which was a note he had written several minutes before after quickly spying out the area. 'Please give him this as soon as he comes in.'

'You can wait if yer want? He'll be home from work in a minute for his lunch.'

That was the last thing Dan wanted. 'Please, just give him the envelope. And remember, as soon as he comes in.'

Mrs Scroggins snatched it and closed the door. Dan hurried off back to the lorry.

'Nell,' he shouted up to her as he arrived, 'there's nobody in. I'll have to hang around for a while.' He glanced around him. 'Look, there's a tea room over there. Why don't you go and have a cup of tea?'

He fished in his pocket and handed her several pennies. 'That should be enough.'

She frowned hard. She hadn't anticipated this. She'd thought she was coming for a nice run, Dan would do his business and they would be well on their way home by now. She exhaled sharply and as she hadn't brought her purse, took the money out of Dan's hand. 'All right,' she said gruffly. 'But I thought I was to stay and guard the bed? And anyway, about this bed . . .'

He quickly interrupted her. 'You get across and have a warm. You must be frozen. I'll go back and check if they've arrived yet.'

Before she could say any more he was gone.

She sat in the tea room nursing a pale-looking mug of warm tea. The tea room, like the rest of the area, was drab to say the least. The tables wanted a wipe and the woman behind the counter looked in dire need of a bath and change of clothes. Nell watched in horror as she wiped her hand under her nose then served a customer with a slice of fruit cake. Dirty cat! she thought disgustedly.

She glanced out of the window, wondering if Dan had finished his business yet. She wanted to be out of this place. She wanted to get home. She turned her gaze to the door as it opened and a man walked in. He paused by the door and looked around at the tables. Nell's hand flew to her throat.

'Sep!' she uttered. It was him. He was much thinner, his face gaunt, and he was shabbily dressed, but it was her husband all right. She slowly rose, her mouth open. 'Sep,' she called, finding her voice. 'Sep.'

His eyes settled on her in disbelief. 'Nell,' he whispered, his face creased in shock. Several moments passed. It took that long for it to dawn on him that he wasn't hallucinating, the woman standing by the table across the room was his beloved wife. His face broke into a broad smile of happiness as he weaved his way through the tables towards her.

He stood before her. 'Nell. Oh, Nell. I can't believe it's you.'

'The same goes for me. You're the last person I expected to walk through that door. Oh, Sep,' she cried, throwing her arms around him, much to the astonishment of the other customers. 'Oh, it is good to see you. Sit down. I'll go and get you a cuppa.'

'I don't want tea, Nell. Just tell me how you found out where I was?'

'Well, I . . .' She stopped as it struck her just what had happened. It was Dan. This was all his doing. Sep had been found and the whole trip was a ruse to get them together. No wonder the back of the lorry looked flat. There never had been a bed under the tarpaulin. 'Never mind about that. It's not important at the moment. I want to know about you. How are you? What have you been doing?' Her voice dropped to a husky whisper. 'Oh, Sep, have you missed me? Why did you go away and leave me like that?'

Sep swallowed hard. 'I had to, Nell. I had no choice.'

'No choice? But I'm your wife. Surely you could have talked to me? I've been through hell, Sep. Pure hell. And so have the children. We thought you were dead.'

'Dead?' He shook his head sadly. 'No, Nell, not dead. But I might as well have been.'

'Well, why then?'

He lowered himself down on a chair and wrung his hands. Nell followed suit, eyes filled with pain, fixed on him.

'I found out, Nell, about you and Cyrus.'

'Me and Cyrus?' she repeated, frowning quizzically. 'What about me and Cyrus?' Fear suddenly raced through her. He had found out about their meetings during the war. He must have. 'Oh, God,' she groaned inwardly. How did she explain to him how that had come about? Would he believe her that nothing happened?

'He saw your legs, Nell.'

'Pardon?' she uttered in disbelief. 'My what?'

'Your legs. He told me he knew you had trouble with your legs. And that could only mean one thing.' He took a deep breath and looked at her hard. 'Did you, Nell? Did you have an affair with Cyrus Crabbe?'

'I did not!' she cried with conviction. 'Septimus Cartwright, how could you think such a thing? He saw my legs when I was having my ankle bandaged by his daughter, Mary. I'd fallen in the snow and twisted it, and if Cyrus hadn't come along when he did, I would have frozen to death. He took me to his house and his daughter did the honours. He saw my legs when he came through with a cup of tea for me and I soon covered them up, I can assure you.' She tightened her lips in anger. 'So if that's what you call having an affair, then yes I did.' Her body sagged. 'Oh, Sep,' she whispered. 'Did he tell you this lie?'

Sep groaned and placed his head in his hands. 'Oh, Nell, how could I have been such a fool? How can you ever forgive me for believing him?' He felt her hand touch his and raised his head. 'Can you ever forgive me, Nell?'

'Sep, there's nothing to forgive. Your absence has made me realise how much I love you. You have my solemn word that we never had an affair. Not ever. Now will you come home. Please?'

Tears sprang to Sep's eyes and rolled unashamedly down his cheeks. 'I'd like nothing better, Nell,' he whispered, wiping his face with his hand.

'Good,' she said firmly. 'Let's get your things.'

She took hold of his hand and together they walked out of the tea rooms.

Five faces stared at him in astonishment when several hours later Sep walked through the door. Shock quickly gave way to joy and three delighted daughters threw themselves on him, shrieking in delight, and his son hobbled over as hurriedly as his crutches would allow. Dan and Wilfred stood at the back and watched.

Questions came thick and fast. In the end Nell had to shush them all and made them give their father at least time to catch his breath.

Later that evening they all sat round the table enjoying the dinner that Nell had worried would be ruined. Sep slowly chewed a delicious piece of beef and looked around, his eyes settling on each individual in turn and especially the two latest additions.

His family had expanded during the months of his absence and he couldn't have been more pleased with the choices his two eldest daughters had made. Especially Peggie's Dan. The man had done wonders in expanding the haulage side of the business and if Sep's instincts were correct, he also owed him a deep debt of gratitude for the part he had played in getting Wilfred and Letty back together, saving her from the Crabbes' clutches. But more importantly, it was through Dan he was sitting at this table now.

Only just that morning he had been trudging wearily back to Mrs Scroggins for the dish of thin soup and dry bread she provided for her lodgers, seriously wondering if he had been wrong not to have thrown himself into the river. His life had stretched before him as a black void, cut off from the people he cared most for. And why? Because he had accepted a lie that he knew deep down, if he had dared to search his soul, could not possibly be true.

He glanced lovingly at Nell sitting by him and rested his hand gently on hers. Never again, he vowed, not for any reason, would he leave her again. Cyrus had lost. And if the man had any sense – any amount of common decency within him – he would now leave them alone. Because if he tried the slightest thing again or Sep heard a whisper he was up to anything that might affect his family, then he would not be responsible for his actions.

Finishing the last morsel, he wiped his plate with a piece of bread then held it out towards Nell. 'Any more left in the dish?' he asked with a grin.

After dinner Sep, Dan, Wilfred and Billy sat round the table discussing the possibilities of the mobile shop and what they needed to do to get the venture up and running. Letty and Primrose sat on the clippy rug in front of the range talking of weddings. Nell pulled Peggie aside.

'Will you pop to Dage's for me?' she said, handing over a half crown coin. 'Get your dad some baccy for his pipe. I bet he ain't had a decent smoke in months.'

''Course I will, Mam,' she replied, grabbing her coat from the back door. 'D'you need anything else while I'm at it?'

Nell glanced over at Sep. 'No, just the baccy.'

Peggie opened the door. 'I shan't be long.'

Jauntily she walked into the store. The bell jangled loudly and Effie Dage, who was just about to close up for the night, glared at her customer angrily.

'What do you want?' she snapped.

Peggie advanced to the counter and slapped down the coin. 'Two ounces of baccy, please, Mrs Dage. And I hope you don't treat all your customers this way. I should remember, if I were you, the Co-op will be opening shortly.'

Tight-lipped, Effie weighed out the baccy, parcelled it up and banged it down on the counter. She grabbed the half crown and gave Peggie her change. She followed her to the door, slammed it shut behind her and shot across the bolts.

On the other side of the door Peggie giggled, and even louder when Effie wrenched down the blind on the door and it shot back up. Effie's face had been a picture. She turned and hurried off home and the prospect of getting back sent a warm glow rushing through her.

Reaching the gate, she halted abruptly as she spotted a figure hovering close by. It was Alice.

'Alice? Alice Hammond?' she said in surprise. 'What are you doing lurking round here? I thought you'd scarpered after the trouble your Bull caused our Billy?'

Hunched over with cold, Alice stepped towards her. 'I didn't mean to startle yer, Peggie. But I 'ad to come. I couldn't stay away no longer. I tried, really I did. But I 'ave to see Billy. I 'ave to see for meself that he's all right.'

'Billy's fine, Alice. He's recovering well. But that's no thanks to your Bull. He left my brother for dead,' said Peggie harshly.

Alice sniffed miserably. 'I know that and 'e's paying for it, Peggie. But it weren't 'is fault really.'

'Weren't his fault! For God's sake, woman. If it weren't his fault, then whose was it?'

Alice looked past Peggie towards the cottage. 'Can I come in, Peggie? Can I just see him?'

'No, Alice,' she replied firmly. 'Our Billy's gone through enough.

265

I don't think you turning up out of the blue will do him any good at all.'

Alice shrank back. 'Please, Peggie. Please?'

'No, Alice. Not now. Maybe when he's fully recovered. But you didn't answer my question. If it wasn't Bull's fault, then whose was it?'

'Cyrus Crabbe,' she replied, surprised that Peggie did not already know. 'It wa' 'im that told Bull. He must 'ave been watchin' us, see. I tried to reason wi' Bull. I tried to tell 'im that it wa' finished between us, but 'e wouldn't listen. Well, 'e were drunk and you know what 'e's like with a drink. 'E made me write a note to Billy asking 'im to come and see me. Then 'e . . . then 'e . . .' She sniffed loudly. 'Set on 'im and I couldn't stop it.' She wiped tears from her eyes at the memory. 'Not long after your dad had gone, Cyrus came back wi' 'is cart. 'E bundled me and the kids on board and drove me over to Coalville, to me sister's. He dumped us in the middle of the street and said if 'e ever saw my face in Barlestone again, 'e'd kill me. I wa' frightened, Peggie. I 'ad me kids to think of.'

Horrorstruck, she placed her hand on Alice's arm. 'Yes, I can see that. It's a pity you never thought of them before you enticed our Billy into your bed,' she said before she could stop herself. She swallowed hard, trying to quell her anger. 'Look, Alice, you seeing Billy now won't do either of you any good. Go back to your sister's. Forget about Billy, just concentrate on your own family. Enough damage has been done and I ain't risking any more, just to satisfy you.' She paused, suddenly feeling pity for this poor unfortunate woman who was saddled for life with a man like Bull, and felt remorse for dealing with her so harshly. But this business was over. Her father was back and Billy was on the mend and she wasn't going to allow it to flare up again to suit Alice.

'I said, go home, Alice,' she commanded.

Alice, tears of remorse rolling down her cheeks, hunched her shoulders and turned into the biting wind, soon to be lost in the darkness. Peggie watched her go and turned into the gate. She paused, staring at the cottage. The flickering lamplight shining through the windows looked so inviting and behind the walls she knew love and laughter were awaiting her.

But so filled with rage was she against Cyrus Crabbe, she could not go in just yet. She had made her decision long before she had sent Alice packing. She was going to see him, tell him she knew what he had done and warn him, warn him strongly, that any further misdemeanours on his part, however small, would not be tolerated. See how it felt for him to be on the receiving end for a change.

She arrived at his door and without hesitation banged loudly, her anger very much in evidence, all set to give Cyrus a piece of her mind.

The door opened and he stood before her. He glared at first then his face broke into a wicked smile. Peggie was horrified at his

266

appearance. He was unshaven, his hair unbrushed, the front of his shirt stained with food, and he stank of stale beer and tobacco. Her stomach turned as he leered at her.

'Well, well, well, the sheep has come to the wolf. Come in, pray,' he sneered, standing aside, his arms held wide in welcome.

'No, thank you,' she said icily. 'I wouldn't cross your doorstep if my life was in danger.'

'Oh, wouldn't you?' he said sarcastically. 'Well, I'm afraid you've got no choice.'

Without warning he grabbed her arm and before she realised what was happening or could retaliate she found herself sprawled upon the floor in the passage, her knee smarting badly from the knock it had received from the skirting board as she had slid across the linoleum. She heard bolts being thrown and a key turning in a lock.

He stood over her menacingly. 'Wouldn't condescend to come into my house, eh? Well, I can tell you straight, Miss stick your nose into other people's business, you're gonna wish you never turned into my street, let alone banged on my door. Reginald!' he shouted. 'Come here now. Come and see who's paying us a visit.'

Peggie crawled a little further along the floor, awkwardly pulled herself up and turned her head to see Reginald smirking at her in the doorway, his appearance no better than his father's. His face carried the remains of dried cuts and bruises, evidence of a beating.

'Don't just stand there like an idiot. Go and get Jesson.'

'What for?' demanded Peggie, confused.

'You'll soon find out.' Cyrus laughed harshly. He strode towards her and pushed her hard on the shoulder. 'Get in there,' he said, pushing her again towards the back room.

She regained her footing, turned and pushed him back. 'Don't you push me!' she cried. 'You're just a bully, Cyrus Crabbe. You want locking up. Now get out of my way.'

He pushed her again. This time she fell into the corner of the door. The sharp edges caught her shin and forehead and she cried out in pain. He grabbed her by her hair and dragged her into the room where he threw her down on a chair by the littered table filled with the remains of many past meals, empty beer bottles and overflowing ashtrays. He strode over and picked up the poker. 'Move and you get this,' he said, eyes narrowing in malice.

He paced before her then stopped. 'Who sent you? Who's hiding behind your skirt now?' he asked savagely.

'No one,' Peggie replied, rubbing her smarting head. 'No one is hiding behind me. I've come of my own accord.' She raised her head defiantly. 'I've come to tell you your plan failed. My father is back home and we know all about you. How you put Bull up to beating our Billy. How you lied to my father about my mother. Well, I've come to warn you, if you don't stop this stupid vendetta against my family, I'm going to involve the police.'

Cyrus's face turned even uglier. 'Warn me!' he erupted. His

anger turned to laughter and he laughed long and hard. 'The police, you say? Oh, my dear Miss Cartwright, I think you're in for a little shock.'

She made to rise. He raised the poker and brought it down on her shoulder. 'I told you to stay put.'

She fell back as searing pain shot through her. She raised her eyes startled as the door opened and Reginald came in. Behind him hovered Constable Jesson. The constable looked at Peggie then at Cyrus.

'She's all yours, Jesson. You know what to do.'

'What to do? What d'you mean?' Peggie stuttered. Her eyes flew to Constable Jesson. 'You're in with him. You are, aren't you?' she cried accusingly, her face contorted in anger. 'But you're supposed to be an officer of the law. You're supposed to guard us against people like him. Not be in league with them.'

Cyrus sprang on her. 'Shuddup!' he cried, waving the poker. 'You should have learned by now to keep that mouth of yours shut. This time it's got you into more trouble than you ever bargained for.' He spun back to Jesson. 'Do it now. You can take my cart.'

Jesson swallowed hard. 'I can't, Crabbe. I won't do this. It was taking a risk before. I can't do it again.'

'You will. You will!' Cyrus shrieked, his eyes ablaze with madness. 'I want her dealt with for good.' His voice lowered to a menacing whisper. 'You know what will happen if you don't.'

Jesson gulped. 'Okay, okay. But this is the last.'

'Oh, you needn't worry on that score. We're leaving this hole. By this time next week we'll be gone. It's never done n'ote for me has this village. And the people in it are worse than dogs. They can burn in hell for all I care.'

Suddenly the seriousness of her situation struck Peggie full force. 'What . . . what do you intend doing with me?' she stuttered. Her eyes flew wildly from one to the other. 'Are you going to kill me, is that it?'

Cyrus stepped forward and pushed his face inches away from hers. 'Oh, no, Peggie Cartwright. Killing is too good for you. Besides, I wouldn't bloody my hands with the likes of you. I have something far better lined up. Take her now, Jesson. I want her out of my sight. And you'll need this,' he said, picking up a long piece of rope that was lying on the floor. He threw it across. 'Reginald, help the constable tie her up. Don't want her escaping, do we?' he laughed wickedly.

'My pleasure, Dad,' Reginald replied.

Tied and secured with a gag over her mouth, Peggie was bundled on to the back of the cart and dirty sacking was thrown over her. She struggled against the bonds, but they were tied so tight they were beginning to cut into her skin. She heard muffled voices. It was Cyrus addressing Jesson.

'You know what to do and you know what to say. Don't fail, Jesson. And make sure no one sees you.'

The cart started off and it seemed like forever that she was thrown painfully up and down as they trundled over the frozen ruts in the road. The bitter cold night air seeped through the sacking and her limbs steadily numbed. She tried desperately to loosen the gag from her mouth. If she could scream at least she might stand a chance of rescue. But the gag would not budge.

Finally, after what seemed like hours, the cart pulled to a stop and for several minutes there was nothing. She lay worried, waiting for something to happen. When nothing did, she began to think she had been abandoned. Then the sound of Jesson's voice reached her ears. She strained but nothing made sense. Moments went by then the sacking was stripped back and a grotesque face peered at her.

'Mad, you say?' the man addressed Jesson.

'Completely.'

'Hanging round impersonating an upstanding village woman, you say?'

Jesson nodded. 'Keeps telling everyone her name's Margaret Cartwright. The real Margaret Cartwright has had enough. Her family's had enough. We've tried to reason with her but she won't go away. She won't tell us either where she comes from, so we can't take her back. She steals from the locals for food, even attacked one woman when she was caught. I've had to tie her up for her own protection. In case she tried anything silly if she happened to realise where I was headed.'

'Mmm.' The man rubbed his hand over his chin. He leaned over and stared at Peggie hard. 'Impersonation, eh? Stealing, eh? Causing a nuisance. Well, we can't have that. We can't have the public in danger.'

Peggie tried to shake her head, her eyes wide in alarm. She tried to talk but the mumbles she produced were inaudible beneath the gag.

As the man walked round the cart, Jesson leaned over.

'I'm sorry, Peggie, really I am, but I had no choice,' he whispered apologetically.

At the bottom of the cart the man leaned right in, clasped her ankles and pulled her bodily out of the back. He untied the rope around her ankles and forced her upright. Grabbing her by the hair, he marched her forward. 'Come on, my dear. Where you're going you can impersonate anyone you like and nobody will care.' He paused and turned to Jesson. 'All right, Constable, you can go now. Leave the rest to me. Safe journey, d'yer hear?'

Peggie tried to struggle, kicking out with her feet, her mind racing frantically. Where on earth was she? Where was the man taking her? Oh, God, how had she got into this mess? She tried to look round but the low-hanging night sky obscured everything. But there were plenty of trees. She could hear the rustle of their leaves in the wind.

The man stopped and shook her hard. 'Now stop this nonsense, do you hear?' He raised his hand and hit her hard on the side of the head. 'If you don't behave yourself, you'll get more of that.'

Peggie's legs buckled as she received the blow. The man lost his grip and she fell heavily to the ground. He wrenched her up and slapped her again. 'You women,' he said savagely, 'never know when to stop.'

Standing before large iron gates the man pulled a bell pull on the wall to the side. Presently another man appeared from the lodge at the side of the gates, carrying a lamp. He shone it at them and nodded in recognition. 'Another one for us, Leonard?'

He nodded. ''Fraid so, Abner. This one apparently likes to impersonate, and she steals. She attacks an' all. She loves that apparently.'

'Oh, does she?' Abner said, opening the gate. 'Well, it'll probably be the wing for her. Poor sod. They can't help it, yer know. They're born that way.'

Peggie was dragged through the gates and along what looked like a sweeping drive. On and on they went until, rounding a bend, a huge red-brick castle-like construction loomed up. It was enormous and extremely forbidding. Peggie shivered as the fear of doom settled upon her.

Leonard stopped and turned to address her.

'Take a good look, me dear. You won't see this view again 'til they carry yer out in a box. Welcome to The Towers.'

Peggie's breath left her body. The Towers was the mental asylum. No, her mind screamed. This couldn't be happening. She struggled in an attempt to make the man listen to her. If he would only give her a moment she would soon make him realise that this was all a terrible mistake. But it was all in vain.

They reached a large oak door and he unlocked it with the aid of an enormous key on the laden ring hanging from his belt. They entered a wide dark passageway. He turned and relocked the door behind them.

Continuing down the dimly lit corridor they passed several closed doors before he stopped before one, opened it and shoved her inside. An enormous woman sitting behind a desk raised her head. She was frighteningly ugly with a large spread nose which seemed to cover half of her heavily jowled face, two small black eyes sunk inside the mounds of fat covering her cheeks and a thick-lipped mouth hiding blackened teeth.

Across the room an extremely thin woman, who had had her back to them, was pouring out two mugs of tea.

''Ello, ladies. I've got one for yer,' Leonard said, pushing Peggie forward.

The woman behind the desk tutted loudly. 'Oh, God, why does it always have to be in the middle of the night? Why can't they bring nutters in at a decent hour?' she grumbled loudly.

'I've always reckoned it's the moon, Esme,' the woman making the tea said knowingly. 'It's that what brings out the madness, you know.'

Esme bellowed loudly. 'You daft bugger! The moon be damned. It's thick cloud tonight, so how can it be the moon? And don't let the doctor hear you talk like that. He'll have you locked up quicker than you pour that blasted tea.' Sighing loudly, she grabbed a pad of paper and picked up a pen. 'What's her name, Leonard?' she asked.

'Dunno. The copper that brought her here says she won't give it.'

'Oh, won't she, eh?' said Esme, rising. She was big. She was as wide as she was tall, and as she approached Peggie could see whiskers growing on her chin. She snatched down the gag covering Peggie's mouth with grubby fat fingers. 'What's yer name, deary?' she asked coldly, a blast of her foul-smelling breath rushing up Peggie's nostrils.

She balked, swallowed hard and licked her lips where the gag had dried them. 'Margaret,' she cried. 'My name is Margaret Cartwright. I'm not mad. Get my father, he'll tell you.'

Leonard looked at Esme and tutted. 'That's the name of the woman the copper said she was impersonating.'

Esme pushed her face into Peggie's. 'Now once again, what's yer name, deary?'

Peggie gasped for breath. 'I've already told you, it's Margaret Cartwright. Constable Jesson is lying,' she blurted. 'He's in the pay of a man called Crabbe. Cyrus Crabbe. They're saying all this to get me out of the way.'

Esme started to laugh and plodded heavily back to her desk, her backside wobbling alarmingly beneath her long black dress. 'Yes, she's a nutter all right,' she said. 'Leave her to us, Leonard. We'll take it from here.'

'No. No,' Peggie screamed. 'I'm telling the truth. You're making a dreadful mistake.'

'Tell that to the doctor,' Esme said flatly. 'And if yer thinking of making a bolt for it, I shouldn't bother. You'd never get out of here in a lifetime of Sundays.' She turned to the other woman leaning against the wall, drinking from her mug. 'A' you gonna stand there all night gawping, Gladys? Untie her hands.'

'I wouldn't mind a cuppa? Leonard asked hopefully.

'Get out.' Esme moved her bulk around the table. 'You can have your share like you usually do when she's safely in a ward. Now clear off.'

Leonard shrugged his shoulders and walked out. Gladys finished her drink and untied Peggie's wrists. She looked at Peggie hard and smirked as she grabbed a handful of her hair.

'Pretty,' she said mockingly. 'Well, that'll have to come off for a start, and if yer've got nits, you'll have to be shaved. Eh, Esme? What d'yer think? Shall we shave her now?'

'Stop it, Gladys. I ain't in the mood tonight. Just get her stripped off and scrubbed down, and hurry up about it.' She looked Peggie over, moved towards some shelving attached to the wall and

271

selected a grey folded garment, a shapeless undershift and a pair of thick grey woollen stockings. She threw them across the room where they scattered on the stone floor. 'Pick 'em up,' she ordered. 'Less you wanna go naked. Makes no difference to us either way.'

Peggie quickly did as she was bid. Clutching the clothes to her chest, she began to shake and tears welled up in her eyes. 'Please,' she cried. 'Please listen to me. The constable was lying. I'm not mad. Honest, I'm not.'

Esme tutted loudly. 'Get her out of here, Gladys.'

She led Peggie towards a door. The room they entered was small and windowless. It was freezing cold, a cold so intense it knocked the breath from Peggie's body. It was tiled from floor to ceiling. Cockroaches scattered as Gladys lit the oil lamp screwed to the wall. She shut the door and leaned against the wall, folding her arms.

'Strip off,' she ordered.

'What!' Peggie exclaimed.

'Look, don't cause trouble. Just do as I say. Scrub yerself down with the water in the bucket and use plenty of that carbolic soap.'

Peggie gulped and turned her head. On the floor to the side of her was a rusty tin bucket filled with murky water, the top of which held a layer of ice. On the floor, covered in black slime, was a block of coarse yellow soap and a stiff scrubbing brush. Still clinging to the bristles were hairs, and embedded on the wooden base a thick layer of dirt.

She raised her head indignantly and threw the clothing she had been given to the floor. 'I will not strip off,' she said defiantly. 'And you can go to hell!'

Gladys burst into laughter. 'Deary, I'd do as you're told if I were you, else me and Esme will do it for yer. And Esme don't stand no nonsense. By the time she's finished wi' that scrubbing brush, you'll have no skin left.'

Peggie shuddered. Resigned, she lowered her head and slowly unbuttoned her coat, then slipped off her skirt and blouse. Dressed only in her body corselet and long drawers, she raised her head and looked over at Gladys who was watching her intently.

Gladys inclined her head. 'And the rest, deary.'

With eyes cast down she slowly removed the rest of her clothes. Naked and vulnerable, she placed one arm across her chest and her other hand across her abdomen.

Gladys grinned. 'You ain't got n'ote I ain't seen before, lady. Now get scrubbed and hurry up about it. I'll catch me death standing here all night waiting for you.'

Shivering violently, and very aware that Gladys was staring at her naked body, she broke the ice of the murky water in the bucket. Several dead insects were floating on the top. She bent down and picked up the soap and hurriedly began to wash.

'No, no, no,' Gladys said, frustrated. 'Use the brush. How d'yer expect to get rid of yer lice without the brush?'

Peggie opened her mouth, then clamped it shut. It was useless. What was the point of protesting? It would fall on deaf ears. Besides, she knew that if she did not hurry she would surely freeze to death. She picked up the brush, ran the soap across it and placed it on her body. Her skin smarted from the hard bristles and she reeked of carbolic. When she had scrubbed every inch of her body she looked around for a towel. There wasn't one. Wet through, she hurriedly dressed.

The woman unfolded her arms and straightened up. 'Now there's a good girl,' she said patronisingly. 'Tip the water down that drain and pick up your clothes.'

Once back inside the warmer office, Esme took the clothes from her and inspected them. After emptying the pockets of her mother's change and her father's baccy, which she slipped inside her desk drawer, she threw Peggie's coat and skirt at Gladys.

'These'll do for your Milly. I'll have the rest for our Sybil.'

'Oh, ta, Esme,' Gladys beamed, delighted. 'She needs a new coat and this don't look half bad,' she said admiringly, holding the coat out.

'You can't!' Peggie said, shocked. 'They're my clothes. They're mine.'

Gladys chuckled. 'Your clothes you have on, deary. These are now ours. 'Sides, you won't be needing 'em again.'

Once more Esme picked up the pad of paper. 'Right, one last chance. What's yer name?'

Peggie clamped her mouth shut, refusing to answer.

Esme looked over at Gladys. 'What d'yer think, Gladys?'

'I dunno,' she replied thoughtfully. 'What did we use last time?'

'Ethel Smith, wannit?'

'Oh, yes.' She paused, deliberating. 'I know, what about Evangeline? I like that name, it's biblical.'

'I can't spell that,' Esme said coldly. 'You always pick names I can't spell.'

'Well, what about Daisy?'

'Daisy?' Esme repeated. 'I can spell that. Yeah, that'll do. Daisy White.'

She picked up a pen and put the nib in the ink well. Slowly and carefully she wrote on the paper: Dasi Wite.

The form completed she handed it to Gladys. 'You take her. Put her in cell six for the night. Then the day shift can take over for assessment. I'm gonna put my feet up and have forty winks. I 'ate this night shift. Fair gets me down it does.' She leaned back in her chair, spread her huge legs wide and closed her eyes.

'Cell six is occupied,' Gladys said scathingly.

Esme's small black eyes flew open. 'Well, use your loaf and put her in ward thirty-six.'

'Can't do that. We ain't allowed.'

'Well, where else a' we 'sposed to put her? Everywhere else is full. Ward thirty-six is the only one left wi' a bed. 'Cos Freda Jackson died, remember?'

Annoyed, Gladys grabbed Peggie's arm. 'Come along, Daisy, let's get you bedded down for the night.' She turned to Esme. 'This is on your head. I shall tell 'em it wa' your idea.'

'Tell 'em what yer like. No one gives a stuff anyway.'

Esme shut her eyes and began to snore.

Down several wide dim passageways they walked until they reached iron gates spanning the width. Gladys unlocked them with a key from the bunch hanging from her leather belt. Once inside she relocked them. As they continued sounds began to filter through. Moaning, crying, wails of anguish. The further they walked, the louder they grew. Peggie froze in horror. She stopped abruptly.

'I can't go further. Please don't make me,' she pleaded. She grabbed Gladys' arm and tried to appeal to her better nature. Telling her to contact her father and Dan. They would confirm the mistake. But Peggie was wasting her breath. Years of working in the asylum, dealing with patients, many incapable of controlling either their own minds or their actions, witnessing the cruelty and harsh treatment that was continually doled out, had sapped any spark of human kindness left in her.

'Now, Daisy. Don't cause a fuss,' she snapped crossly. She placed the flat of her hand on Peggie's back and pushed her forward. She stopped before an iron door and pulled a bell pull on the wall. Several times she had to pull on it before a key sounded in the lock and the door opened.

''Ello, Gladys,' a small thick-set man said, yawning loudly and scratching his head. 'Who's this?'

'Daisy White,' Gladys replied.

'I ain't expecting no Daisy White,' he said, confused. 'Who's authorised her to come in here?'

Gladys pushed Peggie forward. 'Esme has. There ain't nowhere else to put her at the moment. We're full. Loonies falling out the doors. Seems to me that anyone wanting rid of a relative says they're barmy and sticks 'em in here.'

'Yer right about that, Gladys. Okay, hand her over.'

Gladys made to walk away and stopped. 'Eh, no funny business, Bert. She ain't bin assessed yet.'

Bert grimaced and gave Peggie the once over. 'All right, she'll hold. Not bad though, is she?' he said, licking his lips at the thought of his forthcoming pleasure.

The ward was long and grim. Horrific shrieking and anguished wails filled the air. Rows of beds were occupied by pitiful bodies, some comatosed by sedation, some crouching by the bedside, eyes filled with terror, some lying on top huddled in fetal positions, some lying flat staring wildly into space. And from what Peggie could see in the dim light, most were old and withered. The smell of urine and excrement was sickening and she heaved. A wave of misery

274

filled her being. So this was to be her home. She was trapped in this living hell for eternity.

Her body sagged as a vision of her family all gathered in the kitchen laughing happily rose up before her. Amongst them was Dan, his arms wide in welcome. 'Oh, Dan, Dan,' she whispered. Her legs buckled, everything went black and she crumpled to the hard floor.

Chapter Twenty-Six

Sep and Dan walked through the back door and shrugged their shoulders helplessly.

'There's no sign of her,' Dan said worriedly. 'It's as if she's walked off the face of the earth.'

Nell jumped up. 'But that's impossible. Nobody just disappears. She must be somewhere. Did you try Aggie's?'

'We've tried everywhere, Nell,' Sep said, sighing heavily. 'The last person to see her was Wilfred's mother and she says she locked the shop up behind her.'

'Was she alone?'

'As far as we know she was.'

'What does that mean?'

'It means, Nell,' said her husband, 'that as far as we know she was on her way home. But you know our Peggie. She could have took a notion and gone off somewhere.'

Nell shook her head. 'No, Peggie wouldn't have done that. Not with you just coming home and Dan being here. No, she wouldn't have gone off without a word.' Her mouth trembled. 'Oh, Sep, something's happened to her, I know it has. She's been gone hours.'

Letty rushed forward and placed an arm around her mother.

'Now, Mam, don't take on. Don't you think we're making too much of all this? She is a grown woman and hasn't been gone that long.'

'She's been gone six hours. What do you call that then if it's not long?'

Letty tutted loudly. 'You know what our Peggie's like. She gets a bee in her bonnet and all other thoughts fly out of her head. She's probably sitting comfortably somewhere we just haven't thought of, nattering her head off, and has forgotten the time.'

Nell looked up at her. 'Do you think so?'

'Yes, she's right, Nell,' Sep agreed. 'She'll come through that door any minute wondering what all the fuss is about.'

Nell smiled wanly. 'Yes, she will. I'll put the kettle on so the water's boiling when she comes in.'

Dan slipped out of the door and stood by the gate, staring up and down the deserted road.

'Oh, Peggie,' he groaned. 'Where are you?'

Chapter Twenty-Seven

Peggie lifted her head and felt the sun's rays warming her skin. The fragrant aroma of sweet hay and wild flowers filled her nostrils. Butterflies hovered and birdsong filled the air. She breathed deeply as a feeling of wellbeing filled her. Lowering her head, she squinted across the neverending field. In the distance, Dan, his face filled with tenderness, arms wide in welcome, was running slowly towards her, gliding through the long green grass. Behind him, a soft halo of light illuminating them, were her mother and father, Billy, Letty, Primrose and Ronnie. They were waving to her, smiling happily.

She called out in greeting, closed her eyes tightly and opened her arms ready to receive her beloved Dan. As she did so excruciating pain shot through her and her eyes flew open. The field had gone, her family and Dan had vanished. She was huddled on a hard mattress in a long dim room filled with withered bodies all moaning in suffering. The smell of sweet hay and flowers was replaced with a decaying stench so overwhelming she heaved in nausea. Her pain-racked body stiffened as she gripped the sides of the mattress, deeply distressed.

She felt a hand gently close over her own and cried out in fright. Her head jerked to the side. On the floor by her side, huddled in the dark shadows, was an apparition dressed in grey.

Peggie's hand clutched her chest as she stared in terror. It was several moments before recognition struck her.

'Mary,' she uttered. 'Mary Crabbe, is that you?'

'Shush,' Mary whispered. 'The guard. Don't let him hear you. I'm supposed to be in bed.'

Peggie quickly turned her head. Across the room behind an iron grille the guard she knew as Bert was asleep in his chair.

She tried to raise her body but the damage to her shoulder where Cyrus had thrashed her with the poker, and to her legs where she had fallen on the ground, stopped her. She sagged against the hard mattress, her mind racing frantically. She wanted to ask Mary many questions, but so preoccupied was she with her own predicament these questions seemed unimportant for the moment.

'Oh, Mary,' she sobbed, so low it was hardly audible. 'Your father put me in here. Him and Constable Jesson.'

'My father?' Mary gasped.

Peggie nodded. 'How could he do such a thing, Mary? Please tell me I'm dreaming. Please tell me this is a nightmare. Oh, Mary,' she choked, 'they're going to cut off my hair.'

When no reply came Peggie knew without doubt that this was reality. She was in hell and there was no escape.

Mary's hand tightened on hers in commiseration and she sighed deeply. How could she tell Peggie, considering the state she was in, that having her hair cut – losing that beautiful mane of golden curls – was the least of her problems? Inside these walls she would never know peace. Cruelty and lack of human regard ruled here. Outside these confines a face and body such as she possessed were assets; here they were misfortunes. When the male guards had had their fill of her, the females took over. And when someone arrived to take her place, still she wouldn't be free. The constant suffering of the mentally insane never diminished. It was all around whilst they were awake and filled their dreams if lucky enough to sleep.

Any sanity possessed was quickly eroded by days upon months upon years shut away with these poor unfortunate humans. The only daylight visible was through the iron bars at the high windows. She herself had only managed to survive by submission to her cruel guardians. Luckily, for some reason she hadn't appealed to them and had survived by making herself invisible. Quietly accepting set tasks without question, causing no trouble, walking around with her head held low so no one would notice her. And because of her actions she had become a trustee, given work only dished out to the privileged few.

She squeezed Peggie's hand again, desperate to find words of comfort for one of the very few women she had ever known to show her any kindness. But none came to mind. Nothing anyone could say would lessen the traumas she had to face in the future. Unfortunately Peggie wasn't like herself, timid and withdrawn. Peggie was strong, full of vigour, with a mind of her own. She wouldn't take her imprisonment without a fight. That would be her undoing. She would become her own worst enemy.

Now another worry sprang forth. Peggie would soon ask her questions – answers to which she was unwilling to give. How could she begin to explain that these walls offered her sanctuary? How would Peggie understand such an admission? These cold, cheerless surroundings were a haven compared to what she had endured at the place she had called home. Constantly at her father and Reginald's beck and call. Never allowed to be her own person, never allowed to express an opinion or air a view. Continually humiliated and beaten when the mood took them.

Far worse than any of that were the nights her brother would sneak into her room after a night of hard drinking down at the pub. Whenever unable to find an accommodating female, he would satisfy his sexual needs on her body as though it was his right. Making her do things that she knew were wrong. And having no one to turn to, no one interested, these visits continued unchecked, week after week, month after month.

And then she had faced fear and terror like she'd never known before. She was pregnant. She was carrying her own brother's child. She had tried to hide her swelling belly, but nothing she did could obscure it from her father's cunning eyes. He had beaten her to within an inch of her life, accused her of sleeping with all the village men. She had tried to tell him of Reginald but he had branded her a liar, accusing her of covering up for her own lovers. To hide the shame of her evil deeds, he had had her bundled off in the middle of the night and committed to the mental asylum.

On arrival she had been made to strip down and scrub in freezing cold water and had been thrown into an equally icy, windowless, bare cell. And a few hours later, huddled in the corner in the pitch darkness, the pains had started. Pains so severe she thought she was dying. No one heeded her screams, no one came forth to offer her help, and a few hours later she had miscarried. When the guards had found her at daylight they had offered no kind word, no acts of sympathy, she had just been dragged to a ward and put to work scrubbing the floors.

But at least she was free. Free from her father and brother. At liberty to creep in the shadows, unnoticed by anyone, and as long as she stayed submissive her life was bearable.

Her eyes darted to Peggie. Poor girl. She was not free. Her living hell was just beginning. She had to be warned, made to see reason, made to realise how to act in order to survive. She prayed Peggie would listen. She opened her mouth, but too late. She saw Bert at the gate with another orderly. He was placing his key in the lock. Like lightning she moved and was in her bed across the other side of the ward before anyone could realise.

Bert, along with the orderly, walked towards Peggie's bedside. Just before they approached, a skeleton of a human being dressed in filthy rags flung itself on the orderly, wailing loudly. He pushed it away and when it fell to the floor, raised his booted foot and kicked it hard. Screaming in pain, it crawled away and huddled in a corner with several others.

Peggie flinched at the sight.

'Get up,' Bert commanded. 'The doctor's waiting to assess you.'

Peggie was unable to rise because of her stiffness and injuries. Bert, mistaking her action for unwillingness, grabbed her by the throat and pulled her up.

Gasping and spluttering, she was marched down the ward.

The doctor's office was paradise in comparison, and free from the terrible stench, Peggie breathed deeply. Seated behind a desk, scribbling on a form, he addressed her without raising his head.

'Name?' he asked coldly.

She tried to stand proud. 'Margaret Cartwright,' she said firmly.

He wrote on the form, 'Daisy White – Mentally Insane. Recommendation: committal for life.'

He put down his quill pen, raised his head and studied her hard, his eyes cold and cruel.

'That hair will have to come off. And check for infestation,' he said matter-of-factly. 'Then you can put her to work in the laundry.'

'Yes, doctor,' Bert replied.

An intense rage at the injustice of her situation filled her being. She wrenched free from Bert's strong grip and leaped towards the desk. 'No, no,' she screamed wildly. 'I'm not insane. You know I'm not. Why are you doing this to me?'

Bert reached her and with both arms grabbed her round her chest, pulling her backwards. She bent her head and sank her teeth into his hand. He yelped out in pain, brought his arm back, clenched his fist and thumped her on the side of the head. Stunned, she fell to the floor.

The doctor sniffed and addressed the woman orderly sitting on a chair to the side. 'Wilmore, what dentist is on call?'

'Croppin,' she answered.

'Get him. I want all her teeth removed as soon as possible.'

Miss Wilmore smirked down at Peggie sprawled on the floor, rose and walked out of the office.

The doctor addressed Bert. 'Get her hair cut, then put her in a cell until the dentist comes. If she has any more seizures like that, we'll try electric shock treatment. And tonight sedate her just in case she attacks anyone else.'

'Yes, Doctor.'

Miss Wilmore returned. 'I've sent someone to fetch Croppin.'

'Good. Now any more to see?'

'No, Doctor. That's them all for now.'

He rose and began to clear his desk. 'Good. I can get off home.' He handed over Peggie's committal papers. 'See these are filed away.' He looked across at Bert, nursing his hand. 'Well, snap to it, man, before she does someone else an injury.'

Peggie sat strapped to a chair in a room further down the passage. A hard-faced woman stood behind her and raised a pair of large shears. Peggie closed her eyes tightly as the sound of the shears going about their business filled her ears. Blonde curls fell as fat tears squeezed past her eyelids.

Just as the woman had finished her work the door opened and Miss Wilmore stuck her head around.

'She's to be locked up in cell two. Croppin won't be here 'til much later.'

'Righto,' came the reply.

Peggie was unstrapped and marched to the cell, pushed inside into the blackness and the metal door slammed shut behind her.

She felt her way round the wall and on reaching a corner placed her back against the cold painted bricks and slid down until her bottom reached the stone slabs. Hugging her knees to her chest, she doubled over as tears of misery, isolation and desperation fell down her cheeks. Hesitantly she raised her hand and felt what was left of her hair. It had been shorn right up to her ears.

'Oh, Mam,' she wailed in sorrow. 'Oh, Mam, what am I going to do?'

She was still sobbing softly when they fetched her several hours later. A guard she had not seen before silently pulled her up and marched her down many dim corridors until he stopped before a door, opened it and pushed her inside. The room was light and airy and a window on the far wall looked out on to a small spinney. Before Peggie could take in any more she was thrust on a chair, her head forced back and a strap tightened round her throat. She was then strapped at wrists and ankles.

'Right, Mr Croppin,' the orderly said tonelessly. 'She won't cause you no trouble now. I'll leave you to it. Let me know when you've finished.' She gave the dentist a knowing wink and left the room.

Mr Croppin, a wiry, balding, middle-aged man with thick pebble glasses, walked around to the front of the chair. In his hand he held a large instrument, resembling a pair of pliers, and a piece of paper. He studied the paper.

'Biting, eh? Tut, tut, tut. We can't have that.' He raised his head and looked at Peggie hard. His eyes opened wide in surprise and he ran his tongue over his thin lips.

'My,' he said lustily, 'what a beauty we have here. But what have they done to your hair? Still, it would be a shame to waste this opportunity, wouldn't it, my dear?' He put the pliers down on a table and lowered a lever at the back of the chair. The chair tilted backwards until she was lying practically horizontal, her only view of the dirty grey ceiling. He leaned over and began to unbutton the front of her grey shapeless dress. Saliva trickled from the corner of his mouth.

'Don't!' Peggie screamed, trying to shake her head. 'Stop it! Stop it!'

Mr Croppin laughed harshly. 'Oh, a little vixen. Carry on, my dear. I like it when they put up a fight. Scream as much as you like, no one will bother.'

Peggie did not heed him. She opened her mouth and screamed as loudly as her lungs and the strap fastened around her throat would allow.

Unconcerned, he put his hand inside her dress and fondled her bare breast. He inhaled deeply in pleasure as he felt her nipple harden under his probing fingers and licked his lips in excitement.

Defilement and humiliation rose within her. She tried to struggle against her bonds, but as intended she was restrained too tightly for movement.

Mr Croppin withdrew his hand and stood back to unbutton his trousers. He stood before her, his trousers round his ankles, displaying a dingy pair of long johns. He grabbed at the bottom of her dress and lifted it, exposing her knees. He placed his hand on her thigh and stroked it.

'Now, that's nice, isn't it?' he said hoarsely.

A loud commotion sounded from outside, the door burst open and the orderly charged in.

Like lightning a red-faced Mr Croppin pulled up his trousers. 'What the . . .' he spluttered.

'Quick,' the orderly shouted, ignoring the predicament she had caught him in. 'The Governor's been attacked.'

'Well . . . well, get the doctor,' Mr Croppin blurted crossly.

'The doctor's not here and you're needed.'

'But I'm not medical,' he protested.

'Damn it, man. The Governor's bleeding to death. You're the nearest we've got. So get your bag.'

The orderly turned and ran off.

Mr Croppin stood and fumed. 'Oh, really,' he spat angrily. He turned to Peggie. 'I'll be back for you later.'

She shut her eyes, wondering worriedly how long it would be before he returned. She heard the door open and the soft padding of footsteps advancing towards her, and froze. Someone had entered the room. Oh, God, her mind screamed. Dear God, what was going to happen to her now?

She felt the strap on her throat loosen and the belt fall away. She lifted her head in confusion. It was Mary. Peggie eyed her with a mixture of bewilderment and surprise.

'Mary! What the . . . How the . . .?'

Mary placed her finger to her lips to silence her. Deftly she unbuckled the straps on Peggie's wrists and ankles.

'Quick, Miss Cartwright,' she whispered as she flew across to the window, released the catch and heaved it up. Forgetting her injuries, Peggie shot from the chair and followed her, preparing to climb out. 'No,' Mary ordered softly. 'In the cupboard.'

'What . . .'

'Get in the cupboard,' she repeated, pointing her finger to a door at the back of the room.

Bewildered, Peggie for once did as she was told. Before Mary followed she grabbed Mr Croppin's coat from the coat stand.

The large cupboard was filthy from years of disuse, the shelving filled with old files and piles of paper covered in a thick layer of dust. The floor was littered with an assortment of discarded articles. Mary motioned Peggie to sit down. She closed the door, groped her way over and sat down beside her on the hard flooring.

Squatting in pitch darkness, something she was beginning to get accustomed to, Peggie turned to Mary.

'Shush!' Mary whispered before she could speak. 'I'll explain later. They'll be back shortly.'

So they both sat in silence, hardly daring to breathe, acutely aware that at any minute they could be discovered.

Presently they heard angry shouts and Mary placed her hand hurriedly on Peggie's knee as a warning to keep silent. They both held their breaths.

It seemed an age before Peggie heard Mary sigh in relief.

'I think we can safely talk now,' she whispered softly. 'But keep your voice low.'

284

Peggie breathed deeply. 'Mary, why? Why didn't you let us escape when we had the chance. We could have been out of here by now and well away.'

Mary shook her head in the blackness. 'No, Miss Cartwright. That's where you're wrong. As soon as they realised you were gone all the guards would have been after you. And you wouldn't have got far. Especially not dressed like that. It's a dead giveaway.'

Peggie's bottom lip quivered in extreme agitation. 'But what are we going to do? We can't stay in this cupboard forever.' She sniffed loudly as tears of misery sprang to her eyes. 'I'm not going back, Mary. I can't. I just can't.' The tears turned to a stream and poured down her face.

Mary put her arm around her and pulled her close. 'Shush,' she soothed. 'You're not going back. I promise you, Miss Cartwright, you're never going back in there.'

Peggie raised her head hopefully. 'I'm not?' she murmured.

'No,' Mary whispered firmly. 'We stay put in here for at least two days.'

'Two days!' she exclaimed, horrified. 'Oh, Mary, I can't. I can't sit in here two whole days, I'll go mad.'

'You'll have to, Miss Cartwright. You might go mad in here. Out there you'll definitely go mad. After two days they'll think you've got clean away and won't be searching the grounds. That should give you a chance.'

'Oh. Oh, I see.'

'We're safe here. The dentist only comes when he's summoned and the outer door is always kept locked. No one will think to look in here. As far as they're concerned, you escaped out of the window.'

'Oh, Mary. I hope you're right.'

'I am. I've been cleaning these corridors for months now and I know exactly what goes on. That's how I knew where you were. I was on my hands and knees scrubbing the slabs.'

Peggie frowned. 'I never noticed you.'

Mary smiled. No. No one ever noticed her. That's how she had been able to slip in whilst everyone else was occupied. The events leading up to it had been miraculous. No cell to house Miss Cartwright; Mr Croppin's late arrival; the Governor being attacked and no doctor on hand. She had seized the opportunity to help this woman, without question, without regard for her own safety or what could transpire because of her actions. But she couldn't tell her this. Peggie was in no fit state to handle the news that the rest of her life hung by such a fine thread. She still had to get away.

'You were in no state of mind to notice me, Miss Cartwright,' was all Mary said.

'No,' Peggie replied softly. 'No, I wasn't, was I?' Her lip trembled. 'They cut off my hair with a huge pair of shears.'

'Never mind that,' Mary said kindly. 'It's becoming the fashion anyway.'

Peggie managed to smile. 'Yes,' she said lightly, trying her hardest to look on the bright side. 'I've wanted it doing for ages. I suppose it saved me a bob or two.'

Peggie would never know how, considering the situation they were in, but they both started to laugh.

She wiped her eyes on her dress, then peered at Mary in the darkness. 'How come you're here anyway?'

She tightened her lips. She had been expecting this question but not quite yet. She had thought Peggie would have been too preoccupied with her own predicament to bother about her. But regardless, she wasn't going to tell the truth. Loyalty to her father and brother, however misplaced, stopped her.

'As punishment.'

'Punishment? For what? What could you ever have done that was so bad as to warrant being shut away in here?'

'I . . . I stole, Miss Cartwright,' she lied.

'Stole? Stole what?'

'Food, 'cos I was hungry. And when they tried to take it from me I went mad. Kicked and screamed and punched. And the upshot was they stuck me in here.'

'Oh, my God, but that's terrible, 'specially considering you were starving.'

'There's lots of people in here who have done less than I have. Sane people like you and me. Got rid of because they're not wanted or become an embarrassment.' She heard Peggie gasp. 'So maybe I deserved it,' she added softly.

'Deserved it? If your father had treated you better you would never have left home in the first place, then you wouldn't have had to steal, would you? It's him who's to blame.' She felt Mary flinch. 'Oh, I'm so sorry. I didn't mean to speak ill of your father but I have every right.'

Mary gulped. 'Yes, you have,' she whispered.

'When we get away you'll come home with me. My mother will welcome you, 'specially in light of all that you've done. And risked your own neck into the bargain. I ain't stupid, Mary. I know what this will cost you if we get caught.'

Mary froze. How could she explain to Peggie that she could never go home? Not ever. 'Oh, no, Miss Cartwright, I'm not leaving. I can't. I have nothing to leave for. This is my home now.'

'What! Don't be silly, Mary. You have everything to leave for. You shouldn't be in here anyway.' Peggie's body stiffened. 'If you don't come with me, then I won't go either.'

'You can't stay. You *have* to go.'

'I won't,' Peggie said defiantly. 'It's up to you.'

Mary sagged back against the wall. She supposed she could humour her. Let Peggie think she was going, then when she was clear, return and give herself up.

'All right, I'll come.'

Peggie sighed with relief. 'I'm so glad. Because I couldn't go back in there, I'd sooner cut my own throat.' She hugged Mary affectionately and winced as excruciating pain shot through her shoulder.

'Are you all right?' Mary whispered in concern.

'Yes, I'm fine,' she lied. 'I knocked my shoulder earlier and it's hurting a little.' Peggie leaned back heavily against the cold unyielding wall. 'Well, I suppose we may as well try and get some sleep. After all, it's going to be a long wait.'

The two days stretched endlessly inside the cramped pitch black cupboard. Frozen with cold and weakening gradually from lack of water and food, Peggie worried that they would not live long enough to escape. Trapped in such close confines the air soon began to grow stale, the smell made far worse by the fact that for their toilet they humiliatingly had to use a discarded rusty bucket.

The only time Mary opened the door was to check through the window in order to gauge the time. The rest was spent mostly in silence for fear of being caught. Both were still acutely aware that danger lurked close by.

Back in the whitewashed cottage in Barlestone, worry for Peggie's welfare mounted. The uncertainty was driving them all to despair. Why had she gone? What had happened to her? How could she vanish like that, leaving no trace?

To Nell the thought that she may never again see Peggie's beautiful face, never hold her in her arms, never again tell her she loved her, never scold her, never see her face filled with happiness on her wedding day, the birth of her first child and watching it grow, or just going about the daily joy of living – filled her with agonising dread, a feeling she knew would stay with her for the rest of her days. She would sooner die herself than go through that torture day after day, year after year.

She had reached the stage of being unable to control her emotions, not even for the sake of showing a brave face to the rest of her family. She sat, face lined by grief, huddled by the fire, willing good news to arrive.

Trying to be strong for the sake of his wife, Sep kept his feelings to himself. It was hard, so very, very hard. He knew from recent painful experience what it was like to have the ones you loved alienated from you. He knew what it was like to wake every morning worrying about their welfare. He thought those tormenting times had passed and now, almost immediately upon his joyous return, Peggie was gone from them and the nightmare was beginning all over again.

Nell was suffering badly. After all she was Peggie's mother. But he was Peggie's father and the pain he was suffering was equally as bad. But all he could do was continue with the search and try to fathom some place Peggie could be that they hadn't thought of. He would not rest until that search was over. His family would never be at peace until Peggie was safely back amongst them.

Dan was beside himself. His commitment to Peggie was total. Falling in love with her was meant to be. It was his destiny. All the events in his life had been a gradual guiding down the path towards the day of their meeting. Without her by his side he was not whole, he would never be whole again until she was back with him. Without her his life would be meaningless, empty, one that could not be endured.

He never doubted that her absence was enforced. That something or someone was prohibiting her from being here with him. Dan just prayed it was a something, because if it was a someone, then he would not be responsible for his actions. He would kill if any harm had come to his beloved.

All they could do was continue with the search and strive to support each other, comforted by the fact that the villagers were playing their part. They were all rooting for Peggie's safe return.

Had anyone known where she was or who had been behind it, a lynching would have occurred and no one would have shown the slightest remorse or regret as the body swung lifelessly from the gallows.

On the second night of their incarceration inside the cramped confines of the cupboard, when the moon shone high in the night sky, Mary rose and pulled Peggie stiffly to her feet.

'It's time, Miss Cartwright,' she said softly.

She clenched her fists. 'Is it?' she replied anxiously. 'Are you sure it's safe?'

'As safe as it will ever be. Now you know what to do? I'll open the window just wide enough to squeeze through. Then we run quickly over to the spinney opposite.'

'Yes, yes,' Peggie replied, trying to stop her body from shaking. They had gone over their plans so many times she felt she knew them backwards.

'Right. Ready then?'

Peggie took a breath. She grabbed hold of Mary and hugged her tightly. 'Mary, just one thing,' she said softly. 'If anything should happen, I want to thank you with all my heart for what you've done for me.'

She reddened deeply and lowered her head. 'It's nothing, Miss Cartwright. It's the least I can do. You're about the only person who's ever showed me any kindness.'

Peggie hugged her again as tears sprang to her eyes. 'Oh, Mary.' She sniffed, wiping her face on her dress sleeve. 'Will you do me a favour? Call me Peggie, please. This Miss Cartwright lark is so silly. We have never been anything else but equals.'

Mary beamed in pleasure. 'I will, Miss Cartwright, and thank you.'

She put her hand on the door knob and turned gently. 'Don't forget Croppin's coat. You'll need it in this bitter weather.'

'We'll both need it,' Peggie responded, picking it up.

She waited whilst Mary padded softly to the window and heard the sound of it being carefully inched up. Mary climbed out first and Peggie followed, neither realising that the window was six foot above the ground. Peggie fell with a thud and lay motionless for a moment, worried that she had been heard. The fall had worsened the damage to her shoulder and she stifled a cry of pain.

They both reached the safety of the thick undergrowth in the spinney and took several moments to catch their breath before moving off again.

They crept hurriedly from bush to tree across the neverending grounds. Finally they reached the encircling brick wall and Peggie stared up at it in horror. It was at least ten foot high.

'Oh my God,' she whispered in dismay. 'We'll never get over that.'

'Yes, we will,' Mary said firmly. 'We've come too far to give up now.'

Peggie nodded. They had. They had risked everything and she wasn't going to let a simple thing like a ten-foot wall stop her from gaining her freedom.

'Right,' Mary whispered. 'You hook your hands and give me a leg up. I'll sit on the top and help pull you up. The wall has plenty of spaces where the mortar has fallen out so you'll be able to get a foothold.'

Peggie hooked her hands and after several attempts Mary managed to get a hold on the top. Sitting on the wall, legs astride, she leaned over as far as she could without losing her balance and held out her hand.

Suddenly they both froze as sounds of laughter reached their ears. It was two guards patrolling not far off and they were shining a lamp around the undergrowth. Peggie threw herself to the ground as close to the wall as she could. Mary bent over and lay across the top. Both held their breath, fearful that the terrified beating of their hearts could be heard.

'I tell yer, Walter, she'll be long gone. I don't see the point of wastin' time looking round 'ere.'

'Yeah, I agree. Come on. I'm bloody froze. Let's go an' get a cuppa. We'll leave it to the coppers. She's bound to get caught soon. And then won't she wish she never escaped!'

It took several moments for the men's laughter to fade into the distance.

Peggie struggled up. 'You all right, Mary?' she called softly.

'Yes. I thought we'd had it for sure, though. Come on,' she said leaning over again and lowering her arm. 'Let's hurry up in case they come back.'

Peggie handed up Mr Croppin's coat. She put her foot, covered only by a sopping wet woollen stocking, in a niche in the wall and raised her arm. 'So did I, Mary. So did I.'

Her feet cut and bleeding from the scrapes received on the bare brick, she sat with Mary on top of the wall, their legs dangling over, and stared down.

Mary threw down the coat. 'Go on then, Miss Cart . . . Peggie. Go on, jump.'

Peggie gulped to see the space between her and the ground below, wondering if her body would stand another battering. She turned to Mary. 'You first.'

Mary exhaled sharply. 'No. After you.'

Peggie turned her head and stared at her as realisation suddenly struck. 'You're not coming, are you, Mary?'

She shook her head. 'No, I ain't. I've already told you why. And you heard the guards. They only talked of one escaping, not two. I haven't been missed. Now come on, hurry up. Jump before it's too late.'

Peggie felt her temper rise. She gripped the wall tightly and took a deep breath, conscious that every second was precious. 'I've told you, Mary. Either we go together or not at all. I ain't leaving without you and that's final.'

Without waiting for her decision she grabbed Mary's arm and pulled her off the wall.

Chapter Twenty-Eight

Twenty-five miles away, Dan and Sep, after two long days of fruitless searching, had come to the same conclusion and were now interrogating Cyrus Crabbe.

'I'll give you one more chance, Crabbe. Where is she?' Dan spat harshly. 'We know you've done something with her. Now what is it?'

Cyrus, lounging in a chair, grinned mockingly. He turned his head and stared over at Sep. 'Maybe,' he said acidly, 'she just got fed up with living with you lot.' He watched with pleasure as Sep's face contorted in anger, then turned slowly back to Dan. 'I keep telling yer, how should I know?'

'He knows,' Sep cried savagely. 'He knows where she is. What have you done with her, Crabbe? I'll kill you, you bastard. Now tell us!'

Dan eyed him sharply. 'Leave this to me, Sep,' he warned.

'Oh, yeah? And what you gonna do, nancy boy?' Cyrus spoke scornfully. 'Coming in here wi' yer posh accent and la-di-da ways. I ain't scared a' you. I ain't scared a' none of yer. Now I'm telling yer, if you don't get outta my house I'll get Jesson. I'll get you all locked up for trespassing and threatening behaviour.'

Unable to control himself any longer, Sep leapt over, threw his arm around Cyrus's neck, grabbed hold of his hair and pulled back his head.

'You talk or I'll break your neck!'

'No,' Dan said sharply in warning. 'That's what he wants. He wants us to thrash him. Then it's us that's in trouble.'

Sep released his grip and stepped back.

'Go on,' Cyrus urged. 'Beat me black and blue and see how far it gets yer. If I knew 'ote I wouldn't tell yer anyway.' He inclined his head towards Reginald, cowering in the corner, quaking in fear. 'And he won't either.'

Dan grabbed Cyrus by the shoulders and pulled him up, shaking him hard. 'I'll tell you now, Crabbe, and you'd better listen. If I find out you've got the slightest thing to do with Peggie's disappearance you'll wish to God you had never been born.' He threw Cyrus down and eyed Sep. 'Let's get out of here.'

'No, not 'til he tells us,' Sep hissed harshly. 'I'll not leave this house 'til I know what he's done.'

'Sep,' Dan warned. 'I said, let's leave.'

Before he departed, Dan looked at Cyrus threateningly.

'I meant what I said,' he said.

As they walked through the gate Cyrus came to the door.

'Go on,' he bellowed with bravado. 'Get out of here. If yer come back I'll get the law. Besides,' he laughed, 'after tomorrow I don't care what you do. 'Cos I'll be gone to somewhere you'll never find me.'

Sep, his face contorted in anger, made to return, but Dan stopped him. 'Don't. He's not worth hanging for. But mark my words. One day that man will get his just rewards.'

Prudence Jesson put down her sewing and stared across at her husband, seated in the chair opposite, apparently reading the evening paper. What was the matter with the man? This was the third time she had spoken to him and the third time she had been ignored.

She searched his face. Was it her imagination or had her husband aged drastically over the past few days? He looked so tired, as though he hadn't slept for weeks. His usually rosy complexion was tinged with yellow, and he was off his food. He had hardly touched the lamb stew she had prepared for his dinner and it was his favourite. She took a deep breath and tried again, this time raising her voice several decibels.

'Sidney, I said have you heard about Margaret Cartwright? She's gone missing. But of course you'd know all about it, you being a policeman. Her poor mother is going out of her mind with worry. I personally don't know how she's coping. Well, what are you doing about it, that's what I want to know. What if it was one of our four girls?'

He continued to stare blindly at the newspaper. In all the time he had held it in front of him, not one word had he read. His mind was too full of the terrible deed he had performed against Margaret Cartwright, and not just her but Mary Crabbe previously. Those two young women had not deserved such treatment. Being sentenced to a living death with no chance of escape until the day they died. From the moment he had turned his back on Peggie at the asylum gates, boarded the draycart and driven away, his mind had been in a turmoil of remorse and he had had to force himself not to turn round and go back for her.

If he was experiencing such feelings, what about her family? They were beside themselves with worry and had scoured the village and most of the surrounding area in their futile search while he had gone along with them, organising the army of searchers as he fought to cover his own guilt. His mind suddenly listed all the other misdemeanours he had performed in the past on Crabbe's instructions. The consequences of his actions he had always somehow managed to push into his subconscious but this act was different. It was hounding him. He couldn't sleep at night. He kept seeing Peggie's terrified, questioning eyes staring at him. And now her eyes were accompanied by Mary's.

His wife's words echoed in his ears. 'What if it was one of our four girls?'

Suddenly the horror of it all struck with such force the blood drained from his face. He had always blamed Crabbe for the things he had been forced to do, but he was as much to blame as Crabbe. After all, it was never Crabbe's hand that was dirtied, it was always his, and in light of that fact he was worse than Crabbe. He was a coward of the highest calibre, doing anything he was bid in order to save his own skin. Well, it had to stop. Crabbe had to be stopped. Jesson's eyes narrowed. Putting those innocent women inside that dreadful place was the very last deed either of them was going to perform.

Maybe he could not right the misdemeanours he had performed in the past but he could try to redeem these latest incidents. His career would be over, his family ruined, but at least he wouldn't meet his maker carrying the burden of such dreadful sins.

He abruptly rose, the newspaper dropping to the floor. He walked towards his wife and bent and kissed her cheek.

She looked up at him, bewildered. 'What was that for?'

'Just to say I love you, and I'm sorry.'

'Sorry? What for?'

Her question fell on deaf ears. Sidney Jesson grabbed his uniform jacket and walked out of the door.

Sep and Dan arrived back at the cottage to be greeted by hopeful faces. Dan shook his head and they all sighed.

Silently, Letty and Aggie rose and began to make a pot of tea.

Nell sitting in the armchair by the range, Primrose squatting at her feet, raised frantic eyes, red-rimmed from lack of sleep and worry. 'What do we do now?'

Knowing that Sep was in no fit state to take the lead, Dan spoke up. 'We widen the search, that's what we do.' He walked across the room and stood by the range. 'Wilfred can take the bus. Sep and I will go in the lorry. I know it's still dark but I can't sit around doing nothing.'

They all loudly agreed.

Billy grabbed his crutches and struggled up. 'I'll go with you.'

Sep shook his head. 'Don't be stupid, son. You ain't in no fit state. You'll be more use here staying with the women.'

'What about me and Aggie?' Letty piped up.

'Yeah,' Aggie said. 'We can't sit round neither. Primrose can stay with Mrs Cartwright. But we don't all have to wait here for news.'

Wearily Dan scratched his chin in thought. 'I suggest you tag on with the rest of the villagers. Jenny Pegg is organising them along with Constable Jesson. At first light they're going to search the woods and fields at the back of Cables Farm.'

'Oh!' Nell cried. 'You don't think . . . Oh, no, you don't think she's dead, do you? Oh, Peggie, Peggie,' she wailed.

'We don't think anything, Nell,' Sep said, rushing towards her.

'It's just a precaution. Just in case she went over there for some reason and had an accident.'

Desperate to believe her husband, she wiped her eyes and nodded. She struggled to raise her tired body. 'I'll make you some food. You can't go out again in this weather with nothing in your bellies.'

A knock sounded on the door and Sep flew to open it. Cuffy barged through.

'I've just heard the news, boss. Why didn't you tell me earlier? I could have helped.'

'I never thought, Cuffy, I'm sorry.'

'Ah, no worries, boss. I'm here now. I ain't said anything to yer mother. Was that right?'

'Yes, that was right, Cuffy. She would come charging down here and we've enough people looking as it is.'

Cuffy rubbed his hands together. 'Right, then. What d'yer want me to do?'

The dark road stretched endlessly. Hiding in the hedgerow, Peggie stared in either direction, unsure which one to take, wondering if she had the energy to face the arduous journey. She huddled closer to Mary, pulling the coat as far around her as her share would allow.

Running across the asylum grounds and climbing the wall had already sapped what little strength she had possessed. Two days without food and water were affecting her badly.

But she knew she would have to find the energy from somewhere. The consequences otherwise did not bear thinking about.

'I don't think it matters which way we go,' she said, shivering uncontrollably as the Siberian wind whipped through her thin clothes. 'We've just got to get as far away as possible.'

Mary nodded, shivering just as badly as her companion.

They stepped gingerly on to the rutted mud road and turned to the right, hurrying as fast as each painful step would allow, both acutely alert for any sounds of danger. After about half a mile, Peggie stopped, leaned against a tree trunk and examined her feet. The stockings had disintegrated and her feet were already partly skinless and bleeding. She tried hard to shut her mind to the pain and rejoined Mary.

'How's your feet?' she asked.

'All right,' lied Mary.

Huddling close together again they set off, arms entwined for support.

On and on they went as the night turned colder, each dragging step becoming more and more of an effort. Finally they came to a faltering halt and collapsed to the ground, all energy drained and both beyond caring.

'I'm sorry, Mary,' Peggie said with a great effort, 'I can't go any further.'

Her head spun and she blanked out.

Dan drew the lorry carefully into the side of the road in a deserted spot between Barlestone and Desford and switched off the engine. Both he and Sep jumped down and lit the lamps they were carrying.

'Right,' Sep spoke. 'I'll take this side and you that.'

Dan nodded, blinked gritty eyes and held the lamp high.

'Peggie!' they both called, scanning the hedgerows and what they could see of the deserted fields. 'Peggie, PEGGIE!'

'Look, Dan,' Sep shouted excitedly. 'There's a derelict barn over there.'

'Oh, yes,' he replied hopefully. 'You stay by the lorry and I'll take a look.'

'We'll both look,' Sep replied firmly.

Just then a loud bang followed by a cry struck the air. They both jumped and turned towards the lorry.

'What was that?' Sep uttered in astonishment.

Dan shook his head. 'I don't know.'

Gingerly they both tiptoed in the direction of the parked lorry and as they drew nearer blasphemies could be heard.

At the back of the lorry, sprawled on the ground, his bicycle wheels still spinning, was young Constable Tabbett who worked alongside Jesson at the station in Barlestone.

'Who the bloody hell left that there?' he muttered. He stood up, brushing himself down, and looked enquiringly at Sep and Dan.

'Is this yours?' he asked, pointing to the lorry.

Sep nodded. 'Guilty, Constable.'

Constable Tabbett looked at him hard, shielding his eyes from the glare from the lamp. 'Oh, it's you, Mr Cartwright. I'm sorry to hear about your daughter but I'm sure she'll be found soon. Constable Jesson is heading the team of searchers. If anyone can find her, he will.'

Sep sighed deeply. 'Thanks for the confidence, son. I'm sorry about your backside.'

Constable Tabbett grinned sheepishly. 'Oh, that's all right, sir. I wasn't looking where I was going. But to be honest that was the last thing I expected to bump into.'

'Thinking about that lady friend of yours, I expect.'

Tabbett grinned again. 'Something like that, sir.'

He bent down and picked up his bicycle and inspected it. Relieved there was no damage, he boarded and made to set off.

'Oh, Mr Cartwright. I'd be careful if I were you.'

'Careful?' Sep frowned.

'Yes. There's two loonies . . . er . . . two patients escaped from The Towers. And one of 'em is apparently dangerous.'

'Towers?' Dan queried. 'That's the mental asylum, isn't it?'

Sep nodded. 'But we've no need to worry. The Towers is miles away from here. It's right the other side of Leicester.'

'That's maybe so,' Constable Tabbett said firmly. 'But one of 'em comes from around here and the authorities reckon they could be heading this way. We got word via Hinckley Station. I've just been to inform Constable Jesson but his missus said he'd gone out so I'll have to call in again on my way back from telling all the other stations.'

'All right, Constable, we'll be vigilant. And if we see anything suspicious we'll let the station know.'

Dan grabbed Sep's arm. 'You don't think that they're in these parts already and Peggie has been attacked, do you?'

'Oh, God,' Sep groaned despairingly at the thought. He looked at Tabbett in alarm. 'When did you say they escaped?'

'Two days ago. Hang on, I'll tell you precisely.' He fished in his top pocket and pulled out his notebook. He flicked over the pages and squinted at it.

Dan moved over and held up his lamp to enable him to see clearer.

'Ah, here we are. At approximately four-fifteen on the night of the twelfth a Daisy White somehow managed to loosen her bonds and climb out of a window.' Constable Tabbett looked up. 'Damned clever woman if you ask me. She was strapped in a dentist's chair, around the throat, arms and wrists. Must have been a contortionist.' He sniffed and consulted his book again. 'It was then discovered only a few hours ago that another patient had gone. A certain Mary Crabbe. The authorities at The Towers are now certain that they went together and could be headed this way.'

Sep grabbed the constable's arm. 'Repeat that last name.'

'Er . . . Mary Crabbe.' The constable gasped as a thought struck him. 'Oh! You don't think she's any relation to Cyrus Crabbe who has the carting business?'

'I'll bloody say she is,' Sep cried. 'She's his daughter.' He spun to face Dan. 'What the hell is Crabbe's daughter doing in the mental asylum?'

Dan frowned, deep in thought. 'Sep, you don't think . . .'

'Think what?'

'This Daisy White . . .'

He gnawed on his bottom lip, his mind racing frantically. 'It could be. It just could be.'

'Could be what?' Constable Tabbett asked quizzically.

'Nothing, lad,' Dan shouted as simultaneously both he and Sep spun on their heels and ran towards the lorry. 'You just go about your business.'

Hurriedly cranking the engine, Dan climbed aboard and turned to face Sep.

'The asylum?'

'The asylum. And hurry!'

Each deep in their own private thoughts they sat in silence. His foot hard down on the accelerator, Dan drove like a man possessed, the lorry bumping dangerously over the frozen rutted ground, narrowly

296

missing tight high-hedged corners and unexpected buildings.

Five miles from the walls of the imposing Towers Mental Asylum, the headlights picked out a huddled bundle lying in the middle of the road. Dan slammed on the brakes and they both jumped down, racing towards it.

Dan reached it first, threw himself down and cradled the unconscious Peggie in his arms. Unashamed tears of joy poured down his cheeks.

'It's Peggie, Sep, it's her!' he shouted.

'Thank God,' Sep cried, raising his eyes heavenwards. 'Thank God!'

Settled protectively within Dan's comforting arms, Mary nestled at his side, Peggie's eyes flickered open.

'Oh, Dan,' she uttered. 'I had the most awful dream. I dreamt Cyrus Crabbe had me committed to the asylum. Constable Jesson took me there in the cart.'

'Shush,' he soothed. 'It was just a dream, Peggie, my darling. Go back to sleep.'

He watched as her eyes closed then looked across at Sep.

'Did you hear that?'

Eyes fixed on the dark road ahead, Sep silently nodded.

Sidney Jesson stole silently down the side of the house. He knocked loudly on the back door and stood back.

The door shot open and Cyrus glared out. His eyes narrowed icily. 'What d'you want?'

Sidney gulped hard. 'You've got to come with me, Cyrus.'

'Come with you? Where?'

'To the police station, that's where. We have to tell them what we've done with Margaret Cartwright and also your daughter Mary. We've got to get them out of there, Crabbe. It isn't human what we've done.'

Cyrus stared in disbelief. 'A' you outta your mind, man?'

'Yes, I think I must be. But I'll never rest again 'til those women are back home.'

'And you realise what they'll do to us?'

'Yes, I do. I'm fully aware of what will happen.'

'You're mad. Well, I'll tell yer, I ain't going anywhere and if anybody questions me I shall deny everything. After all, it was you who took them, not me. The asylum guard will recognise you, not me.' He laughed. 'They can't recognise me, can they? I wasn't there. It's Mary's and Peggie's word against mine and I shall make them out to be such blatant liars nobody will ever believe them again. Now go home to yer wife, there's a good man, and forget about all this,' he said patronisingly.

Cyrus studied Jesson hard. It suddenly struck him that the policeman was serious. He was going to confess all and expected him to do likewise. He stepped over the threshold and placed himself right up against Jesson, his eyes glaring madly. 'Breathe a

297

word of this to anyone and drag me into it and your life won't be worth living. I shall make them believe that I was in your pay. That it was you behind everything, right from the beginning when we stole Cartwright's brake. I shall tell them it was your idea and that you've demanded a share in the profits ever since. By the time I've finished, the authorities – and don't forget that you happen to represent them – will be so confused they won't know what to believe. But one thing's for sure. If I go down, I shall make sure you're so far ahead of me you'll never claw your way out. Your wife and daughters will be a laughing stock and hounded out of the village.'

Cyrus pushed him on the shoulder with the flat of his hand. 'Maybe I should have had *you* put away in the asylum. If you carry on talking like this I shall think very seriously about doing just that. After all, you do know how easy it is to get someone committed.' He eyed Jesson mockingly before turning on his heel and slamming shut the door, his loud laughter ringing in the air.

Jesson stood rigid, staring at the closed door, his face reddening in humiliation. Crabbe was leaving tomorrow, or at least he said he was leaving. Nothing the man said could be taken for gospel. His mind raced frantically. He had achieved nothing by coming here. And Cyrus was right. He would lie so convincingly Jesson's bosses wouldn't know what to think.

He closed his eyes wearily and shook his head. He hadn't solved any of his problems or relieved his guilt, if anything he felt worse, and he knew then that for the rest of his life he would live in the fear that even if Cyrus did leave the vicinity, one day he would reappear and make demands on him. He would never be free, never. He would always be peering over his shoulder.

Suddenly he raised his head as something Cyrus had said surfaced. His eyes glinted. Without realising Cyrus himself had handed him the solution. He unhooked his truncheon from his belt, hammered on the door and stood to the side, the truncheon raised. When the door opened the weapon came down heavily on Cyrus' head. He fell unconscious on to the hard slabs.

Sidney stared down at him for a moment, shocked at what he had done. He quickly gathered his wits. He had come too far now to back out. He took his handcuffs from his pockets and pushed Crabbe over with his heavy-booted foot, securing his wrists behind his back. He tied a large handkerchief as a gag around his mouth and, searching around, found a thick piece of discarded rope with which to strap his ankles together.

Quietly he stole across the yard and into the barn where he harnessed the horse to the brake. With difficulty he dragged Cyrus across the yard and heaved him on to the back. Just in time. Cyrus began to stir. Without hesitation Jesson raised his truncheon and whacked him over the head again.

Satisfied that Cyrus was out cold he made his way back across the yard and walked into the house. He found Reginald the worse for drink slumped in a chair. He shook his arm. Reginald jumped, alarmed.

Jesson gripped his arm and leaned menacingly over him. 'I'm giving you a chance, Reginald. Get out. Get out while you can, else you'll suffer the same fate as your father.'

He stared up, bewildered, his eyes glazed with drink. 'Fate?' he slurred. 'What fate?'

'Never you mind,' Jesson hissed. 'If you value your sanity, your life, leave now. Get your belongings and go and don't ever, ever show your face within a thirty-mile radius of this village or you won't like the consequences. I'll be back later and I don't want to find any trace of you, I want nothing left to show you've ever lived here.' He released his grip and straightened up. 'Is that understood?'

Reginald gulped. He had never seen Jesson like this, so menacing, so frightening. He did not doubt he meant every word he was saying. He jumped up from his chair. 'Don't worry, I'm going,' he shouted, stumbling around, grabbing at anything he could lay hands on and throwing it into a bag.

Satisfied his threats had been heeded, Jesson hurriedly left the house, climbed into the driving seat and whipped the horse. The brake shot out into the night.

Several hours later he arrived at his destination and pulled the brake to a halt. He climbed down and walked round to the back.

A pair of frantic eyes glared up at him as Cyrus wriggled furiously to free his bonds.

Jesson took a breath. 'I'm sorry, Crabbe, but I have no alternative. I cannot leave you free. You see, I'm giving myself up. I'm going to see my superiors. It will be up to them what they decide to do with me. And to be honest, any punishment they dish out, I'll deserve. The only thing is, my family will suffer. But I have to bear that. What I cannot do is leave you free to menace some other poor unsuspecting bugger.' He smiled and nodded. 'Yes, Cyrus, you've guessed it. We're at the asylum and I'm going to make sure you never get out. I'm doing humanity a service. Yes, that's what I'm doing, saving other poor souls from suffering the same fate as me and all your other victims.'

Ignoring Cyrus's frantic mumbles from beneath the gag he turned, walked towards the wall and pulled hard on the iron bell pull.

Chapter Twenty-Nine

Peggie's return was greeted with jubilation, Mary's with astonishment. But regardless the two were quickly deposited in armchairs at the side of the range and covered with thick blankets.

Nell raised her eyes thankfully to the ceiling. 'Thank God,' she cried. 'Oh, thank you, God.'

Motherly instinct overtook all else. Questions would receive answers when she was positive her daughter was comfortable. The most important thing was that her beloved Peggie was back. As far as she was concerned, an account of what had happened to her could wait for the moment. She quickly gave her instructions and soon the two girls had their feet soaking in bowls of warm salted water whilst the others busied themselves making drinks and hot sustaining food, and stripped clean linen to bandage their badly bruised feet.

As the rest of the family fussed, Dan and Sep stole quietly out of the cottage, making sure no one noticed their departure. They were met at the gate by Cuffy and Wilfred who looked at them enquiringly.

Dan quickly told them the good news and instructed them that after they had had something to eat, they should go and tell all the people who had led search parties and thank them for their help. But he stressed that no mention of the mental asylum was to be made. That was to be kept quiet for Peggie's and Mary's sake.

Wilfred went into the cottage. As Dan made to walk away, Cuffy stopped him. 'If Peggie's safe, where are you two going?'

'To see Crabbe. We're going to make sure he leaves the village. He's done his last vile act in this vicinity.'

'I'll come with yer.'

'There's no need, Cuffy, there won't be any violence. Sep and I can handle this. Now go and get yourself inside and something to eat. You've been out hours and you must be exhausted.'

Cuffy pulled himself up to his full height and puffed out his broad chest. 'Boss, I'm coming with yer whether you like it or not. I saved yer life, remember. I'm responsible for yer. Besides a bit of muscle might be needed. A man like Crabbe ain't gonna leave willingly.'

'He's right, Dan,' Sep said. 'Cuffy's presence will convince Crabbe we mean business.'

Dan thought. 'Yes, all right.' He smiled at Cuffy. The best thing that had come out of the terrible war was his friendship with this man. He took a deep breath. 'Well, let's get this over with.'

All three made their way in silence. They reached the Crabbe household to find the place in darkness and no sign of life.

'Strange,' Sep said, frowning deeply, casting his eyes over the darkened building.

'Maybe not so strange,' Dan replied thoughtfully. 'I think they've gone while they could. Maybe they heard that Peggie and Mary had returned and realised it was only a matter of time before they had a visit from the police. And you'll remember, they were already leaving. They've gone tonight instead of tomorrow.'

Cuffy tutted, dismayed, rubbing his fists. Secretly he'd been looking forward to another confrontation with Crabbe. He wanted the man to suffer for what he had done to his boss's lady and all the other misdeeds in the past.

Sep stroked his chin. 'Well, it looks like our job's been done for us. And talking of police, let's get around to Jesson's. I want to hear what story he's concocted about his part in having our Peggie committed.'

'Yes, and it better be good,' Dan said icily.

They were met at Jesson's gate by Sergeant Armstrong. A cart was already partly loaded with belongings. Dan, Sep and Cuffy stared at it, mystified.

Sergeant Armstrong cleared his throat as he barred the way through the gate. 'I know why you're all here,' he said, addressing Sep.

'Do you?'

'I do. Jesson confessed all down at the station. It seems grave injustices have been done over the years, to your family in particular. In respect of that we'll need to talk to you later to clarify a few things. But in the meantime, go home. Let us handle this.'

'And what about Crabbe? What are you doing about him?'

Sergeant Armstrong stroked his chin. 'We'd like to talk to him . . .'

'Talk to him? Is that all?' Dan erupted.

'For the moment that's all we can do. Jesson has no proof to back his allegations. But it seems that Crabbe and his son have disappeared.'

'Yes, cowards they are,' Sep hissed. 'Does Jesson have any idea where they are? After all, it seems they were all in league together.'

'He says not. But they're bound to surface somewhere and when they do we'll be waiting. We'll need to speak to Peggie later. That's if she's able.'

'She'll be able. She'll give you all the proof you need for when you do catch up with him. And Mary also. Did you know Mary Crabbe was in the asylum too?'

'Jesson has told us. But I shouldn't bank on her giving evidence. After all, Crabbe is her father.'

Sep sighed. 'No, I suppose not. Misplaced loyalty, eh?'

'Something like that, sir.'

Dan gestured towards the cart. 'What is going on here, Sergeant?'

He squared his shoulders. 'We feel it wisest Mrs Jesson and her family leave the village. When this news breaks, we think it won't be very pleasant for her.'

They all nodded in agreement.

'No,' Sep said. 'It won't. Shame she has to bear the brunt of her husband's deeds. She's a nice woman. And her daughters are good lasses.'

'Get off home,' Sergeant Armstrong said wearily, wishing wholeheartedly he could, remembering the warm bed he shared with his wife that he had hurriedly left when he had received the summons from the station about Jesson's revelations. It was hard work dealing with any sort of criminal but when one turned out to be an officer of the law it was worse and the punishments far harsher. 'You've all been through a terrible time yourselves and those at home will be needing you.'

As they walked back to the cottage, Sep raised his eyes towards the dark sky. Dawn would soon rise. A new day would unfold. Suddenly an overwhelming sense of relief came over him. It was over. All the years of looking over his shoulder, wondering what Cyrus had planned for them next, were finished. Somehow Sep knew that he would never see him again. Cyrus was gone, gone from their lives forever. Sep did not care where the man was, or what had happened to him. The most important thing was that he was no longer around to blight his own or his family's lives. They could get on with the job of living, forging new ground without fear of that man's interference.

He turned towards Dan and Cuffy walking silently beside him. 'Come on, let's get a move on. The others will be waiting.'

303

Chapter Thirty

Several days later, propped up in bed, Peggie blew her nose noisily and looked at Dan through streaming red eyes.

'I feel awful,' she moaned.

He took her hand. 'Darling, you look fine to me,' he said tenderly. 'If a cold is all you're suffering then I would be thankful if I were you, because believe me, at the least I'd have expected pneumonia.'

'Yes, I suppose,' she grumbled, adjusting the sling supporting her painful shoulder. She blew her nose again and sniffed loudly. 'How's Mary?' she asked.

'She's fine. She's helping Billy learn how to balance the books.' Dan grinned mischievously. 'Those two are getting on very well.'

'Are they? Good. Mary's just the type of woman our Billy needs and he's just the kind of man for her. They'll be good for each other. Let's hope they realise it.' She smiled warmly. 'It was good of my mam to take her in and I've never seen Mary look so happy, despite her poor feet.' She screwed up her eyes. 'It's funny about Cyrus and Reginald disappearing like that, though. What d'you think has happened to them?'

Dan shrugged. 'I've no idea, Peggie, and to be honest I don't really care. I think we can safely say we won't ever see them again.'

'What, never?' she asked hopefully.

'Never, Peggie. Cyrus wouldn't dare show his face around here again. If he does, you have me to care for you now and I wouldn't let him harm a hair on your head.'

She smiled as his loving protectiveness enveloped her. He was a prop for her to lean on, someone she knew would be there for the rest of her life. Suddenly her eyes filled with tears as guilt at her own happy state filled her. 'Oh, Dan. I can't help thinking of all those poor people in that horrible place. I know they're ill in their minds but they're treated worse than animals. I don't think I'll ever get over it.'

Dan put his arms round her and pulled her close. 'Hey, hey,' he soothed. 'You will, Peggie, believe me.'

'No, I won't,' she cried.

Dan pulled away and looked at her hard. 'Oh yes you will,' he ordered firmly. 'I was in the trenches, remember? I and thousands of others saw atrocities that made the asylum look like a picnic.

305

Now if we can put all that to the back of our minds, then so can you. We've a lot of living to do, Peggie Cartwright, and I do not want this business to mar our happiness.'

She gazed at him adoringly. He was right. If she was ever to get on with her life she would have to put the events of the last week out of her mind. It would be a hard struggle to forget, the memory of those pitiful creatures kept creeping into her thoughts, but with work she should be able to shut those pictures out and get on with living. And with Dan at her side, her future was going to be such a joy.

She smiled at him. 'I love you,' she whispered sincerely.

'And I you, Maggie,' he said, grinning wickedly.

'Eh, I'll have less of that,' she said sharply. 'I don't care what your dad calls your mother. My name is Peggie. Got that?'

Dan laughed loudly. 'I've got that,' he replied, grinning. He pulled her close again and kissed her cheek. 'I want us to set a date for the wedding,' he said.

'Wedding!' she exclaimed in alarm. 'I can't.'

'What?'

Peggie gulped. 'Not 'til my hair grows. I ain't going out of the house 'til my hair grows. And besides, me feet hurt that much I doubt I'll ever walk again.'

'Oh, for goodness' sake, Peggie. Your mother is coming through when she's prepared the dinner to trim your hair properly. It'll look fine once she's finished. And, besides, I'm marrying you, not whatever hair style you've got.' He stared at her. 'All right?'

She gulped. 'All right.' She took a deep breath. 'I'll marry you as soon as you like, providing my mother makes a good job of it.' She paused and grinned at him. 'I do want to marry you as soon as possible,' she admitted, ''cos I've missed you like hell since you and Wilfred went to lodge with Aggie's mother.'

'Well, we had no choice. Now that your father's back and Wilfred and Mary moved in we were falling out of the doors. Even though your mother did try her best to accommodate us all.' He laughed loudly at the memory of Nell ordering the move round of the rooms, but try as she might she couldn't fit them all in. 'But I'll keep you to that promise, Peggie. I'll go and see the Reverend tomorrow.'

She smiled happily at the thought. 'Now that's settled, tell me your plans for the car business? When are we going to get started?' she asked excitedly.

'Oh, I'm not doing that now.'

'You're not? Oh, Dan, why not? It was your dream, remember. You can't not do it.'

'I'm not doing it because I've got something else more exciting in mind, that's why.' He took her hands. 'I'm going to talk to your father, Peggie.'

She frowned quizzically. 'Talk to Dad? What about?'

'About us forming a partnership. With my capital and what

you've already got, we could build a bus and haulage business to be envied.'

Peggie gasped. 'Oh, Dan,' she cried happily, seeing loaded buses and lorries flashing before her eyes. 'I think that's a wonderful idea. And I would be part of it, wouldn't I?'

'You'd all be part of it, like you are now. Only we could have proper coaches, like the ones the Loughborough Brush Company are building, and several lorries. There's stacks of business out there, Peggie, just waiting for the right people to handle it. And we'd be the right ones with our combined efforts.'

'Oh, yes, without a doubt. My father will love the idea, I know he will. He thinks the world of you, Dan.'

'And me him. In fact, I couldn't wish to be marrying into a better family.'

A warm glow of happiness settled over her.

'Go on then. Go and speak to him now. And tell my mother to hurry and get the scissors.' She ran her hand over her shorn locks. 'The sooner she does something with this, the better.'

Just then the door opened and Letty burst through with a mug of tea, slopping some of it on to the linoleum, her face like thunder.

'What's up?' Peggie asked.

'That woman!' she spat. 'That Effie Dage is threatening to put a stop to the mobile shop. She reckons she's going to the parish council.'

Peggie pulled herself painfully up in her bed, 'Oh, she is, is she? Well, we'll see about that,' she said angrily.

Dan grabbed her arm. 'Peggie Cartwright, do you never learn? There you go again, like a bull to a red rag.'

Peggie slank back against the pillows and grinned sheepishly.

'Don't worry,' Dan addressed Letty. 'There's nothing she can do. You and Wilfred go ahead as planned.'

Letty beamed in relief, ramming her spectacles against her nose. 'Thanks, Dan. And I hope we pinch all her bloody customers. Serves her right for treating them all so badly over the years 'cos they had nowhere else to go. Well, now they'll have us and the new Co-op.' Giggling gleefully, she left the room.

Dan rose.

'Eh, not so quickly,' Peggie said. 'Haven't you something to tell me?'

'Pardon?'

'Don't "pardon" me, Daniel Dixon. I know.'

'Know what?'

'I know that it's your money at the back of this mobile shop. I had my suspicions when Wilfred announced that his mother had given him money and it didn't take me long to suss out that it wasn't her at all, it was you.'

Dan sat back down on the bed. 'Well, yes, you're right, Peggie. I can see I'm not going to be able to keep anything from your astute mind, but that's where it stays. This agreement was between me

307

and Wilfred, no one else is to find out. He wouldn't be able to hold his head up.'

Peggie nodded. 'I won't say a word.' She leaned over and kissed him tenderly on the cheek. 'You're a lovely man, Daniel Dixon. I'm so lucky to have you.'

Outside in the kitchen, Nell put the finishing touches to the shepherd's pie she had made and pushed it into the hot oven. She wiped her hands and walked over to the welsh dresser, staring at it crossly. 'Now how the hell am I supposed to find the scissors amongst this mess?' She turned abruptly to Primrose, lounging comfortably in the armchair, thumbing through her comic. 'Sort this mess out. Throw out all the rubbish and 'ote you think's worth saving, put in a pile on the floor.'

Primrose pouted sulkily. 'Oh, why is it always me?'

Mary, who was sitting next to Billy at the end of the table, jumped up. 'I'll do it, Mrs Cartwright.'

Nell tutted loudly. 'Mary, for goodness' sake, will you stop offering to help every time something wants doing? You're supposed to be resting. I've told you before, you're to act as one of the family. And none of them does anything voluntary, I can assure you.'

Mary sank back on her chair and stared around at them all. From the moment she had been brought into this cottage she had been welcomed and treated by all as one of their own. Never before in her life had she experienced such a feeling of belonging, of being wanted. Never before had she experienced the feeling of happiness. She understood fully now what Peggie had meant by a home. A home was made up of four walls and the people who resided within them. It didn't matter what possessions adorned the floors or walls or what money was coming in. It was the people who mattered and these people she was with now were the best possible. The love and respect they held for each other radiated forth and the circle that enclosed them had been opened and extended to include herself. She never, never wanted to have to leave them.

Billy interrupted her thoughts as he raised his head from the business ledgers he was struggling over and laughed. 'You're wasting your time anyway, Mam. By the time it's all been sorted there'll be more on top than there is now.'

Nell frowned, then smiled as she spotted the scissors. ''Spose yer right,' she said grudgingly.

She made towards the stairs and stopped as the back door shot open and Sep charged through.

'Nell,' he shouted on spotting her. 'Come outside, quick.'

'Why? What's happened?' she gasped, clasping her hand to her mouth in worry.

'Nothing's happened. Just come with me now.'

She hurried over and stood in the doorway, staring in astonishment at the lorry parked by the gate. Strapped on the back was an upright piano. Sep put his arm around her and pulled her close.

'Well, what d'you think?' he asked proudly.

'Oh, Sep,' she cried in delight, wriggling free and rushing to the gate. 'You got me a piano!' she exclaimed.

'I did. I've just come back from Leicester with it. And it was a bargain.'

Nell turned to him, her eyes twinkling merrily. 'And did you drive round the village before you came home.'

Sep puffed out his chest proudly. 'I did. Now all the villagers will know that my wife owns a piano.' He turned to her and hugged her tightly. 'So, my girl, you'd just better get those piano lessons booked, 'cos come Christmas we're all going to be standing round it singing and you'd better be playing the music. So be warned.'

'Where you gonna put that, Mam? I wouldn't a' thought we'd any room?' a voice enquired.

Nell turned her head. Her mouth dropped open in shocked surprise. 'Ronnie!' she shrieked in delight. 'Ronnie, you've come home.' She wrenched open the gate and threw herself on him.

'Oh, ged off, Mam. All the neighbours are looking,' he said, blushing deeply.

Nell held him at arm's length and stared at him. 'Why, Ronnie, you've grown. We sent away a boy and you've come back a man. Well, I'll be blowed.'

Primrose, who had come out to see what all the fuss was about, laughed loudly. 'And he shaves, Mam. Look, he's covered in cuts. I bet he's got a girl friend,' she giggled.

'That's enough, young lady,' Sep scolded. He prised Nell off their son and picked up his luggage. 'Come on in, son, I bet you've lots to tell us.'

'I have that,' Ronnie said excitedly. 'I've finished at Rugby. Got a glowing report, and I'm gonna be working at Bag'orth again to finish my apprenticeship.'

'Oh, good. So you'll be living at home, son?' Nell said excitedly. 'Oh, I have missed yer.'

Ronnie grimaced fiercely. The last thing he was going to admit was that he had missed all his family dreadfully, even Primrose. He was a man now and men kept their own counsel on such matters.

Nell and Sep put their arms round their son and guided him up the path. As they walked, Ronnie stared at the cottage.

'Well, I don't suppose much has been happening round here since I left,' he said flatly.

Sep and Nell looked at each other.

'No, not much, son,' Sep responded, hiding a smile. 'Not much at all.'

Chapter Thirty-One

Peggie arrived at the bottom of the aisle and glanced quickly around the congregation through the misty cloud of netting that formed her creamy white veil. All eyes were upon her. Happy smiling eyes for a wonderfully happy occasion.

At the top of the aisle she could see her mother, dressed in her finery. Even from this distance Peggie could see the tears glistening in her mother's eyes and the handkerchief she was holding at the ready. Alongside her were Letty and Wilfred, Primrose and Ronnie. Beside them, Billy and Mary, and if Peggie's eyes were not deceiving her she could swear they were holding hands.

Behind them sat Cuffy and Aggie. Aggie turned and gazed at the huge man beside her adoringly, quickly jerking back when she received a sharp nudge from her own mother. Yes, very shortly, if Peggie wasn't mistaken, the Reverend was going to be busy. Very busy indeed. And she herself couldn't be more pleased.

On the other side of the aisle, Dan's family were gathered, delight at this match apparent on all their faces.

But more important than all of them was her Dan, standing facing her at the other end of the long aisle, smart in his wedding attire, his face filled with such pride, such happiness, he looked about to explode. She wanted to gather her dress and run to him and have him draw her in to his protective arms and crush her against him. But she could wait. In a very short time, they would be joined for ever.

She felt her father take her arm.

'You look beautiful, Peggie,' he said, with proud tears in his eyes.

'Oh, Dad,' she whispered. 'I do love you.'

He nodded. 'And there's another man not far away who loves you as well. Now we'd best be off before he gets fed up with waiting and decides to go home.'

Peggie stifled a laugh at the very thought. The wedding march struck up and she took a breath.

'Ready, then?' Sep asked, his voice quivering.

Peggie breathed deeply. 'I've never been more ready for anything in all my life, Dad.'